Only a Chapter

Only a Chapter

Heather Tracy

Trigger Warnings: Cancer, emotional abuse, death of parents.

Space Wizard Science Fantasy
Raleigh, NC
www.spacewizardsciencefantasy.com

Cover Design by Abra Millsaps
Editing by Courtney Brooks
Book Layout © 2015 BookDesignTemplates.com

Only a Chapter/Heather Tracy.— 1st ed.
ISBN 978-1-960247-38-4

Author's website: https://www.spacewizardsciencefantasy.com

In loving memory of my grandmother, Denise Zuege, who fought breast cancer and won...twice. To all my other pink siblings surviving and thriving, I sincerely hope a cure is right around the corner.

And, to my amazing husband, Bill Tracy. Quite literally the person of my dreams.

AUTHOR'S NOTE

This book is a work of fiction; however, it is influenced by my personal journey not only with breast cancer, but also with dreams.

I was diagnosed with breast cancer in 2022. The breast cancer journey in this story is very similar to my own but adapted for the fictional story I wanted to tell. As anyone who has ever had cancer—breast or otherwise—can tell you, no one's story is exactly the same. **Mild Spoiler Alert**: My story has a happy ending as I am a three-year survivor as of this printing.

The title comes from when I announced my diagnosis on social media by saying that "Cancer is only going to be a chapter in my life, and not the whole story."

Onto the dreams…I've had very vivid dreams all my life. In fact, many of the dreams featured in the book are adapted from those of my teen years through college that seemingly predicted the future. No, I'm not claiming to be psychic. But most, if not all, of my dreams of a faceless person did come true in one way or another after I met Bill Tracy (aka William C. Tracy). I've wanted to write them into a novel for many years.

This novel is the combination of both of these personal journeys, and I hope you enjoy it!

Heather Tracy
April 2025

CONTENTS

Chapter 1: "Unwritten" ____ 7

Part 1: "Set Fire to the Rain" ___________________________________ 8

Part A: "Here Comes the Rain Again" ____________________________ 15

Part 2: "Sail On" ____ 22

Part B: "Curse the Love Songs" __________________________________ 38

Part 3: "Uninvited" ____ 50

Part C: "Unintended" ____ 63

Part 4: "Déjà Vu" ____ 72

Part D: "Taking Over Me" ______________________________________ 79

Part 5: "Shivers" ____ 87

Part E: "Touch of Your Hand" ___________________________________ 96

Part 6: "Umbrella" ____ 105

Part F: "That's What Friends Are For" ___________________________ 121

Part 7: "Falling into You" ______________________________________ 131

Part G: "Truly, Madly, Deeply" _________________________________ 142

Part 8: "All of the Stars" _______________________________________ 153

Part H: "Written in the Stars" __________________________________ 163

Part 9: "Easy on Me" ____ 172

Part I: "Between the World & You" ______________________________ 182

Part 10: "Where the Light Shines Through" _______________________ 194

Part J: "Dare You to Move" _____________________________________ 208

Part 11: "Remember When it Rained" ____________________________ 215

Part K: "About Damn Time" _____________________________________ 227

Part 12: "Part of Me" ____ 234

Part L: "Broken Pieces Shine" ___________________________________ 242

Part 13: "Shut Up & Dance" _____________________________________ 254

Part M: "I Wanna Dance with Somebody" ________________________ 265

Part 14: "Padam Padam" ____ 273

Part N: "Hold on to Now" _______________________________________ 284

"Dream On" ____ 293

Chapter 2: "Come What May" ___________________________________ 302

Chapter 1

"Unwritten"

April

"Ms. O'Donnell, the pathology of your right axillary lymph node came back consistent with adenocarcinoma. As this is a malignancy, we'll need you to come in for further testing..."

That night I dreamed again of the faceless one, but this time, he was more clearly defined except for his face. He was waiting for me in the rain in a tuxedo with his hand out, gesturing for me to stand under the shelter of his umbrella...

* * *   * * *

"Ms. O'Donnell, the pathology of your right axillary lymph node came back benign. There's nothing to worry about."

That night I dreamed again of the faceless one, but this time, she was more clearly defined except for her face. She was sitting in a car in her tuxedo dress, patting the seat next to her for me to join her...

Part 1

"Set Fire to the Rain"

April

"Suz! Are you listening to me?" I yell down the hall as I throw the last few items into my suitcase. No response. I'm sure she can't hear me since those wireless, noise-cancelling headphones I got her last Christmas drown out everything in the world except that insipid video game.

Zipping up the bag, I take one last look around the room we've shared for the past five years. Believe me, I'm not taking inventory of all the warm fuzzy memories held in this room. I'm not even sure there are any. And there definitely wouldn't be any if I tried to stay here through whatever treatment I'm going to need. She wasn't there for me during the last few torturous days waiting for my results, so how could she be there for me through whatever my diagnosis is going to throw at me. No, I'm just making sure I don't leave anything valuable to me behind, because she'll just throw it away...when she gets around to it.

I turn away and head for the bathroom. All my beauty products are lined up neatly on the rickety, plastic shelving system over the toilet. I hold a tote bag open with one hand and sweep my other arm across the shelf. Miraculously, everything falls directly into the bag. I grab a couple items out of the shower, then start searching for the cat.

Shelley has been especially skittish today, not that I can blame her. I've been running around like a mad woman ever since I got home from work, and all the fruitless yelling at Suz hasn't helped either. Not wanting to scare Shelley any more than I already have, I don't get the carrier right away. Instead, I grab the canister of treats from the kitchen and walk quietly to the guest bedroom. She loves hiding in the closet when we're freaking her out.

"Shelley," I coo. "Would you like some fishy treats?" I shake the treats, and the sound has the desired effect. Slowly but surely, I see one fluffy, grey paw emerge, followed closely by a pair of beautiful blue eyes. She blinks at me once. I blink slowly back at her, and I know she's forgiven me for scaring her. As long as I relinquish a couple of the stinky salmon treats, of course.

While she's munching, I very gingerly step around her to grab the carrier from the top shelf of the closet. She's just finished the last treat when I scoop her up and shove her in the dreaded box. If looks could kill, I'd have been dead years ago. I won't be forgiven for this one for a while. Oh well. I throw a few more treats into the carrier and haul her out to the living room.

"Suz!" Still no response. She hasn't looked up from the screen since I got home. I doubt she's even registered that I'm here. I grab my other two bags from the bedroom and put them by the front door with Shelley. She's started to "meyowl," which is something akin to a cat howling at the moon.

I think about calling Suz's name one more time to try to get her attention, but realize it would be futile. The *Star Trek* quote, "resistance is futile," pops into my head, and I know I have to get out of this place. Soon.

"I'm setting them on fire," Suz says to her gaming companions over the internet. "We get one if we turn in the hair."

I walk over to the sofa where she's sitting and stand there with my hands on my hips, staring at her. Still nothing. Fed up, I pick up the remote and turn the TV off.

"What the—?" Suz shouts, still oblivious to my presence. She continues to press buttons on her controller, thinking she's somehow killed the TV while fighting off the bad guys.

"Suz," I say. She finally looks up.

"You turned off the television," she accuses.

Of course she blames me. The TV could have died or something, but instead, I must have done it. And, yes, I did do it, but it's her assumption that drives me insane. One more nail in the coffin.

"I did," I say with just an ounce of calm. "Suz, we need to talk."

"Clare," she whines, "why'd you have to turn off the TV? We were right in the middle of a level." The sound is so grating I wonder how I've survived this long without going insane. "I mean, at least let us get to a save point or something."

I just continue as if she's said nothing. "I'm leaving. I can't stay here anymore. I'm not happy and I've finally decided it's time to move on. I'm going to go stay with Abby for a while until I can find a place."

And she continues as if *I've* said nothing. "Now we're going to have to start all over. It took forever to get past the Mines of—"

"Suz! Did you hear what I just said?" I ask, exasperated. "Of course you didn't, because you don't care as much about me as you do that stupid game."

"What?!" she exclaims. "You said you were going to hang out with Abby tonight. Have fun."

I take a deep breath and count to ten on the exhale. Then I take another. Finally, by the third breath I'm ready to repeat myself. "No, Suz. I said I'm leaving, as in moving out. I'm breaking up with you and moving out. See?" I gesture to my bags and the poor kitty locked in the torture chamber.

"But... We just re-upped the lease. How am I supposed to pay for this place on my own?"

"It's nice to know I've meant that much to you," I reply. I'm not sure what I expected to happen during this conversation, but her complete lack of thought for me really hurts. After nearly eight years together, you'd think she'd be a little upset about me leaving, not just about the rent. "Good-bye, Suz."

I pick up my purse off the kitchen island on my way to the front door. It's not until I've picked up my bags that she calls out to me. "Can you at least give me a prorated check for this month?"

I don't even bother to respond. Knowing how anal she is about us paying exactly half of every single thing in this apartment—except for the things we don't share, like certain foods and beauty products—I already left a check on her desk. And she makes more than enough to cover our apartment on her own. I also put a note in there explaining more fully why I'm leaving her. Not that she'll read it, or understand it, if she does. It just made me feel better to get it all out.

After I slam the door behind me, I hear the telltale beeps that mean the TV's been turned back on. I shake my head then start making my way down the stairs. It figures I would decide to move out right when the landlord finally decides to do maintenance on the ancient elevator.

It doesn't hit me until I've gone down two flights that I've just broken up with my girlfriend and I'm essentially homeless. Not to mention the echoes of the word "cancer" bouncing around in my mind. Sure, Abby's going to let me stay at her place, but that's just temporary. Tears well up in my eyes and I try to shrug it off as I continue down the next two flights. I needed to do this. I couldn't stay there anymore because I'm not happy. I deserve to be happy.

It's just... She didn't care. We've been together for so long, and she didn't care that I was leaving. I really don't know what I expected to happen, but I thought she'd at least ask me one time not to go. Some tiny expression of sorrow that I wouldn't be there tomorrow would have made me feel better. But I got nothing from her. She didn't even ask if I'd gotten my results yet. Almost eight years, and nothing to show for it.

I step out onto the sidewalk only to find out it's raining. And, by raining, I mean pouring. Typical. I cower beneath the pitiful excuse for an awning and reach in my purse for my phone. It's not there. Then it dawns on me, I left it charging at work. I never charge my phone at work, but with all the extra phone calls to make appointments and checking for updates on my portal every five seconds, I ran out of battery. A whimper escapes my throat. What am I going to do now? I'm homeless and getting wetter by the second, and I have no way to get to Abby's on my own.

Shelley is losing it in the crate. Her treats have long since disappeared and she's getting wet too. "I'm sorry, sweetie. I'll get us somewhere dry in a second."

I look up the street, but there aren't really payphones anymore. Not that I have change in my wallet anyway. There's a coffee shop across the street, but the owner goes nuts about people asking to use his phone or his restroom if you don't buy anything. I don't have enough hands to carry a drink I don't want. The tears have really started to flow now.

I think about going back upstairs to use Suz's phone, but I just can't face her and her indifference. No, I need to do this on my own. I decide to make a run for the coffee shop, and I'll just buy a tea to use the phone.

I'm near the entrance when I see a guy walking out of the shop, nice and dry under his golf umbrella. With nothing left to lose, I call out to him, "Excuse me?"

He turns toward me, and I see he's in a tuxedo—tails, no less. "Can I help you?" he asks, dubious.

"I'm sorry to bother you, but would you happen to have a phone I could borrow? I just had a bad breakup, and I was supposed to call my friend to come get me, but I left my phone at work," I beg.

He takes in my bags, poor imprisoned kitty and my drenched appearance, and figuring I'm safe, he walks toward me. He reaches into his jacket pocket and pulls out his phone. "Here," he says, handing me the phone.

As he looks at me and I see his face, I feel an intense sensation of déjà vu. But I've never seen this guy before in my life. I set the suitcase down, take the phone from him and dial Abby's number. She finally answers on the fourth ring. After a brief explanation of why I'm calling from a strange number, I quickly ask her to pick me up and she says she'll be here in ten minutes. I hang up and hand the phone back to him.

"Thanks," I say, wiping at the wet hair plastered to my forehead. I'm still unable to shake the feeling that I know him from somewhere.

"No problem. Would you like me to wait with you until your friend gets here?" he offers.

I notice he's stepped closer to me while I was on the phone such that Shelley and I are now mostly covered by his umbrella. "Um... No, that's okay. I'll just wait in the coffee shop."

"If you're sure," he replies. "Let me at least walk you to the shop so you don't get even more soaked."

We walk the half-block to the shop door, and I thank him. He turns to leave, and I realize I don't even know his name. I shrug, then set my suitcase, tote bag and cat down at a table. I walk to the counter to order something, then the world comes to a complete halt. I can only vaguely hear the owner's protests at my having brought a cat into his restaurant. I turn back toward the entrance, and I know what I must do.

I turn toward the older woman at the table next to where Shelley is meyowling in her crate. "It's an emergency. I'll be right back. Can you please watch my stuff?"

Without waiting for a response, I step back out in the rain and see him standing at the crosswalk a block away. I break into a run, shoes flinging water on the back of my pants. I'm silently praying the light doesn't change before I get there. I take a brief look before I cross the first intersection and even though it says, "Don't Walk," I run across anyway. I'm halfway down the next block when I see the crosswalk signal change. He starts striding purposefully across the street, completely unaware I'm chasing him.

I somehow manage to make it across before the light changes again. I'm getting closer. Only a few feet left.

"Hey!" I call out, slowing to a walk. Since he's the only one on this side of the street, he turns around slowly.

I step up to him and hear my heart pounding in my chest. I know it's not just from the run. I hesitate ever so slightly. But I know I must do this or I will regret it forever.

He looks at me questioningly. "Did you need to make another call?"

"No," I reply, shaking my head.

I look into his eyes one more second before grabbing his lapels and pulling him into a kiss.

Part A

"Here Comes the Rain Again"

April

"Suz? I'm home," I call as I enter our apartment. My cat, Shelley, greets me at the door with her usual sad eyes for treats. Still not hearing Suz reply, I set my purse down on the table by the door, and head to kitchen to feed the starving kitty. She's thirteen pounds, but pretends like she's skin and bones.

"Suz? Are you home?" I call from the kitchen. Shelley devours her treats as if she hasn't been fed all day—she has—then proceeds to wash her face. I walk into the living room to find Suz playing her video game with her noise-cancelling headphones on. *I'm ruing the day I got those for her for Christmas.* She's in her usual position, legs crossed, leaning forward with her elbows on her knees, gaming controller in hand. Her golden-brown hair falls in a chin-length cut that's almost too straight. She doesn't believe in layers, so all her hair has to be exactly the same length. Unfortunately, it accentuates the severity of her heavy eyebrows and Aquiline nose.

"I'm setting them on fire," Suz says to her gaming companions over the internet. "We get one if we turn in the hair."

I have this intense feeling of déjà vu but chalk it up to having heard Suz play this particular level before or something. I roll my eyes and head to the bedroom to change into loungewear. It'll be at least half an hour before Suz hits pause on the game, and I don't want to deal with the repercussions of interrupting her absolutely *riveting* adventure. Don't get me wrong, I do enjoy playing a video game every now and again—Suz and I even play some together—but I'm not as obsessed with them as she is, and I don't play the ones that take hundreds of hours to complete and have very few save points.

I remove my blouse and dressy jeans to put on my comfiest yoga pants from Torrid and my favorite Muse T-shirt that's seen better days. Though we don't see many clients in person at work—which is in my friend and boss Nate's house—he prefers us to look put together. He says it keeps us motivated as well. I'm not sure about that, but at least he doesn't require us to be super stuffy. Shelley walks by, rubbing her fluffy grey tail against my legs, and I reach down to pet her. She's a fairly affectionate cat to me, but she's not one who likes to be picked up, and she doesn't like other people all that much. She simply tolerates Suz's existence, but she never gets to pet her. Not that Suz has ever wanted to.

I pick up my phone—which I nearly left charging at work but remembered to grab at the last second—and check for any notifications. Just one email from my doctor's office telling me again that my biopsy was negative. What an absolute relief that was when I got the call yesterday. I seriously didn't know what I was going to do if they had told me it was cancer. Those were the worst thirty-six hours of my life waiting for that call. Suz was just as relieved as I was—possibly because she knew she wasn't going to have to take care of me during whatever treatment I went through. I know she cares for me, but she's not the most nurturing soul on the planet.

Honestly, I've been contemplating breaking up with her for months now, but something keeps holding me back. It's not that things aren't good with her, but I'm just not completely happy in the relationship. We still enjoy watching movies and shows together, and there's no one else in my life who can help me with my computer or my taxes the way she can. But I know there's got to be more than this monotony we've fallen into. We've been together for eight years and living together for the last five, but some days it feels more like we're roommates than girlfriends. And Suz won't even use the term "girlfriends" or partners. If she introduces me at all, she just says my name. "This is Clare."

It all comes back to Suz and I being very different people. They say opposites attract, but we might be too opposite. I'm an affectionate person and Suz is very much not. She "doesn't understand the point of kissing." I'm tidy but Suz takes it to extremes, to the point where I can't move any of her things for fear she'll completely lose it. I'm vegetarian and Suz loves meat. I like to pay my own way, but Suz needs everything split exactly—to the penny. Heaven forbid our water bill comes and it's an odd number.

With all our differences, she was there for me when my parents died in the car accident, and I'll never forget that. She helped me plan the memorial service while I was in the hospital recovering from my own injuries, handle the estate and go through their things. And I wouldn't have made it through the long car ride back from the mountains without her—not to mention that I'd stopped driving as soon as I recovered. One could say I feel indebted to her for all that.

This has led to me expressing interest in things I don't really enjoy to try to find some common ground and deepen our relationship. My best friend, Abby, gets on me all the time about being a Trekkie now, just because I watch some *Star Trek* shows with Suz. Do I like *Star Trek*? Not really. But in pretending to like some of Suz's favorite things, I did find some new things I do like, such as the new *Doctor Who*. C'mon, David Tennant and Jodie Whitaker are hot!

Bleep, bleep, bleep. My phone chirps with a new text message. It's from Abby, confirming our plans to hang out tonight. Abby's been my best friend since we were kids. We met in elementary school when we were both in the Academically Gifted program and bonded when we were somehow the only girls in the class. If I do decide to break up with Suz, I will most likely move in with her.

> Abby: What time did you want me to pick you up?
> Clare: 7 work for you?
> Abby: Sounds good. Getting ice cream. What flavor do you want?
> Clare: Vanilla Caramel Fudge, please! :-)
> Abby: You got it! See you at 7.
> Clare: Btw, I want to talk to you about your guest bedroom again.
> Abby: Really? You're finally going to do it?
> Clare: We'll see, but I think it might be time.
> Abby: YAY!!

Shelley jumps up on the bed wanting pets. I can't say no to her beautiful blue eyes, so I sit down next to her and rub her cheeks. She purrs contentedly, then twirls around to settle herself away from me on the bed—her signal that my job is done, and she'd like to be left alone now, thank you very much. She was my parents' cat and came to live with me after the accident. I know she loves me, but I also know she was much more affectionate to my parents. It could also be she's getting on in years and is simply getting grumpy.

Looking at my watch, I see I've got just enough time to heat up leftovers for dinner, eat them and maybe talk to Suz for a couple minutes before Abby comes to pick me up. Suz and I used to eat together, but our schedules don't sync anymore now that she gets home earlier than me and immediately jumps online to play her games. So, we eat when we feel like it. It's not like we eat the same things anyway. In fact, the fridge is literally separated down the middle with tape to denote her side and mine. Although I do like that her meat products aren't touching my vegetarian food.

Walking past the bedroom window on the way to the kitchen, I notice it started raining. There's a handsome guy in a full-on tuxedo coming out of the coffee shop across the street. *I wonder if he's going to a ball*, I think as he pops open his huge golf umbrella, and I chuckle to myself.

After eating my leftovers, I hear Suz wrap up her play session in the living room and the *beep-beep* that signals the TV has been turned off. I go into the living room and find Suz setting her headphones on the stand next to the game controller.

"Hey," I say.

She looks up, probably realizing for the first time that I'm home. "Oh, hey."

"Good game?" I ask, not really caring but trying to show an interest.

She nods. "Yeah, we got to level twelve, and my character has some new armor that will come in handy."

"Great," I reply.

Silence.

"So, I'm going to Abby's tonight to watch a movie. Need anything before I go?"

She thinks for a moment. "Nah. I'm gonna eat then the gang is going to play some more."

"Okay. Have fun. I'll be back later."

"Sounds good," she says, then she saunters off into the kitchen to make her dinner.

We're basically just roommates, but I want more. I need more. I'm forty-two years old, and the woman I thought was my girlfriend is just my roommate. I might be an idiot for staying here this long.

* * *

"Come on in," Abby says, opening the door to her apartment.

She works in property management, and one of the perks is getting a big discount on this swanky two-bedroom apartment in the Village District. It's got hardwood floors, an open-plan kitchen/dining/living area, separate bathrooms and huge walk-in closets for each bedroom. Plus, there are floor-to-ceiling windows in the living area that look out on the courtyard below. She does make good money, but there's no way she could afford a place like this without the discount. It makes the place Suz and I are living in look like a dump.

"So, are you really going to do it?" Abby asks. "I mean, you keep saying you're going to break up with her…"

"Maybe. I…I'm seriously considering it." I actually packed an overnight bag before I left so I could stay the night at Abby's and think things over. I texted Suz from the car and told her I'd be back tomorrow after work, but haven't gotten a response yet.

"What's different this time? Did Suz do something? Or, more likely, *not* do something?"

"Nothing's different with her, which is part of the problem." I shrug, which sends a sting of pain through my right underarm where they did the biopsy. I'm glad I brought the tiny ice packs along to dull the pain. I'll have to put those in again soon. "But, finding out I might have cancer really shook me. And Suz was very blasé about the whole thing. I know she wouldn't have been particularly caring and nurturing if I did have to go through any kind of treatment." I wipe my hands down my face. "I don't know if I can sit around in a dead-end relationship anymore."

"Good for you!" Abby pats me on the back. "You gave it your all. No one can say you didn't. But she just isn't right for you. Someday you'll find the person you're meant to be with."

"Thanks. I feel kinda rotten about it. Not 'cause Suz will care, but because I stayed too long where I wasn't wanted. I wasted too much time."

Abby envelops me in a hug. "You'll find them, I know you will. And it will be magical."

In her arms, I feel safer than I've ever felt. And I don't know if it's the stress of the last few days, my impending breakup, or the dream I had about the faceless one again last night, but I have this overwhelming feeling that maybe the person I'm meant to be with has been here in front of me all along. *That would just be too easy,* I think.

We break apart, and I look into her eyes. Even though the dream girl didn't have a face, I feel exactly what I felt for the dream woman while I look at Abby: safety, hope, love. I tear my eyes away and shake my head to clear it. There's no way the faceless one is Abby. I don't know if it's Suz either, but if my best friend was the one I was supposed to be with, I think I'd have already figured that out in over thirty years of friendship, wouldn't I?

Part 2

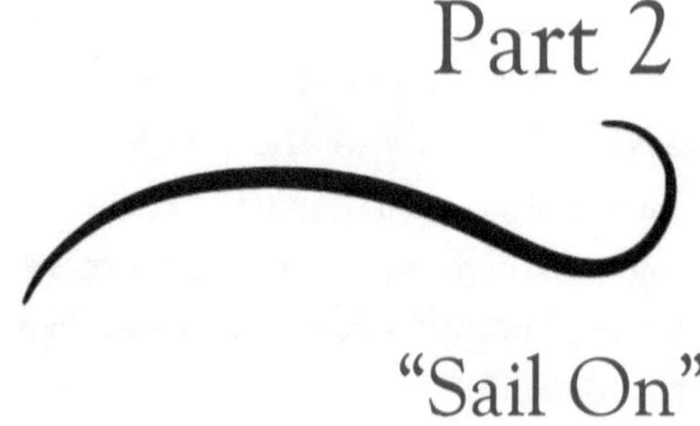

"Sail On"

April

"Why are you so out of breath?" Abby asks as I close the door to her red Mini Cooper. "I mean, I get that you ran out from the shop, but it's like three feet away."

I take a moment to collect myself, which isn't that easy considering I just made a complete fool out of myself, sprinted back to the coffee shop, grabbed my things and my cat, and practically threw them into her waiting car. My heart is still racing, but I breathe deeply and by the time we make it to the second stoplight, I'm feeling better. "I ran a little farther than that," I say, but Abby continues as if I haven't answered her.

"And whose phone was that you called me from? Did you lose your phone or something? Drop it in a puddle? Did Suz keep it as collateral so she could get half her money back?" Abby is nothing if not inquisitive.

"If you'd let me answer just one of your questions..." I sigh, then proceed to explain to her how I ended up calling her. Her eyebrows go up when I mention asking a random guy on the street to borrow his phone, but I plow through. That's a story to tell over a pint of ice cream. Come to think of it, I have many such stories for tonight.

Abby turns into the parking garage of her apartment building and parks in her assigned space. "Alright, let's get you gals inside and dried off!"

We get my stuff out of the backseat, and I grab Shelley, who was fine, but is now starting to freak out again. She's the only cat I've ever known to be calmed by riding in the car. "It's okay, sweetie. We're almost to Aunt Abby's," I say as we get on the elevator. Shelley ignores me and continues having her hissy fit.

When we reach the third floor, I follow Abby down the hall to her apartment. I've been here so many times before, but never thought I'd be living here. Of course, I never thought I'd kiss some random man on the street in the rain either, so I guess it's a day for firsts.

"Here we are, ladies. Home, sweet home," Abby sing-songs. "I've got the litter box all set up in the bathroom."

"Thanks, Abby," I say, putting down the carrier. I open the door, and Shelley flies out like she's been holed up in there for days. "Yeah, we won't see her for a while."

I put the tiny ice packs the radiologist gave me in the freezer for later, and we take the rest of my things to my new room, Abby's guestroom. It's a lovely room with a queen-sized bed and a small walk-in closet. The attached bath is small, especially with the litter box in the corner, but it's more high-end than my old place. I feel a pang of loneliness when I think of not being with Suz anymore. I turn around and walk back into the bedroom. I look up over the bed and see a framed poster of Monet's *The Walk, Woman with a Parasol*. It is one of my favorite paintings and I can't believe Abby remembered. Her idea of art is more along the lines of cells from animated films. "Abby," I call.

"Yeah?" she says, coming back to my room holding a dish towel. "What's up?"

I point to the poster. "Did you get that for me?"

"I thought you needed a little something of you in this room, so you'd feel at home," she shrugs. "Hooray for same-day delivery! Is that the right one? I remembered there was a woman in it, but..."

"Yes," I squeak, fighting back tears, "it's the right one." I pull her into a hug, trying desperately not to cry all over her.

"Aww, Clare. Today's been a rough one, hasn't it?" Abby asks, gently rubbing my back. "Just cry it out."

I sob into her shoulder, relishing the warmth of a good friend's embrace. Eventually, I pull back, wiping the tears from my eyes. "I think I needed that."

"Of course. Whatever you need."

"It's so hard, you know? One day, you're minding your own business, getting your annual mammogram like you're supposed to, then *blam!* Cancer." I shake my head. "I haven't had any symptoms. I couldn't even feel this 'chunky' lymph node the radiologist found on the ultrasound, but what do you know, it's malignant."

Abby pats me on the shoulder. "I'm so sorry. I can't imagine what you're going through."

I shrug. "I don't really know what to think right now because they still have more tests to run to figure out where it's coming from, but it's scary as hell." Tears well up again and my next words come out choked. "I could die."

"You're not going to die," Abby says immediately, shaking her head emphatically with tears running down her own cheeks. "Nope. It's not going to happen."

"But I really could."

My words hang heavy in the air for what feels like hours but is probably only a few seconds. I hope in my heart this is not the most likely scenario, but when anyone hears the word cancer, the word death is not too far behind. I also cannot spend this evening dwelling on that, or we'll be crying all night long. Plus, my heart is beginning to pound in my ears.

"Okay, I think I need to not talk about this any more today. There's nothing I can do about it until I see my doctor tomorrow and get more tests done, so let's try to do something else to take my mind off of it. I really don't want to work myself up into another panic attack like I had yesterday when I got the call." I've had panic attacks ever since my parents passed away, and it took my coworker Nate quite a while to calm me down yesterday. I'd rather not go through that again tonight.

"Good idea, because we should celebrate!" she announces.

"Celebrate what?" I ask. You really never know with Abby. One night it could be the celebration of her boss giving her a raise and the next a celebration of her favorite show being renewed for a fifth season. To her, almost anything is a celebration. Maybe she wants to celebrate that we're roommates again after all these years.

She looks at me as if I'm totally dense. "Celebrate you finally getting out of that relationship with Suz that was going absolutely nowhere. You're finally free!"

So, not exactly what I thought she was going to say. "Um...I don't actually feel like celebrating tonight," I mutter.

She nods. "I get that with the news you got you probably don't feel like celebrating much, but you finally got up the courage to get out of that dead-end relationship and we should celebrate it. Wanna go out somewhere and pick up some cute guys...or girls?"

I shake my head, thinking briefly of the guy I did almost "pick up" tonight. Just wait till Abby hears about that one. Then I'll have two celebrations to deal with.

"C'mon. We have to do something. I can't let you just sit in here all night organizing all your clothes in the closet or wallowing about the biopsy," she whines, then puts a hand up. "Not that you don't deserve all the wallowing in the world about your test results, but I still think we should do something fun tonight. What do you want to do?"

I think for a moment. The only thing I really want to do right now is lay on my bed and cry, but I won't let myself do that. Not to mention the fact that Abby's not going to take no for an answer. So, I come up with the only solution I think we can both agree to.

* * *

After a quick trip to the store for emotional support ice cream, we're sitting in our pajamas on the sofa eating pints of Ben & Jerry's with giant spoons. Abby got her usual Coffee Caramel Buzz, and I got Chocolate Therapy, which seems very appropriate for the occasion. Each spoonful is filled with all the chocolaty goodness one person can possibly stand, and it's working miracles on my mood.

"Alright, Clare. Out with it," Abby says over a mouthful of coffee ice cream. She's wearing her favorite Winnie the Pooh pajamas and has her long brown hair pulled up into a loose ponytail. She's one of those classically beautiful women, whereas I'm more grow-on-you beautiful with my short coppery hair and freckles. I'm just your typical Irish-American stereotype.

I swallow. "Out with what?"

"Out with whatever it is you're feeling that required this ice cream social." She knows me too well. Yes, it's a cliché that girls eat ice cream when they're upset about something, but Abby knows I only go for the hard stuff—and by that, I mean the chocolate, chocolate, chocolate stuff—when something really big is bothering me. If it's just a little mild sadness over a bad week at work or a spat with Suz, I'd get something a little more normal like Peanut Butter Cup. But, if it's full-on depression or biting-my-nails kind of worry, it's chocolate overload all the way. "Is it just the biopsy results or is there something else?" she asks.

Biding my time, I take another big spoonful and let the flavor melt away my anxiety over telling her. "Mostly, but there's...something else."

She tucks her legs underneath her and faces me, her eyes asking all the questions I know are swirling around in that head of hers. When I don't continue immediately, she starts peppering me with "whats."

I take a deep breath and begin to recount for her the entire evening. The mad rush to pack and leave Suz's, her lack of concern over me leaving, her abundance of concern over the rent, the pouring rain and the coffee shop.

"What a jerk," she says. "She didn't know what she had when she had you. I'll bet she comes crawling back once she realizes she's not just missing your rent check."

"Thanks," I reply. I seriously doubt that will happen, but it certainly would make me feel better if it did. Not that it will make me change my mind. Well, not really.

"So, then you called me from that guy's phone, and I picked you up. What else is there to be upset about?" she asks, then quickly adds, "Not that that isn't plenty to be upset about. But you said it was more than just Suz and the biopsy, right?"

"Yeah. Something happened after I called you." My pause is evidently a little too long here and Abby tries to get another question in, but I raise my hand to stop her. "Please, just let me get this out without interruption. Okay?" She nods.

"After I called you, the guy offered to walk me to the coffee place so I wouldn't get more wet. He had one of those big golf umbrellas. Did I mention that already?" I'm stalling, I know I am. I'm just not sure how to tell my best friend that I did something so impulsive and crazy as to kiss some random guy on the street. I am *so* not that girl. Abby is that girl, but I am as far from that as Earth is from the Sun.

Okay, Clare. Just rip off the Band-Aid. "You remember those dreams I have sometimes?" I ask, then gesture that it's okay for her to reply.

"The ones where a faceless person does all sorts of romantic things for you?"

"Yeah. Well, when I got into the coffee house, I had this extreme sense of déjà vu. You know, like I'd seen that guy before. But it didn't seem like I'd seen him just anywhere—"

"You mean, like you'd seen him in your dreams?" As soon as the question was out, Abby clapped her hands over her mouth, her eyes wide.

"Something like that. I...I'm not sure if I even fully registered what I was feeling at the time. I just felt this overwhelming sense of someone or something pushing me toward him." I trail off and take another bite of my ice cream. Abby looks at me expectantly, hands still over her mouth. A gentle shake of my head tells her I'm not done. Her eyes get even wider.

"Without much thought, I left all my stuff in the coffee house and ran after him. And, when I caught up to him, I..." Her eyes impel me to continue. "I kissed him." The words are barely audible, even to my own ears.

"YOU WHAT?!" Abby shouts.

"I kissed him," I repeat, louder.

"You...you...kissed him? You kissed him? You, Clare O'Donnell, kissed a guy you've never met before, on the street, in the rain? On the day you broke up with your long-time, live-in girlfriend?"

"Yes." It's all I can think to say.

Abby lies back on the sofa, draping her arm across her face. I'm barely able to rescue her spoon, full of ice cream, from falling to the floor. After a moment, she peeks at me from under her arm. "You really kissed him?"

"Yep."

"On the lips?"

"On the lips."

Her breath gushes out of her as if she'd been holding it this whole time. "Wow."

"I know."

"I just can't believe it. You are like the least impulsive person I know. I mean, it took you how many years to break up with Suz?"

I cringe at the sound of her name. "I know. I can't believe I did it either."

"So, how was it?" she asks, sitting up again, eager for the juicy details.

"I...uh...well," I stammer, but something on my face must tell her exactly what she wants to know.

"That good, huh?"

I know I'm blushing fifteen shades of red, and I look down at the couch as if the sage green fabric just caught my attention.

"Did he kiss you back?" she probes.

"I think so?" It comes out as a question, but really, I know the answer. Yes. He most definitely kissed me back. It was, in fact, the best kiss I've ever had in my life. The best kiss I've ever dreamed of having in my life. I felt that kiss down to my toes. But I can't tell Abby this detail because she'll blow this even more out of proportion than she's already doing.

"So, what happened next?"

"I ran."

"You ran?"

"All the way back to the coffee house, where you were just pulling up. That's why I was out of breath when I got in the car."

Recognition dawns on her face. "But you left without getting his name? Without seeing if he liked the kiss too?"

"Abby, I was just so embarrassed. Once the kiss was over, I could not get away from there fast enough. I've never done anything like that in my life." And it's true. I never do anything without looking at every single scenario at least ten times. I've made mistakes, mind you, but at least I know I've thought about them a lot before I decide to commit them. "I'm sure he thinks I'm some love-starved fool who was just really happy he let her use his phone."

Abby looks over at the coffee table, contemplating, then looks back at me with mischief in her eyes. "You know, I have his number in my phone."

"Um...no," I reply, matter-of-factly.

"But you have to. You can't just leave it like this."

I get up from the couch and walk to the kitchen to wash my spoon and put the rest of my ice cream in the freezer. "I most certainly can and will leave it like this. Do you have any idea how mortifying that was? And, by extension, how mortifying it would be to see him again?"

"I can only imagine," she says, then holds up her hand to keep me from interrupting her. "But what if he is literally the man of your dreams? Can you really let this chance go by? After all you've been through with your parents and Suz and..."—she gestures widely—"...everything. You so deserve to be happy."

At the mention of my parents, I feel the burn of tears in my eyes, but I will them not to fall. "I just...can't," I whisper.

Without another word, Abby comes to the kitchen and embraces me, rubbing my back. When she releases me, she puts her hands up in surrender. "Okay. I won't push. I just think you might be missing the opportunity of a—" Her phone starts vibrating across the coffee table. "Probably another telemarketer. I'll be right back."

She grabs her phone and glances down at the number. "Um...Clare?" She looks up at me. "Remember that missed opportunity? It's calling."

I immediately run toward her in a vain attempt to dismiss the call before she can answer it. But I'm too late.

"Hello?" she says, grinning at me like the Cheshire Cat. "Yep. Uh huh. I'm Abby and her name is Clare."

"Say I'm not here," I mouth, waving my hands like I'm landing a plane.

But, of course, Abby says, "Yeah, she's right here. Hang on." So much for not pushing me.

She thrusts the phone at me, still grinning like a fool, and I take it with my hand that has suddenly gotten very sweaty. "Hello?" I croak. My knees buckle and I'm grateful to have been standing right in front of a chair.

"So, what was all that about back there?" he asks with no introduction.

"I...uh...well...I..." I stammer.

"Well, that's just not going to cut it now, is it?" he says, not unkindly. In fact, I can almost hear him smiling on the other end of the line. "You see, I can't just ignore that I was kissed in the middle of the street by a complete stranger."

His voice reminds me so much of the one I heard in the dream the other night that I try to say something—anything— but nothing comes out. Abby whispers for me to put him on speakerphone, but I shake my head. Slightly annoyed, she sits down on the arm of the chair and puts her ear next to the phone. As if I wasn't overheated enough.

"Clare? Are you still there?" he asks.

"Yeah. Still here," I manage.

"Why don't we meet at the coffee shop tomorrow around four?" Sensing my hesitation, he adds, "It'll give you a chance to explain yourself."

I nod my head, then when Abby pokes me, I realize he can't see that through the phone. "Okay," I answer.

"Ask his name," Abby stage whispers in my ear.

Before I get the chance to ask, he says, "Tell your friend my name's Roddy Vaughn."

* * *

Before I've even thought about where I'm going to put all my stuff in Abby's guestroom, she starts riffling through my clothes trying to pick out the perfect outfit for my meeting with Roddy. I flatly refuse to call it a date since I don't even know the guy and he's probably just meeting up with me to find out just how crazy I am so he can share a good laugh with his friends later. Abby, on the other hand, is in full-on Date Preparation Mode. You'd think I was going out on a date with Chris Evans or Scarlett Johansson the way she's going on about it.

"Clare?" she calls from the bedroom. "Would you like to explain to me why I just found this in your suitcase?"

I come out from the bathroom, where I was trying to unpack my toiletries, to see Abby holding up a *Star Trek* t-shirt. More specifically, a purple shirt with the words "Make Trek Not Wars" emblazoned across the chest in both *Star Trek: The Next Generation* and *Star Wars* lettering. The fact that I know this shames me to my core. "Um...I don't know how that got in there. I must have grabbed one of Suz's shirts by mistake."

Abby gives me a knowing look, and I think she's going to let me off the hook. Then she holds the shirt up against herself and says, "Suz hates purple, if I remember correctly. Want to try again?"

"Alright," I sigh heavily before continuing. "Suz gave it to me for my birthday last year. I've only worn it once and it must have still been in the drawer with my other shirts. Happy?"

"I'm happy that you admitted it, and I'm happy that you didn't buy it for yourself, but I'm not happy that it's in my apartment. You need to purge all the Suz-ness out of your life for good," she says, balling up the t-shirt and throwing it into the trash can. "I have no problem with people being nerdy. But you don't even like *Star Trek...Wars...*whatever, so you shouldn't pretend to just to make Suz happy. Especially now that you're not together anymore."

She's right. Throughout the entirety of my relationship with Suz, I pretended to like the things that she liked in order for us to get closer to one another. I watched her shows, I read her books, I tried playing her video games. I even went to an Anime convention with her—just one, mind you. Not only did it not work to bring us closer together, it backfired in that she thought I really liked all those things. I pray Abby doesn't find the *Doctor Who* socks in the bottom of that suitcase. They're actually my favorite socks, and I couldn't bear it if she threw them out. And, I genuinely like *Doctor Who*...the new ones, at least.

"I know. But seeing as I just broke up with her today and you're so proud of me for doing that, could you just let me throw them out when I'm ready to?" I plead. It's been a hard enough day without having to go through all my stuff and rid it of anything that reminds me of her.

"Sure," she says, coming to give me a hug. "I'm sorry I threw out your Trek shirt. Shall I fish it out of the trash?"

I laugh a little. "Well, we could at least donate it somewhere. It's a nice shirt."

"Goodwill for Nerds?" she asks.

"Something like that," I say. I pull the shirt out of the trash can and start a pile of items to donate, knowing full well that the pile will be huge by the time I'm done going through my things.

Abby walks back over to the suitcase and starts sorting through my clothes. "Now, let's find something for you to wear on your date."

I roll my eyes and just go with it.

* * *

An hour later, the doorbell rings and Abby goes to answer it. I hear a flurry of male voices, coupled with Abby's, and though I can't hear them clearly through my closed door, I suspect it's our friends Isaac and Nate. I've known Isaac since high school when we were in sophomore English class together. We worked on a group project where we had to do a modern retelling of a legend or fairy tale, and I decided we should do a puppet show about Robin Hood. Isaac loved the idea and the two of us carried the group to an A, even though our group mates were completely useless.

I met Nate when I was working at a boring office job about ten years ago. We talked a little over the years, but really hit it off about six years ago when he came back from vacation to Salzburg—somewhere I'd always wanted to go because of my love for *The Sound of Music*—and we got to talking about all the places we'd love to visit. We started having lunch together, talking about anything and everything. Then, we would hang out on the weekends to go to the movies. He came out to me one such weekend, and I was so proud of him and happy that he felt he could be his authentic self around me.

Eventually, Nate decided to leave the office job to start his own travel agency. Once it got going, he asked if I wanted to join his company. I didn't think twice. I turned in my two weeks' notice and started working with him thereafter. I've never looked back because being a travel agent is the most rewarding and wonderful job I could have ever imagined. Plus, I get to work with one of my best friends every single day and dream about travel, even if I never actually go anywhere myself.

Now, I walk to the doorway of my bedroom and hear a bit of their conversation.

"...wanted to check to see how she was doing," Nate says.

"She's doing okay," Abby replies, sotto voce. "She didn't really want to talk much about the results."

"We won't even bring it up," Isaac says, putting his finger to his lips. "Is she here, though? We have some exciting news to share that might cheer her up."

"Clare? Nate and Isaac are here," Abby calls. "They have exciting news!"

I head to the living room and see my friends standing next to Abby. Nate's very tall and lanky—though not quite as tall as Roddy—with a full head of dark blond wavy hair. With golden skin, rugged features and one of those close-cropped beards that are all the rage, he's very handsome. Isaac is a little shorter, but very muscular. He is bald by choice and his rich tawny complexion sets off his deep brown eyes. Abby has always said if she wasn't a lesbian and they weren't gay, she'd be all over them both. I have to admit, if they weren't gay, I would be too.

"Hi, guys," I say with a weird wave I couldn't seem to hold back.

"Oh, Clare," Isaac says, and runs toward me with his arms flung wide, tears in his eyes. He embraces me and I wrap my arms around him. The tears come even though I will them to stop. I feel Nate hug me from behind as well.

"Make room for me in there," I hear Abby say as she comes over to join the hugging. Nate shifts to the left so she can come in from the right side to make a circle around me. I am completely enveloped by my friends' warm arms, safe and secure.

"We are all here for you," Nate encourages.

Isaac kisses my cheek and adds, "Yes. Anything you need, you just call. We love you, Clare."

"I love you all too," I say through my tears.

Isaac is the first to step back, then Abby, then Nate, and I see that we've all been crying.

"I'm going to see my doctor tomorrow morning, and we'll see what happens from there. I know there are going to be more tests, so I know there will be a lot of opportunities for everyone to help me out." Desperately wanting to change the subject, I wipe my eyes and ask, "So, what's this news? I'd love to hear something happy."

Nate gives Isaac a knowing glance, and Isaac shrugs. Abby sees this exchange as well and, never one to mince words, says, "Well, c'mon. One of you tell us."

Isaac holds his hand out for Nate to spill the beans. Nate takes Isaac's hand in his before he speaks. "We were going to wait until a slightly better time, when you aren't dealing with quite so much, what with the biopsy and the—"

"Oh, we know, just get on with it," Abby interrupts. "She wants happy news, not a rehashing of all the bad stuff."

"I'm getting there," Nate replies, abashed. Abby and Nate are good friends, really, but she gets really annoyed with his tendency to ramble and restate the obvious. Apparently, today, she's had enough.

"Nate, I'm sorry. Please, continue," Abby says.

"It's okay. I'll get to the good stuff." Nate smiles. "Tonight—just an hour or so ago, in fact—I proposed to Isaac and he said, 'yes'!"

"Oh my God! I'm so happy for you!" I squeal. Now that I think about it, Nate isn't merely smiling, he's positively glowing. How did I not notice this before? And Isaac is beaming back at Nate as well. The two of them are so cute together and absolutely made for each other.

"Congratulations!" Abby adds. "I knew you two would tie the knot eventually."

"Thank you, thank you," Nate replies. "We're both really excited."

"And, Clare, I wanted to ask you something," Isaac starts, "would you be my Best Woman?"

Tears spring to my eyes again, but happy ones this time. "Absolutely!"

Nate turns to Abby. "And, Abby, would you be my Best Woman?"

"Really?" Abby asks, shocked. "You want me?"

"Of course I do," Nate replies. "You two are our best friends in the world and we want both of you up there with us."

Nate nudges Isaac, and they both look back at me again. "Clare, we had another favor to ask," Isaac says, eyes gleaming. "Would you be willing to sing for the wedding?"

Nate jumps in before I can respond, "Your voice is so heavenly, and it would make our day truly special if you would grace us with a song."

I wipe the tears from my cheeks. "I would be honored. Just please don't make me sing 'I Will Always Love You' by Dolly or Whitney." We all laugh.

"You got it," Isaac replies. "You'll have full artistic approval."

"I think we need to do that group hug again," I say. Everyone obliges and soon we're hugging and laughing. In the back of my mind, however, is a fleeting thought that I hope I am around to sing at their wedding.

Part B

"Curse the Love Songs"

April

When I get back to my...our...Suz's apartment at ten o'clock the next evening, she's not in her usual position on the sofa. I assume she's taking a bathroom break or a shower and will be back soon to rejoin her game, since Friday nights are one of her group's customary times to play. But, when I get back to the bedroom to put my stuff away, she's sitting on the bed reading. She's got music playing quietly on her phone.

"Hey," I say. I set my overnight bag on the end of the bed and start unpacking.

Suz looks up from her eReader. "Where have you been?" she asks.

"I was at Abby's last night. I texted you I was going to stay over."

She shrugs. "I never got your text. But, my phone did some sort of update yesterday, so I wonder if I just missed it."

"You could have texted *me* you know." No response. I put the last of my things in the hamper, then change into my nightshirt. Suz is back to reading her book and I don't know what to say to her anymore. So, I go to the bathroom to get ready for bed.

When I come back to the bedroom, I trip on the rug next to her side of the bed and am barely able to keep myself from falling by pressing my hands into the mattress next to her. "Aaaccck!" I shout. I clutch my right wrist, which took the brunt of the impact. I know it's not badly injured, but it still hurts a bit. Suz doesn't look up at all.

"Do you have eyes on top of your head to know I'm fine, or do you just not care?" I ask, irritated. "I mean, you had to have felt me hit the bed, even if you didn't see anything."

She slowly drags her gaze away from her eReader to look at me. "I saw, I felt, and I heard, but you seemed like you had it handled. What did you want me to do?"

I sigh heavily. "Care? At least ask if I was okay. Something. Anything."

"Are you okay?" she asks with as little feeling as possible.

I throw up my hands. "I don't want you to ask me because I told you to. I want you to be concerned about me." I pause to see if she'll have any reaction. "But you aren't, so that's just *fine*."

"I really don't understand what you're so upset about," she replies, still not putting her eReader aside.

As a love song plays from her phone, it dawns on me that I'm not upset about her not checking on me from this little incident, I'm upset because she doesn't care about me in general. She didn't check to see where I was when I didn't come home last night. We've been living completely separate lives and it's taken this long for me to come to terms with it.

"No, you don't, do you? I think I'm going to sleep in the guest room tonight," I reply, finally. I walk to my side of the bed, pick up my pillow and walk out of the room.

* * *

"Well, you know my feelings on the matter," Abby says, taking a bite of her salad. "You should have done this months or even years ago."

I convened a summit of my closest friends at our favorite lunch spot, Denise's Café, the next day to discuss the "Suz Situation." Abby and Isaac both had the day off, and Nate and I decided to play hooky today as well. Nate and Isaac were only too eager to give their two—or make that four—cents and eat the delicious food. Especially after they came over last night to give us the news about their impending nuptials. I'm sure they'd rather talk more about the wedding today. Abby came for the food since we'd already hashed this out last night. But I knew she would probably throw in some more opinions before the lunch was over. We're gathered around our favorite table by the window, and I'm growing more certain of what I must do as the conversation wears on.

"I don't know about years," Nate interjects. "Things were good there for a while. And she really was there for Clare after the…you know…"—he lowers his voice to a whisper—"*accident*."

Isaac puts down his sandwich and wipes his hands on his napkin before speaking. "Was she though? I mean, yeah, she helped out with the planning aspects of the funeral and the estate and stuff, but that's what she's good at. Technical and organizational stuff, you know? Was she *really* there for Clare in the emotional sense?" He shrugs. "Jury's still out on that one."

"Helping me out with all the arrangements did take a huge burden off while I was healing and gave me more space to grieve, so in that sense, I think you could say she was there for me emotionally," I reply. "However, I do see your point, Isaac. So, if she wasn't there for me emotionally then, then she hasn't really been there for me…ever." This realization weighs heavily on me, and I put my head into my hands. Nate and Abby each lightly rub my back.

"Oh, girl," Nate begins. "I know it's hard. You put your heart into something—someone—and it just wasn't reciprocated."

I slowly lift my head. "It's not that. I mean, it sort of is, but I feel like such an idiot for believing in us for so long when it's obvious to everyone around me that there was nothing to believe in. Hell, it's even obvious to Suz! She has never once called me her girlfriend, partner, significant other, or anything to show that I mean anything to her other than a rent check."

"You're not an idiot," Abby and Isaac say at the same time as Nate says, "That's not true."

"But it is, and I am. It's over, if it ever was anything to begin with." I take a big bite of my grilled cheese sandwich in an attempt to drown my sorrows in copious amounts of cheese. Denise's makes the best grilled cheese sandwiches. I swallow and say, "Alright, enough about Suz and me. Let's talk about your wedding or something else fun."

"Well," Isaac begins, "we talked and looked at our calendars last night, and we settled on a date."

"Really?" Abby and I say almost in unison.

Nate nods. "Yep. We're getting married on November fifth." To me he adds, "You know how I've always wanted to get married in the fall."

"I can't believe you let almost this whole lunch go on with me droning on about Suz and you sitting on this amazing news," I say. "You should have cut me off sooner. I don't want to be Carrie Bradshaw, always talking about my stuff and never anyone else's."

Isaac tsks, then adds, "No, you needed us and we're here for you. You're nothing like Carrie. Believe me, Abby would call you on it if you were. Isn't that right?"

Abby laughs heartily. "You got that right."

She winks at me, and all those feelings from last night start flooding back. *No, Clare, that was just one of her regular winks. Get a grip!* I manage a smile back, but it's tentative at best. I probably look like I've got something in my eye.

Abby looks down at her watch. "Oh, I have to run. I'm meeting my parents for coffee in like thirty minutes." She rolls her eyes. "Clare, can you make your own way back to the apartment?"

"Sure. Is everything okay?" I ask, concerned. Abby's relationship with her parents is stilted at best, and she tries to avoid seeing them when they're in town.

"Yeah." She shrugs. "Nothing major."

I take the hint that she doesn't really want to share too much in front of Nate and Isaac, so I let it drop. "Okay, well, I'll see you back at your place later then."

"See you then. And congrats on setting the date, guys!" She picks up her jacket and purse and heads out the door to her car.

"I wonder what that was all about," Isaac says. "I take it from your bewildered expression that you don't know either."

I shake my head. "I have no idea. She usually avoids her parents when they come to town, so it's a little strange."

"Oh, she's probably doing the coffee date just to avoid a longer visit with them later," Nate adds. "I'm sure she'll fill you in later when the menfolk aren't around."

Isaac and I laugh at that. "Menfolk?" Isaac queries. "When did you turn country?"

"I've lived in North Carolina all my life. Occasionally a little hillbilly slips in."

To me, Isaac says, "Am I making the right choice? Should I back out now?"

"Haha," I chuckle. "You're making the right choice. He's just got to keep you on your toes is all. You can't know everything about each other already."

Isaac looks over at Nate who is making puppy dog eyes at him. "How can I not love this man? Even if he does say crazy things like 'menfolk' out of nowhere." They kiss and it's incredibly sweet to see, although it does make my heart hurt slightly with the fact that I've just decided to break up with Suz.

Crap. I still have to break up with Suz.

"Alright, I need to go rip the Band-Aid off and deal with the Suz situation," I say, taking a last sip of my iced tea. I wipe my hands on my napkin, gather my things and stand up.

"Do you want us to come with you? I'm not sure if it would help or not, but we're happy to be there for moral support," Nate offers, and Isaac nods his agreement.

"Thanks, but I need to do this on my own. I'll text you later and let you know how it went." I put on my hoodie and sling the strap of my cross-body purse over my head and onto my shoulder.

"Good luck!" Isaac calls as I walk out of the café.

* * *

I step off the bus at the stop in front of my apartment. Really, it's Suz's apartment as only her name is on the lease—a fact that she loves pointing out to me—but I feel like it was a tiny bit mine for a while. My nerves are so jangled I almost drop my keys when I hear the squeal of the bus pulling away. On the one hand, I can't believe I am breaking up with Suz, and on the other, I can't believe I've waited this long.

I put the key in the lock of the downstairs door, then climb the four flights of concrete stairs to our floor. When I reach the first landing, I hear the telltale banging of the construction crew working on the dilapidated elevator. Of course I decide to move out right when the landlord is finally fixing it.

When I reach our floor, I'm a little winded, so I walk at a leisurely pace to our…her door to allow me time to catch my breath. Being real, I'm not entirely sure what I'm planning to say to her when I get in there either, so I should use the extra time to figure that out. Am I? Nope. I am, however, fretting over whether I should open the door with my key or knock. *Why are you being an idiot, Clare? Just open the door.*

I fumble with my keys so much when I do finally make it to the apartment door that the sound must be enough for Suz to hear from the other side, because she opens the door before I can get my key in the lock.

"Clare?" she says, confused.

"Hey. Yeah, I was having trouble getting my keys out. Sorry," I reply.

"Oh." She steps back so I can come in.

Sticking my keys back in my purse, I walk in, and she shuts the door behind us.

"I was just getting ready to have lunch. Are you having anything?" Suz asks.

I shake my head. "I had lunch already."

She walks into the kitchen. "Cool. I'm just going to make—"

"We need to talk," I interrupt. My heart is racing and I'm willing myself not to panic. Most of the time, my panic attacks are brought on by severe stress, but sometimes they can be triggered by more minor things. Although, breaking up with one's "girlfriend" is not all that minor, in the grand scheme of things.

She turns, her mouth still open from speaking. She closes it, then says, "Uh. Okay."

"Sorry. I need to get this out. Then you can make your sandwich or whatever, I just need you to listen for a few minutes."

"Fine," she replies. She leans against the counter, crossing her arms over her chest.

I take a deep breath to calm myself down. I take another and feel a little relief. One more deep breath, cleansing exhale out and I feel okay to begin. "Suz, I can't do this anymore. I feel like I have given all I can to this relationship, but I'm not being given anything in return. Hell, you don't even call me your girlfriend. I need to be happy and find someone who will acknowledge me and love me for who I am."

She looks askance for a moment, and I turn to see that Shelley has jumped up onto the couch in Suz's favorite spot. "Can you get your cat off the couch?"

My blood boils with frustration. "I'm breaking up with you and you're worried about the cat? Seriously? Were you even listening to me?"

She looks back at me. "I heard you, but then I saw your cat jump up onto the couch—where she's not supposed to be— and thought you could deal with that while I work on what to say in response to what you said."

"Fine," I say, exasperated. Thankfully, my heart rate has slowed down and I'm not feeling panicky anymore. Just angry. I stalk over to the couch and gingerly pick Shelley up from her relaxed position there. She's not happy with me for disturbing her, even though I relocate her to her favorite window perch with a beautiful sunbeam. "Blame Suz," I mouth to Shelley.

I return to the kitchen to find Suz in the exact same position, but her eyes are closed in contemplation. I know this look well as whenever she's coming up with what to say, she simply closes her eyes while she formulates her response instead of engaging with the person on the other end of the conversation. It's unnerving.

I'm settling down on one of the chairs in the breakfast nook, knowing this could still take a while, when Suz's eyes suddenly pop open. She turns slightly to face me anew before she speaks. "I have to say this feels like it's coming out of the blue for me, so I'm having a hard time wrapping my head around it." She starts to pace and counts with her fingers as she recaps what I've said. "You aren't given enough back from what you put in. You want to be happy. You're upset because I don't call you my girlfriend. You can't do *this* anymore. And, what do you mean by 'this,' exactly?"

"This," I reply, waving my arms between the two of us. "Our relationship. We've been together for how many years now and you don't seem to comprehend any of it. This is exactly my point."

Suz stops pacing and sighs. "Clare, I'm afraid I don't understand what you mean by 'relationship,'" she says using air quotes. "I thought we mutually decided we weren't so much dating as just rooming together. You know, after we tried and failed our experiment to..." She trails off gesturing vaguely with her hand.

Naturally she's bringing up our one "failed experiment"— as she puts it—or attempt at sex as most others would call it. It was shortly after we moved in together and it *was* pretty awful, I'll give her that much. It wasn't either of our faults really, but I think we just needed to work on things in that department. Suz, on the other hand, didn't want to. She said, "I'm fine if we just never do that again." But I certainly don't remember anything about us deciding we weren't in a relationship anymore after that. I definitely missed that memo.

"I do not remember mutually deciding we weren't in a relationship anymore," I reply. "If that's the case, then why do we still share a bed?"

It takes a while for her to respond to this. "Convenience?" She shrugs.

"Really?" Flabbergasted would be an understatement.

"You know I hate change." Another shrug.

I throw up my hands. "I could have moved into the other bedroom. Did you ever think of that?"

"I guess not," she replies, crossing her arms again.

"I'm basically just a rent check to you then, aren't I?"

Silence except for the sound of cars passing by on the street outside.

"Ugh," I huff. "This isn't making me want to stay, and is, in fact, making me want to bolt even more." I stand up, the legs of the chair scraping as I do—the sound of the end. I walk to the hall closet to get my suitcases, and I expect her to say something, anything, in response. Instead, I hear her open the fridge and know she's making her lunch. Discussion over.

More resolved than ever, I pack as many bags as I can, as quickly as possible. I know I'll need to come back later to get some larger items, but at least I can take all my clothes, toiletries and such now. *Maybe I can get Abby, Nate, or Isaac to help me with the rest when Suz is at work one day,* I think. I don't know if I can bear to see her again after this. At least not for quite a while.

Once I have everything packed, I realize there's no way I can carry all this down the stairs by myself, plus I need to get Shelley in her crate. I can't imagine the bus driver's face when I try to shove multiple suitcases, two duffel bags, a toiletry case and a cat crate on the bus. I sit on the bed in our room and unlock my phone to call Abby, but I realize she's probably still out with her parents. So, I call Isaac instead to see if their offer of help is still available. Thankfully, they are free and will be here in ten minutes with their car.

I think about going back into the living room to wait for them, but I can't face Suz. I survey our room and bathroom, to make sure I haven't missed anything, and find a tiny picture of my parents sitting on the windowsill. I'd almost forgotten about it. My mom always said it was good luck to put pictures of people you'd lost in the window so their spirits would be reflected back to you. I have no idea where she got that from, as I've searched Irish myths and legends and never came across that one, but knowing her, she could have made it up. Regardless, I wanted to believe it was true, so I did it.

I pick up the small frame and hold it lovingly in my hands as I sit back on the bed. They were so happy in this photo—taken on their thirtieth wedding anniversary—both of them laughing at something, eyes sparkling, and the photographer captured their perfect joy forever. More than anything, I want what they had: someone to laugh with, someone to cry with, someone to love and never let go.

Suddenly, I'm thinking about the latest dream again of the faceless one. My father used to tell me when I was a young girl that they would make sure I was taken care of and loved even if they were gone. He said they'd always show me the way, which was a comforting idea, but I never thought much about it until the dreams started.

On the day they died, I chalked it up to too many pain meds for my own injuries from the accident, but when I kept getting the dreams long after I recovered, I couldn't help but wonder if my parents were sending me messages from the beyond, guiding me toward the one I was supposed to be with.

The dreams always started off with a genderless, faceless person doing romantic things for me like taking me to the opera, a romantic walk in the park, a trip to California, and on and on. I don't really remember the first one, probably because of the meds, and some of the others are kind of fuzzy as well. When they kept recurring, I started a dream journal so I could record them. The person's face would be blurred out like on TV, and their body was completely androgynous, but they were wearing a tuxedo. Always a tuxedo no matter what we were doing.

The other night was the first night where I could tell it was a woman, even though the face was still blurred, and the first time I got the feeling it might not be Suz.

Part 3

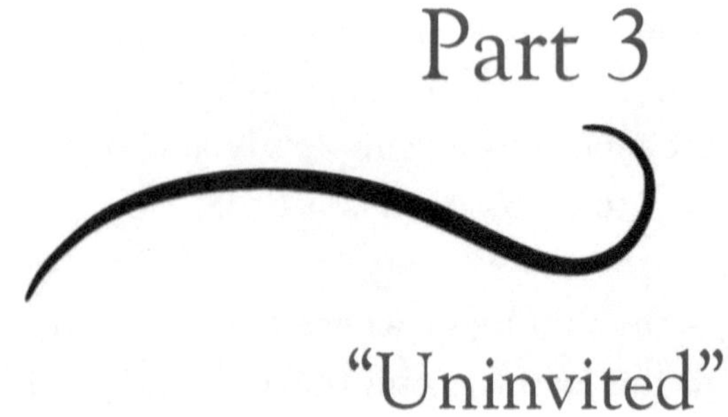

"Uninvited"

April

"How are you feeling, Clare?" my GP, Dr. Nouri asks the next morning.

I shrug. "I *feel* fine, but I'm freaking out a bit. And I haven't slept great since I had the biopsy. Even worse last night after I got the call, if I'm honest."

She nods. "That's understandable. I can send over a prescription for Xanax, and you can take even just a quarter tablet to help you sleep, because sleep is definitely important. Just don't drive or anything while you're taking it."

"I don't drive so that's not a problem," I assure her.

She types things into her laptop—sending the prescription to the pharmacy, most likely—then turns back to me. "I'm happy to answer any questions you have as best I can, but I wanted to go over the game plan first, if that's okay."

I nod, unconsciously picking at the skin around my thumbnail.

"Since adenocarcinoma can come from multiple places, we need to find the source. Most likely—given the location of the affected lymph nodes—it is breast, so I'm going to send you for a breast MRI since nothing showed on the mammogram or ultrasound. I'm also going to refer you for a chest and abdominal CT scan, to make sure there's nothing coming from somewhere else. With me so far?"

"Yes," I reply. "It's a lot to take in, but that sounds like a good plan."

She nods. "It is a lot, but before I refer you to oncology, I want to make sure I'm sending you to the right team. If it's breast, then I want to send you to the breast care team. If it's something else, then I want to get you to them. Once we get the results back from these scans, I'll get you to the right place and they'll get you moving with biopsies and treatment."

"Treatment," I repeat. My left knee starts bouncing up and down, unbidden. "That word just sounds so overwhelming." I think about Roddy and our coffee "date," and how much I'd really like to go on a proper date with him sometime. But is that something you can do when you're going through what I'm about to go through?

"I know," Dr. Nouri says, putting a reassuring hand on mine. "Hopefully, when we get the results back from the scans, the news will be the best possible and mean less in the way of 'treatment' for you."

"Fingers crossed," I say, crossing the fingers of my other hand and attempting a smile. We talk some more about what to expect from the tests I'll be undergoing and how long it could take to get everything scheduled.

"I know it's really scary. I won't pretend that it's not. But, I'm here if you need me. Just send a message through the portal or call the office and set up an appointment to come chat with me. We can even do telehealth, if it's more convenient. I can also refer you to a counselor or therapist, if you feel like you would benefit from that."

"I really appreciate you taking the time to meet with me. This has been really helpful," I reply sincerely.

We both stand up and she pats me gently on the back as she opens the door to the exam room. "I wish you the best and I will keep in touch as I receive the results from the scans. As I said, though, don't hesitate to reach out if you need anything in the meantime."

"Thanks." I exit the exam room and head for the checkout. Once I'm outside, I take a few deep breaths of spring air before I walk to the bus stop to head back to Abby's since Nate told me to take the rest of the week off from work. Although I did swing by to pick up my phone, which was still sitting on my desk in his office, right where I left it. I know I'm going to need a nice warm shower and some time to wrap my mind around everything before I meet Roddy this afternoon.

* * *

Sitting in the coffee shop, I'm willing myself to settle down. I don't think my left knee has stopped jumping since I left the doctor's office this morning, and while I'm not a particularly nervous person most of the time, I can really work myself up into a frenzy. I remind myself to get an herbal tea when I order. Ordinarily, I loathe herbal tea—and coffee, for that matter—but I know the caffeine will just make me more jittery. And, a hot chocolate might make me seem too self-indulgent. *For goodness' sake, Clare, just be yourself!*

The tinkle of the bell on the door signals the entry of yet another person that is not him. I'm beginning to think he isn't coming. Why should he come and face the person who embarrassed herself, and him, last night? I still can't believe I did what I did. Who kisses someone they don't even know just because of déjà vu from a dream? I wonder what my father would say if he knew what I did. I bet he'd think I lost my last ounce of sanity. "Clare," he'd say, "you've gone and lost your last marble, now haven't ya?"

"Clare?" I hear from a deep, male voice beside me and nearly jump out of my chair. Leave it to me to be daydreaming when he shows up so that I look even more the fool. At least I didn't have a drink to spill. I look up and see a hint of a smile playing at his lips. Was he this tall last night?

"Sorry, I didn't mean to startle you," he says after a moment. He puts his hand out. "I'm Roddy."

Eventually I realize that I haven't said anything or made any move to get up to greet him. "Oh...uh...that's okay," I stammer, standing and taking his hand. "I'm Clare."

"Well, Clare, it's nice to meet you...formally," he replies. He pats my hand with his left hand, presumably to remind me that we're still shaking hands since I seem to have forgotten. I not so gracefully take my hand back and sit down. Gesturing at the chair opposite me, he asks, "May I join you?"

I nod. He removes his jacket and sits down. I feel like I should say something, but I have no words. Last night, I really didn't register just how handsome he is. Even now, it's hard to pinpoint. His curly, medium brown hair is definitely a turn-on—I've always been partial to people with curly hair, although Suz has straight hair—and I wish I could run my fingers through it, but I'm sure that would scare him off even more. He's wearing dark-wash jeans which are not too loose, not too tight, and a simple blue polo shirt that indicates a well-defined chest underneath. He has strong features—a chiseled jawline, Roman nose and dark hazel eyes. And his lips are not too full and not too thin, perfect for kissing.

Get a grip, Clare! I wake myself out of my reverie and try to think of something to say to him. "Should we order?" I ask.

"Sure. What would you like?" he asks, standing.

"Oh, I can get mine," I say, not wanting him to think he has to buy the drink I still haven't decided on just because I kissed him last night. I'm not that kind of girl.

"There's really no point in both of us going up there to order. Plus, I forced you to come down here to explain yourself, so the least I can do is buy you a cup of coffee."

"Okay," I relent. "I actually don't care for coffee, but an herbal tea would be nice." As soon as the words are out of my mouth, I realize I really want the hot cocoa with all the whipped cream and chocolate shavings on top. But, my inner personal trainer tells me to save the calories.

"Huh," he says. "I don't like coffee either. Thought I was the only one." He smiles and walks up to the counter to place the order.

I silently pray that it takes the staff a while to make our drinks, so I'll have more time to think of what to say to him when he returns. Abby coached me last night after we came up with a few different plausible scenarios in which a girl might chase a guy down the street to kiss him. I know I can't tell him the real reason because he would never believe me, and he'd probably drive me straight to the psych ward and leave me there. I'm not sure he'll believe these other stories either, but they're all I've got. And I'm certainly not going to tell him about the "Big C Word," especially since I don't have any concrete information yet myself. I'm just deciding on which story I'm going to go with when he arrives back at the table with three steaming mugs.

"So, they didn't have any herbal tea," he says, placing two mugs in front of me. "I wasn't sure what you'd prefer instead, so I got you an English Breakfast tea—my personal favorite— and a hot chocolate. I didn't get any whipped cream on it, but if you want some, I'd be happy to go back and get them to add it."

I stare at him, astonished. "The hot chocolate looks great," I reply. "And English Breakfast is my favorite tea, too."

He sits down, looking relieved, and squirts some honey into his tea. "Alright, no more beating around the bush. What was that last night?"

I pick up my mug of cocoa and blow the steam away. I know if I take a sip now, I'll regret it, but it comforts me to just hold the warm mug in my hands. "I...you see...I had a bad breakup, as I mentioned last night. And, I...uh...went temporarily insane?" It comes out as a question, but it wasn't supposed to. And, this isn't at all how Abby coached me. But, when I was looking at her and explaining myself, it was easy. Looking at Roddy now, I can't seem to remember anything. "And I know I should have at least asked if it was okay to...you know...kiss you, but I got caught up in the momentary insanity of it all, and...didn't."

"I see." He leans back in his chair and places his hands behind his head. He looks thoughtful for a moment, looking up at the ceiling. I almost think he's bought it, but then he looks me straight in the eyes and starts laughing. It's not an I'm-making-fun-of-you kind of laugh, but a laugh like we're sharing in the joke. And I guess we sort of are. I know my "explanation" made no sense and was tentative at best. He knows it's a lie, and I know it's a lie, but maybe he's going to let it go.

"Did you really break up with your boyfriend?" he asks.

"Girlfriend, actually, but yes." Seeing his raised eyebrow, I add, "I'm bisexual."

"Oh, that's cool. My brother-in-law is bi or maybe pan. I'm not really sure." He takes a sip of his tea while I'm thinking this is the shortest conversation I've ever had about my sexuality with anyone. "So, when exactly did you break up with your girlfriend?"

"Last night. About five minutes before I asked to borrow your phone," I say sheepishly.

His eyes widen. "Tell me you're joking."

I shake my head. Now he thinks I'm the biggest slut in the world, in addition to being completely insane.

"Did you break up with her or did she break up with you?"

"I broke up with her."

"So, you broke up with your girlfriend and thought 'I'll just kiss the next person I see, and it'll make me feel better?'"

"No, that wasn't it at all," I say, emphatically. "I think I just lost my mind for a moment. It was pouring down rain and you were so kind to lend me your phone, and I just...I just really appreciated it."

He laughs again. "So, what do you do when someone off the street helps you up if you fall? Or do I even want to know?"

I can feel the heat building on my cheeks, and I want to crawl under the table. I don't know what to say to him. I'm about to stammer something when my phone rings. The Caller ID says it's from the hospital system, and I can tell from a quick glance that Roddy has noticed this also. "I'm sorry," I say. "I need to take this."

"No problem," he replies and gestures for me to answer.

Under normal circumstances, I would answer it outside, but the rain from yesterday still hasn't let up, so my options are to either answer it in a relatively quiet coffee house or outside on a busy street in the rain. I opt for the quiet coffee house and just hope that I won't have to give any potentially embarrassing details over the phone. "Hello?"

"Good afternoon. This is Maggie from Wake Radiology. May I speak with Clare O'Donnell, please?"

"This is she," I reply. I pull out my pocket calendar, knowing that this is probably a call to schedule those tests my doctor wanted me to have. And, yes, I'm old-school and have a physical calendar in my purse still even though our phones can do everything but make us meals these days.

"Ms. O'Donnell, I'm calling to get you scheduled for the bilateral breast MRI, and chest and abdominal CT scan ordered by Dr. Nouri. For the MRI, I can get you in next Tuesday at ten AM in the Raleigh office. Will that work for you?"

"Yes, that will work." I write that down.

"Great. I have you scheduled for that. There's no prep you'll need to do for that test and you won't need a driver or anything. You'll get a message in the portal with directions and a link to pre-register. Now, for the CT..." She pauses and I hear her typing something. "I can actually get you in today at five-thirty in the Wake Forest office. Would you be able to make that? Keep in mind, you can't have had anything to eat or drink two hours prior to the procedure."

I look at my watch: four-twenty. "You mean in an hour and ten minutes? Um...I don't... Do you have anything next week?"

She types again. "No. Nothing for next week. The earliest I'd be able to get you in would be in two weeks. We had a cancellation for this evening, so that's why we have this spot available."

I really don't want to wait for two weeks to have this test done because that will just prolong everything. But, for me to get to Wake Forest from Raleigh via rideshare in the middle of rush hour is going to cost a fortune, because there's no way I'll be able to figure out the bus transfers in time. Plus, I actually haven't had anything to eat or drink for the last couple of hours, since I never took a sip of any of the drinks Roddy brought me after all.

While all this is going through my mind, I feel a hand on my shoulder. I start and remember Roddy is still sitting across from me. And he's probably heard this entire exchange because this woman is speaking so loudly. If only the ground could swallow me whole...

"I can take you wherever you need to go," he says, giving my shoulder a gentle squeeze.

"I can't ask you to do that," I reply. "You don't even know me."

"Ms. O'Donnell?" Maggie says on the phone. "Are you going to take the appointment today?"

"I...uh..." I stammer.

Roddy nods his head and starts collecting the various mugs on the table.

"Yes, I'll take the appointment."

"Okay. I'll email you with the pre-registration link so you can fill out the forms on your way here, if possible. That will just speed up the process once you arrive."

I get the other details about the appointment from her and end the call. Meanwhile, Roddy has put all the drinks into to-go cups and a drink carrier tray so we can, presumably, take them with us. I collect my things, and we get ready to leave.

"Thank you," I say, knowing it is nowhere near enough.

"It seemed like it was really important for you to get there today, and it didn't sound like you had another way to do so. I'm happy to do it." He waves a hand in a gesture that says it's nothing. "Plus, it means I get to spend a little more time with you."

I know I'm blushing as we walk out into the rain and open our respective umbrellas. He indicates with a nod of his head the direction to his car, and we walk in silence. On the way there, he puts up a finger for me to pause, and he stops to hand my two drinks to a homeless woman sitting under an awning on the corner. She thanks him, gratefully. My heart absolutely melts.

He walks back over to me with just his cup. "I hope you don't mind, but they wouldn't be any good cold. I'll get you a fresh one once your test is over."

"I don't mind at all," I say honestly.

We arrive at his car—a grey hybrid SUV—and he opens the passenger door for me. I have to fiddle a bit with my umbrella to get it closed, then climb into the car. He closes my door then heads around to the driver's side.

"So, where exactly are we headed?" he asks once he's settled and buckled in.

I give him the address—hoping against hope he doesn't balk when he finds out it's all the way up in Wake Forest, and we're going to be driving there in the rain during rush hour—and he plugs it into the GPS in his dash.

"Got it. ETA: thirty-five minutes." He puts the car in drive, checks for cars and pulls out of his parking space.

I'm about to tell him again how much I appreciate this when he asks, "So, not to pry, but do you not have a car or something? I mean, I noticed that you needed Abby to come pick you up the other night and now you were struggling to make it to this appointment. Feel free to tell me to mind my own business if you don't want to answer."

"It's okay," I say. I'm so used to answering this line of questioning, it's rote now. "I haven't driven since my parents were killed in a car accident five years ago. I was in the backseat and was pretty banged up myself. Once I recovered enough to be able to drive again, I found I just couldn't. Most of the time, I take the bus, or I use rideshare if I have to."

When we stop at the next light, he looks over at me with sincere sympathy. "I'm so sorry. I can't imagine how hard that must have been for you."

"Thanks. I'm tempted, at times, to try to get my license again. But I haven't quite gotten to that point yet."

We sit in silence for a while as he navigates through downtown traffic on our way out of the city. Thankfully, everyone seems to be driving well despite the rain—not always a safe bet in North Carolina—and we haven't hit a major slowdown yet.

I keep thinking I should be incredibly nervous about this scan I'm about to have, but instead, I'm more nervous about telling this man I barely know in the car next to me *why* I'm having the scan I'm about to have. He hasn't asked, and he's probably too polite to ask, but I feel like he has the right to know since he's driving me all the way out there.

"Um...in case you were wondering, you're driving me to a CT scan," I say.

His right eyebrow lifts slightly, though he stays focused on the road. "Oh?"

He's not going to make this easy on me, is he? Or, is he just being polite so you don't have to tell him all the details? "I had to have a biopsy earlier this week on one of my lymph nodes, and it came back positive for cancer. They're not sure where it's coming from, hence the CT scan."

"Clare, I don't know what to say. That really sucks," he replies.

"It really does."

He reaches over and squeezes my shoulder. I will myself not to burst into tears.

The GPS breaks the tension by giving him instructions, and he puts his hand back on the wheel. We go back to companionable silence until we get to the radiology office.

Once he puts the car into park, I start to unbuckle my seatbelt, but he puts his hand over mine to stop me. "Clare, I have something I want to say before we go in there."

We? I hadn't thought he would go in with me. "Yes?"

"Just so you know, that was one hell of a kiss."

* * *

The scan itself is relatively easy, and the nursing staff is so kind that they put me mostly at ease. I get changed into a gown, they insert the IV for the contrast, and I lay down on the table. You're not supposed to move during a scan, so I'm conscious of not fidgeting, and instead my mind is whirring with all the possibilities of things they could find, and I'm silently praying the whole time I'm being scanned that nothing comes up.

Once the scan is complete, I get dressed and meet Roddy in the waiting room. The waiting room chair looks too small for his height, but he somehow manages to look comfortable flipping through a copy of *Better Homes & Gardens*. There's a photo of snowflake cookies on the cover so it must be several months, or years, old.

"Anything interesting in there?" I ask when I get close to his chair.

He looks up, his eyes fixing me with both interest and concern. "Lots of tips on how to decorate both your home and your cookies for the holidays. I'm not the biggest fan of plain sugar cookies and all white Christmas décor, though my sister would probably be all over this as an interior designer." He sets the magazine aside. "All finished? Ready to get out of here?"

"Yes." I nod.

We walk out to the parking lot, but before we make it to his car, I'm suddenly overcome with all the fears I've been tamping down all day. Tears fill my eyes, and I have to stop walking when I can no longer see. I feel Roddy's strong arms around me in an instant and I break down.

"I'm...so-rry," I sob into his chest.

"Shhh," he soothes, rubbing my back in gentle circles. "Don't apologize. It's alright. Let it all out."

The safety of being in his arms calms me until my breathing gets closer to normal and my tears subside. I give him a squeeze, then step back from his embrace, but he keeps a steadying hand on my shoulder.

"I'm..." I begin then start again. "It's been a lot the last couple of days."

He nods. "Understandable."

I take in another shaky breath. "Okay, I think I'm better now. We can go."

Roddy takes my hand, and we walk the rest of the way to the car. I have never before felt more scared or safer in my life.

Part C

"Unintended"

April

"Did the Brooks family send back their signed agreement?" Nate asks me at work on Monday morning.

"Yep. I put it in their folder," I reply, turning in my chair to face him. "They said they would pay the planning fee invoice by today."

"Great. That should be a fun one for you and they're really nice people."

I nod. "I'm looking forward to working with them. I haven't worked on a National Parks trip in a while, so it will be good to do one of those again."

Nate's travel agency is called Nerds on a Plane, and we specialize in set-jetting—travel to locations where shows and movies were filmed—literary trips, history trips, nature trips, and more. Basically, whatever someone is nerdy about, we can build a trip for them. There are the obvious ones like going to New Zealand to see Hobbiton or Los Angeles to see…everything, but the ones I love are the more complex ones where the people don't know quite how we're going to make it work, then we do. Like the time we planned a three-week, self-drive trip across Europe for a couple to do a cheese and chocolate Nerdventure.

"You're still working on the London trip for the Gazaks, right?"

"Uh huh. Should be finished with that one tomorrow. I'm really liking how it's coming together. I found some cool activities for them I think they're really going to like." Nate pulls up the pages on his computer to show me. "Like this day trip to Highclere Castle. They're gonna be so excited about that. Oh, and Buckingham Palace is going to be open during their dates, so I've already put that on hold for them."

"They are going to be so excited!" I've met this couple, and they have wanted nothing more than to do both of those things, along with the regular touristy things in London.

We both turn back to our computers and get back to working on our respective tasks: Nate on the London trip and me on answering a few emails that came in from prospective clients through our website.

"Oh, Clare, did Isaac tell you we decided on a song for you to sing for the wedding?"

I turn in my chair. "No, but I'm intrigued. Last I heard, you were still trying to convince him that 'Black or White' was a good idea, even though I said there was no way I'd be able to do MJ justice."

Nate rolls his eyes. "Yeah, yeah. We abandoned Mr. Jackson. Then Isaac suggested 'Love on Top' by Beyoncé, and even though I love the song, it's just not what I envisioned for our first dance."

"You're at least getting warmer with something I could actually sing, though," I reply.

"Exactly. To that end," he says, eyes sparkling, "we thought something more classic would work best for your more classic voice. How would you feel about 'Only You' by the Platters?"

"That's perfect! I'm just annoyed I didn't think of it myself." I'm thrilled because I know I can do that song justice and it shouldn't require a ton of practicing since I've known it all my life. "I'm so glad you found something you both love and will be happy with."

Nate sighs. "Me too. Let's hope the rest of the wedding planning goes this smoothly."

We go back to our respective tasks for a while, and Nate brings me a cup of tea a little while later when he gets himself a cup of coffee.

"Hey, did you ever find out how Abby's coffee date went with her parents on Friday?" Nate asks, handing me the mug.

I shake my head. "She didn't tell me, and I didn't think to ask." I feel awful. I was so caught up in my whole emotional rollercoaster of deciding whether or not to stay with Suz that I didn't think to ask her the entire weekend.

"It's understandable. You had a lot going on yourself."

"Yes, but I should have checked in since I know it's always such a kerfuffle every time they come into town. I know she would have been there for me if my biopsy had turned out to be cancer. I'm definitely going to ask her about it tonight since we're having dinner."

* * *

When I get to Abby's that evening, she's curled up in her favorite armchair in the living room reading a paperback. Not wanting to disturb her—because I absolutely hate it when someone disturbs me when I'm reading a good book—I head to my room to drop off my things.

Abby's guestroom, or I guess I should call it my room, looks like a tornado went through it since I haven't had a chance to fully unpack yet. My suitcases are open across the back wall and the duffel bags have clothes spilling out of them. Shelley is currently napping on top of one of said duffels, so I know my formerly clean clothes will be covered in grey cat hair. Not like everything I own isn't covered in her fur, but these will be particularly well coated.

I start putting things away since I have some time now, and I can't live with this mess. Suz might have been the ridiculously neat one of the two of us—to the point of having all our clothes in the walk-in closet organized not only by type, but also in order of the rainbow spectrum—but I at least like to have my things put away.

An hour later, I'm just putting the last empty suitcase in the closet when Abby knocks on my open door. "Hey. Just wanted to see if you had thought about where you wanted to get dinner."

I shake my head. "Nope. But I'm starving after getting all my clothes put away."

She takes in the clean floors and the neatly hung clothes. "Nice work! I would have helped you with that, you know."

"I know, but you looked pretty engrossed in your book, so I didn't want to disturb you."

She smiles. "I appreciate that."

"I hadn't really thought much about where to eat. Did you have anything in mind?" I ask.

Her eyes drift up to the ceiling as she contemplates. Then she grins as she says, "I could totally go for Mexican food."

I laugh. "I mean, I'm not going to say no to that." Abby and I both love Mexican food. Any time. Anywhere. Chips and queso, bean burritos, cheese enchiladas, tostadas, rice, the list goes on. "Let me just check Shelley's litter box, then we can go."

"Sounds good. I'll grab my jacket."

Once we reconvene in the living room, we grab our purses and head out for our favorite Mexican place: Fiesta Mexicana. Although it's a little farther away from Abby's apartment, it's the place we used to go back when we were in college at North Carolina State University. Their décor hasn't changed much in twenty years, though the dated brown booths have gotten a couple new coats of paint. The murals on the walls of Mexico are just as kitschy as ever, but they have a great menu, and the service is excellent.

"Hola, amigas!" Miguel, our favorite server, greets us as we arrive. He puts his fist out and we each bump it in turn. You know you're regulars when the staff greets you with fist bumps. "Right this way."

We sit down in our booth and set the menus down because we've long since memorized them. Chips and salsa are delivered by the owner's niece, Daniela, and we dive right in. Shortly after, Miguel brings our iced teas—he doesn't even have to ask anymore—and he takes our orders.

"I'll have the vegetarian combo with a bean tostada, cheese enchilada and rice, please," I say.

"And for you, amiga?"

"I think I'll do the enchiladas rancheras, please. But, can I get one chicken, one bean and one cheese, please?" Abby asks.

Miguel nods as he scribbles on his order pad. "Of course." He takes our menus and runs off to place our orders.

I take a sip of my tea. "I've been meaning to ask you, how did your coffee date go with your parents the other day? Is everything okay?"

Abby nods as she finishes chewing the chip she just ate, then takes a sip of her own drink. "Yeah, they were just in town and wanted to have some 'face time.' It wasn't any big deal, this time. The place was actually so busy and loud that we could hardly talk at all. So, a lot less pressuring me about my job and my love life. But, they did at least try to tell me all about some friend's kid who is a gazillionaire and married with five kids. As if I want any kids, let alone five." She rolls her eyes.

"You know I'm with you there." Neither Abby nor I have ever really wanted kids. I have thought at times it would be nice to have one, maybe. To know what it feels like to bring new life into the world and to get to mold and shape the next generation. But then I see people with their unruly kids in stores and that feeling quickly melts away. I wouldn't mind being an aunt, though, if I was with someone who had nieces or nephews. "Any word on when they're coming into town next time?"

She shakes her head, dipping another chip in the salsa. "Nothing yet. But you know them, they love to tell me the day before they're coming to town."

Abby's lawyer parents technically "live" in Raleigh, but they spend most of their time at their vacation home in Florida. They pop back and forth as they please and drive their daughter nuts in the process.

"That is their MO." I also eat another chip with the fresh salsa and savor the salty acidity. "At least they didn't try to pressure you into any more blind dates."

"Well, not exactly," she says, taking a sip of her tea.

"Oh yeah? Who did they try to set you up with this time?" I ask, a little concerned about her going on yet another blind date. Not only do her parents have horrendous taste, but I'm also worried that Abby might finally like one of them herself, then where would that leave me? *You literally* just *broke up with your girlfriend and you haven't even mentioned to Abby that you like her.*

"Some woman named Lily. Apparently, she went to NC State, then transferred to Wake Forest for law school." Abby rolls her eyes. "God, I don't know if I can take another stuffy lawyer—male or female—with questionable morals and terrible taste in clothes. I know they're hoping they'll rub off on me to get me to go into law, but c'mon. Can't they find anyone…you know…cute and an environmentalist or something?"

I laugh. "Would your parents know what an environmentalist is?"

"Probably not," she agrees. "Ugh. Just because I'm in my early forties and not married doesn't mean I'm an old maid or something. This isn't the 1800s!"

"I'll drink to that." We clink our cups. "So, are you going to go…on the date?"

"Yeah, I texted her and she's got tickets to some soccer game next week. I can't think of anything I'd rather do less than go on a blind date with a lawyer to watch sports, but at least it's women's soccer, so maybe there will be cute girls on the field." She shrugs.

"That's the spirit," I reply. At least this Lily woman doesn't have a clue what Abby likes, so that's one strike against her.

"Speaking of relationships, how are you doing? You know, with all the Suz stuff," she asks, as she takes a bite of her own chip.

Swallowing, I try to compose my thoughts. "I'm doing okay, I guess. I dunno. It's strange. On the one hand, I feel like I should be wallowing and crying all the time because I just ended an eight-year relationship last week, but on the other, I think I know in my heart that we weren't really in a 'relationship' at all." I examine the faux-wood table and ask quietly, "Was it all in my head?"

"Pardon?"

I look back up at Abby, my eyes brimming with tears. "Was it all in my head? Was my relationship with Suz all in my head?"

"No." Abby puts her hand on mine, and I feel a warmth there that's more than just her body heat. "It wasn't all in your head, and Suz was a bitch—I know you hate that word, but it's the best word for her—for stringing you along all that time. She wanted a roommate, pure and simple, but even I thought she wanted more from you."

"But you knew before I did."

She shrugs. "We see what we want to, sometimes." I think about this and wonder if she means that I saw what I wanted to or that she, Abby, saw what she wanted to. In that, she wanted Suz to not be in a real relationship with me. And, if that's the case, what does that mean?

I look at Abby's hand on mine and think about how comfortable it is. How Suz and I never held hands across a table like this. How much I want someone to want to hold my hand like this and mean it. Abby's blue eyes are warm as she looks at me and I wonder if she could be feeling this too. However, she suddenly averts her gaze and takes her hand back, picking up another chip and dunking it in the salsa.

"So, there was another reason I wanted us to have dinner tonight," Abby says, changing the subject.

I raise my eyebrows. "And that is?"

"I was thinking we should plan a surprise engagement party for Nate and Isaac. What do you think?"

I feel a hint of disappointment and wonder what I was expecting. Abby doesn't know about these feelings I've been having. She doesn't have a clue about the latest turn the dreams have taken. I mean, it's possible she could feel something for me, but it's probable that she will never consider us as more than just friends, especially since she's continuing to go on blind dates set up by her parents.

I paste on a smile as I reply, "Sure, I'd love to."

Part 4

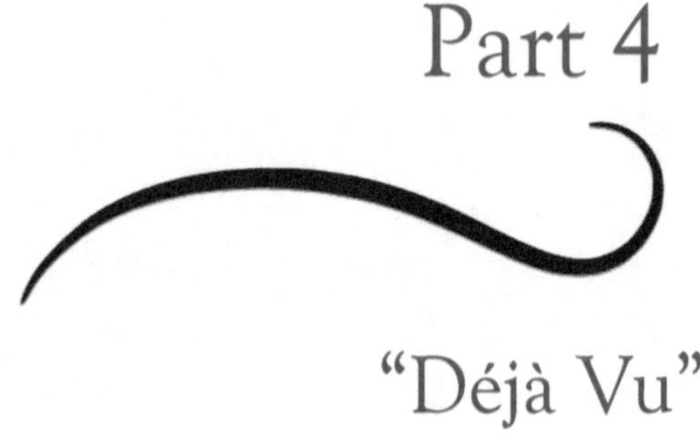

"Déjà Vu"

April

The faceless one appeared again in a tuxedo, as always, and we were walking the streets of a city I've never been to before. It was definitely European, but I couldn't put my finger on which country. Most of the scenes were like out of old photographs—a bit blurry and the color was off—but it felt like home. He walked me to the center of an iron bridge that was painted white. As I tried looking at his nonexistent face for any hint as to who he was, he produced a padlock from his pocket and attached it to the bridge...

* * *

"Excuse us," Isaac says as he leads the way to our seats in the back of the upper balcony of Meymandi Concert Hall on Saturday evening. We walk around two more people, careful not to step on their toes, and arrive at our seats. "Here we are. You want your usual seat, right?"

"Yes, please." Seat 205 was always my father's seat when he'd buy us season tickets for the North Carolina Symphony. My mother wasn't a classical music fan, so it was something my dad and I always did together. I think I was seven or eight when he took me to my first symphony concert. I remember wearing my favorite purple dress with a lace collar. After they died, I continued getting the same seats for the symphony to carry on the tradition. Isaac is usually my "date," but if he's not available then Abby or Nate accompany me. Once, I tried bringing Suz, but the only music she likes is soundtracks to video games, so Mozart's Requiem wasn't really her thing.

"I forgot to tell you how nice you look this evening. The color of that blouse really sets off your red hair." Isaac smiles at me then opens his program.

"Thanks," I reply. I'm wearing a simple black pencil skirt with a frilly green blouse. To this day I still dress up for symphony concerts, even though a lot of people come in more casual clothing. My father always said it was a sign of respect for the artists that you dress up to hear them play. Isaac's wearing a dark grey suit—perfectly tailored to his well-built frame—which looks really great against his dark skin. Isaac was voted prom king, and for good reason. Nate says he looks like a cross between Jason George and Shemar Moore. Any way you slice it, Isaac is a really good-looking man. And he's one of the sweetest people you could ever hope to meet. "You don't look too bad yourself."

Tonight, we're going to hear Beethoven and Mozart, two of my favorite composers. I flip open my program as well to read the conductor's notes about the pieces we're about to hear. I'm totally immersed in my reading when the symphony starts tuning. I close my eyes and listen to the familiar sound. I try to hear if anyone is actually out of tune, but don't detect anything amiss. Sometimes I can pick out that one violin or cello that's just a little bit sharp or flat.

Isaac leans over and whispers in my ear, "Guess what? I actually remembered my binoculars this time." He holds them up triumphantly.

I stifle a giggle because he always says he's going to bring his binoculars and has never once remembered. I was beginning to think he didn't have any.

Conductor Charles Carew enters the stage, and Isaac immediately starts using the binoculars. He thinks Mr. Carew is incredibly handsome and jokes to Nate sometimes about throwing him over for the conductor. Nate takes it in stride, mostly because I think he's secretly got a crush as well.

Once the music starts, I steal the binoculars away from Isaac so I can watch the strings play. The string section has always been my favorite part of the symphony. The fluidity of their movements and their notes. The way some of the performers sway when they get to their favorite parts. You can see the gentleness of the softer sections and the fierceness of the more vibrant sections as their bows dance upon the strings.

I scan the violins first and see some familiar faces among them. My parents donated a lot of money to the symphony, so we got to go to a couple cocktail parties with the artists over the years. They even set aside some money in their will for the symphony, so I still get invited to their functions from time to time. I haven't been to one since they passed away because it's still too painful.

I tear myself away from the violins to scan the musicians on the other side of the conductor. Scanning the cello section, I'm astonished to see a face more familiar to me than all the others. My heart starts pounding and my hands shake so hard I nearly drop the binoculars. Feeling like I might faint, I lean over to put my head between my legs. I close my eyes and all I can see is the faceless person from my dreams transforming into a female who seriously looks like Abby, then into Roddy, back and forth, until it finally lands on Roddy. Feeling like I can't catch my breath, I sit upright again. I feel Isaac touching my shoulder and I hear him whispering to me, but I can't make out the words. I see his pained expression as he tries again to speak to me. I just shake my head, knowing he's asking if I'm alright. He takes my arm to stand me up. I barely register the people I'm walking—more like stumbling—over on the way to the lobby.

Once we're out of the concert hall, I settle on a bench and try to collect myself. Slowly, the sounds around me become clear. I hear the music of Beethoven drifting through the balcony doors and the sound of my own breathing.

"Clare? Clare? Are you alright?" I finally hear Isaac say, obviously completely confused as to why I'm having a panic attack at the symphony. He's kneeling down on the floor in front of me with concern covering his features. *Roddy plays the cello.* This means I've seen him numerous times before. I've seen him from a distance but never been close enough to see his face. My thoughts keep threatening to overwhelm me. I will myself to focus on my breathing, to calm myself down.

In response to Isaac, I nod. My breathing has slowed, and I no longer feel like my heart is going to jump out of my chest, but I'm not feeling much like talking. And, anyway, what am I going to tell Isaac? He doesn't know about the dreams or that I kissed Roddy on the street right after we first met. Abby is the only one who knows all the details. But I have to tell him something. I've never had a panic attack in front of him before, and now I've had one in a public place with one of my best friends.

"I just..." I begin but still can't get the words out.

"Is it your dad?" Isaac volunteers. "Was that his favorite piece or something?"

I really don't want to lie to Isaac, but I just can't face telling him the truth. Not yet. Not until I figure out what the heck is wrong with me. "Yes," I say, finally, tears welling up in my eyes, but not for the reason he thinks.

Isaac hugs me and I start to feel calmer. At his suggestion, we sit there until after intermission to go back in so that I won't have to hear more of my dad's favorite piece. I hope that when we get back inside, I'm able to enjoy the rest of the concert without having another panic attack. I'll just have to forget Isaac has binoculars.

* * *

When Isaac drops me off after the concert, I practically run up the three flights stairs to the apartment—because the elevator in her building *is* pretty slow—anxious to tell Abby everything I couldn't tell Isaac. I'm completely out of breath when I reach the door and have a hard time finding my keys in my purse. Thankfully, Abby must have heard me panting because she opens the door. I'm bent over with my hands on my knees, only to look up and see she's holding a frying pan like a baseball bat ready to knock one out of the park.

"It's...just...me," I say between gasps.

"Why the heck didn't you just use your key instead of standing in the hallway panting like a rapist?"

I scrunch up my eyes and shake my head. "That doesn't make any sense."

"Well? I heard a noise, and it startled me," she explains, finally lowering the pan and stepping aside to let me in. "Then, when I got to the door, all I could hear was heavy breathing, so I grabbed the frying pan before opening it."

"Why didn't you just look through the peephole?" I'm able to stand upright now but still clutching my left side.

She opens her mouth to answer and closes it again. "I don't know."

I hang my jacket on the hook near the door, along with my purse. Abby takes the frying pan back to the kitchen, then turns to me. "So, why were you panting anyway?"

"I just ran up the stairs."

"And why would you do something silly like that?" Abby pretty much lives her life avoiding exercise. Oh, she's been known to take walks from time to time, but nothing that would count as a full-on workout. She only takes the stairs if she's forced to, and I don't think she knows how to do a crunch or sit-up. And, she's always been thin, which bugs the heck out of me sometimes.

"I had a panic attack at the symphony," I say bluntly.

"What?" She steps back to take a better look at me. "Hmm... Yeah, you don't look so hot. Here, come sit down."

We walk to the living room and sit down in our usual places—her on the couch, me on the chair. "So, Isaac brought his binoculars tonight."

"Really? I thought you said you didn't think he had a pair."

"Not really the point, but he does." I take a slow breath. "I was looking around the string section and saw a rather familiar face in the cello section."

"Who?" Abby asks, literally scooting to the edge of her seat.

"Roddy."

"Roddy?"

"Yes, Roddy. Evidently, he plays the cello for the symphony." As I say the words out loud, it hits me again how insane this is. How insane I must be. I feel my heart start to beat faster, but I take a cleansing breath and will it to slow down. I'm home and I'm fine. Everything is going to be just fine. "And, when I closed my eyes, I could see the faceless person from my dreams literally turning into Roddy. They turned into a female, briefly, but settled on Roddy in the end."

"Whoa."

"I know."

"I mean… Well, what does this *mean?*"

"I have no idea." I'm telling the complete truth.

Abby slumps back on the couch. "Whoa."

"You can stop saying that now."

She shakes her head as if to clear it. "Sorry. I'm just…shocked, is all."

I shrug. "How do ya think I feel?"

"I can completely understand why you had a panic attack. What did you tell Isaac?"

"That I freaked out 'cause it was my dad's favorite piece. He guessed that and I didn't correct him."

"Probably for the best." We sit there in silence for a moment or two, then Abby asks the question I've been dreading. "Do you think this is a sign the dreams are coming true?"

I don't answer her. I can't physically answer her. For the second time that night, I'm in tears, and my best friend wraps her arms around me while I sob, unsure what's wrong with me and what I'm going to do about it.

Part D

"Taking Over Me"

April

The faceless one walked with me through the streets of Paris; the tuxedo she wore perfectly hugging her curves. We wandered into the Musée de l'Orangerie where Monet's Water Lilies *surrounded us. Suddenly, we were outside in the dark, but the glittering lights of the Eiffel Tower illuminated our promenade through the Champ-de-Mars. I kept trying to catch a glimpse of some feature on her face, but as always, there was nothing…*

* * *

"You doing okay after the biopsy and everything? I mean, I know it was all okay, but sometimes it can still be traumatic." Isaac asks me as we take the stairs to the upper balcony of Meymandi Concert Hall on Saturday night.

Reaching the top of the stairs, I nod. "Thanks, but I'm really okay." I raise my index finger and say meaningfully, "I don't want to have to go through that again anytime soon—or ever, if I'm wishing for stuff—but I'm good right now."

"That's good to hear." Isaac keeps his arm around my shoulder, guiding me into the seating area. Even though I've walked these halls dozens of times since my parents died, I still find it hard sometimes to come to the symphony without my dad. This was our special time each month, and I miss him so much each time I'm here without him. Isaac knows all this and keeps his arm around me as we walk in.

"Excuse us," Isaac says, walking down the row to our seats: 205 and 206. "Here we are. You want your usual seat, right?"

"Yes, please."

"I forgot to tell you how nice you look this evening. The color of that blouse really sets off your red hair." Isaac smiles at me then opens his program.

"Thanks," I reply, feeling this intense sensation of déjà vu. *This is really weird. But, maybe he's said that to me at another symphony concert.* "You look nice too."

I try to dispel the strangeness and open my program as well, but the only thing that happens is I start thinking about the faceless person…woman dreams. I'm staring down at the words on the page about Beethoven and Mozart—two of my favorite composers—however my mind is saying, *Is it Abby or Suz? Or someone else? Why now? Are Mom and Dad sending me these dreams?* I set the program down on my lap and rub my eyes. It doesn't help as the thoughts keep swirling around my head on a loop.

Isaac pulls me out of my downward spiral by leaning over and whispering, "Guess what?"

Out of absolutely nowhere, I finish his thought, "You remembered your binoculars this time."

"I…uh…how did you know?" he asks, tentatively holding up the binoculars in question.

How did *I know? Am I psychic now?* "Lucky guess?" I say, though it comes out as a question.

Isaac shrugs and hands them to me as the symphony starts tuning. I start with the first chair violin as he leads everyone in the tuning process and scan the string section. I love seeing how the men are all in tuxes and the women are all in black dresses, but there are so many shades of black and different styles of dresses out there when you look closer. Right when I get to the cello section, I hear applause as the conductor comes out, and Isaac is nudging me to get the binoculars back, but I can't tear my eyes away from one particular cello player. If I didn't know any better, I'd swear it was that guy I saw out on the street outside Suz's apartment the other night. The night after I got my biopsy results back and had the first of the faceless person dreams that showed them specifically as a woman.

So, what is it about this guy? I've probably seen him countless times before at concerts, if he's been with the symphony for any length of time. Not needing to stare at this guy anymore, I pass the binoculars back to Isaac so he can ogle the conductor. I close my eyes and try to just get lost in Beethoven's Symphony No. 7. In my head, though, all I can see is the faceless one morphing from a genderless person into the cello guy, into Suz, then into Abby. This happens over and over like someone pressing rewind and fast forward on a video, until it finally settles on Abby.

When I open my eyes, I'm having trouble catching my breath and I see Isaac looking at me with concern. I can't hear anything but the thoughts swirling around my head and my pounding heart. Add to that the feeling that this has all happened before and I'm in a full-blown panic attack.

I stand up and press my way through the legs and feet of the people next to me, desperate to get out of there as quickly as possible. I push through the double doors into the relative quiet of the lobby. I see a bench on the landing and rush toward it, feeling I could collapse at any moment as my breathing comes in a staccato rhythm—not unlike the "Poco sostenuto – Vivace" movement the symphony is playing now—and my head starts spinning. As soon as I sit down, I fold forward and let my head fall between my legs.

"Clare? Clare? Are you alright?" Isaac asks frantically. I shake my head. Although I can't see him, I can feel that he's kneeling in front of me. He gently rubs my back as I try desperately to control my breathing and my rapidly pounding heart. "It's going to be okay," he adds in his soothing baritone.

Gradually, I start to feel better, and I very slowly start to lift back upright. Isaac comes to sit beside me and continues rubbing my back while my breathing comes back to normal. "Sorry. I didn't mean to ruin your evening," I manage in a hoarse whisper.

He gives me a soothing hug. "Don't worry about me. I'm worried about you. Are you okay? Was this something to do with your dad? His favorite piece or something?"

I could lie and just tell him that was all it was. But I so want to confide in someone about what's been happening with the déjà vu, the dreams and everything. Abby is the only one who knows about the dreams, but I don't feel like I can talk to her about them anymore. Not now. Now when I suspect she's the one they're pointing me toward.

I look in Isaac's kind eyes. "Do you mind if we blow off the symphony tonight? Maybe we could get dessert or something and talk?"

He nods. "Sure. Whatever you need." Then, tentatively, "Should we get Nate and Abby to meet us?"

I know I don't hide the look of anxiety on my face when he mentions Abby.

"Got it. I'll take that as a no then."

We decide to go to the coffee house across the street from my old building since it's within walking distance and would still be open for a while. When we stand up, I realize I left my purse in the concert hall. "I'll just go back and get it."

"No need," he says, holding up my purse that was apparently sitting beside him on the floor this whole time.

"Thanks," I reply, blowing out a sigh of relief and taking the bag from him, leading the way down the stairs to the warm spring air outside.

* * *

"Let me get this straight," Isaac begins as he sets his cup of coffee down on the table. He holds his right hand up and starts ticking things off on his fingers. "You've been having dreams of some romantic, faceless person since your parents died. You feel like they might be from your parents pointing you toward the person you're supposed to be with. Recently, the faceless person has started looking more feminine. You think that person might be Abby. And, you've been having episodes of déjà vu. Does that about cover it?"

I swallow a bite of the chocolate chip scone I got to go with my chai latte. "Yep, pretty much." I nod. "You think I've lost my mind, right?"

He shakes his head rather noncommittally. "Not entirely. I'm just having a hard time wrapping my head around some of the more out-there aspects. You know me. I'm probably the most practically minded of all of us." Then quickly, he adds, "Not that I don't think you're having these dreams or feelings, or that they are any less legitimate."

I chuckle. "I know. If I weren't the one this was happening to, I would be struggling to believe it too. It's a lot to take in."

He takes a sip of his cappuccino and continues to hold the cup in both hands, pondering.

"Have you mentioned any of this to Abby?"

"She knows about the original dreams, but not about the latest ones, and definitely not that I think it could be her."

"What has she said in response to them before?" he asks, finally setting down his cup.

I shrug. "I dunno. She kinda had the same reaction you did, at first, but the more of them I had, the more she started to think they could be pointing me toward my future partner. But she never believed they were pointing me to Suz."

Isaac smirks. "I'd have to agree with her there."

"Yeah, well," I sigh. "That's over now, if it ever was anything to begin with." I savor the warmth of my latte, soothed by both the spices and the cream.

"Hang on," he begins, interrupting my pity party over the Suz breakup. "You never told me what precipitated your panic attack tonight. Was there something specific at the concert that triggered all this?"

How do I explain I was experiencing déjà vu already, then saw some guy I've never met before with Isaac's binoculars, and for whatever reason, that set off a feeling like either he or Abby could be the one in my dreams? Is it déjà vu if it's more than seeing something again but reliving the same activity? I don't remember much of my high school French, but maybe something like "déjà faire" or "déjà fait" or something? Regardless, just thinking about all of this again is making my breath come quicker, and if I don't watch it, I'm going to be in the midst of another full-blown panic attack.

"I...I...can't explain it," I stammer, breath coming in short gasps.

Isaac comes around the table and rubs my back. "Then don't. I believe you. Just take deep breaths for me." He takes in an audible breath through his nose, then blows out heavily through his mouth. He does this a couple more times as I try to mimic him. "There. That's good." He moves back to his side of the table but holds onto my hand.

I start to calm back down and my pulse rate slowly starts to return to normal. "I'm so sorry. It's just—"

He puts up his other hand. "Nope. Say no more. I don't want you hyperventilating on me for the third time tonight."

I sigh. "Thanks. And thank you for believing me."

"Always, Clare. I will always believe you and believe in you. You are my best friend, aside from Nate. But he's my fiancé, so that hardly counts." We both laugh.

"I have a piece of advice I don't think you're going to want to hear right now," he says, "but I'm going to give it anyway. You ready?"

I nod almost imperceptibly.

"You should tell Abby everything." At my immediate look of disagreement, he continues, "I know. I said you weren't going to like it, but I'm telling you anyway. You should tell her. She'll understand—probably even better than I—and even if her feelings aren't the same, you'll feel better for having gotten it off your chest."

"I doubt that," I mutter.

"Maybe not right away, but it will be better than it causing panic attacks, right?"

"I guess you're right," I relent. "But I still think she's going to think I'm as crazy as I feel."

He shakes his head. "She loves you, even if just as a best friend, and she already knows about the dreams, so I don't think this will be as big of a leap for her."

"How about this: I'll think about it. Will that work for you?" I offer.

He nods. "That's as good a plan as any."

"Oh, and would you mind keeping this a secret from Nate? At least until I figure out what I'm going to do about Abby."

"I'll do my best," he agrees.

I take the last bite of my scone and wonder how I will ever face my best friend and roommate again.

Part 5

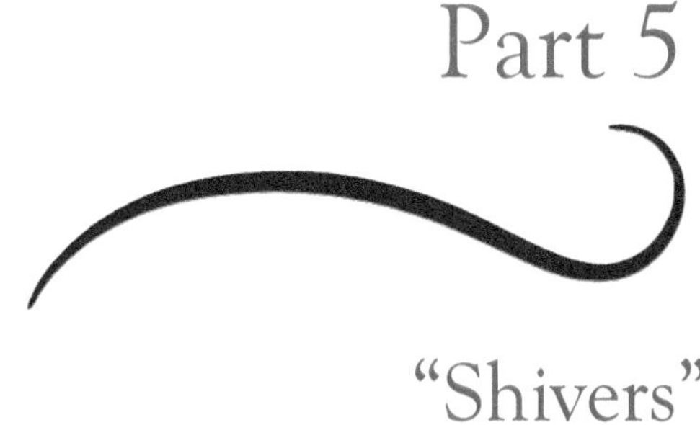

"Shivers"

April

I'm just on my way out the door on Monday for my lunch break when my cell phone rings. I don't recognize the number, but since it's a 919 area code I answer, hoping against hope that it's Roddy and not a telemarketer. If I'd been smart, I would have entered it into my phone from Abby's. Or, I would have gotten it from him when he drove me to the CT scan on Friday evening, but you know what they say about hindsight.

"Hello?" I answer.

"Hi, Clare, it's Roddy."

I'm instantly both thrilled and panicked. I try to think of something remarkable to say, but all that comes out is, "Oh, hi."

"I'm sorry I didn't call sooner, but this weekend was insane," he explains. "Any results yet from the scan on Friday?"

"That's okay. I was pretty busy myself," I lie. I mean, I did spend a while unpacking, but most of the weekend was spent watching movies with Abby in our pajamas. And, even if he had called over the weekend, I was still feeling so terrified over the biopsy results and the CT scan—not to mention the realization Roddy might literally be the man of my dreams—that I wouldn't have been a great person to talk with. I'm still feeling pretty panicked, but talking things out with Abby helped and I'm trying to take things one day at a time. "No, nothing yet from the CT. I've been refreshing my portal all day to no avail."

"Sorry, that must be hard. Hopefully you'll hear something soon," he says with genuine concern. "Probably just them catching up from over the weekend."

I nod, then realize he can't see that and reply, "Probably."

"So, listen," he begins, "I'd really like to take you out for that proper date sometime. Are you free this week at all?"

My heart flutters as I flip open my calendar and do a quick scan. "I'm free every night except Friday," I reply. Friday is the night Abby and I are taking Nate and Isaac out to celebrate their engagement. We're going to throw them a real engagement party later on, but with everything going on with me, Abby thought it would be good to do a nice dinner with just the four of us for now.

"Hmm. I could do tomorrow, but it would be kinda late." He's silent for a moment. "How do you feel about dinner Saturday night? I could pick you up around six-thirty."

"That sounds perfect," I say. I'm secretly thrilled he offered to pick me up, so I don't have to smell like public transit on our date. I'm sure Abby would be willing to drive me, but it's probably just as embarrassing to be dropped off by a friend as it is to smell like bus.

"Great. I'll see you on Saturday." I think he's about to say good-bye, but then he adds, "I'm really looking forward to it."

"Me, too."

As soon as we hang up, I text him Abby's address—in case he forgot from dropping me off on Friday—then sit back in my chair with a huge smile on my face.

"And just what is that big ole smile about?" Nate asks, startling me. He must have come back downstairs while I was on the phone. I wonder how much he heard.

"Well...uh..."

"You weren't just talking to Suz, were you?" He gives me a reproving look. "You need to move on from her, Clare. She didn't make you happy."

I sigh. "No, I wasn't on the phone with Suz. And, you'll be happy to know that I am moving on. I...have a date on Saturday night." I smile, triumphantly.

Nate gasps. "Really? This soon after the breakup?"

Shaking my head, I say, "C'mon now. You can't have it both ways. You can't tell me I need to move on from Suz and then tell me I'm moving too fast when I do."

"You're absolutely right." He puts a hand on my shoulder. "You deserve to be happy."

"Thank you," I reply, patting his hand with mine. "Now, if you'll excuse me, I was just heading out for lunch. Can I get you anything?" I stand up and grab my purse.

"Can you get me anything? Uh uh. You're taking me with you and giving me all the details of this mystery person you're seeing on Saturday," Nate declares, hooking his arm in mine and leading me toward his front door.

"Oh, I'm sorry, Nate. Would you like to come to lunch?" I mock while he ushers me to his car, a late model Camry Hybrid. He opens the passenger door for me, and I get in.

Nate starts up the car, then turns to me. "So, where are we going?"

"Well, I was just going to walk to Noodles..."

"Oh, you eat there all the time," he interrupts. "Let's go to Element instead."

We ride in silence for the four minutes it takes to get there. Nate parks in the deck closest to the restaurant and we walk the half block to our destination. Element Gastropub is one of my favorite restaurants in downtown Raleigh. They are completely vegan, and even if you aren't vegetarian, their food is just as delicious as their meat counterparts. Unfortunately, it's always very crowded, unless you come at an off time. Thankfully, though, there is a sidewalk table available, so we don't have to wait long. The hostess seats us, then leaves so we can peruse the menu.

Nate puts his menu down on the table without giving it so much as a glance and checks his phone. "So, I want you to tell me about this new person, but you'll have to wait until Isaac gets here."

"Isaac's coming?" It's not that unusual for Isaac to meet Nate for lunch, but it's surprising he didn't tell me until now.

"Of course he's coming," Nate replies. "I texted him while we were walking to the car. You didn't think I was going to keep him out of the loop, did you?"

"No, but I figured you'd just tell him later on. Hey, how does he know where to meet us?" I ask, since Nate texted him before he decided where we were going.

"I texted him again in the parking deck," he answers, sighing. "You know I'm a wizard at texting with one hand."

I laugh. "Yeah, and half the time I can't understand your texts because the words you misspell get autocorrected into something completely different. Like when you texted me: 'You defibrillator need to raff the hogging post toady.'"

"You always seem to figure it out," he says. Then he waves his hand high above his head, and I turn to see Isaac striding toward us down the sidewalk.

"There's my handsome fiancé," Isaac says, as Nate stands up to hug him. Isaac gives Nate a quick kiss on the cheek, then turns to give me a hug as well. "And, my beautiful friend, Clare. How are you doing?"

I pull back. "I'm doing okay. Everything is still so overwhelming, but I'm trying to take deep breaths and just take things as they come right now."

Isaac nods. "That's all you can do. Until you have all the information, that is. I know it's scary, though. We're here, if you need us."

"We are," Nate echoes.

"I know. And I love you guys." I do my best not to let the tears well up in my eyes, but it's hard. "All the waiting and wondering is so difficult, not to mention all the testing appointments. Thankfully I have the best boss in the world who doesn't question when I need to schedule one."

Nate shoots me an "aw shucks" expression. "You are one of our best friends and that's what we do for one another. Plus, I'd like to think I'd be this understanding of a boss regardless." He looks at Isaac. "Wouldn't I?"

"Of course you would, but we're not here to stoke your ego, dear," Isaac replies, then turns to me. "I've got plenty of PTO built up, so if you need someone to take you, let me know. I know Nate and Abby are at the ready too, but you can never have too many drivers."

I thank him as the server comes over for our drink orders. We all end up ordering as well, since we know what we want, and she heads off to place our orders.

"Now, what did Nate drag me all the way down here for?" Isaac asks, smiling.

"All the way down here? You work like two blocks from here," I reply. Isaac works at a software company doing some sort of computery thing I couldn't begin to describe. He's evidently really good at it because he keeps getting promoted.

"Anyway," Nate interjects, dragging out the word. "So, you remember how our little Clare successfully broke up with Suz last week?"

"Yes," Isaac replies taking my hand. "I'm still so proud of you for actually doing it."

I nod. Thankfully, the server comes back at just that moment with our drinks, which allows me not to say anything on the topic of Suz. I take a sip of my ginger ale and remain silent.

"And that's not all," Nate says, sounding a bit like a game show host introducing the new car after the contestant has seen the boring living room set. "She's got a date Saturday night."

"What?!" Isaac looks at each of us as if he must have misunderstood. "Who are you going on a date with? Have we met her? Him? Them?"

Nate pats Isaac's knee. "That's exactly what we're here to find out."

* * *

At the end of the day, I'm really ready to go home. I'm feeling emotionally drained after telling Nate and Isaac some of the details of meeting Roddy—conveniently leaving out the part about kissing him—and holding in my feelings about Suz. Plus, you know, everything else going on in my life right now. Also, they wanted to discuss the song I'm going to sing at their wedding for their first dance, and it took a while. There were a lot of little arguments while they discussed everything from Michael Jackson to Beyoncé. In the end, they settled for something classic: "Only You" by the Platters. What I'd like to do is take a long hot shower and curl up on my bed with Shelley to watch a sappy chick flick.

Back at the apartment, I just want to crash. I know if I see Abby, she'll want to talk to me, and I just can't talk anymore today. So, I come in as quietly as I can and walk straight to my room. Shelley is asleep on my pillow—her favorite naptime location—which makes things easier since her food, water and litter are all in my bathroom. I close my door quietly and drop into the blue club chair in the corner, my purse falling to the floor. I close my eyes and just sit there, enjoying the silence.

About five minutes pass like that, then my phone bleeps, signaling a new text message. I contemplate ignoring it, but curiosity gets the better of me. I pull my phone out of my purse and look at the screen. My heart jumps when I see that it's a text from Roddy.

Roddy: How are you doing? Any results yet?

My heart is full at the fact that he keeps checking in. I realize I'm grinning ear to ear and he's only asked me about test results.

Clare: I'm doing okay. No results yet.
Roddy: Hope that means it's good news.
Roddy: Changing the subject...How does Asian food sound for dinner Saturday?
Clare: Sounds great.
Roddy: Ever been to Yo Ho?
Clare: Like, "and a bottle of rum"??

I giggle.

Roddy: ☺ No. Yo Ho Asian Bistro, in Cary.
Clare: Oh, haha. Can't say that I have.
Roddy: Well, if you like Asian food, it's one of the best places in the area.
Clare: Then, by all means, let's go! ☺ And, thanks for asking.
Roddy: Of course.

A few seconds later:

Roddy: (My sister suggested I subtly let you know where we were going so you wouldn't stress out about what to wear quite so much.)

Hmm. So, he's told his sister about me. *Did he tell her about the kiss?* I shake off the thought. At least he's close with his family.

Clare: Tell your sister thanks.
Roddy: Will do. See you Saturday.
Clare: See you then.

Just as I'm about to close my texting app, I see the link of my conversation with Suz. I realize I haven't communicated with her in any way since I left—not that she's tried to talk to me either—and I do need to go back to move the rest of my stuff out at some point. Hesitantly, I open our conversation and start a new text. It takes a couple tries before I get out exactly what I want to send.

Clare: Hey. ~~Hope you're doing okay.~~ When would be a good time for me to come by to get the rest of my stuff?

I wait a few minutes, but get no response. This is a little odd because Suz is practically glued to her phone. *Except when she's playing one of her annoying video games.* She must be in the middle of one of those very involved RPGs with her crew. I send another text anyway.

Clare: ~~Guess you can't be bothered to answer right now. Figures.~~ I can come when you're at work sometime, if you don't want to see me.
Clare: Just let me know.

I give up for tonight since this still garners no response from her. Instead, I focus on my upcoming date with Roddy. Saturday certainly can't come soon enough for me.

Part E

"Touch of Your Hand"

April/May

As I enter Nate's house on Monday, I can see he's flustered. He's pacing the office, obviously on the phone with someone, and his hair is sticking up every which way. Papers have fallen—or were thrown—onto the floor, and he gesticulates wildly at me to look at something on his computer. I don't even bother putting my stuff down at my desk before going to peer at his screen. His browser is loaded with tabs—all for airline websites and Google flights searches—so I know something has gone wrong with someone's flights. Airlines, the bane of our existence.

"You have *got* to be kidding me!" Nate yells into the phone. "Well, they have to have some way for them to get home."

He points at the tab open on the screen, I see the problem. Our clients, the McClellans, are supposed to be heading back from Ireland tomorrow, but the airline, Skyways, has decided to cancel their flight for some unknown reason.

Nate punches the mute button on his phone and says to me, "There aren't any weather issues forecast, no upcoming strikes, no staffing issues I've seen in the news, nothing to indicate why they're cancelling this flight. Nothing except they're jerks!" His face is beet red and there's a vein threatening to pop right out of his forehead.

"Deep breaths," I reply. "Let me put my stuff down and I'll take a look."

Nate nods. "Sorry, I didn't mean to take it out on you. I just hate dealing with this shit time and time again. They can just screw people over all the time without any consequen—" He quickly unmutes himself and says to the agent on the phone, "Yes, I'm here. What did you find out?"

Meanwhile, I set my lunch and my purse next to my desk and open up my laptop. Nate's computer is too chaotic for me and don't get me started on his desk. I love him and he's a great travel agent, but we have very different organizational styles. I pull up the McClellans' itinerary in our CRM, and find their original schedule. Then, I pull up their current itinerary on Skyways' website to see what new flight they've scheduled them for. Therein lies the problem. They've neglected to offer another flight option after cancelling the original one.

"Thursday?!" Nate exclaims. "No, no, no. That will not work at all. They have a connecting flight tomorrow and they can't stay in Ireland for another two days because *you people* cancelled their flight for no reason. This is unacceptable."

"Nate," I say, with a warning tone. Although the airline in general deserves all he can dish out, the specific person he's talking to didn't cancel the flight and is probably doing everything they can to help.

"I'm sorry. This isn't your fault, but there has to be something you all can do to get them home before Thursday."

He looks at me as if to say, "Is that better?" I smile and nod before going back to the task at hand. Scrolling through all the flights Skyways has tomorrow, I see a schedule that might work. It's a gnarly one with two connections, but it would get our clients home tomorrow instead of two days late. It's basically the only option I can see without us having to force the airline to refund the clients and trying to rebook them on another carrier.

"Hey, look at this," I say, pointing at my screen.

Nate comes over to look, and nods. "It's not ideal, but at least they get home the same day. Is that all they have?"

"Yeah. I couldn't find anything else that would get them back tomorrow."

"Well, that's what they're going to do then. Assuming this guy ever gets back on the line with me." He stalks back over to his desk. "Can you send that to me?"

"Sure thing," I reply. I send it to him, then go put my lunch in the fridge, finally.

About five minutes later, I'm stirring honey into two mugs of tea when Nate comes into the kitchen. "I'm so sorry I got so upset back there. I didn't mean to take my frustrations out on you or the guy on the phone," he says, taking the mug I offer him. "Thanks for looking up the alternative schedule. And for the tea."

"It's okay," I reply, taking a sip of mine to see if there's enough honey in it. I add a tiny bit more because the day is certainly starting out to be one where a little extra honey could go a long way. "Any particular reason you're extra touchy today?"

Nate rolls his eyes as he swallows a gulp of tea. "We heard back from our wedding planner that The Cannon Room is booked for every weekend for the rest of the year, not to mention November fifth, and Isaac is having an absolute meltdown. Which means that I'm having a meltdown because if he's not happy, I'm not happy. He really had his heart set on getting married there."

"Oh, I am so sorry. I know he's dreamed of getting married there since Andrew and Suzanna's wedding."

Nate nods. "It's not that he wanted to one-up his brother, but we both really liked the vibe of the place, you know?"

"I know he's really upset right now, but do you think he'd be open to another suggestion?"

Nate shrugs. "If he's not, I am. We need to get this show on the road if we're going to get married in seven months."

"That's exactly what I was thinking." I set down my mug and pull out my phone from my pocket. I open my browser and pull up the site of the venue I'm thinking of. "So, I was thinking I'd get married here myself at some point, but that doesn't sound like it will be happening anytime soon, and I—" My voice cracks and even though I wasn't expecting it, tears spring to my eyes.

"Clare," Nate says, sympathetically. "Your someone is out there. She, or he, might be right in front of you before you know it."

I nod and wipe the tears away with a napkin from the counter. "I know. And I really thought I was over it. I thought I'd moved on from Suz, but…well…here we are."

"I know this is going to sound like a cliché, but these things take time. It's only been a little over a week. Give yourself the grace to feel your feelings."

"I will. Thank you." I take a deep breath, then focus back on my phone. "Alright, back to the task at hand. What about the NC Art Museum for your wedding?"

Nate's eyes widen. "I'm intrigued. Tell me more."

* * *

That night, I text Suz to see when a good time would be to pick up the rest of my things from our…her place. She answers back almost immediately.

Suz: I guess sometime when I'm at work. You still have your key?
Clare: Yeah. I'll see when N&I are free to help with the furniture and come then.
Suz: K

I see the little ellipsis that means she's typing something else, but it keeps disappearing. I wonder what she's thinking about saying and not. Does she wish I'd come back? Is she missing me? Does she wish she'd told me she loved me or called me her girlfriend? Did I make a mistake by leaving?

Finally, her next texts come through.

Suz: Don't forget to take that godawful chair in the guestroom.
Suz: And leave the prorated rent/utilities check on the kitchen counter.

So, yeah. None of those things. I made the absolute best decision.

* * *

On Thursday evening, I'm doing an online dance workout with my favorite instructor, Gina B. of Up to the Beat Fitness. I'm in my usual sneakers, black biker shorts (with pockets), and my favorite Up to the Beat branded tank, which says "Be Active Be Happy Be You."

I'm currently doing the cha-cha-cha in her Power Walk through the Decades '80s mix and sweating buckets, but having a great time. I'm pumping my chest and my arms as I step forward on one side, then chassé to the other side and repeat. The music is fast, so I'm having to really focus on my footwork. I'm singing along as well, which helps me focus on my breathing.

"Do you think the boys would like Caffè Luna for their engagement party?" Abby asks abruptly, nearly making me lose my balance. "Whoops. Sorry. I didn't notice you were working out."

Out of breath, I hit pause on the video and take a sip of water before responding. "It's…okay," I pant.

Abby waves her hands. "Never mind. I can come back later. Go ahead and finish."

"It's fine. I was almost done. What did you need?" I reply, drinking some more water and walking in place to cool down.

"I was just looking at venues for the engagement party and wondered if you thought they'd like Caffè Luna."

I think about this for a moment. "Nate and Isaac have always loved Caffè Luna, so that sounds like a great plan to me."

"Wonderful. I will give them a call tomorrow and get it booked," she says.

"Was that all you needed?" I ask—now stepping side to side, doing arm stretches—wondering why she interrupted my workout to ask such a simple question.

"Yeah… Well, no." She chews on her lower lip and sits down, then stands right back up again. I haven't seen her this nervous in a while.

I stop my stretching and walk closer to her. "Abby, what's up?"

"My parents are coming for a visit again," she replies. "They want to take me out for a full dinner next week to 'catch up.' My mom said she'd make a reservation 'someplace quieter.' Ugh!"

"Ugh is right," I say. The Cassidys' idea of catching up is usually grilling Abby about her nonexistent love life, why she didn't go into law like them, how she expects to support herself doing property management for the rest of her life, why she won't let them fix her up with one of their friends' handsome sons, etc. Lately, they've come to terms with the fact that Abby is a lesbian, but that only means that they have then tried to fix her up with eligible daughters of their rich friends. Like Lily. I'd almost forgotten about Lily.

"Yeah. I don't think I have the bandwidth to deal with them again so soon. Things have been crazy at work, and I haven't had a real date in I don't know how long—that soccer thing with Lily was *so* not a date—and I don't even know what to tell them on that front." She sighs heavily.

"Really? You didn't tell me the date with Lily didn't go well," I reply, secretly cheering on the inside.

She scoffs. "We planned to meet there, which was fine, but then she left my ticket at the box office. Didn't even meet me at the front gate or anything. Who does that?" She throws her hands out to the side forcefully. "Then, I tried to talk to her during the game, you know, to get to know her at least a little. She shushed me! Can you believe that?"

"Wow. Sounds like she was more interested in the game than in you."

"Exactly. I mean, I was only doing this to get my parents off my back, but I was at least trying to be polite and talk with her a little."

I ponder this for a moment. "Maybe, she was on the date for the same reason. To get her parents off her back, so she didn't really have any interest in moving things forward with you." I hold up a hand as Abby starts to object. "Not a reason at all for her to be rude to you, but that might be the explanation."

She scrunches up her face, then says, "Yeah, you're probably right. But, what do I tell my parents? You know how they are. They're going to grill me about the date and not understand that it didn't go well cause Lily and I didn't hit it off. And I just… Would you go with me? You know, take the edge off?"

"Of course I will. Just tell me where and when," I reply with all sincerity.

Abby throws her arms around me. "Thank you, thank you, thank you!"

"You're welcome, but I'm all sweaty and gross, are you sure you want to hug me right now?" I say, laughing and hugging her back. I have to say I'm not the least bit upset by her hug, quite the contrary. Our bodies fit together in such an easy way, whereas Suz and I were so awkward whenever we hugged or touched. *Stop comparing Abby to Suz. They're two different people.*

"I do not care," she says, hugging me tighter. "You lifted an enormous weight off my shoulders and as long as you take a shower between now and next Tuesday, we're golden."

We both laugh as we pull apart. "Hey, while we're asking for favors…"

Abby raises an eyebrow. I find it so attractive when people can do that, and I'm only about forty percent jealous that I can't. "Yeeaaah?"

"Since the biopsy was negative—thank God—and I've gotten out of the dead-end relationship, I thought maybe it was time for me to make some other life changes."

"Oooo! Tell me more." Abby's face lights up.

"Well…I was thinking maybe I could try to get my driver's license again. Would you help me?" I brace for whatever Abby might say or do when I drop this bomb. My friends have been incredibly supportive over the last five years, and they've never pressured me in any way, but I know it's a burden to have a friend who doesn't drive. I do take the bus as many places as I can, and rideshare is always an option, if money isn't too tight, but I rely on my friends an awful lot to get me from place to place. Since the five-year mark of the accident passed, I've been seriously thinking about getting my license again, and I think it's finally time.

Abby's squeal is almost deafening. She throws her arms around my neck and wiggles me back and forth with glee. Letting me go, she says, "Nothing would make me happier than to help you get your license again." She puts her hand up. "Don't get me wrong, I'm not saying that *I* want you to get your license, I'm happy that you feel like you're *ready* to get your license again."

I smile as tears start to well up in my eyes. "Thank you. That means a lot."

"It means a lot that you asked me." Abby's eyes shimmer with tears as well.

I wipe my eyes and change the subject before we're both sobbing. "Okay, let me go take a shower, then you can tell me more about your plans for the engagement party."

As I turn to go to my bedroom, Abby calls after me, "I love hearing you sing when you're working out. I don't think I ever knew all the words to 'Livin' on a Prayer' until now."

I smile to myself and have no doubt about the song I'll be singing in the shower.

Part 6

"Umbrella"

April

This morning, I received a call from my doctor's office that the CT scan was clear except for something suspicious near my liver. My doctor reassured me that it was most likely nothing, but she referred me for an abdominal MRI, just to be safe. *Great, yet another appointment in the growing list.*

I don't have time to worry about the CT results or the upcoming abdominal MRI, though, because I'm on my way to have a breast MRI. I briefly break my "don't Google anything about this process" rule I made with myself and look up what that entails while Abby drives me to yet another radiology office.

"Oh my gosh. Not only am I going to be in a giant tube, but I'm going to be face down with my breasts in some sort of contraption," I tell Abby as I scroll through images of breast MRIs on my phone.

She stops at a red light and glances over at the picture I'm showing her. "Looks like they're going to put your boobs in some kind of jail!"

I can't help but laugh at that. "Yep." I put my phone away before I get freaked out any more about this impending test. "I wonder if it will be easier having an MRI being face down.

Like, I won't be able to tell that I'm in a confined space, maybe?"

Abby shrugs. "It's possible. I've never had an MRI, so I have no clue what to expect. I've heard they're really loud, though, but they let you have music to drown it out."

"Yeah, I had one done on my knee after the accident, and I got to pick a radio station to listen to while they did it. But, I went in feet first, so my head never went in it. It was really loud, though. Almost drowned out the music."

When we arrive at the office, Abby parks in the very full parking lot, and we go into the two-story brick medical building. I locate the suite I'm supposed to go to on the first floor, and we walk down the hall in silence. Once there, I check in, and we take our seats in the waiting room. Thankfully, it's empty except for us, so I hopefully won't have to wait very long. I grip the arms of the chair in a death grip and my knee starts bouncing up and down.

Abby faces me and puts her hand over mine. "You know this is only a chapter, right?"

"Huh?" With the blood pounding in my ears, I'm not sure I've heard her correctly. I turn to look at her so I can see her words as well as hear them.

"This is only a chapter. It's not your whole story," she says reassuringly.

I suddenly have this feeling of not only calm but of something else I can't quite place. Almost like I've heard her say that before, but I know that's not true.

However, I don't have time to sort out those feelings because a nurse calls me back then for my test. Abby gives me a hug and wishes me luck as I head off for the next test in my journey.

The nurses get me changed into yet another itchy gown that's been washed a thousand times. Not like it matters because they're going to have me practically take it off as soon as I get in for the test anyway. In the testing room, the giant MRI machine looms like a coffin with the world's worst drummer playing inside it. On the patient table is the "boob jail" I saw online, along with several pillows, wedges and bolsters of varying sizes.

The nurses get me positioned on my knees, with a pillow underneath them for comfort, and with all the other supportive things under me that I need to keep my back flat while my breasts dangle down into this metal "jail." There's a face cradle, like on a massage table, and they pull my arms out in front of me like Superman. It's not as uncomfortable as I thought, and with the headphones, I'm able to listen to '80s music to try to drown out the hammering of the scanner.

My mind wanders as I'm taken in and out, in and out of the machine, but mostly I'm thinking I hope they find something and that it's small and treatable.

* * *

"Just wear the first outfit you tried on," Abby says, exasperated.

I look back at the bed to see my favorite jeans, and swirly navy blue and pink top lying on my pillow. "Are you sure?"

"Yes. You already said it's your favorite outfit. And I listened to you expound on how soft the peachskin fabric is and how all clothes should be made out of cotton and peachskin. Just wear your favorite outfit and let me get dressed for my evening."

I take another look in the mirror at the black A-line skirt and purple blouse I'm wearing currently, and decide Abby is right. Of course she's right. I should be happy and comfortable on my date. I looked up the restaurant online the day Roddy texted me and found out it's a fairly casual place. Which is the whole reason he said he texted in the first place—so that I would know what I should wear. And did it help? Nope.

"Okay," I relent, pulling off the skirt and blouse, to put on the more comfortable outfit. "Thank you for your help. Now, go put on your PJ's and enjoy your marathon of *Veronica Mars*."

"I will. And I want *you* to have a great time on your date. Just be yourself and stop obsessing over the dreams and the kiss," she says, giving me a pointed look. "Pretend it's just a regular old first date and you can save that whole nervousness thing for whether he'll kiss you goodnight or not."

"That's not really helping, you know."

"I know. You're going to worry regardless. Just *try* to relax and enjoy it."

I nod and finish getting ready. I put on my pink teardrop earrings and clip the right side of my hair back with a sparkly clip. Shelley brushes against my legs and meows, letting me know it's dinnertime. I want to scoop her up in my arms and squeeze her but resist the urge. Not only would she probably try to bite me, but I also don't want to have cat hair all over myself for the date. Instead, I pat her on the head and rub her ears briefly before filling her bowl with the salmon-flavored kibbles she loves. She tucks in immediately, barely coming up for air.

I hear a knock at the door, so I take one last quick look in the mirror before going to answer it. I grab my purse from the table in the entryway and open the door, planning to run out to greet Roddy so I can get away from the embarrassment of introducing him to Abby. She means well, but I know she'll mention something about the kiss.

"Hi!" Nate and Isaac exclaim in unison as they push past me into the apartment. They look around, then turn back to me.

"What are you guys doing here?" I ask, figuring I already know the answer.

Nate takes their jackets and hangs them on the coat rack. "We're here to spy on your new mystery man, of course."

"You know, it's not spying if you're standing in the middle of the apartment where he can see you, right?"

"Sure it is," Isaac chimes in. "We just came over to visit our good friend Abby and take her out for a drink. Isn't that right, Abby?"

Abby appears at her bedroom door still wearing the trousers and blouse she had on when she said she was going to change. And she's touched up her makeup. "That's right. Just three friends getting ready to go out for a drink."

"Oh, so you did this?" I look pointedly at Abby. In answer, she pretends to check her phone for a message. Of course she invited Nate and Isaac over to see Roddy. And of course she isn't wearing her PJ's because she's just dying to meet him too. I guess my plan to rush out of the apartment is out of the question now. "Fine. But, please, don't be weird."

They all promise to just say hello and let us go on our date. But, if I know these three like I think I do, Roddy's not going to know what hit him. We also make plans to go pick up the rest of my furniture next Tuesday while Suz is at work since I haven't heard back from her. I assume she's just in a snit because I left, but I'll make sure not to disturb her things and only take what's mine. Mostly, I really want to pick up my mother's rocking chair from the guest room, and just get everything else out of there so I don't have to keep thinking about it. I have enough on my plate as it is.

Sure enough, there's a knock at the door and as I go to answer it, I hear the three of them gathering behind me like that scene in *Love Actually* where the Prime Minister goes to Natalie's house to tell her he misses her, and her entire family is crowded around on the stairs staring at them. Now, of course, this is only three people, not ten, but it still isn't what I had in mind.

I take a deep breath and open the door, and Roddy is standing there holding three orange tulips. "Hello, Clare. These are for you," he says, handing me the delicate flowers.

I take them and my hand brushes his. My heart beats a little faster. "Thank you. Tulips are my favorite flower."

He smiles. "Mmm. I just had a feeling you weren't a rose kind of girl."

I hear Nate swoon and Isaac clear his throat to remind me, yet again, that they are here.

"Oh, Roddy, this is my roommate, Abby. And our friend Isaac and his fiancé Nate." I gesture to each one in turn, and they all grin like fools at him. I actually see Nate looking Roddy up and down, and I give him a surreptitious glare.

"Hello, everyone," Roddy replies, and gives them a nervous little wave.

Nate steps forward and asks, "What, exactly, are your intentions with Clare?"

"Nate," I say with a warning tone.

Before I can say anything else, Roddy puts his arm around my shoulder. "It's okay," he says to me. Then, turning to Nate, Isaac and Abby, he says, "I intend to take Clare out for a nice dinner where I hope to get to know her better. Anything beyond that will be up to her. Does that sound alright?"

"Yes, that sounds just fine," Nate agrees, looking a little sheepish. He takes the flowers from me. "I'll put these in water for you. Now, you two run along and have a good time."

"Shall we?" Roddy asks putting out his arm which I take as we head down the stairs.

* * *

YoHo Asian Bistro is a cozy restaurant in Cary. I've ridden past it a few times, but with having to walk, take the bus or rely on the kindness of friends to get me places, I don't spend much time outside of downtown Raleigh. The hostess takes us to a booth in the corner of the restaurant. The benches have high backs, and the tables are made of thick knotted wood that looks like it could have been part of an old ship or something.

"So, do you come here a lot?" I ask then shake my head. "Sorry, that sounds so cliché."

Roddy laughs. "Pretty regularly. I live right down the road, so it's convenient. And their take-out is quick and good."

"I didn't know you lived over this way. If I'd known that, I could have just met you here."

"Nonsense. It was no trouble at all."

"Seriously? It was nearly twenty minutes out of your way to come all the way to the Village District and back." Of course, I'm happy he went to all the effort, and it's not like there's rush hour on a Saturday, but still.

"Sorry, but I wasn't raised to meet a girl at a restaurant for a first date. My mother would be appalled if she heard I did something like that."

So, he's close with his mother and his sister then. That's almost always a good sign. Suz wasn't close with anyone in her family really. Maybe you could say she was close with her dad, but it's not like they actually talked about anything meaningful. Don't get me wrong, Suz's parents are really nice people, but they're not big on emotions. The apple certainly didn't fall far from the tree there.

"Well, I thank you for going out of your way to get me." I pick up my menu and am pleasantly surprised by the heft of it. They've got everything from Lo Mein to sushi, Pad Thai to edamame. It's an Asian food lover's dream!

"See anything that looks good?" Roddy asks.

"Everything looks good. So good I have no idea how to narrow it down."

He smiles. "Yeah, I have that trouble sometimes too. If you like, we could get a couple different things and share them. And do you like sushi? I usually get a couple rolls as an appetizer."

"That sounds good. I will say that I'm vegetarian, so it would need to be veggie-friendly sushi." I shiver slightly at the thought of raw fish.

He looks surprised. "Something else we have in common. I'm vegetarian as well. I usually stick with the avocado maki and the fried sweet potato maki."

"Wow. How long have you been a vegetarian?"

"Since college," he replies, taking a sip of water. "My mother didn't really understand at first, because she's French and she couldn't imagine any meal without meat, but she's slowly warmed to the idea. She even does Meatless Mondays every week for her and my dad. What about you?"

"I've been vegetarian all my life. My parents were, and I've never really considered anything else." I glance at the menu again, secretly beaming inside that he's also vegetarian. "As for the food, I'll defer to you since it all just looks so good."

When the server comes, Roddy orders the sushi, spring rolls, an order of vegetable Lo Mein, sesame tofu, and some extra plates so we can try some of everything. The server writes it all down, then hustles off to put in the order. And, we're left alone without menus to distract us from looking at each other. The room suddenly feels very warm.

Roddy says, "I was going to ask," at the same time I manage the very intelligent, "So." I gesture for him to continue.

"I was going to ask, if you're comfortable answering, how did everything turn out with the test that I took you to?" he asks.

That was not what I thought he was going to ask, but I assumed it would come up at some point. "It was fine. Only one thing showed up that my doctor's not too concerned about, but they're sending me for another MRI to be sure," I reply.

He nods. "That's good, I hope. And have they determined the cause of the malignant lymph node yet or a course of treatment? Sorry, my father is a doctor, so I grew up hearing about his medical cases."

"I actually just got the results back of the breast MRI I had done earlier this week and—" My voice hitches, and I'm not really sure how I feel talking about the breast cancer diagnosis I just received with this man I barely know on our first date. Roddy puts his hand on mine.

"It's okay. We don't have to talk about this, now or ever. Let's just enjoy our evening, shall we?" Both his voice and his eyes are very reassuring.

I nod, collecting myself.

"Clare, what is it that you do for a living?" Roddy asks, changing the subject.

"I'm a travel agent. My friend and business partner, Nate—who you just met—and I run our own agency: Nerds on a Plane," I reply, feeling on steadier ground. "We specialize in travel adventures for people who want to see where their favorite movies and tv shows were filmed, or want to learn more about their favorite authors. I mean, really, we can turn any trip into something nerdy."

"Really? That sounds amazing. I might have to get you to plan a trip for me sometime. I've always wanted to go to Austria to learn more about Mozart and Strauss."

"We'd be happy to!" I say, meaning it. I try to think of a smooth way to confirm my suspicions about his line of work, but nothing "smooth" comes to mind. "And you were about to tell me where you work the other day when we were interrupted."

He nods. "Yes. I was going to say that I play cello for the North Carolina Symphony."

Even though I already knew this, I can feel my eyes widen as if I'm actually surprised. "Really?"

"Yep. I've been playing with them for about five and a half years now."

That hits me like a ton of bricks. He's been playing with the symphony since just before my parents died. As in, I most likely just started seeing him—but not really since I never had binoculars—right before they passed away. And the dreams didn't start until after they were gone. Again, I feel like I'm losing my mind. But I can't let myself get bogged down with this now. Not on our date. I remind myself to do as Abby said stop thinking about all of this and get back to the here and now.

"Clare?" Roddy says. "You seemed a million miles away for a second there."

"Sorry, I was just...I was actually at the symphony concert on Friday night."

Now it's his turn to look surprised. He looks about ready to say something, then doesn't for a few beats. "Did you enjoy it?"

"I did," I half lie since we only heard part of it, what with my panic attack. "Isaac and I really enjoyed it. Beethoven and Mozart are two of my favorite composers."

"Mine too," he says. "So...uh...did you already know I played for the symphony, and you went to the concert to—"

"Stalk you?" I interrupt, smiling.

He nods.

"No. I've actually been going since I was a kid, and my dad would get season tickets and take me. Now, I get season tickets myself. Isaac usually goes with me."

"Ah, well, it's a relief that I don't have to run screaming from the restaurant." He smirks.

"I'm sure." I'm glad he can have a sense of humor, considering how all this began. Honestly, I'm not sure if I'd have a sense of humor about this if I were in his shoes. There are so many coincidences that this all seems too good to be true. He seems too good to be true.

I'm about to ask him whether he has a day job or if he just plays for the symphony when the server arrives with our appetizers. I'm so hungry I don't really think about anything but the delicious food in front of me. Roddy graciously holds each plate up for me to take some, then serves himself.

"Do you have a day job too or...?" I ask then shove an avocado maki into my mouth to hide the fact that I can't come up with a way to finish the question.

Roddy swallows. "Not so much a day job, but I do teach music lessons on the side. I have about fifteen students, though not all of them come on a regular basis. Some of them I'm tutoring, so to speak, for their regular school classes."

"Wow, that's a lot of students. Do you enjoy teaching?"

"Most of the time. I really love when they start to get it, you know? But the first several months can be brutal when they have no clue what they're doing and everything sounds very scratchy." He grimaces. "I know I sounded like that when I first started playing, so I get it. But once they really start to get how to play, their faces light up and it's a great feeling to know you've helped them achieve that."

I smile at him. "I'm sure that must be beautiful to see."

We eat in silence for a while, until I hear a disturbance near the entrance. There's some older lady who seems to be shouting across the restaurant. Over the music playing, it sounds like she's shouting, "A goose!" But, that can't be right. As if in slow motion, she starts walking toward our side of the restaurant, with a younger woman in tow, and now she's waving and continuing to repeat "Oh-gooo-st!" As she comes closer, I glance at Roddy to give him a "can you believe this lady" sort of look, and I see he's trying desperately to fold his body in on itself while looking at the wall. Almost as if he's trying to hide himself from what's going on. Then, I realize he must know this woman.

"Auguste," she says, the word finally becoming clear as she's now standing at our table, the younger woman standing behind her. "Auguste, why did you not respond when you heard me calling to you?"

Why the heck does she keep calling Roddy that? Is she actually a crazy, French, orchestra stalker who gave him some kind of different name for when she sneaks up on him in restaurants?

"You know I hate that name," Roddy says, through gritted teeth. "Why can you never call me Roddy, Mother?"

Mother? The crazy orchestra stalker lady is his mother? Of course, she's not a stalker then but maybe still a bit crazy. And, her French accent is there, but not overwhelming, like she's been in America for quite some time.

"Fine, darling. I'll call you by that silly nickname your father picked out." She waves her hand as if to brush away the thought. "Now, come give ta mère a kiss."

Roddy stands up and kisses her lightly on the cheek, then turns toward me. "Clare, I'd love to introduce you to my mother, Sabine."

Unsure whether I'm supposed to kiss her too or what, I quickly place my napkin on the table and stand up with my hand out. "It's lovely to meet you."

Sabine shakes my hand firmly, then releases it while looking me up and down. Self-consciously, I glance down at the floor. "Ah, Clare, you are just as lovely as Roddy described. But he simply did not say just how beautifully vibrant your hair truly is. Red hair is so becoming for some. I myself have tried to pull it off—with dye, you know—but it never worked for my complexion the way it does for you. Très magnifique!"

I can't help but smile. I've always loved my hair and even though I'm complimented about it all the time, no one has ever said it quite like that. Although, this is bittersweet these days as the thought swirls in the back of my mind that I might lose my beautiful hair if I have to do chemo. I shake that thought from my mind as I hear Roddy speak again.

"I'd also like to introduce you to my sister, Camille."

Camille steps out from behind Sabine and gives a small wave. "Nice to meet you, Clare."

"You, too," I say. Then I remember to add, "Thanks for having him text me the restaurant ahead of time."

Camille grins. "Sure thing. Glad to be of service."

We all stand there by the table awkwardly for a few moments, until Camille finally breaks the silence. "Mother, we really should let them get back to their date. Their food is getting cold."

"Ah, yes," Sabine relents. "Enjoy your evening, Clare and...Roddy."

"Thank you, Mother," he replies, kissing her on the cheek again.

Sabine and Camille head back to the cashier to pick up their take-out and leave. Roddy and I sit back down, and I put my napkin back on my lap. I'm just about to say something about how nice his mother and sister seemed, when he says, "My full name is Auguste Rodin Vaughn."

I look up at him and see the flush on his cheeks as he admits this. I think about saying something corny like "interesting" or "that's neat," but decide against it. I just try to give him a reassuring smile and reach my hand out for his across the table—which is not an easy task considering how many plates of food are sitting between us. He takes my hand and gives it a little squeeze.

"As I mentioned before and I'm sure you could tell from meeting her, my mother is French, and she takes art *very* seriously. She swears up and down that my first word was Monet." He chuckles. "My mother has a very dominant personality, and my father doesn't like to argue, so she won out. But my father gave me the nickname Roddy, and has never called me anything else. Most of my school career, my teachers would only call me by what was on the class roster, but they always pronounced it August, and my mother would speak with the principal, and it just always turned into this whole big thing. I liked the name my father gave me—less pretentious—so I went with it."

"So, Camille's middle name is? Monet?" I venture.

"Claudel. She went for the sculptors slash lovers." He rolls his eyes.

"Ah. Well, I won't say it isn't a bit quirky to name your children after famous artists, but my dad named me after the county where his mother was born in Ireland, which I always thought was a bit strange."

"But it's a beautiful name. And a beautiful county."

"Alas, I have never been. My father always said he'd take me, but there was either no time, no money or something else would come up." I feel the tears threaten, but I will them back down. "He and my mom passed away before we ever got to go."

Roddy squeezes my hand again and I see true sympathy in his eyes. "I'm so sorry to hear that. If you don't mind me asking, how long have they been gone?"

I nearly blurt out the number of months, weeks and days, but simply say, "About five years."

"I'm so sorry, again." He gently rubs his thumb on my hand.

I take a deep breath, because I know we cannot continue to talk about this or I'm going to lose it. Instead, I pick up my fork with my other hand and start eating again. "This sesame tofu is amazing."

Taking my cue, he gives my hand another squeeze, then releases it so he can start eating again too. "It really is. But I have to say, the Lo Mein is my favorite."

* * *

When we get back to Abby's apartment—err, my apartment, I guess—Roddy walks me to the door, holding my hand. My hand feels like it fits with his so well, it astounds me. I'm giddy as we exit the elevator, but also a little sad because our date is over. I know Abby will be home and I don't want him to have to go through the third degree again tonight.

As we reach the apartment, I see a note stuck to the door.

Gone out with the boys for drinks.
Don't wait up. –A

I pull the note off and grab my keys from my purse. I turn back to Roddy, my heart in my throat. "Do you want to come in for tea?"

He nods and runs his hand down my cheek before pulling me into a kiss. His lips feel so soft and warm against mine. Everything about the kiss feels right and perfect. It sounds so cliché, but it feels like we were meant to be. And that both thrills and scares me to death.

He pulls back and I reluctantly turn back to the door. My hand shakes as I put the key in the lock. I open the door and before I know what's happening, I grab him and kiss him again, just like that first night in the rain. Only, this time, the skies are clear.

Part F

"That's What Friends Are For"

May

Isaac wasn't available to help me move the rest of my stuff out of Suz's, but Nate and Abby could come, so we head over there on Tuesday during the day to get it over with. Both Nate and Abby drove so we'd have plenty of room for everything. Abby's little Mini won't hold furniture, but Nate's SUV can hold a ton.

When I walk in, everything looks the same with one big difference: all my stuff is piled neatly in the corner next to the front door—with the exception of the aforementioned "godawful chair." The chair that was my mother's and was the one she rocked me to sleep in as a child. Yes, it's a little worn, but I could never part with it.

"Well, that's convenient," Abby says, taking in the boxes labelled "Clare's stuff."

"Yeah, I guess she really didn't want us going through her things," I say. I'm not surprised and a little bit miffed that she packed up all my stuff like this. Is this just because she didn't care or because she doesn't like people going through her stuff? Or was she trying to make it faster for us?

"Alright," Nate begins, "let's get the furniture out of the way first, then we can put the boxes wherever else there's space."

We work quickly and efficiently, packing Nate's SUV to the hilt, then putting the remaining few boxes in Abby's car. Thankfully, the landlord fixed the elevator since I've been gone so we didn't have to cart everything up and down stairs.

When the last box is packed into the cars, I go back to the apartment I shared with Suz one last time. I walk through each room one by one, place the check and my key on the kitchen counter as requested, lock the bottom lock from the inside, and exit for the last time.

* * *

"Are you sure I look okay?" Abby asks for the hundredth time, smoothing her black pencil skirt and picking invisible lint off her floral blouse. We're standing about a block down the street from the French bistro—Jolie—her parents chose for this evening's festivities. Abby wanted to wait until she saw her parents arrive at the restaurant before we went in, and she wanted time to calm her nerves as well. Frankly, I think we should go in first so her parents would see she was early, but this is Abby's call.

I take Abby's hands and attempt to relax them down by her sides. "You look wonderful." And she does. Some might say radiant, but I'm not sure if that comment would be helpful at this exact moment as Abby is too nervous about dealing with her parents to deal with any of my mixed-up feelings. Not to mention the fact that I haven't decided if and when I will ever say anything to her in the first place. "Tonight is going to go just fine. And I'm here if you need anything."

She gives me a half-hearted smile. "Thanks. I am so glad you came with me. I don't think I could stand to face them otherwise."

"Oh, you're much stronger than you—" I stop speaking as my eyes catch sight of Suz striding down the street toward us. She's looking at something on her phone, so I don't think she's seen us.

"What?" Abby asks, turning around so she can see what I'm reacting to. "Oh. Has she seen us? Do you want to hide?"

I shake my head. "No, it's okay. We can stay here." I haven't seen Suz since the breakup and, though I think I would like to hide, my feet feel rooted to the spot. I can feel my pulse racing and my palms are starting to sweat. *Deep breaths, Clare.*

Suz comes closer and finally spots us, putting her phone in her pocket. "Hey, Clare."

My mouth feels like I just ate a handful of sand, but I manage to croak out, "Hey."

"We're having dinner with my parents," Abby puts in helpfully.

Suz nods. "Great."

I nod as well because no words will come out.

"I see you got your stuff out today," Suz says matter-of-factly.

Abby answers because I can still only nod. "Yep. No problems there."

"Okay, well," Suz says. "I'm on my way home and I want to get logged in before everyone else. Have fun at dinner." She walks on by as if she'd never stopped.

As soon as she's out of earshot, I fold forward and wrap my arms around the backs of my legs. With all the blood whooshing in my ears, I breathe deeply in and out. Slowly, the panic subsides and I'm able to stand back up again, slowly.

"Feeling better?" Abby asks. She's been with me through enough panic attacks to know that this was a relatively mild one. She rubs my back just the same and a shiver runs down my spine that I don't think has anything to do with the panic attack.

"Yeah," I reply weakly. "I just...it was the first time I've seen her since the breakup and...I just didn't expect that kind of reaction."

Abby tilts her head to one side in a look of understanding. "You know this is only a chapter, right?"

"What?" I ask, feeling a sense that I've heard those words somewhere before, but uncertain as to where.

"This is only a chapter," she says again. "It's not your whole story. You'll get past this Suz thing, and the next chapter will begin."

Even though I'm racking my brain trying to figure out when or where I've heard that before, I'm feeling more relaxed than I have in days.

"Thanks," I say, giving Abby's hand a squeeze. "Now, let's go tackle this dinner."

* * *

The restaurant is decorated beautifully in a classic bistro style with white tablecloths, black chairs, and hints of blue all around to complement the white. The mirrors on the wall give the illusion that the room is larger than it is, and the kitchen is right behind the bar so you can smell all the wonderful dishes being prepared.

It's not too busy since it's a Tuesday night. The host seats us at a table for four near the back next to a wall with navy blue and white floral wallpaper. The Cassidys take the bench side, leaving Abby and I with the chairs. Abby's father, Jack, is over six feet tall and combined with his broad shoulders, he cuts an imposing figure. On the other hand, Lynnette, Abby's mom, is shorter than her husband by nearly a foot, but her icy stare has a commanding presence all its own.

Picking up his menu, Jack says, "So, Clare, are you still in the travel game?"

I am barely able to keep from rolling my eyes, but I reply, "I am still a travel agent, yes, sir." Even though I've known the man for years upon years, he has never allowed me to refer to him as anything other than "sir" or "Mr. Cassidy."

Lynnette looks up from her menu and asks, "And is that going well? Do people still use travel agents?"

Abby pats my thigh under the table and a shiver runs up my spine. While she knows how much I loathe this question about my line of work, she doesn't know how it feels when she touches me. At least, I don't think she does. Shrugging that off, I reply, "Yes, many people still use travel agents because we provide personalized services that online companies don't give you. We can customize your itinerary to your needs, and we're there for you if something goes wrong. The internet guys just send you to a call center. Our clients really value our services, and we have a lot of repeat clients."

Lynnette looks slightly abashed. "Oh. Well, that's wonderful. I'm sure your parents would be very proud."

At the mention of my parents, my face flushes. Though Abby and I have been friends for years, our parents weren't the best of friends. They were friendly since their girls were friends, but they didn't socialize or really talk much unless the two of us were around. Abby would be the first to admit that my parents were much more down to earth than hers. Still, Lynnette and Jack were very kind to me when they died and hosted the funeral luncheon. "Thank you, Mrs. Cassidy."

The server comes over to take our orders and Jack speaks first, in his boisterous baritone, "Yes, we're actually ready to order. We'd like to get a charcuterie board and the steamed mussels for the table. Then I'll have the steak frites, medium well. My wife will have the trout almondine, and my daughter will have the poulet roti."

Abby shakes her head. "Um..." she begins meekly. "Actually, I'd like to have the crispy eggplant, please."

I silently applaud her for standing up for herself, even a tiny bit. I add, "Make that two crispy eggplants, please."

Jack grimaces. "I stand corrected."

The server furiously scribbles everything down, and Jack lets us all make our own drink orders, thankfully, or we'd all be forced to drink some ridiculously expensive wine he'd order "for the table." Every time I dine with him, I have to remind him, rather forcefully sometimes, that I neither eat meat nor drink alcohol. Two facts he cannot understand or respect. I have been at plenty of dinners at their house when I could only have bread, salad and water, and was chastised for not eating enough of their delicious food. If we're dining elsewhere, I'm darn well ordering something I can eat, and I'll just pick cheese off the charcuterie board.

Abby isn't a vegetarian, but she hates it when her father presumes to order for her, so I think she ordered the eggplant just to spite him. Or maybe she really did want it. She does love the ratatouille I make.

There's not a lot of conversation until the hors d'oeuvres come, at which point Lynnette starts telling us all about their recent trip to France and how much better the food was there. I'm sure the entire restaurant can hear her since her volume is akin to her husband's. Abby and I grin and try to engage with them, but anyone could tell we don't really care about their opinions of France or the food. But the food I'm eating must be different from what they're having on the other side of the table, because I think it's delicious—what I can eat of the charcuterie board, anyway.

Once the entrees arrive, Jack clears his throat as he cuts into his steak. "So, Abigail, when are you going to buckle down and go back to school for your law degree?"

"Dad, I…uh…" Abby stutters.

"'Dad, I…uh,' what?" Jack mimics. "You're forty-one years old. Enough of this property management bullshit. Excuse my French," he says this last part to me as if I'm the one he needs to apologize to. "We want you to make something of yourself. You've spent too long dilly-dallying and wasting your life. Enough, already."

I really want to punch his lights out for speaking that way to my best friend, but I want to give her a chance to stand up for herself first. She only asked me here for moral support, not to assault her father—and it's doubtful I could take him anyway—so I don't want to overstep.

Abby looks to her mother. "Mom, do you feel this way too?"

Lynnette looks at her trout like she's never seen a fish before. Her nod is infinitesimal, but it's there. "We only want the best for our little girl," she almost whispers.

"I really like my job, and I think I'm doing pretty well for myself," Abby replies in that weak tone of voice she only uses for her parents.

"All the money we wasted sending you to college," Jack mumbles under his breath.

I think about trying to change the subject, but Lynnette beats me to it, unfortunately. "Do you have a new boyfr— oops! Sorry, sweetheart—girlfriend we should know about? How did things go with Lily?"

Abby quickly darts her eyes to look at me, eyes wide with fear, then looks down at the table. She whispers, "No. No one. Lily and I didn't really hit it off."

"Didn't hit it off? What is that supposed to mean?" Jack scoffs.

Abby wrings her napkin nervously in her lap. "We didn't have much in common. She wouldn't even talk to me—"

"When the hell are you going to settle down?" Jack shouts and there's a rattle of cutlery around the tiny restaurant as everyone stops to stare at our table.

Lynnette puts her hand on his arm. "Jack, please, lower your voice."

He has the decency to look apologetically around the room and gestures for everyone to continue on with their meals. But he doesn't apologize to his daughter. "Abigail, your mother and I want to see you settled down with a good job and a family. You aren't getting any younger and if you intend on having children—with invitro, adoption, what have you—you need to get on it or else you're going to be eighty at your kid's graduation."

"I have a good job," Abby replies, meekly.

"She does, sir," I interject.

"Not good enough," Jack says, taking a swig of his wine. "Nowhere near good enough."

* * *

Back at Abby's, we're drowning our sorrows in crackers and spray cheese.

"I just cannot believe them. I'm over forty and they're still treating me like I'm fourteen." Abby pops a cracker particularly loaded with the orange goo into her mouth. She immediately grabs another cracker and squirts a big dollop of the processed cheese on top.

I pick up my own cracker piled with the stuff, and we knock them together like we're clinking champagne flutes. "I know. I completely understand why you spent so much time at my house growing up. Not that my parents were perfect."

"They were pretty darn close," Abby replies around a mouthful of cracker. "At least they supported you no matter what and didn't try to press their agenda on you."

I nod, tears pricking my eyes. "I miss them so much."

She puts her arm around my back, and I lean my head on her shoulder. "I miss them too."

We sit like that for a while, and somehow, I manage not to cry. There's a level of comfort only a best friend can give you, and I hope Abby feels the same way about me, even if she doesn't think of me romantically.

I sit back up and drink some water. "So, if your parents had no say and left you alone, where would you see yourself in five years?"

She thinks about this for a moment while she twirls a cracker around in her hands. "Theoretically, I'd like to still be working for Marshall Realty, unless some other amazing job came along. I could see myself still living here because I don't want to have to maintain a yard and all that, plus I love being so close to the shopping center and downtown." She bites her lower lip. "I guess all of that is the same as what I have now. So, what I think I'd like most of all is to be married or in a relationship with someone I truly love who loves me for who I am and not who they want me to be."

"You deserve all that and more," I say.

"Oh, and absolutely no kids," she adds.

I laugh. "Duly noted."

"What about you? Where do you see yourself in five years?"

I don't even have to think about it. "I want to keep working at Nerds on a Plane, but I want to have actually seen some of these places I book. More than that though, I want someone to share my life and my travels with. Someone to share the ups and downs with. Someone who feels like home."

"Mmm. That sounds lovely." There's a glint in Abby's eye, and I can't tell if it's the light or if she's responding to what I just said. I think about how comfortable it felt with my head on her shoulder earlier, and I think about how nice it would be to snuggle with her again.

"Clare?" Abby says, bringing me out of my daydream.

"Yeah, sorry, what did you say?"

"Do you remember that time we played Girl Talk until two in the morning? Your dad had to come in and tell us to quiet down twice before we finally went to sleep."

I giggle. "Oh my gosh. Yes! He was so annoyed with us that night, but we were having so much fun."

We spend the rest of the evening reminiscing about the fun times we had growing up until there isn't a bit of spray cheese left in the can.

Part 7

"Falling into You"

May

Glass shattered and flew in every direction. Pain rose up my arm and into my chest like a lightning strike. My mother's screams and the crunch of metal merged together in a cacophony of sound. My father's last words–"We'll always look out for you"–echoed in my mind as I was taken off on a stretcher. The beeps of the hospital equipment nearly drowned out the message that my mother was gone. The tears flowed until there were no more left.

Suddenly, I was sitting in a wheelchair being pushed toward the hospital exit. A man waited for me on the other side of the sliding doors, but I couldn't make out his face. I shuddered in fear and begged the nurse to take me back to my room. She reassured me and kept propelling me forward. I realized this was the same person I'd seen in my dreams before, though I still couldn't make out any discernable features. He handed me my favorite flowers as he helped me get into the car, and my heart softened a little.

Seated at a diner together, he held the menu for me. We both ordered comfort food–macaroni and cheese, and chocolate cake–not worrying about calories. He paid the check and drove me home. He helped me into my apartment, and I heard myself invite him in for tea. He accepted and we talked on the sofa for hours. When he left, he hugged me, and I felt safe in his arms.

* * *

"Feeling loopy yet?" Nate asks as we drive across town to yet another radiologist's office a few weeks later.

This will make the fifth branch of Wake Radiology I've been to since this whole thing began. I keep suggesting to the receptionists that they should have a punch card and for every five visits, you get a free massage or something equally enjoyable. They've laughed, but no one has given me a punch card, a massage or even a free fro-yo yet.

Come to think of it, maybe that Valium has started to kick in.

"A little bit," I slur. My doctor prescribed drugs for this test since it is not only another breast MRI, but I'll be having multiple biopsies during it. She said it could take over an hour, and even though they use local anesthetic, it can still be quite painful. I was only too happy to take some Valium on my way, so I hopefully won't care about what they're doing to me and my poor breasts that feel more like pin cushions these days. This will be my fourth round of biopsies and the third type I've had. I started with ultrasound guided—had two rounds of those—then moved on to mammogram guided, now MRI guided.

"That's good," Nate chuckles. "I'm sure you're going to want to be good and drugged for this one."

I try to nod, but it feels like my head isn't quite as attached to my neck as it used to be. "Yep. Afther the mamm-o-gram one, I don thin I wanna rememer thisss." Wow. Even to my own ears that sounds terrible.

Nate parks the car and comes around to my side to help me out. "Whoa, there. Let me help you. Put your arm around my shoulder."

I do as he says, but I can still barely stand up. I've never taken Valium before, but I didn't think it would have this much effect on me. A nurse must see Nate struggling with me because she rushes out with a wheelchair. Soon, I'm seated and being pushed into the office.

"Thanksh," I say.

"Yes, thank you," Nate adds.

We get inside the office, and they check me in, all the while I'm feeling like my head is floating somewhere away from my body, and my legs feel like lead weights in the wheelchair. I'm fairly sure I'm going to sleep through this whole procedure, which is fine by me.

"O'Donnell," a nurse calls from the doorway.

I try to raise my hand, but there's no way. Thankfully, Nate answers her, and the nurse whisks me off to the changing area. She helps me get changed into a gown—which I'm sure is not part of her job description—and she wheels me to the area just outside of the MRI room.

"Dan, I'm gonna need help with this one," she says to a burly man sitting at a computer.

He turns around and must see that the Valium has taken hold. "You're hoping not to remember this at all, aren't you?"

"Naht if I ca-an hep it," I slur.

Dan helps the other nurse get me into position on the MRI machine—on my knees with my boobs in that jail contraption like they were in before—and the rest is just flashes. At some point, I feel them squeezing some sort of plastic thing around my breasts, which really hurts, but I don't really care either. And I am pushed into and out of the MRI machine over and over again. Eventually, they announce that they are going to do the actual biopsies—which I thought they'd already done—and I can feel the needles going into my breasts. This time, I do care because it hurts like hell, and it takes them a long time and a lot of pressure to stop the bleeding. My poor breasts feel like they've been in a bar fight.

Once it's all over, Nate takes me back to Abby's, gets me changed into my pajamas, and I collapse on the couch—with more tiny ice packs in my bra—and fall into a deep sleep.

* * *

When I wake up, it's dark in the living room and I can see the last remnants of daylight disappearing through the window. I roll to one side and immediately regret it, as I'm very sore from the procedure and the ice packs have long since thawed. I reach for my water bottle on the table, but another hand grabs it first.

"You're awake," a voice says, and it takes me a few groggy seconds to realize it's Roddy's voice. He helps me sit up before handing me the water bottle.

"Thanks," I reply, taking a good, long sip as he turns on the light next to the couch.

He holds out some Tylenol. "Would you like these? Nate said you could have some"—he looks at his watch—"before now, actually."

I take the pills and drink a lot more water as my throat is very dry. "What are you doing here?" I realize how that must sound and start over. "Sorry, not that I'm not happy to see you, but where's Nate?"

He grins. "Nate had to go because of a client emergency he needed to deal with, he couldn't reach Isaac, and Abby had some dinner thing, so he called me a couple hours ago." Abby must have given Nate Roddy's number. Sensing I'm done with the water for now, he takes it and sets it back on the table. "How are you feeling?"

"I'm...okay," I say. "This one was definitely worse than the others, and I'm still feeling a little loopy. What time is it?"

"It's about seven forty-five," he answers. "Can I get you anything? Are you hungry? Do you need more ice packs?"

I smile at his thoughtfulness. "Yes and yes. But, first, I think I'm going to need help getting up to...you know. Not that I'll need help in there, just help to and from."

"Ah, yes. Can do," he says masking any discomfort he might be feeling. He comes beside me and bends down so I can put my arms around his strong shoulders just long enough to stand up. Then he stands slowly, supporting me at the waist with his arms. I feel so incredibly safe and supported, and if it weren't bordering on an emergency and my arms and chest weren't so sore, I would stand here and relish his touch for a bit longer. I lower my arms and put one around his waist as he helps me walk to the bathroom.

Once I've taken care of business, Roddy helps me back to the couch and retrieves more tiny pink ice packs from the freezer for me. I swap them with the ones in my bra so he can refreeze those.

"Any requests for dinner?" he asks, taking the ice packs back to the freezer.

"I'm not super picky, but I am ravenous since I haven't had anything since breakfast." Nate offered to pick up something for lunch on the way home, but I was too groggy to care and just wanted to sleep.

"Understood. I'll make us something quick." He shuffles some things around in the cabinets and the fridge, then I hear him getting pots and pans out from under the stove.

"Do you need any help?" I offer, though I'm not sure how much help I'd be considering how unsteady I was just now getting to and from the bathroom.

His head pops back up over the bar top and he says, "Nope. You just relax."

I leave the food in his, hopefully, capable hands and prop my feet up on the ottoman, snuggling the blanket around myself a little more since the ice packs are sending shivers down my spine. Or maybe it's the handsome man in the kitchen making me dinner. Shelley deigns to walk by the couch, and I give her some chin scritches before she hops up onto Abby's chair to have a nap.

To keep myself from dwelling on how attracted to him I am, I turn on the TV and find some old episodes of *The Great British Baking Show*, the most comforting program on the planet. It doesn't matter how many times I've watched them, I can always watch them again. Everyone is just so friendly to each other, their accents are so delightful, and they bake up such delicious-looking treats that it makes you want to grab a cup of tea and dunk your shortbread into it just like Paul Hollywood does.

I'm in the middle of an episode where they're making chocolate tea cakes for the technical challenge when Roddy appears with a tray of food. "I thought grilled cheese and tomato soup might be my best bet, based on what you had in the kitchen," he says as he sets the tray down on the coffee table and I hit pause on the show.

He says this very nonchalantly, but the grilled cheese is made with thick cut French bread, and I can see spinach, tomatoes and at least two kinds of cheese oozing out of it. Not to mention it's grilled to perfection. And the tomato soup has croutons and a tiny bit of shredded cheese on top.

"I think you've undersold your skills in the kitchen." I smile up at him.

"Anyone can make grilled cheese and tomato soup."

I gesture at the beautifully laid out tray and reply, "Not like this they can't. My dad could barely boil water. Thankfully, my mom was an excellent cook."

Roddy shrugs and sits down beside me on the sofa. "When your mother is French, you pick up a thing or two. Even though she's not a chef or anything, she still learned how to cook and bake from her mother."

I pick up my grilled cheese and take a bite. The crunchy, buttery bread filled with the melted cheeses tastes even better than it looks. "Remind me to thank your mom the next time I see her," I say once I swallow.

He chuckles. "I'll do that and I'm sure she'll appreciate it."

We tuck into our food, and I can't help but notice that he's sitting so close his arm brushes mine every so often while we eat. *I hope he can't see the goosebumps on my arms.* Even though I'm self-conscious about sitting here in my pj's probably looking like crap in front of a handsome man I barely know, I also think how comfortable this all feels at the same time.

I swallow the last spoonful of soup and dare to start the conversation I've been dreading. "So, um, this might seem like a random time to ask this..." I begin hesitantly, "but are we friends? Dating? Helpful acquaintances?"

He nearly chokes on his soup in what I hope is laughter. I hand him a napkin, and he composes himself before answering. "Considering that when we first met you practically attacked me by kissing me in broad daylight, I think we're way past acquaintances."

I put up my hands in protest. "I did not 'practically attack' you!"

"C'mon, you have to admit it was pretty close to an attack," he replies.

I think back on that time, and even in my drug-addled state, I can see where he's coming from. "Okay, it was pretty close," I concede.

He grins. "Getting back to your original question. I'd say we're definitely friends"—my heart drops a little—"but I'd say we're also dating, as...unorthodox as it has been so far."

"Sorry about that." I look back down at the food on my plate.

From the corner of my eye, I see him shake his head. "Don't apologize. It doesn't matter to me if we're going out for dinner or a movie, or just sitting here on your...err...Abby's couch eating grilled cheese sandwiches. I love spending time with you."

I feel the heat rise to my cheeks as I tilt my head to look back up at him. "I love spending time with you too."

He gives me a sly smile as he reaches over and brushes the hair back from my face. "This part isn't bad either."

Our lips meet and I feel the warmth from my cheeks spread through the rest of me. The kiss is warm and tender at first, becoming more urgent as it continues. I feel his one hand tangled up in my hair and the other pulling me closer—the perfect mixture of passion and safety. The bristles of his stubble tickle my chin and it's another sensation to add to the growing list of things I love about this man.

Wait, love? We both said love. The stray thought makes me almost lose my balance, even though I'm sitting down. I recover and don't think Roddy is the wiser. The overwhelming feelings I have for him after such a short time are hard to reconcile in this moment, but I'm glad we're on the same page, at least, with where our relationship stands.

The doorbell rings, and we break apart. We stare at each other for a long moment until the doorbell rings again.

"Shall I go see who it is?" Roddy asks, finally.

"Sure," I reply. Not having any clue who could be coming by at this hour, and knowing it's not Nate or Isaac because they would have texted first, and it's not Abby because it's her apartment so she would have used her key, unless she was carrying something.

Roddy opens the door, and there stands his mother. "Mother. What are you doing here?"

"I came to bring Clare this cake I baked to help with her recovery, of course," she says, handing him an enormous cake carrier. Without waiting for an invitation, she brushes past him and coming straight into the living room. "Clare, darling, how are you *feeling?*"

"Hi, Sabine," I say. I see Roddy mouthing "I don't know," from the kitchen as he puts the cake on the counter. "I'm doing okay. Your son has been taking great care of me."

Sabine beams at me, then at Roddy. "Auguste, sorry, Roddy is very good at taking care of people. His father and I raised him well. Didn't we, mon chou?" As an aside to me, she adds, "I used to call him mon petit chou, but he is no longer so petit, n'est-ce pas?"

I laugh as Roddy arrives back in the living room to stand next to his mom. "Yes, you did," he says, either not having heard her last comment or choosing to ignore it.

"I can't thank you enough for teaching him to cook. The dinner he made me tonight was just what I needed," I tell her.

She gives Roddy another proud smile. "It is in the French nature to cook. My mother taught me, and I taught my children. Food is...how do the children say it these days...my love language."

"I'm sure Clare will really appreciate the cake, but maybe we should let her rest," Roddy says, trying to shoo Sabine from the apartment.

"Yes, Sabine, it was really good of you to stop by and to bring a cake," I echo. I shift with my blanket and feel a jolt of pain in my breast. It must show on my face because Roddy is there in two quick strides to check on me. "I'm fine. I just moved wrong. I think my ice packs might need a refresh again."

"On it," he says, taking the thawed ones I hand him. "Be right back. Mom, I can walk you out."

He puts a hand on his mother's shoulder and nudges her toward the door. She goes, unwillingly, but calls back to me, "Take care of yourself and enjoy the cake, ma chérie."

"Thank you, Sabine," I call back as Roddy practically shoves her out the door.

He comes back with the new ice packs a few moments later. "I'm so sorry about that. I texted that I was going to stay with you after your procedure, but I had no idea she'd just show up here. She must have tracked my phone since we're on one of those family plans."

I shrug. "It's fine. Plus, she brought cake." I turn away to get the ice packs situated, then turn back to him. "Do you not get along well with your mom?"

He shakes his head. "It's not that. She can just be...a lot, as you've seen. I didn't want her to scare you off, and she does have this habit of showing up at inopportune moments."

I blush, remembering his lips on mine. "I see."

There's a beat of silence as I gather he's remembering as well. He gives a sharp nod of his head then says, "Right. Let me clear these dishes, then I'll cut us some cake. Sound good?"

"Perfect. What kind is it?" I ask, not really caring because I haven't met a cake I didn't like.

"If I know my mother," he says, taking the tray to the kitchen, "it's probably a fraisier cake. That's her go-to unless someone is allergic to strawberries." He looks up from the counter. "You aren't allergic to anything, are you?"

"Nope, no food allergies here."

He opens the cake carrier and it's most definitely a fraisier cake. I've seen them made on baking shows enough times to recognize the cake, cream and strawberry halves lining the outside. "Oh, it's gorgeous!" I exclaim.

Roddy cuts slices and brings them over. It's even more beautiful close up. "You won't find a better fraisier outside of Paris, I can guarantee that."

"I'm sure," I agree. I take one bite, and it's absolute heaven. The delicate sponge is the perfect complement to the cream and the sharpness from the strawberries.

"Is this the one with the gingerbread strooctures?" Roddy asks in his best Paul Hollywood impression, indicating the show on pause.

I let out a giggle. "Oh my god, yes!" I reply, thrilled to have a subject I could talk for hours about. "Do you watch Bake Off too?"

"Who doesn't?"

"Do you want to watch the rest of the episode?" I ask, not sure how long he's staying.

In response, he picks up the remote from the ottoman where I left it and presses play. He moves to the corner of the sofa and puts his arm across the back, gesturing for me to come closer. I slide over and snuggle in next to him, using the blanket to cover both of us. Shelley comes over and curls up next to me on the blanket and purrs. We end up watching the last two episodes of that season before Abby returns from dinner with her parents.

Part G

"Truly, Madly, Deeply"

May

"Good evening and welcome to Meymandi Concert Hall and your North Carolina Symphony in concert. Please take a moment to silence all electronic devices and remember that no flash photography is allowed during the performance. Now sit back, relax and enjoy the concert."

The familiar announcement before any symphony concert played over the speakers. I was sitting in my usual seat in the concert hall in the upper balcony. But, instead of my dad sitting next to me, I saw the faceless woman sitting in his seat. I gasped and felt my heart start to race. Why was she sitting next to me? Were we on some kind of date?

She muttered something unintelligible right as the concert master began to tune the symphony. I tried to ask her what she said, but still couldn't hear or understand her. We listened intently to the concert as they began to play a piece I couldn't name.

Throughout the whole concert, I kept feeling like something was missing. I thought, at first, I was just missing my dad, but I could tell it was more than that. I looked around me, but all the seats were filled with other people. I scanned the stage and noticed an open spot on the right side of the symphony. There was a chair in the cello section, but no one sitting in it. Maybe someone was sick, and they couldn't find anyone to fill in for them.

After the show, we walked to a coffee shop and sat at a table in front of the window. We drank our beverages in alternating silence or more muttered musings I couldn't understand. Even though it was strange, and I couldn't understand what she actually said at all, I felt like I knew her and trusted her. I was growing very fond of her.

* * *

"Are you sure you have everything?" Abby asks for the fourth time as we head out the door on the way to Nate & Isaac's engagement party. She's been more than a little bit stressed since taking this on mostly by herself—even though I helped her as much as she'd let me—and I will never hear the end of it if I forget anything we're meant to bring.

I check my tote bag for what feels like the hundredth time this week. Laptop, check. USB with photos and videos of the two of them, check. Tiny projector, check. Various cables and cords to hook everything together, check. Notecards for my speech, check. "Yes, I am positive I have everything. Do you have *your* speech?"

She checks her tote bag, which is no doubt filled with more than we could possibly need for this dinner party, and gives me a thumbs up.

"Great. Let's go," I say walking toward the front door.

"Wait!" she exclaims running back toward her room. "I forgot the bag with the party favors."

I sigh. "I thought we decided not to do party favors."

Abby comes back from her bedroom hoisting a bag above her shoulder. "Got it! And, yes, I know we said we weren't going to do them, but I got this great deal on personalized M&M's, and I couldn't pass that up. They're so cute and you know how much Isaac loves M&M's." She pulls out one of the tiny bundles from the bag to show me.

"When did you have time to put these all into individual bags?" I ask thinking back over the last couple weeks and having no recollection of her doing something like this. "I would have helped you, you know."

"I know, but it didn't take very long. I actually did them on my day off last week while you were at work."

I examine the little bundle and see Isaac and Nate's faces printed on the chocolate candies. "They really are cute. Although some of them came out a little weird."

She nods. "Yeah, I know. Some of them are a little wonky with smooshed faces and such, but they're still cute."

I put a reassuring hand on her shoulder. "They are, and I'm sure the guys will love them. Now, can we go? If we don't leave soon, we're going to be late."

* * *

When we arrive at Caffé Luna, there's a flurry of activity getting the private room set up for us. Abby is off directing and instructing—politely, I might add—everyone so that it's all perfect for when Nate and Isaac arrive. I busy myself with setting up the laptop and projector so that will be all ready to go when Abby gives the signal. Why she didn't become a party planner when it was something she always said she'd love to do, I'll never know, but considering I changed my career in the last few years, there's still time if she still wants to pursue it. I'm sure her parents would hate that even more than her working in property management, but it's her life.

As the time gets closer to Nate & Isaac's arrival, guests start to arrive and they all take their seats, leaving the two center seats at the long banquet table for the guests of honor. The restaurant did such a great job with decorations and the place settings, and everyone is having a great time.

At six-thirty on the dot, Nate's sister, Sophia, pops her head in to say the boys are on their way in. Sophia was tasked with getting them here under the pretense that she and her friend, Adam, were taking them out for dinner to celebrate their engagement—which was mostly true.

"Okay, everyone, showtime," Abby stage-whispers.

We all take our seats, and Abby turns out the lights while we wait for them to walk in the door. I feel like my heart is pounding in my throat, I'm so excited with the anticipation. Soon enough, though, we hear Nate say, "I thought this room was for private parties only," as the door is flung open and we all yell, "Surprise!"

Nate's arms fly around in shock and he nearly knocks his fiancé over. Isaac, meanwhile, is smiling like he knew all along we were planning this party. Everyone cheers, and Nate and Isaac take bows.

Nate walks over to me and waggles his finger. "Do we have you to thank for this?"

I sort of shake my head noncommittally. "Partially, but it was Abby's idea."

"Abby," Nate says in a warning tone walking toward her. "What have I told you about surprise parties?"

Abby doesn't miss a beat and replies, "Nothing. You've never mentioned surprise parties to me, ever."

"Oh." He shrugs like he didn't expect that answer at all, then continues, "Well, I would have said that I *love* them!"

He wraps Abby in a bear hug, then they start wiggling back and forth, which eventually devolves into them holding hands, jumping up and down. Isaac looks at me seriously for a moment, then grabs my hands and we start doing the same until we're all jumping and laughing.

"Speech, speech!" someone calls out, then starts everyone else to tapping their utensils on their glasses.

Nate looks at his fiancé, and Isaac nods. He steps behind the chair with his name card at the center of the table. "Thank you all so much for being here to help us celebrate our engagement. We couldn't be happier to be getting married and to share our joy with our closest friends and family." He picks up his glass, even though there's nothing in it at the moment, and raises it high.

A young server who looks like he couldn't be more than fifteen, but who is also totally on point, runs over and fills it with champagne. The other waitstaff start filling everyone else's glasses with their choice of champagne or sparkling cider.

"Thank you," Isaac says to the server. To everyone else, he proclaims, "A toast! To true love in any form and the people who support you no matter what."

Everyone echoes the toast happily and clinks glasses with those around them before drinking some of their chosen beverage. I clink my glass with Nate and Isaac, then turn to Abby to do the same, and there's this unexplainable feeling I get when I look at her. We see each other all the time now that we're roommates, but it's more than that. It's like I'm being drawn to her. Or more like propelled toward her. She and I have been friends for so long that these feelings almost feel like a betrayal of that friendship. Like my heart is trying to overstep the boundaries and forgetting that the unwritten rules of friendship shouldn't be broken.

These dreams are driving me crazy because I cannot see the face of the person in them, and up until a couple weeks ago, the person was neither male nor female. Now, though, they are definitely female and the feeling that Abby could be the one in the dreams is so strong. Especially since that night at the symphony when I saw the faceless one morph into her as I closed my eyes. I keep thinking I should talk to her about all of this, especially since she already knows about the dreams, but the right moment hasn't presented itself.

"Alright, everyone, let's take our seats because the dinner is about to begin," Abby announces, and I realize I've been staring at her this whole time. *Knock it off, Clare, or she's going to think you're insane.* Just as I go to tear my eyes away from her, she's looking right back at me. *Oh no! Play it cool.* I give her a little wave, even though we're standing right next to each other. *Smooth. I'm sure she doesn't suspect a thing.* She raises an eyebrow, then gestures for me to go first toward our seats.

We sit across from the happy couple, and the grooms' parents sit to either side of them. Sophia and Adam are sitting next to me, and Isaac's brother and his wife are sitting next to Abby. Other family members and friends are arranged meticulously around the long table, and there's plenty of good conversation happening from what I can tell. We start with salads, then the entrees are served family-style around the table. There's bread in abundance, and everyone seems to be having a great time.

"So, Clare, how have you been?" Sophia asks while she holds out the fettuccini alfredo dish for me. "You're still working with Nate at the travel agency, right?"

I serve myself some of the creamy pasta, then say, "I've been doing pretty well. And, yes, I'm still working with your crazy brother." I flash a grin at Nate which causes him to look questioningly at me, and I just wave my hand in a dismissive gesture. "How have you been doing, Sophia?"

She passes the dish across the table to her aunt and shuffles a bit with her napkin before responding. "Good. Still working with my dad at the architecture firm. I like it, though," she replies. "Are you still with…Sam? No, that's not right. Syd?"

I shift uncomfortably in my seat. "Suz. And, no, we're not together anymore."

She looks crestfallen for having asked. "I'm so sorry. Are you doing okay since the breakup?"

I nod. "Yeah, I'm actually doing alright. It's only been a few weeks, but it was time. We just weren't suited for one another, and I think I'm in a much better place now." Oddly enough, that's the complete truth. I thought it would take me ages to get over Suz and to mourn our relationship, but since seeing her when I went to dinner with Abby's parents, I've been feeling much better about my decision to end things.

Sophia puts her hand on mine. "Good for you. I'm glad everything's working out for you."

"And you? Are you"—I lean in conspiratorially to whisper—"seeing Adam?"

Sophia shakes her head. "No. We're just good friends. I'm not seeing anyone, at the moment."

"So, we're both single then," I reply. "Nothing wrong with that."

Sophia nods in agreement. "I'm absolutely stuffed. This pasta is delicious!"

"Isn't it though? This is one of our favorite restaurants," Nate interjects.

"I can see why," Sophia adds pushing her plate away.

Just then, I feel a nudge from Abby. I turn, and she leans in close to my ear. "It's almost time for the video."

"I'm ready when you are," I say wiping my mouth with my napkin and pulling the thumb drive out of my pocket. "Just say the word."

"As soon as everyone has their desserts, we can get up and hop to it."

I nod my assent as I hand my plate to the server.

The desserts are served, but before Abby and I can enjoy our chocolate mousse cake, we get up and walk to the projector I set up earlier. I pop in the thumb drive and turn on the projector so a white screen appears on the wall at the end of the table.

"If we could have everyone's attention while you enjoy your desserts, we have a little something special to share from the best women," Abby says, gesturing for everyone to turn toward the "screen."

After everyone scoots their chairs so they can see, I add, "We made this video to show how much we love Nate and Isaac, and how happy we are that they are finally getting married. Please enjoy: Nate and Isaac, Through the Years."

I press play, and the song "True Colors" by Cyndi Lauper begins to play as photos of Nate and Isaac as children alternate in the video. Their parents were instrumental in providing some great, and sometimes very funny, photos of them through their childhoods. Abby and I were able to scour social media for some great photos and videos of them once they met. My particular favorite is a photo of the two of them embracing on the Ha'penny Bridge in Dublin—somewhere I've always wanted to go. As I see the photo now, I have this feeling like I've been on that bridge before, even though I've never been to Ireland. But that photo is quickly exchanged for a video of the boys at Raleigh Pride last year, and all thoughts of Dublin and the bridge are whisked away.

When the video ends, there are more than a few tears being wiped away among the guests. Nate and Isaac look particularly moved, and Isaac mouths, "Thank you."

"Now, if you're all finished with your desserts, it's time to dance!" Abby declares.

I turn off the projector and turn on the playlist we set up for this occasion. A mix of love songs and fun pop hits suitable for a celebration. The restaurant was okay with us having some music and dancing, as long as it wasn't so loud that it would disturb the guests in other areas. I make sure the volume is still reasonable, then head out to dance with everyone else to Kool & the Gang's "Get Down on It."

Most of the party is up and dancing, but a few of the older crowd are still finishing up their desserts and might be waiting on a slower song. Meanwhile, the rest of us are singing, dancing and grooving our hearts out. Isaac is doing the Bump with Nate, and they look really cute. Abby and I are doing more of a side-to-side step because while we love dancing, neither of us are adept with the more complex moves. Not that the Bump is particularly complex, but it does require some amount of coordination and style to pull off. I might do my Up to the Beat workouts nearly every day, but that doesn't mean I'm a great dancer.

Several other fast songs play in a row, and we keep right on dancing. When the "Electric Slide" comes on, everyone joins in and soon we're all laughing and singing along together while line dancing our butts off. Nate's parents look a little self-conscious, but they roll with it and by the end seem like they've loosened up a bit.

Abby and I are bouncing around together until the end of the song, smiling and laughing at each other. After a brief pause, I hear the first chord of "Truly, Madly, Deeply," and I'm not sure what to do. Nate and Isaac immediately begin slow dancing, along with most of the other couples in the room. Sophia and Adam go back to their seats—though it looks like Adam wanted to stay and dance more. I want to dance with Abby so badly, and I realize the only way to make that happen is to suck it up and make the first move.

I put my hand out and it's shaking like a leaf. She's glancing over at our friends, so I ask, "Would you like to dance?"

She turns back to meet my gaze, and her eyes are wide with shock? Excitement? Fear? I can't tell. I think she's about to say no when she surprises me by saying, "I'd love to."

She takes my hand in hers and wraps her other arm around my waist to pull me closer. I put my other hand on her shoulder, and we begin to sway along with the music. I've only slow danced with someone else a few times—Suz wasn't a fan of dancing—so this feels completely new to me. I'm very aware of how sweaty I've gotten during the last few dances. However, looking at Abby's brow, I can see a sheen there too, so at least I'm not alone. It also explains the heat radiating between us, or maybe that's this overwhelming feeling I have to want to kiss her right here, right now.

"I love this song," Abby says her eyes never having left mine. "I know it's a little old school, but it's so pretty, you know?"

"I know," I breathe.

"What made you want to dance with me?" she asks.

"I…" This is the perfect time to tell her about the dreams, but my mouth won't form the words. "I…don't know," I finally manage.

She lets go of my hand and I fear she's going to pull away, but instead, she wraps both arms around my neck and rests her head on my shoulder. "It's actually really nice dancing with you, Clare."

Oh my god, oh my god, ohmygod, ohmygod! This feels so right and the fact that she is enjoying it too is fantastic. I steal a glance over at Isaac and he gives me a wink. Nate, on the other hand, is completely confused, but seems no less happy.

"What's going on?" Nate mouths.

"I'm not sure," I mouth back. And I'm not. Does this mean she would be open to dating? Does she feel the things that I'm feeling? Or does she just like dancing with me?

The music goes on, we keep dancing, and I close my eyes to let the moment take me. I start singing along without realizing it.

"Wow," Abby says lifting her head up to look at me. "Hearing you sing this song takes me back to senior prom. Remember?"

"Dancing together because we were too dorky to have dates of our own? Of course I remember," I say. It strikes me that we danced to this very song, only we were standing about two feet apart with our hands on each other's shoulders at the time. "I think prom was more fun with you than it would have been with a date."

"Everything is more fun with you, Clare," Abby replies, then rests her head back on my shoulder.

No matter where this leads, I'm just going to be happy to be dancing with her tonight.

Part 8

"All of the Stars"

June

"Ms. O'Donnell," Dr. Dayal begins, "through all the biopsies, we've identified three areas of concern." She starts counting on her fingers. "The first is the enlarged right axillary lymph node originally found on your mammogram. The second is an IDC—invasive ductal carcinoma—in your right breast, which explains the enlarged lymph node. The third is a DCIS—ductal carcinoma in situ—in your left breast. This means it has not spread to the lymph nodes. With me so far?"

I nod along with the diagnoses as the doctor goes through them. I've already seen all this through my patient portal as each biopsy was completed, but it's the first time I've met with this doctor to discuss the game plan. Roddy came with me to be my support and to hold my hand. I'd also asked him to take notes, but there is a nurse here who is taking down all that the doctor is saying so that Roddy and I can focus on what she's telling us.

Dr. Dayal is beautiful, with tawny skin and dark brown hair pulled back in a clip at the base of her neck. She's also very slight compared to my larger frame, but something about the way she moves her hands as she speaks tells me she's a great surgeon. Her fingers gesture with a fluidity and dexterity I do not possess.

"Good," she continues flipping through my file. "I see that your CT scan was negative and the abdominal MRI showed nothing remarkable regarding the liver, which is great news."

Roddy gives me a smile and squeezes my hand in reassurance. I give him a squeeze back and what I'm sure is more of a grimace than a smile. I know the doctor has to recap everything, but I'm more interested in getting to the game plan so we can get this cancer out of me.

Dr. Dayal continues going through all my previous tests, including the one where they determined that I don't have any genetic markers for breast cancer—fantastic news. Though, that was a hard test for me to take even though it was a simple blood draw, because I could only think of my parents not being here to tell me my genetic history, and more importantly, to help me through all this. Isaac said they probably would have done the blood test anyway, but that was only minor consolation.

"Alright, I think that's everything. Do you have any questions so far?"

I shake my head. "No, nothing yet."

She pulls out a legal pad from behind my file and proceeds to draw a neck, shoulders, chest and breasts. With the speed at which she does this, I know she does this several times per week, if not per day. She turns the pad toward us, gesturing and drawing as she speaks. "My first thought for your treatment plan is to do a bilateral lumpectomy with axillary lymph node dissection. I'll make an incision here"—line by the right armpit—"for the lymph nodes. Here for the tumor in the right breast"—another line on the outside of the right breast. "For the left breast, since the tumor is right behind the nipple region, my plan is to make my incision right around the areola, to hopefully hide the scar." She draws a semicircle around the bottom of the left areola.

I try hard not to flinch as she talks so specifically about my breasts in front of my boyfriend who hasn't even seen them yet. "Are you saying I don't need to get a double mastectomy?" I ask, tentatively. "I was just assuming with cancer in both breasts that I'd need to have them both removed, then look at reconstruction options."

"You have to choose the surgical option that's right for you. However, because both of your tumors are small, and your cancer is estrogen and progesterone receptor positive— meaning you can go on hormone blockers after treatment— the least invasive option is lumpectomy. But, if you want to do a double mastectomy, we can explore that option as well." She goes on to explain the benefits and survival rates of both for my particular case. She also explains the ins and outs of the two types of reconstruction: implants and tissue reconstruction.

"The choice is ultimately up to you. We've found that those for whom lumpectomy is a viable option tend to do better emotionally after treatment because of the retention of the breasts. Those who opt for mastectomy—with or without reconstruction—can still lead full lives, but studies have shown that some who undergo mastectomy can carry more emotional scars, along with the physical ones," Dr. Dahal says. "You can take a few days to decide and give my office a call once you've made a decision. Then we can work on scheduling you for surgery."

* * *

On Sunday evening, Isaac picks me up at seven so we can attend a donor event for the NC Symphony. This is the first one I've been to without my parents, but when Roddy invited me, I couldn't say no. Plus, it's time I came back to things like this because I really enjoyed them. Dad and Mom would want me to keep doing the things we once loved together, even though they can't be here with me. Plus, I have an extra incentive to go now.

Roddy said he would have picked me up, but he needed to be there early to glad-hand some of the higher-level donors. Although, he said I was the only donor he was interested in seeing tonight. Plus, Isaac goes with me to most of the symphony concerts and wanted to meet some of the artists, so I didn't want to take that away from him.

"How are you doing?" Isaac asks, holding the car door open for me.

I know he means well, but I'm already tired of this question. I paste on a smile, though, and tamp down the exasperation. "I'm doing fine. It's just been a lot to take in and think about."

It only took me one partially sleepless night to decide I wanted to go with the lumpectomy as my doctor suggested, so I called her office the next day to get it scheduled. They scheduled my surgery in three weeks, and I'm filled with a mixture of dread and simply wanting to get this horrible cancer out of my body.

"I'd like to say I understand, but I don't. I can't imagine what this is like for you," he replies, putting his hand on my shoulder. "You know Nate and I are here for you."

I rest my hand atop his and nod. "I do, and I appreciate it more than you know."

"Good, because whatever you need, you just call us."

"Thank you," I say sincerely. "Now, can we not focus on my diagnosis or upcoming surgery tonight? I'd really like to go and have fun."

He sweeps his arm out in a gesture for me to get into the car. "Your wish is my command."

I laugh at his silliness and slide in, as much as my somewhat bulky dress will allow. I only have a few fancy dresses, so I rotate them for more formal events like this. The crinoline under my black brocade dress gives just enough volume to make it harder to cram into tight spaces than less poofy ones. But I absolutely love the pink and gold pattern of the fabric and the way the seaming hugs my curves in such a way that I don't feel as self-conscious about my size.

Isaac gets in on his side and starts the car.

"Welcome back to My Big Gay Wedding..."
"We're your hosts, Tomathy Thomlinson..."
"And Julian Flaubert. On this week's episode, we'll be talking about..."

Isaac hits the power button on the sound system. "Sorry about that. Nate's got me listening to this podcast while we plan the wedding..."

The rest of what he says is drowned out by the whooshing of blood in my ears. I know I've heard all this before, from the podcast starting in the car to Isaac's explanation. However, this experience of déjà vu is short-lived, comparatively, and I'm able to hear Isaac again.

"...Is Roddy going to be there tonight?"

It takes me a moment to recover from the disorienting experience I had moments ago. Still, I manage to stammer out, "Y-es...h-he is."

"Great. Then maybe I can talk to him for longer than the three seconds you allowed on your first date." Isaac gives me a sideways glance.

"Keep your eyes on the road," I caution. "But, yes, I'd be happy to more properly introduce you tonight."

Once we arrive at the parking deck, Isaac hurries out to open my door again—ever the perfect gentleman. I take his arm, and we walk into the venue. Inside is a sea of people dressed in mostly black and white, with the occasional splash of color here and there. The invitations don't say anything about the attire, other than "cocktail dress," but as the symphony members normally dress in black and white, it seems the most logical choice.

Isaac and I line up for the buffet of heavy hors d'oeuvres because we both skipped dinner knowing they would have a delectable spread of goodies, including plenty of vegetarian options. The whole time we're in line, I'm keeping an eye out for Roddy, but I haven't spotted him yet.

"I don't see him either," Isaac says, sensing what I'm doing.

I shrug. "I'm sure he's here somewhere. Probably talking with another donor."

"It does seem odd that we haven't seen him, though, because he should be easy to find with his height."

We arrive at the buffet table and begin piling our plates with wonderful morsels. Isaac spots one of the high tables that's empty nearby and goes over to claim it for us while I get some punch.

"Let me help you with that," I hear a deep voice say from behind me.

I turn around to find Roddy there in his tuxedo, and I'm struck both by how hot he looks in the tux and by how much he looks like the man in my dreams. Goose bumps break out on my arms and a shiver runs down my spine.

Roddy must sense something is off because he says, "Clare, are you alright?"

I take a deep breath and compose myself before answering. "Yes, I was just startled is all."

"I'm sorry. I didn't mean to scare you," he replies gently. "I'm so glad to see you. You look amazing."

"Thank you. I'm glad to see you too."

We stand there, staring at each other for what feels like hours, but must only be a few seconds. Roddy shakes himself out of it faster.

"Let me get you a glass of punch, then we can find Isaac." He fills a glass and walks with me to the table.

Isaac is just finishing a bite of food as we approach. He swallows quickly and puts his hand out for Roddy. "I'm Isaac Johnson. Nice to formally meet you."

Roddy sets down the glass and shakes Isaac's hand. "Roddy Vaughn. The pleasure is all mine." They release the shake and Roddy claps Isaac on the shoulder. "Oh, and I hear congratulations are in order."

Isaac beams. "Yes. Thank you very much. Nate and I are very excited to finally be making it official."

"Do you have a date yet?" Roddy asks.

"Even I don't know that," I say realizing I haven't heard much at all since they got engaged. But, then, I've been a bit wrapped up in my own life to pay attention to my friends. Suddenly, I feel extremely guilty.

Isaac shakes his head. "We haven't set a date yet. We're waiting until—"

"Waiting for what?" I ask.

"We...uh..."

"Isaac, what is it?" All sorts of things are flooding through my mind like that they eloped without telling anyone—which Abby and I would absolutely lose our minds over—or their chosen venue isn't available for the foreseeable future.

Isaac sighs heavily. "We're waiting until your treatment plan is settled so we can pick a time when you'll be feeling up to it."

Tears well up in my eyes and I throw my arms around Isaac's neck. He whispers in my ear, "We said we weren't going to talk about it anymore tonight, so I was trying not to say anything."

"I appreciate that. And I appreciate you postponing the wedding for me too. But you don't have to do that. I'll be happy for you two no matter how I'm feeling physically." I step back and see his cheeks are streaked with tears as well. I use my napkin to dab my eyes, and Isaac pulls out a handkerchief to wipe his face.

Isaac shakes his head resolutely. "No, we want both of our Best Women feeling their best because this is going to be the celebration of the year. No, check that. The century!" He pumps his hands up in the air in a "raise the roof" gesture. All three of us laugh.

Roddy leans conspiratorially over to Isaac and asks, "I'd hate to miss out on the party of the century. What do I need to do to get an invite to this wedding?"

"Keep treating our girl here right, and I'm sure she'll bring you as her plus one," Isaac replies.

"Deal." Roddy winks at me, then he and Isaac shake hands for the second time this evening.

We continue chatting while Isaac and I enjoy our food, until one of the members of the philanthropy department, Rebecca Wilson, gets up to make a speech.

"Good evening, everyone. I hope you are all enjoying the wonderful food, drinks and time to share with your North Carolina Symphony." She spreads her hands wide to encompass the whole gathering. "I wanted to take this moment to thank you all for your generous contributions over the years. Your support helps us bring great music not only to you and other patrons like yourselves, but out into the community at large through our unsurpassed education programs..."

Everyone listens while she continues thanking the donors of each level that are afforded the opportunity to attend this event, the symphony musicians for coming out, and so on and so forth. The speech itself isn't particularly remarkable, but I have another feeling that I've heard it before. And not just the fact that I've been to these events before and there's always a speech.

Rebecca concludes by introducing the quintet of musicians who will be performing tonight's musical selection. "...and Roddy Vaughn, performing the first movement of Schubert's String Quintet in C major."

"That's my cue," Roddy says, giving me a kiss on the cheek before dashing off to get on the stage with the others.

Isaac leans over and whispers, "Did you know he was playing tonight?"

I shake my head. I didn't know but I'm absolutely thrilled to hear him perform. This is the first time hearing him since I had the panic attack at the symphony. Plus, I'll be able to hear him even better in a quintet than when playing with the whole orchestra.

I grab Isaac's hand as I practically run toward the small stage at the front of the room. "C'mon. I want to be at the front for this."

"Hey...I wasn't finished with my punch," he whines but follows me anyway.

We get as close to the front as possible—apparently some others had the same idea, although I doubt these older folks just started dating one of the performers—and I make sure I can see Roddy perfectly as they tune their instruments. He looks so at one with his cello, like it is an extension of him. He catches my eye right before they begin and gives me a smile. *I am falling for this man hook, line and sinker.*

The musicians start to play, and I'm mesmerized. Not only by watching Roddy, but with all of it. The piece is beautiful. First, the violin has the melody, then one of the cellos takes over—Roddy!—then it goes back to the violins, but all the instruments are integral in such a small group. I'm watching them all sway and move with the music, digging in with their bows on the faster, louder parts, and ebbing away as the notes get softer.

Out of nowhere, my vision blurs and I nearly stumble even though I'm standing still. It's almost like I'm looking through those glasses that overlay something on top of the real world. What are they called? Oh yeah, augmented reality glasses. The quintet looks the same, but I'm seeing random people standing practically on top of Isaac and me...only they're not really here. It's bewildering, to say the least. I take a look around and see all the people standing in a slightly different place from where they are in my reality. Not only that, but I see Isaac and me standing back at a table looking at something on Isaac's phone while the musicians play.

Just as suddenly as they appeared, the glasses fall away and everything is "normal" again. My breath hitches, but I pull my focus on Roddy and the beautiful music, and manage to stave off another panic attack.

My mind is drawn back to the day I met Roddy—that overwhelming feeling he was the one in the dreams, and how I chased him in the rain. Then, I remember the phone call from the day before that, the endless testing, and my upcoming surgery. *I could die*, pops into my thoughts, uninvited. I try shaking it off and going back to the music, but the intrusive thoughts just keep coming. *I'm never going to be the same. I might have to do chemo. I might lose my hair. Will Roddy, or anyone, want me anymore?*

Suddenly, I feel a warm hand grab mine. I look over at Isaac and I can feel the tears, unbidden, on my cheeks for the second time. He releases my hand and puts his arm around my shoulder, drawing me close into him.

"It's going to be okay," he whispers.

I lean my head on my friend's shoulder and hope that he's right.

Part H

"Written in the Stars"

June

I've been riding on an absolute high ever since my dance with Abby at Nate and Isaac's engagement party. I came so close to telling Abby everything right there on the dance floor. But I just couldn't. It's not that I think she won't believe me or think I'm crazy or something, I'm mostly scared to find out that she doesn't feel the same way. It's like Schrödinger's feelings: right now, she both does and doesn't feel the same. If I say something, I'll have to know the outcome.

I'm thinking about all of this while I get my workout clothes on to do my morning Up to the Beat dance workout. I hear Abby moving around in the living room while I'm tying my shoelaces, and I'm half hoping she is on her way out the door by the time I get there. It's not like I'm avoiding her all the time, per se. But the memory of our dance together is still fresh in my mind and dancing in front of her would send me into a bit of a panic.

Pulling on my headband, I give a quick pat to Shelley who is sleeping in the sunbeam on the floor, and I tentatively walk out into the living room. To my surprise, Abby's sitting on the sofa wearing her workout clothes, punching buttons on the TV remote.

"Good morning!" she says exuberantly. "I thought I'd join you for one of your Gina B workouts, if that's okay."

Abby has never wanted to work out with me before—she might take a walk while listening to an audiobook on her lunch break but nothing as heart-pumping as aerobics or dance—so I'm a little taken aback. "Um…sure…yeah. Of course."

"I know. I don't usually do aerobics." She shrugs, laughing. "Okay, I never do aerobics. But I've been under so much stress lately with my parents and planning the engagement party—though that's over now—and work, that I just wanted to do something a bit more up tempo, that wasn't like running. Ick!"

"You know I agree with you on the running thing." We both laugh. "I'm happy to have you dance with me. Did you find one you wanted to do already?" I point to the YouTube channel displayed on the TV.

"Not really. I think maybe something with great retro music that's not too hard for my first one would be good. Not feeling weight training today." She hands me the remote.

"Just give me one second…" I go back a couple screens so I can scroll through the playlists I've curated and try to find the workout I'm thinking of. "Aha! I think you'll like this one."

"Cool. Why don't you stand in front so I can watch both of you. Also, I have no clue what I'm doing, and I don't want you to laugh at me," Abby says gesturing for me to being in front. Of course, that means she'll be staring at my backside the whole time, but I try not to think about it too much.

After a five-minute warmup, a remix of Joan Jett & the Blackhearts' "I Love Rock 'n' Roll" echoes from the speakers as Gina leads us through a fast-paced walking workout to classic rock hits. This video is followed by a George Michael and Wham workout and cooldown. We're both concentrating on the moves and the quick walking sections, but also laughing when we inevitably get our feet tangled up doing some of the dances.

"This…is…hard," Abby pants behind me as we walk forward and back, our arms going up and out to work the whole body. "Why aren't you…more winded?"

"Maybe because I do these all the time," I reply. "I am sweating buckets up here, though."

"There aren't enough towels in the world for all my sweat. Oh no!" Abby cries. "Not more triple-step!"

"Yep. It's her favorite dance, so you'll hardly find any of her workouts that doesn't feature at least a little cha-cha dancing." I throw my arms out as my feet somehow find the rhythm of the quick three-step between the two step backs on either side. The cha-cha hasn't always been a favorite of mine, but the more I do in the workouts, the more I see the benefits because it really works your whole body. Something Abby is hating right about now.

All of a sudden, Abby flops onto the sofa and throws her hand over her head. "Apologies to Mr. Michael and Mr. Ridgeley, but I cannot do any more. Carry on without me," she says dramatically. "Let me know how it ends."

Giving her side eye with a smile, I reply, "Hang on. I can fast forward to the cool down. I think you're going to like this one." I pick up the remote and skip to the next video.

"I don't even think I can bear a cool down. I'm so exhausted." She still has her arm draped over her face and has slumped down even further on the couch as if she's melting.

"Give it a moment."

When the first guitar riffs of "Faith" play, she slowly uncovers one eye, then the other. Almost imperceptibly, her hips start swaying from side to side.

"Come on. You know you want to," I say, waving my hands from side to side as I sashay toward her singing the lyrics.

"Oh, alright," she concedes. "I can't say no to this song."

She slides the rest of the way off the couch and joins me in the cool down. We both belt out the song while stretching and doing slower dances to bring our heartrates down gradually. By the end, I know we're both feeling pretty good about our workout.

"Thanks for letting me work out with you," Abby says, wiping the sweat off her face with the bottom of her shirt. I can just see the pale skin of her belly and the top of her belly button above her shorts.

"Um…yeah," I stammer. *Get it together, Clare.* "It was fun. You're welcome to join me whenever."

"Great. Though, I might need some slower ones to build up to your level."

"We can do that." I take a quick sip of water, then say, "Hey, not to change the subject, but do you think we could try driving next week? I know we've both been super busy, but my calendar is pretty open."

She grins. "Yeah, I think I'm pretty free next week too. I'll check for sure, but that sounds like a great plan. I'm so excited you're still wanting to do that."

"Did you think I was going to back out or give up before we'd even started?"

"No, not really." She shrugs. "I was only concerned you might be having second thoughts, but I wanted to give you space to work through your feelings."

"I appreciate that. But no. No second thoughts."

"Great!" She pats me on my arm. "Right now, though, I suggest we hit the showers."

My brain does a double take as I realize she doesn't mean for us to take a shower together, but for us each to take our own shower in our own bathrooms. I turn around and down the rest of my water to hide the flush on my cheeks that has nothing to do with the workout. "Yeah. I'm just gonna go fill up my water first."

"Cool. Guess I'll see you tonight sometime? We can compare calendars."

"Yeah. See you then," I reply as I head for the kitchen.

* * *

"Don't you look lovely this evening," Isaac says as he holds his car door open for me.

"Thank you," I reply, getting in and smoothing down the embroidered black brocade fabric of my dress. "But you've seen me in this dress several times before."

Isaac nods. "I know. Just…for whatever reason, you look particularly stunning in it tonight. Maybe it's the hair?"

He's picked me up for the annual symphony cocktail party for donors of a certain level. This is the first one of these parties we're going to since my parents died. I've been invited every year, but the thought of going has been too painful. When the invitation came this year, I felt something propelling me to RSVP yes. Maybe it was the thought that since my biopsy was negative, I should stop saying no to things. Maybe it was my parents giving me a gentle nudge that it's time to move on.

"Who knows, but I'll take the compliment," I say once he's ensconced in the driver's seat. "And you look rather dashing in your suit tonight as well. Is that a new tie?"

"It is. And a new pocket square to match." He practically preens.

"Ooh la la! Did your fiancé get those for you?"

"Heavens, no!" he exclaims. "You know I'm the fashionista in this relationship."

I throw my hands up in surrender. "Sorry. I thought it might have been an engagement gift or something. And maybe he got some help from the sales staff."

"Girl, I would have to tell him what to buy." He laughs heartily. "No, this was a present to myself, from myself, just because."

I place my hand on his shoulder. "And a well-deserved gift to yourself, I might add."

"Why, thank you." He turns on the car and a podcast starts playing.

"Welcome back to My Big Gay Wedding…*"*
"We're your hosts, Tomathy Thomlinson…"

After a lot of fumbling, Isaac finally hits the pause button.

"Wait! What are they talking about this week?" I ask, feigning genuine interest, and feeling a hint of déjà vu. I think I'd remember listening to a podcast called *My Big Gay Wedding*, though.

"Sorry about that. Nate recommended this silly thing to help with our planning." Isaac starts driving. "Who knows what they're talking about this week. Probably something stupid like rainbow centerpieces to really drive it home that we're queer, we're here and we're getting married."

I chuckle. "I have no problem with the podcast in general, but *Tomathy?*"

Isaac nods. "I actually looked it up and that's his legal name. No idea if he changed it or what, but it's not a 'stage name' or anything."

"There are no words to explain how…bizarre that sounds." I shake my head. "I mean, I'm all for being who you are, but who chooses Tomathy for a name?"

"That guy, apparently." We drive for a few moments in silence, then Isaac says, "I wonder what he looks like."

"When you looked him up, there wasn't a photo?"

"Nope. Not in his bio for the show or on his Wikipedia page. I didn't find any socials for him—separate from the show, that is—which either means he's got them super-duper locked down and private, or he's a ghost."

I pull out my phone to see what I can find. I see everything Isaac said, or lack thereof, but then I scroll farther down on the podcast social media page. "Oooo, I might have found something."

"What? What?" Thankfully we're at a stoplight because Isaac looks ready to jump over the center console to get a look at my phone.

"Keep your eyes on the road. It's a pretty blurry shot of two guys standing on a beach. I'm trying to zoom, but it just gets blurrier." I'm squinting as hard as I can, and I cannot make out either man's face enough to tell whether the one guy is Julian or not, based off the photo on the podcast's website.

"I'll have to text Nate when we get there. He's been listening to these guys for years 'cause they have several podcasts he likes. This is the only one he's ever asked me to listen to."

"Yeah, maybe something happened and Tomathy had to take down all his photos." I put my phone away since the search didn't bear any fruit. "Or he's a ghost."

We arrive at the venue, and Isaac texts Nate immediately but hasn't heard anything yet. So, we take our time enjoying the food and drinks, waiting for the entertainment to begin. Usually, there is a group of performers who will do a short piece after some speeches, but the selection of music is not told to us in advance. I'm hoping it's something truly classical and not some modern classical composer who basically just throws all the notes together and calls it music.

I'm savoring a stuffed mushroom cap when the speeches begin, and another one of those intense feelings of déjà vu hits me. I look over at Isaac and he's typing away at his phone, which means Nate probably answered him back. But that's not the thing that seems familiar. No, I'm feeling like I've heard Rebecca give this exact same speech before.

All of a sudden, it's as if I'm looking through AR goggles with another party overlaid on this one. It's exactly the same, but there's one man standing next to Rebecca in my reality who isn't there in the other one. Or wait, he is there, but he's standing next to me.

Looking at him more carefully, I see that it's the same cello player I noticed at the last symphony concert. *Wasn't he triggering a memory of the dreams then?* Yes, the dream sequence I saw that night was flipping between him and Abby, which I thought was weird at the time since I've never met that guy before—that I know of. So, why's he standing next to this other me in the other reality?

Another reality? *God, am I going insane?* Should I just call it a Multiverse and assume that I'm in a Marvel movie now? Suz would love that. She always wanted there to be different universes layered on top of one another where we'd do different things and be different people. I kinda wanted that too, but for different reasons.

The musicians are introduced, and the man standing next to me in the other reality goes up to the stage where he "joins" with the version of himself in my reality. *This is wild.* I also see my other self pulling Isaac forward toward the stage to get a better look. As the musicians—a quintet—play, my mind is enveloped by the music. It's Schubert's String Quintet in C major and it's lovely. This man that my other self seems to be with is a really accomplished cello player. And, I wonder, *Am I supposed to be with him?*

Isaac nudges me and the "goggles" drop away, though the feeling of confusion lingers for hours.

"Apparently, Tomathy had a stalker, so he had to take down all his photos," Isaac's saying while scrolling through his texts from Nate. "But, Nate does have a screenshot from last year when they had a photo of the two of them as the cover photo for the podcast."

He shows me the photo, but I can only pretend to be interested. This experience has shaken me to my core, and I don't know what I'm going to do about it.

Part 9

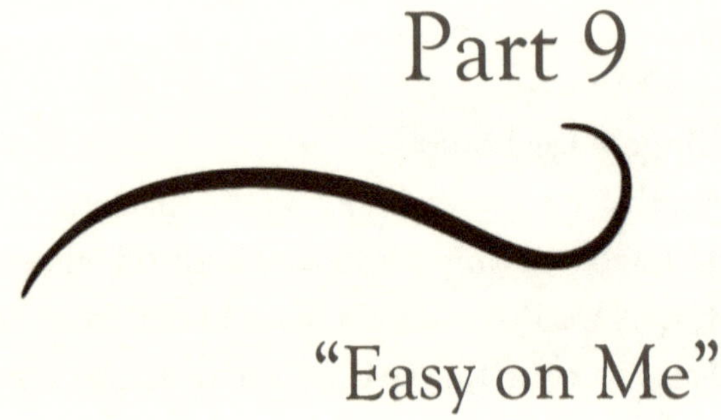

"Easy on Me"

June

My eyes open and I am momentarily confused as to where I am. The bright lights overhead and beeping machines around me tell me I'm in the hospital, which means my surgery must be over. Here I am in a hospital bed with scratchy sheets and one of those delightfully breezy gowns everyone loves.

My body feels stiff, as if I haven't moved in days, even though it's only been a few hours. I shift slightly and feel pain rocket through my chest. A whine escapes my lips.

Abby's face comes into view on my right. "You're awake. How are you feeling?"

My throat feels like I gargled with sand, but I manage to croak out, "Okay, I guess. Thirsty."

"Here's some water," Roddy says, appearing on the other side of the bed with a plastic cup complete with a bendy straw. "The surgeon said everything went really well."

I take a couple small sips of the water. "They got it all out?"

Roddy nods. "They think so. It will take a little bit for the full pathology to come back, she said, but she's pretty sure the margins are clear."

I give what I hope is a smile, but I can already feel the drowsiness threatening to overtake me again. "What about the lymph nodes?"

Abby answers this time, "They had to take eight, which was more than they expected."

"So, chemo then," I sigh.

"Most likely," Abby replies, putting her hand on my shoulder. "But they haven't gotten the final pathology, as Roddy said, so there's a small chance not."

"Dr. Dayal said she'd come by before they discharge you, so you can hear it all from her," Roddy adds. "The main thing now is that you're through surgery and the cancer is out."

"Yes, the cancer is out," I repeat, drifting back off to sleep.

* * *

"Please fasten your safety belt, ma'am," the flight attendant said. "We're about to take off."

Uncertain where I was, I looked around and saw I was sitting in a private jet. Sitting next to me was the faceless man. He reached up to take a warm towel from the flight attendant. I managed to buckle my seat belt and took my own warm towel from her. Not entirely sure what to do with it, I wiped my hands with it and placed it back on her tray.

"Are you ready?" the faceless man asked.

"Yes," I said, tentatively. I wasn't sure whether he just meant ready for the plane to take off or for something beyond that.

Even though I couldn't see his face, I could hear the smile in his voice as he said, "Just relax. You'll know where we're going soon enough."

The rest of the flight sped by in a blur, and soon we were landing. As we exited the plane, I saw a black limousine waiting for us. The driver opened the door, and we got in. Once the limo was under way, the faceless man pulled two champagne flutes and a bottle from the mini-fridge, and poured us both a glass of champagne.

"To us," he said, clinking his glass against mine.

"To us," I repeated. "So, you really aren't going to tell me where we are?"

"I'm really not."

Just as with the flight, the limo ride went by very quickly. The door opened and I saw glimpses of Times Square. My jaw dropped open. "We're in New York City?"

He laughed. "Yes. Right in front of Richard Rodgers Theatre to be exact."

"And we're going to a show?" I could hardly contain my excitement.

"We are."

He took my hand and led me into the theater. He grabbed a Playbill, but wouldn't let me see it until we sat down. We were in one of those private boxes to the side of the stage and I felt like I was going to burst with joy. I managed to snatch the program from him and found out that we were going to see The Sound of Music *starring none other than Dame Julie Andrews and Christopher Plummer, along with the entire original cast of the movie.*

I turned to him and tears flooded out of my eyes. "You remembered."

"So these are tears of joy?"

"Most definitely."

We held hands throughout the play, which is also a bit of a blur. Once it was over, he led me outside and we walked to Central Park. He sat me down on the edge of the Bethesda Fountain and took my left hand in both of his.

"Clare," he began, getting down on one knee, "will you marry me?"

* * *

The dream is so vivid this time, I fully expect to wake up in Central Park. But I'm here in my own bed at Abby's, propped up on a wedge pillow Nate let me borrow. I'm not a back sleeper, so I was hoping this would help keep me from rolling onto my side while I'm healing from the surgery. It worked this time, probably because the anesthesia is still in my system. Tonight will be the true test.

I attempt to stretch but realize quickly that is a bad idea as everything from my chest to my shoulders to my arms hurts. It feels like I've been in a fight or done some really heavy weightlifting. Yeah, right, the most I can do is five pounds. Or...could...before all this.

"Uhnnh," I groan as I relax back down into the wedge pillow.

"Hey," Roddy says from my mother's old rocking chair in the corner. He gets up and walks around the bed to stand beside me. "How're you doing?"

With no idea how to answer that question, I simply say, "It hurts."

"You're overdue for a pain pill, but Abby and I thought it best to let you sleep. Let me go get one and some water." Before he does, he pushes the hair from my face and gives me a kiss on my forehead. "I'll be right back."

I would like to sit up before he gets back, but I'm not sure if I can manage it by myself. I try swinging my legs over to the side of the bed, but they only move a couple of inches. Then, I press my hands into the bed to see if I can push myself up, but the only thing I get is more pain. I do manage to throw the covers back to make sure I'm at least dressed, since everything after the hospital is a blur. I'm wearing my Winnie the Pooh pajamas. Pulling the neck of the shirt up, I see the compression bra they sent me home in from the hospital. It's stuffed with gauze, and I can't take it off for a couple days. That's perfectly fine with me because I'm not sure how much I want to see what it all looks like.

Roddy comes back in and sees the pitiful attempt I've made to get up. "Here, let me help." He puts down the pill and the water on my nightstand, then puts his arm around my back to help me sit up. From there, I'm able to turn and sit on the side of the bed.

"Thanks," I say. I take the pill he offers and swallow it with a big gulp of water. "What time is it?"

He checks his watch. "About three-thirty. Are you hungry?"

"A little," I reply. "Like, maybe just a snack or something."

"I think we can handle that." He grins.

After some effort on his part—because I'm still pretty unsteady on my feet from the drugs—I'm sitting on the sofa in the living room and Abby's handing me a tray with various snack options.

"Alright, you've got your run-of-the-mill saltines, if you're feeling nauseated from the anesthesia. Then, there's a banana for some fruit. A tiny bit of cheese if you're feeling good. And, if you're feeling really, really good, there's a couple chocolate truffles," she says, pointing to each thing in turn as if I've never seen any of these foods before.

I smile up at her. "Thank you, Abby."

"You're welcome. Now, do you need anything else? Would you like the ice packs?" She's hovering around me like a mother hen, and I'd like to tell her to calm down, but I appreciate everything she's doing to make me feel better.

"The ice packs would probably be good, but let me try eating something first." I've got that feeling of either being really hungry because I haven't had anything but fluids since last night or nausea from the anesthesia, and I can't tell which quite yet. I peel the banana and take a small bite. It goes down well, and I try another. So far so good, but I take things slowly. As much as I love cheese and chocolate, I think those are going to have to wait until later. Banana and saltines it is.

Roddy sets a glass of herbal tea on the end table along with a glass of juice. "I wasn't sure which you'd prefer, but I thought something other than water might be nice."

I'm reminded of our first "date" in the coffee house where he brought me the tea and hot cocoa. Seems like he thinks I can't decide on just one beverage at a time. Does he think just because I'm bisexual that I need multiple drink choices at all times? Come to think of it, maybe there's something to that.

He sits down next to me as I continue eating, and I notice he and Abby keep staring at me. I use the napkin to brush any food off my face, but they're still staring.

"Guys, is something wrong?" I ask.

Abby shakes her head. "No. Sorry, I didn't realize I was staring. Just thinking about how glad I am that you're okay."

"Me too," Roddy adds, tenderly rubbing my back.

"Well, it's creeping me out. Please stop staring at me like I'm going to break apart," I request. "I feel okay—as long as I'm not moving around too much. I appreciate the concern and everything you're doing, but really, I'm okay."

They both nod apologetically.

"How about we watch some Bake Off?" Roddy asks.

"That would be wonderful," I say. I reach for the remote on the end table, but in an effort not to knock over my beverages, I fumble the remote onto the floor. "Oops!"

"I'll get it!" both Abby and Roddy say, but Roddy is closer and faster to that side of the couch.

He kneels down on the floor and when he goes to hand me the remote, he's offering it to me on one knee. Suddenly,

I can't catch my breath and my eyes can't seem to focus. My heartbeat pounds in my swollen breasts and my ears are full of static. *The faceless man just proposed in the dream today, and here Roddy is down on one knee. Does this mean anything or am I insane?* I take some slow, deep breaths to calm myself down and, thankfully, the panic attack is short-lived. But I see the grin on Roddy's face melt away to concern.

"I'm okay," I lie. "I just overstretched and had a little pain is all."

He makes his way back to the couch again and puts his arm around my back. "Are you sure? You look a little flushed."

"Yeah, Clare, you do look a bit off. Maybe you should go lie down," Abby adds.

"Gee, thanks." I shake my head. "I promise, I'm fine. But maybe those ice packs would be good before we get involved in the show."

"On it!" Abby exclaims, already on her way to the kitchen.

After putting the ice packs in the compression bra—very carefully—I lean back on the couch and take a sip of the juice while Roddy hits play on the next episode.

I get a text while the contestants are presenting their signature Cornish pasties and I see that it's from Nate's sister, Sophia, who lives in Charlotte.

Sophia: Nate mentioned you were having surgery today.
Sophia: I thought I'd check in to see how you were doing.
Clare: I'm doing okay. Still pretty loopy from the drugs.
Sophia: I'm sure. Glad to hear you're doing okay.
Sophia: I did send you a couple eBooks I enjoyed to give you something fun to read.
Clare: That's sweet! I look forward to reading them.
Sophia: If you need anything, let me know.

Clare: Thanks for checking in. <3
Sophia: Anytime. Take care of yourself!

"Who was that?" Abby asks when I put my phone down.

"Sophia," I reply, then add for Roddy's benefit, "Nate's sister. She was just checking to see how I was doing. She said she sent over a couple eBooks as well."

"She's so sweet," Abby says. "I wish she lived here so we could see her more often."

"Where does she live?" Roddy asks.

"Charlotte," Abby and I say in unison.

"Ah," he replies.

We watch a few more episodes of Bake Off until I'm too exhausted to stay awake anymore, but I still feel them both eyeing me from time to time.

* * *

Since I'm already in my pajamas, that makes getting ready for bed much easier. Abby went to her room to read, and it's just Roddy and me. He escorts me into my room, and I complete my nightly rituals while he waits patiently in the chair. I'm really torn because I desperately want to ask him to stay with me so I'm not alone my first night after surgery—even though Abby's not far away—and not appearing like a hypocrite since I kept going on about how fine I am all afternoon. I resolve to put on my big-girl panties and spend the night alone when I come out of the bathroom.

Roddy is busy typing something on his phone but looks up when I enter the room. "All good?"

"Yep. Pain pill taken and all ready for bed," I reply.

"So, I was thinking..." he begins at the same time I start to say, "Thanks so much..."

We both laugh. I gesture for him to go first.

"I was just thinking that if you wanted me to, I could...you know...stay tonight. You know, if you wanted," he stammers. Then adds, "No funny business. I could sleep on the floor."

"You don't need to sleep on the floor. I think my queen bed should be big enough for both of us." I smile and wonder if he knows this was what I wanted him to say. "But you don't have to if you have somewhere else to be."

"I don't want to be anywhere but here, with you," he says and my heart melts.

"Full disclosure," I begin in a half-whisper, "I haven't...uh...haven't slept with anyone but Suz."

He tilts his head. "That's understandable. You haven't been broken up that long. I mean, we hadn't really defined anything until recently, but I didn't think you were dating anyone else."

Realizing his misunderstanding, I am torn with whether to correct him or not. On the one hand, it's not a lie that I haven't slept with anyone *since* Suz, but that doesn't get to the root of what I meant. I did say "full disclosure," so I decide to hold myself to that and not chicken out.

"Actually, while that's also true, I meant I haven't slept with *anyone* but Suz." My cheeks feel immeasurably hot, and I wonder if he can tell. His face is impassive, so I continue, "I mean, I have dated men—and other women—before, but it's just never...you know, progressed...that far with anyone else but her."

"Ah," he says. His expression is still unreadable.

"I hope that's not a dealbreaker or something." I don't see how it could be, but who knows. "I just thought you should know."

He gets up and strides over to me. His gaze on me is warm. "I will admit, I am surprised. But it's nothing I would consider a dealbreaker." He places his hands lightly on my shoulders and rubs them up and down my arms. "Maybe someday we can change all that. Tonight, though, I just want to be here for you."

"Thank you. I think I will sleep better with someone here," I reply. I lean into his arms, and he gives me the gentlest hug. We pull apart, and I walk over to the bed.

He helps me get situated on the wedge pillow and pulls the covers up. "Comfortable?"

"As much as I can be, considering."

"Maybe this will help." He leans in and presses his lips to mine. It's a brief, comforting kiss. When he pulls away, he caresses the side of my face and kisses my forehead. "Good night, Clare."

"Good night. And thank you."

He turns the light off, and I hear the rustling as he removes his clothing and slips into the bed. A thought runs through my brain about what he looks like naked, but between my exhaustion and the drugs, it's fleeting. I feel him take my hand right before I drift off to sleep.

Part I

"Between the World & You"

June

I was sitting at my desk in my college dorm room, writing a paper for English class, when hands came from behind me and covered my eyes. I gasped, then heard a familiar voice say, "Guess who?"

I turned around and it was her. This time, she wasn't wearing a tux, but she was wearing a buffalo plaid button-down shirt, with some well-fitting khakis. I still couldn't see her face, but I could tell she was smiling as she spoke.

"I'm kidnapping you for the afternoon," she said.

"But I have a ton of work to do," I replied, gesturing at my computer.

She took my hand in hers and pulled me up. "Nonsense. You can spare a couple hours, and you'll come back refreshed and ready to work."

This was the most conversation we'd ever had in one of these dreams. I couldn't figure out how to describe her voice, though. But when she spoke I felt warm and safe—like I was home.

"Alright," I relented, not really put off by my schoolwork that much. I mean, why wouldn't I want to spend the day with—what I assumed to be—a beautiful woman who was obviously crazy about me?

Suddenly, we were in Hyde Park in London. I'd never been to London before, but had always wanted to go. She held my hand as we walked around the gardens, finally coming to a secluded spot where a picnic was laid out. We sat down and began enjoying the delicious lunch of sandwiches, fruit and cheese.

After lunch, she produced a wrapped bakery package with two perfect scones inside, complete with strawberry jam and tons of cream. The scones were divine, like nothing I'd ever tasted before. When we were finished, she looked over at me and said, "You have a little cream right there." She wiped it from the corner of my mouth with her finger. The next thing I knew, we were kissing like it was going out of style.

Eventually, we pulled apart and gathered up the remains of the picnic. "I'd better get you back so you can get your work done," she said, and suddenly we were back in my dorm room. As she was getting ready to leave, she leaned in and whispered, "I love you," in my ear.

* * *

"I don't think y'all are at all ready for this!"

I'm startled back to the present by Abby's exclamation emanating from the dressing room of the bridal shop. While we wait on a luxurious sofa for her to change each time, my mind keeps wandering back to the dream I had last night with the faceless woman. I cannot shake the feeling that Abby had that exact same outfit when we were in college, but it's been so long ago that the memory is as fuzzy as the dream-woman's face.

It's a beautiful Saturday, and the light streaming in through the floor-to-ceiling windows of the shop is giving everyone's mood a boost. Nate and Isaac brought us both here to try on dresses for the wedding to see if we can figure out what would work best for our Best Woman ensembles. The guys have both taken advantage of the champagne being offered, and I'm sticking with water. Abby's been too busy trying on outfits for the last thirty minutes to have anything to drink.

"Well, get on out here so we can see it!" Nate returns. He's been practically acting like an Olympic judge with all the dresses she's tried on so far. I keep expecting him to hold up a sign with "9" as if she's doing gymnastics or ice skating.

"Are you sure you're ready?" she asks, poking her head around the corner of the mirrored wall facing us.

"Yes!" Isaac replies.

I add, "Please, show us before Nate blows a gasket."

Before she appears, I wonder what she's going to come out in this time. So far, she's tried on a red sheath (too dark and simple), a yellow mermaid dress (too washed out), and a pink princess dress (it was a tulle nightmare). Seriously, she looks great in anything, but we have to find something I can coordinate my look with and something that will set the tone for Nate and Isaac's wedding since they've decided to wear white tuxes with rainbow vests and bowties.

The first things I see are a flash of teal and the sparkle of sequins. When Abby steps around the corner, we hear the opening bars to Cyndi Lauper's "Girls Just Want to Have Fun." With each dress she's tried on, Abby has come out doing a dance number with a different song playing on her phone. As she bebops out and onto the riser in front of the mirrors, I think we can all tell there's no way to take this dress in all at once. The whole thing is teal satin with a black shimmer. Sequins cover the entire bodice and spill onto the skirt, which opens out into a wide asymmetrical arc to the right. And the sleeves. Oh, the sleeves look like they're going to engulf her head they're so poofy.

Nate is the first to speak. "I think I'm going to vomit."

Abby smirks. "I told you you weren't ready."

"Why on earth would you put that on?" Isaac asks. "It's hideous."

None of us can control ourselves anymore and we all start laughing hysterically. A couple of the shop workers stare at us, and I wave them off to let them know we're okay, really. Tears are rolling down my cheeks and I grab a tissue from the box on the table next to the sofa to dry my eyes. It's not lost on me that the tissues are for people so moved by their loved one coming out in a beautiful wedding dress that they're crying, and this makes me laugh even harder.

Once we're all able to compose ourselves, Abby explains the dress. "I saw it back there on the rack, and thought it was hilarious, so I thought I'd try it on for fun. Plus, I thought if I showed you how hideous this one was, it would make the one I really want to wear seem even better."

"If you love whatever it is, I'm sure we'll love it," Isaac says.

"Please, anything but this," Nate pleads, shivering. "Absolutely anything."

"Do you want help burning that?" I call as Abby disappears into the dressing room, but one of the twenty-something sales people overhears me and shakes her head disapprovingly. "I was just kidding. It's...lovely."

"It's vintage," she returns. "It's from the '80s."

Nate, Isaac and I all share a look, and we shake our heads. Once she's out of earshot, Nate stage whispers, "If that dress is vintage, then what are we?"

"Old, apparently," I reply, sighing at the thought that something forty years old is "vintage."

"I don't know. But the '80s were twenty years ago, so I don't think she knows what she's talking about." Isaac shakes his head, and we all laugh.

The three of us remain silent until Abby alerts us that she's coming back out with her preferred outfit. We all wait with bated breath. Isaac leans forward with his elbow on his knee. Nate is literally bouncing on the edge of his seat. I'm hoping against hope that this is "the one" so I can start trying on dresses myself.

Abby emerges from the dressing room with the opening bars to "New York, New York" playing on her phone, doing what can only be described as a Broadway-style dance number. She's kicking up her legs and mimicking having a top hat, and grinning ear to ear. She steps up onto the platform, doing a few more moves before twirling to a stop in the center. Her hands go out to the side in jazz hands and she says, "Ta-da!"

Our mouths collectively drop open. I think we were all caught up in the dance number to realize what she's actually wearing. It's a tuxedo but made for a woman. The pants are more like tuxedo leggings, but still have satin stripes up the sides. The shirt is crisp and clean, with black rhinestone buttons. She's wearing a plain, black satin vest underneath, and the jacket looks like it was tailored just for her already. It hugs her curves in all the right places, and it has beautiful detailing all around the cuffs and lapels.

"Oh, Abby, it's perfect!" Nate exclaims.

"I absolutely love—"

Isaac's comment is drowned out by the whooshing sound of the blood rushing to my ears. Suddenly, I can't see anything but Abby in that tuxedo. *Abby in a tuxedo. The faceless one in a tuxedo. The rhinestone buttons are identical, as is the vest. In the dreams, the woman was sometimes wearing a skirt, but sometimes they were leggings. They must be the same. How could Abby not be the one in the dreams now?* My thoughts come a mile a minute and I can't process anything else. *You have to tell her. You have to tell her.*

"Clare? Are you all right?" Nate says from beside me.

I feel him shaking me gently and slowly my vision starts to come back. I look around at everyone, and they all share the same concerned expression. Abby's come down off the platform to stand in front of me. *When did that happen?*

"I'm fine. I'm so sorry, guys," I say. "I just…I don't know what happened."

"Is it the tux?" Abby asks. "Did it repulse you that much?"

I shake my head. "Oh, god no. You look amazing in it. I think I might just have low blood sugar or something," I lie.

Nate pats my hand. "Look, why don't we break for lunch"—he looks at his watch—"since it is almost two o'clock. Then we can come back, and Clare can strut her stuff for us? If you're feeling up to it, that is."

"That sounds like a great plan, dear," Isaac replies. "Why don't you two go to the café next door and get a table, while Abby and I put this fabulous tux on hold for her?"

"Great plan," I agree.

* * *

"I can't believe that took all day," Abby says, as we finally walk into her—or is it our?—apartment at about five-thirty that evening.

"I know. My arms and chest are somehow sore from trying on so many dresses," I reply. It sort of makes sense because we were putting ourselves in awkward positions to get into and out of these clothes all day, but also there's this tingling sensation running up my right arm and it feels a little numb. I rub it a little to try to wake it up.

"I'm exhausted too. Do you wanna just order pizza for dinner?"

"Sure," I reply, my feet also complaining at spending nearly eight hours at the bridal store, not counting the hour break we had for lunch. I had no idea picking out our outfits for the wedding would take that long. "I'll just go hang my dress in the closet and I can place the order through the app, unless you want something different than last time."

"That sounds great," she calls from her bedroom door. "I think I'm gonna lie down until the pizza gets here."

"Cool. I'll let you know when it arrives."

I order the pizza, then head into my room and hang up my dress in its grey zippered bag in my walk-in closet. After trying on more dresses than I can count, I ended up with a Kelly green, satin A-line dress that hits just below my knees. It has a V-neck and gauzy sleeves that come down almost to my elbows. The color really sets off my red hair, and the cut is very flattering for my voluptuous figure. While I did try on a tuxedo, it just didn't look as amazing on me as Abby's did on her, and I didn't want to feel self-conscious standing in front of a large group of people.

I hang out on my bed with Shelley while waiting for the pizza to get here. Poor kitty hasn't seen me all day, so she's lying upside down on my bed wanting belly rubs and chin scritches. I oblige, of course, because it's not often that she allows me to rub her tummy.

With my hand stroking Shelley's warm fur, I ponder telling Abby about the dreams again. The one I had last night was so vivid and seeing her in that tux today was a sign if there ever was one. *Wait a minute,* I think. *I* know *I've seen Abby in the outfit from the dream last night.*

I leave Shelley on the bed and start riffling through my old photo albums on the bookshelf. Finding the one with our photos from college, I thumb through until I find the photo I'm thinking about. And there Abby is wearing a buffalo plaid shirt with khaki pants while we flew kites in Pullen Park.

I sink back onto the bed and stare at the photo. Abby's hair is blown back by the wind, her eyes are closed because she's laughing so hard. Her kite is falling out of the sky behind her, even as she runs to keep it aloft. She looks so free and happy.

I look at the next photo in the album, and it's one of the two of us holding the broken kite. In the picture, I'm laughing at how mangled the kite became, and Abby is looking at me and smiling. Huh. I never noticed before that she was looking at me in this photo and not at the camera or the disintegrating kite. *This is the first time where the dream has already happened…well, sort of.*

With determination, I pull the photos out of the album and head out toward the living room. I open my door, saying, "Abby, I have something I need—"

"No! I really can't tonight." I hear Abby practically shout from her room.

Not wanting to pry, but still wanting to make sure she's okay, I close my bedroom door slightly, but peek through the crack to see if she's in distress. She's pacing back and forth from her bedroom into the living room with her cell phone pressed against her ear.

"I don't know. Maybe," she says. "I'll need to check my calendar."

She looks up and sees me. I open my door a little wider and mouth, "Can I help?" She shakes her head.

"Okay. I'll text you. Yeah. Yeah. Yeah." She mimes talking with her hand and rolls her eyes. "You too. Bye."

"What was that about? Are you okay?" I ask, crossing the distance through the living room to her.

"Yeah, I'm fine." She sighs heavily. "My parents are in town again, for a week this time. They wanted to have dinner tonight, but I'm just too exhausted to deal with them. Plus, they gave me like zero notice. This is literally the first I'm hearing about them being in town."

"That sucks." I put my hand on her shoulder. "I wish dinner with them was just dinner and not all the drama."

"Yeah, and I just don't want to go at all, you know? But I can't avoid them forever." She shrugs.

"I'm sorry." I honestly don't know what else to say because their relationship will always be a mystery to me. I had such a great relationship with my parents, and she has such an awful one with hers. Really, it always makes me miss my parents even more when she's dealing with or avoiding the Cassidys. "I could go with you again, if you need me to."

"Thanks, but I might see if I can get out of this one. They were just here, and I don't think I have the bandwidth to deal with them again this soon," she says. "I'll see if I can invent some kind of work crisis or meeting to use to get out of it."

"You could always use the wedding," I suggest.

"That's a great idea! I'll figure out something before they call again tomorrow."

The doorbell rings, signaling the arrival of the pizza. I answer the door, take the food and thank the delivery guy, who was actually kinda cute—if he'd only been a little bit older. The box is very hot, so I set it down on the stove. Wordlessly, we grab plates and napkins and grab some piping-hot slices of mushroom and black olive pizza. Abby took the liberty of getting us each sodas from the fridge while I was answering the door, so those are waiting for us next to our spots on the sofa.

"What do you want to watch tonight?" Abby asks, turning on the TV.

I swallow the bite of pizza I shouldn't have eaten yet because I knew the cheese was too hot, but I did it anyway and burned the roof of my mouth. Still worth it. "I dunno. Something brainless."

We both think for a moment, then say at the same time, "*27 Dresses?*"

She doesn't wait for a response and just hits play on the movie. We enjoy our pizza, one of our favorite chick-flicks—which is insanely apropos—and just hanging out after a long day.

All thoughts of telling her about the dreams are put off for another time.

* * *

The next day, Abby drives us to an empty parking lot where I can practice driving. While I certainly remember the basics and I assume muscle memory will take over at some point, five years is a long time, and I don't want to be out on the street with other people just yet. I also have no idea what my emotional state is going to be when I get behind the wheel again, so I'm so glad Abby's here with me.

"Are you ready?" she asks, turning off her Mini and unbuckling her seatbelt.

"I think so?" It comes out as a question, though I don't mean for it to.

We both get out of the car and switch sides. I slide into the driver's seat and buckle my seatbelt. I check the mirrors and only need to adjust the rear view one slightly.

"How does the seat feel?" Abby asks. "I mean, we're about the same height, but if you need to adjust it, feel free. Just make sure to put it back after." She laughs.

I shake my head. "No, it feels fine."

"Good. Then, go ahead and push the start button."

I do, and the car comes to life. "I just don't know what to do with all these screens everywhere. My old car didn't have all this fancy stuff."

"You can ignore most of it for now. The only one you need to worry about is the one right in front of the steering wheel with the speedometer, odometer, et cetera." She points to the screen in question.

I put my hands on the wheel and feel the vibration of the car from my palms all the way up through my arms. Suddenly, it feels like the breath has been knocked out of me, and my vision is blurred. All I can think about is the accident with my parents. Even though I wasn't driving that day, it was my car we were in, and I was sitting right behind my father, who was driving. Five years and I don't think I've sat on this side of a car or held a steering wheel since then.

"Clare, are you alright?" Abby asks with concern.

"I...don't...know...if I...can...do...this," I eke out while panting. My back feels sweaty and there are tears running down my cheeks.

Abby turns the car off and starts rubbing my right arm. "Deep breaths. It's okay."

I try doing as she says, but I end up sobbing instead. My hands are still in a death grip on the steering wheel.

"Clare, it's alright. I'm here, nothing's going to happen," Abby says. She pries the fingers of my right hand off the wheel and pulls me toward her. "C'mere."

I release my left hand from the wheel as well and let myself lean over into Abby's arms. She rubs my back while I cry. I let the tears flow. I think about my parents, about how if that patch of black ice hadn't been there, they might be alive today. Everything might be different.

"Shhh. I've got you," Abby soothes.

Between her words and her embrace, I feel supported and cared for. If my parents were here, they would be doing exactly what Abby is, then encouraging me to try again. And I know since they aren't here, that they'd want me not to let their death stand in the way of me moving on with my life.

"Maybe we started too quickly. Perhaps we should have done the signs part first," Abby says.

I sit up and wipe the wetness from my face. "No, I'm okay. I think I'm better now."

"You're sure?" Her face betrays her surprise.

"I'm sure. I promise if my emotions threaten to overtake me again, I will stop, turn the car off, and you can drive us home. Deal?" I say, putting my hand out.

She takes it. "Deal."

I turn the car back on, figure out how to get it into drive, and I drive for the first time since the accident. It's an empty parking lot, but the accomplishment is anything but empty.

Part 10

"Where the Light Shines Through"

July

Recovery from surgery goes faster than I expected. As the doctor ordered, I make sure to move around every day and build my stamina back up little by little. The incisions aren't as gnarly as I thought they'd be, once I'm able to take the Steri-Strips off, and I can tell my surgeon knows what she's doing by how quickly everything starts to heal. I'm still a little concerned about how everything will look and feel later on, but for now, I'm feeling pretty good.

I've started back to work this week, and Nate has me mostly working on admin—emails, invoices, inquiry forms, etc. I told him I could do more, but he's juggling everything else for the time being since I'm "supposed to be taking it easy at home." I tried pointing out to him that we work out of his home, so it shouldn't matter if I'm working from here or there, but he wouldn't hear of it.

I'm just getting ready to send the Bon Voyage email to the Goffin family for their New Zealand trip, when I receive a text from Roddy. He's been checking in every day about this time to see how I'm doing, which is so sweet, especially since he's been in New York City all this week for some solo concerts up there. He's also sent me chocolates and eBooks to make the recovery more bearable.

> Roddy: My mother asked me to invite you to dinner at their house on Saturday evening.
> Roddy: You don't have to if you don't want to, but I'd love to see you.
> Roddy: Camille and her husband will also be there, if that helps anything.

Dinner with his parents? Are we really to that stage? I honestly don't know why I'm panicking about this. I've already met his mother and his sister, and they both seemed to like me. But meeting both parents seems to be a big step. After a couple of deep breaths, I respond.

> Clare: I'd love to. What time?
> Roddy: 5:30. Unfortunately, I'll be coming straight from the airport and won't be able to pick you up. Do you mind meeting there?
> Clare: Not a problem. Just send me their address. Anything I can bring?
> Roddy: She said you don't need to bring anything.
> Clare: Okay. But I will anyway, so is there something in particular they like?
> Roddy: I'll think about that and get back to you.
> Clare: Sounds good.
> Roddy: Sorry, I gotta go get ready for my next concert. Talk later?
> Clare: Sure thing. Play well.
> Roddy: ☺

So, now not only am I having dinner with his parents, I'm also going to have to take the bus there. I really hope they live close to a bus stop. If not, I guess I'll have to wear my good walking shoes or ask someone to drive me.

* * *

Thankfully, his parents do live within a quarter mile of a bus stop, so I didn't need to wear my clunky sneakers to dinner. When I get off at the stop, I'm about thirty minutes early, so I walk around their neighborhood a little bit before locating their house. They live in one of those great older neighborhoods where all the houses look different, and you can tell in what era each one was built. There are some Cape Cod-style homes, some standard ranch homes, some bungalows and some that were definitely built in the 1980s. Even with all the diversity in housing styles, they all feature mature trees and well-maintained lawns that give a sense of community.

The Vaughn house is a two-story home that reminds me of the house featured in *Father of the Bride* with Steve Martin. But, it's more of a whitewashed brick with navy shutters and a red front door—which all goes well with the dual French and American flags flying out front. They have numerous garden areas, which are full to bursting with flowers. I walk up the brick driveway and up the two steps to the small front porch. I'm about to push the doorbell, when the door flies open suddenly. I make a startled "oh" sound and am face-to-face with a very tall Indian man, who I can only assume is Camille's husband.

"You must be Clare," he says, and puts out his hand. "I'm Dilip. Sorry for scaring you."

I shake his hand. "No problem. You saved me the trouble of ringing the doorbell." I smile. "It's nice to meet you as well."

"Well, I was just sent out to the store for some camembert. Somehow, Sabine is all out." He goes to step past me, but I put a hand on his arm to stop him.

"Actually, I brought some camembert and water crackers with me." I hold up the small cooler I'm carrying.

"Great," he says. "You saved me from the hell that is the grocery store on Saturday night."

"Happy to be of service."

"Well, let's not just stand here on the porch. Come on inside." Dilip pushes open the door the rest of the way and leads me into the foyer. "It's great to have another bi person here, by the way." He gives me a sidelong look. "Now I won't be the only one they tease about sitting weird. Anyway, I think they're all in the kitchen. Follow me."

We walk past the stairs and into an absolutely stunning dining room which is open to the enormous kitchen. Sure enough, Sabine, Camille and a man I can only assume is Roddy's father—purely based on stature since they're all facing away from us—are gathered around a large island covered in white marble. There's a large pot simmering on the stove and if I'm not mistaken, we're having ratatouille for dinner.

"You have to be joking, mother," Camille says, taking a bite of apple. "There is no way I'm going to have this baby in a wading pool in your living room. I'm going to be at the hospital with all the sterile equipment and most especially, the drugs."

Sabine walks around the counter and puts her hand on Camille's shoulder. "Darling, did you not read all the studies on childbirth— Oh, Clare, you're here!"

Camille and the man—who I'm absolutely sure is Roddy's father now—turn around to also see Dilip and me. Camille gets up and comes over to hug me. "Hi, Clare. How are you feeling?"

I hug her back and say, "I'm doing really well. Healing nicely. How are you?"

She steps back and gestures to her stomach, and a teeny tiny baby bump. "Oh, we're doing just fine. I don't know if Roddy told you, but Dilip and I are expecting our first child early next year."

"No, he hasn't. Congratulations! That's wonderful news," I say.

"He probably thought I didn't want him to tell anyone because we're not quite out of the first trimester yet, which is sweet of him." Then, to Dilip she asks, "Honey, weren't you going to the store?"

"No need. Clare anticipated us and brought camembert and water crackers." He takes the cooler from me, holds it up and beams at his wife like a man who was pardoned from a death sentence at the last moment.

"How wonderful, Clare," Sabine says as she too comes over to hug me. When we separate, she holds out her hand to her husband as he walks over. "This is my husband, George."

"It's very nice to meet you," I say to him, holding out my hand. He takes it and gives a firm but not too firm handshake.

"Pleased to meet you as well. You are more lovely than Roddy described."

I know I'm blushing ten shades of pink right now. "Thank you."

"Clare, please come in and have a seat. Thanks to you we now have plenty of hors d'oeuvres to tide us over until Augus—I mean, Roddy, gets here." I could tell how much it pained her to use the name he prefers versus the one she chose, but she caught herself admirably.

Sabine arranges the crackers and cheese on a glass platter, and we all tuck in. I have always loved camembert—and really all cheese—and since I splurged and got a kind of expensive one at Whole Foods, this one is particularly lovely. Sabine seems pleased as well, and if you can please a French woman with French cheese, then you must be doing something right. As much as I'm enjoying being here so far, I do glance down at my watch and notice it's about half an hour past the time Roddy told me he'd be here.

"I'm sure he'll be here soon," Camille whispers to me, obviously having seen me look at the time. "You know how much of a pain airports can be."

"Yes, definitely." Maybe not personally, but I've heard from my clients. I take another bite of my cracker. "So, how did you two meet?"

"It is such a lovely story," Sabine answers, not realizing I was actually asking Camille and Dilip. Oh well, I'd like to know how Roddy's parents met as well, of course. Camille shrugs at me, then gets some fruit for her plate. "I was just a young woman studying art at Les Beaux-Arts de Paris, of course. One day, I'm sitting at a café sipping un café au lait, and suddenly a plate with a slice of chocolate cake is placed in front of me. I turn to tell the waiter I didn't order anything to eat—even though I was ever so hungry and chocolate cake is my favorite dessert—but I see the person who put the cake in front of me wasn't a waiter at all, but a young man. A very handsome young man, I might add." Here she pauses and looks meaningfully at George. "And what did you say to me, my darling?"

"I told her she looked hungry, and I couldn't see such a beautiful woman go hungry," George says.

"So, I asked this American boy to sit down with me and share the cake. He got another fork and sat down next to me, and we talked all afternoon. We walked around the streets of Paris, avoiding all the touristy things, and just talked. I knew right then that he was the man for me. For, any man who will bring me chocolate cake has the key to my heart." She takes George's hand and holds it to her heart.

George smiles at his wife, then turns back to me. "And, the rest, as they say, is history."

I smile back at them. "What a lovely story."

"Camille," Sabine says, "do tell Clare how you and Dilip met."

Camille winks at me. "It wasn't quite as romantic as all that, but I like our story." She places a hand on Dilip's knee. "I'm an interior decorator, and I was at a client's home discussing her new living room. Color swatches, fabric samples, that kind of thing. Well, I'd just gotten Ms. Reinmiller to decide on the fabric for the sofa, when the general contractor for the kitchen remodel shows up. Now, I've spoken to this man countless times on the phone, but never met him in person. I had pictured this tall, burly man in his mid-sixties, but he's actually this frail-looking, balding little man who's probably in his eighties."

My face must have shown my confusion, because she quickly says, "Just wait, I'm getting there," and I nod my head for her to continue.

"So, I talk to the contractor—Raj—and find out his grandson will be joining us soon to take over the project, because he—Raj—is retiring. Sure enough, his grandson shows up and he's this beautiful, tall man with these dark brown eyes. His smile lit up my entire world. I know it sounds totally corny, but I just knew I had to get to know him better."

"And I was carried away by the beauty of this woman with her fabric samples and designs for a fireplace that could only be described as the Versailles of fireplaces." Dilip shakes his head. "I thought that thing was going to be the death of me, but my lovely wife knew exactly what she was doing."

"I always do," Camille says, smiling.

"I asked her to dinner once the dreaded fireplace was behind me."

Just then, I hear the front door open and close. "That'll be Roddy," Camille points out. "If I know him, he'll probably go up to his old room to change clothes first before joining us."

I nod. Feeling the call of nature, I ask, "Actually, is there a bathroom I could use?"

"Of course," Sabine answers. "The downstairs powder room is currently out of service, but there's a full bath at the top of the stairs and to the left you are welcome to."

I set my plate down on the counter and head to the foyer. Next to the door, I see Roddy's cello case propped against the wall. At the top of the stairs, I see the bathroom, and to the right, I see a partially open door. Wondering if that's Roddy's room, I step a little closer. I can very slightly hear movement from that room. My curiosity gets the better of me, and I walk closer still. I can see Roddy in there with his back to me. And he's shirtless. He has a large tattoo of a cello spanning the space between his well-defined shoulders. I've never really seen the appeal of tattoos, but I do in this case.

Suddenly, he turns around and sees me standing here gaping. I expect him to shut the door all the way, but instead, he opens it more and gestures for me to come in. I walk into the room, and he shuts the door behind us. "I was hoping you'd come up to find me."

I can feel myself blushing, heat rising to my face and neck. "I actually just came up to use the bathroom."

"Ah," he says, smirking. "Did my mother or Camille not tell you it's on the other side of the landing?"

The blushing continues as he walks closer toward me. And, if seeing his muscular back and tattoo weren't enough, his chest and arms are just as muscular. He puts his arms around me, and I place my hands on his warm back. Our kiss in that moment is more urgent than any of our previous kisses. His hands move up into my hair and I hook my arms around him, grabbing the back of his shoulders. Finally, when the intensity of the kiss has worked its way down to my toes, we pull apart.

"Clare," he whispers into my hair, still holding me close.

It takes a few moments, but I remember that we are in his parents' house, and we're expected back downstairs. "I should really let you finish getting changed. Dinner will probably be ready soon."

"Yeah. I'll only be a moment, then I'll walk you downstairs." He picks up his shirt from the bed and starts to pull it on.

"You are going to have to tell me more about that tattoo sometime," I say, going back out into the hallway and the original reason I came upstairs.

When I come out of the bathroom, Roddy is waiting for me on the landing. He puts his hand behind my back, and we descend the stairs together. His touch reminds me of the kiss we just shared, and I'm wishing we weren't at his parents' house anymore. At the bottom of the stairs, he whispers in my ear, "How much do you wish we weren't here right now?" I simply nod, and he kisses my cheek.

Upon entering the kitchen, I see Sabine pulling two pie pans out of the oven, placing them on the stove next to the large pot that was there earlier. The aroma emanating from everything smells heavenly, and I am suddenly famished.

"The quiches are ready, everyone. Please take your seats in the dining room," she announces.

"Quiche Lorraine is mother's specialty," Roddy says.

"If it tastes as good as it smells, then I'm excited to try it."

On the way to the dining room, Roddy goes over to give his mother a kiss on the cheek while she arranges the quiches on a platter. She asks Roddy to carry the large pot for her and shoos the rest of us into the dining room again. Once he's set down the ratatouille, Roddy hugs his father, sister and brother-in-law in turn. Then, he pulls out a chair and gestures for me to sit there. Once I'm settled, he seats himself to my right. Dilip and Camille sit across from us, and George sits at the head of the table between his children.

Shortly after, Sabine comes to the table bearing a platter with the two quiches, and she places it on the table. I notice there is already a basket with bread and a bowl of leafy green salad on the table as well. In the center of the table sits a tall vase with long-stemmed roses in various shades of red and pink, and elegant crystal candlesticks hold tall taper candles. Each place setting includes both an entrée and salad plate with a folded red napkin on top, a bread plate, soup bowl, water and wine glasses, and all the appropriate cutlery. I don't think I've ever been to dinner with such a beautiful table.

"Mon chéri, would you do the honors," Sabine says to George.

George stands up and picks up a long lighter from the end of the table. "This evening, we celebrate the gathering together of family and friends." He lights the candle closest to him. Walking around the table, he comes to stand next to Sabine. "We are grateful for all our many blessings and celebrate those who have gone before us." He lights the second candle. "And we celebrate our hope for the future: that all may be healthy and wealthy in whatever life they may choose." George kisses his wife sweetly, then returns to his seat.

Tears well up in my eyes, but I blink them back. Tonight is a night to get to know Roddy's family, not to dwell on my loss. I place my napkin on my lap as I see everyone else do the same.

Roddy picks up the bread basket and offers it to me. "Thank you," I say, taking a dinner roll and placing it on my bread plate. I pass the basket in turn to Sabine.

"So, Clare," Dilip begins, "Roddy tells us you are a travel agent."

I look up from buttering my roll. "Yes. I work with my friend, Nate." I explain to them the concept of Nerds on a Plane.

"Oh, that sounds like so much fun," Camille replies. "What's the craziest one you've ever had to plan?"

"There was this one couple who wanted to go to Dublin with their instruments and fully recreate the movie *Once*. Have you seen that one?" Everyone nods except George, so I continue. "So, I scouted out all the outdoor locations, found out how to get them a busking permit, how best to get his guitar and her keyboard transported on the flights, and booked them. It was an ordeal, but they had a fantastic time. And they posted about it on socials and the stars of the movie—Glen Hansard and Markéta Irglová—saw it and gave them a shoutout."

Camille's eyes go wide. "You're kidding! I love that movie so much, but I don't think I would ever have gone to those lengths."

"Of course, you also don't sing or play an instrument," Dilip says. Seeing Camille's crestfallen expression, he adds, "But you are multitalented in so many other ways, my love."

"Good save," Roddy murmurs.

"And can you just imagine what that must have cost? But each to their own," George pipes in then goes back to eating his quiche.

"Where is your favorite place in the world you've travelled to, Clare?" Sabine asks as she walks around the table serving everyone ladles of ratatouille. "Knowing of course that France is the most wonderful country in the world."

The others roll their eyes at Sabine's joke, but I shift uncomfortably in my seat. "Well, I really liked the Grand Canyon when I went there with my family as a teenager.

Niagara Falls and Toronto are lovely too. My friend, Abby, and I went there during college."

"Oh? Have you not been outside of North America?" George asks.

I shake my head. "No. My family couldn't really afford it or couldn't get the time off work when I was growing up, and there either hasn't been money, time or someone to go with since then." I sigh and fidget with my hands in my lap. "I know it's crazy. A travel agent who hasn't travelled. But I do want to travel when I can..."

Roddy puts his arm around my shoulder and pulls me close.

"I'm sure Roddy would love to take you travelling, wouldn't you?" Camille says, winking.

Roddy shoots her a look that must be some sort of sibling thing, then says to me, "Of course I would."

"Gotta finish this pesky treatment first," I say too brightly. Everyone silently goes back to the delicious meal. *Great, now I've put a damper on the whole meal. Way to go, Clare!*

"It's been a long time since we've had a full table at dinner," Sabine jumps in, changing the subject. "It's so nice to have a sixth person to round out the party."

Not sure where she's going with this, I just nod and take a bite of my salad.

"Roddy hasn't brought a girlfriend home in more than five years. Since Jillian, I believe," she says, looking pointedly at Roddy.

Five years? My mind is reeling at the thought that his last long-term relationship ended five years ago, but as I turn to Roddy, all I can think to say is, "Jillian?"

Roddy closes his eyes firmly for a second, then opens them again. "Jillian was just an old girlfriend. Mother was quite fond of her."

"I think she was a little more than that, brother," Camille says quietly, spearing a tomato slice in her salad.

"Yes," Sabine replies. "They were affianced for over a year—"

"Mother," Roddy says with a warning tone. "I asked you not to bring her up...ever again. And we were never engaged."

Sabine looks taken aback but recovers quickly. "Sorry, mon chou, I was just mentioning because it's so lovely to have someone here that you obviously care about because we would love to see you happy."

I must look shell-shocked because Roddy takes my hand under the table and says quietly, "I'm sorry, Clare. I was waiting for the right moment to tell you about Jill."

I shake my head a little to clear it. "It's okay. We can talk about this later."

"Je suis désolée, Clare. I'm so sorry—" Sabine's words are drowned out by whooshing of blood in my ears. The burning starts behind my eyes, and I know I won't be able to stop the tears from falling this time.

"Excuse me," I say as I practically run to the front door.

"Clare!" Roddy calls as he chases after me.

Throwing open the front door, I inhale deeply and feel the warm summer air dry my tear-stained face. Roddy is beside me in an instant and his strong hands turn me to face him. He closes the front door, so we have some privacy.

"I'm so sorry you had to find out this way," he begins.

"Listen, it's okay, really—" I start to explain that I'm not upset about him having a previous relationship—even though I'm not sure how I'll explain that I'm really upset about the fact it was five years ago—but Roddy continues on.

"And let me start by reiterating that Jill and I were *never* engaged," he says firmly. "She and I met in college, but we didn't start dating until we reconnected after she moved back here from Texas. We did move in together, briefly, until I found out she was cheating on me with some other guy she knew from her time in Dallas." He sighs heavily. "When I found out, I left and as far as I know, she moved back to Texas to be with him. It was five years ago."

Five years ago. So many things happened five years ago: my parents died, the dreams started, this man's heart was broken by this woman. There has to be something to all these coincidences. Something to explain why everything is drawing me to this man standing in front of me. I'm not mad at him because this happened so long ago and it doesn't really matter in the grand scheme of things. Plus, with the chaotic way our relationship has gone, there hasn't been time to go through every single detail of our previous lives. But I'm not ready to tell him about the dreams and everything that's been pushing me toward him. So, I'll play along.

"Clare?" Roddy says. He looks as if he might cry at any moment. "Please say something, anything."

"It's okay," I reply, and his face brightens if only a little. "Our relationship has been anything but 'normal.'"

He nods. "But I should have told you before my mother did."

I laugh. "Yes, that is definitely true." I pause before I ask the question I don't know if I want the answer to. "Do you miss her?"

"Not at all," he responds with no hesitation. "I didn't know how great life could be until I met you."

He wraps his arms around me, and we kiss on his parents' porch, until we finally go back inside to rejoin his family.

Part J

"Dare You to Move"

July

A month has gone by, and I still haven't told Abby about the dreams. It feels like there's just one thing after another preventing me from talking with her, from her parents calling the night we went dress shopping to "driver's ed" to work stress for me to wedding details taking up a lot of our free time. Or maybe I'm letting things get in the way because I'm scared. Either way, the more I put it off, the harder it feels being around her without telling her, and the more I know I need to rip the proverbial Band-Aid off.

Sitting at my desk where I'm supposed to be confirming all the details of the Goffins' *Lord of the Rings* Nerdventure, and my mind has again wandered to Abby. My hands are on my keyboard, but my head is lolled back and I'm staring off into space. This is where Nate finds me when he comes back from his lunch break.

"Clare? Earth to Clare," he says, waving his hand in front of my face.

I snap out of my stupor and automatically hit all the keys my fingers were on. My laptop makes the "what the hell are you doing, woman" beeping sound. "Oh my god. I'm so sorry."

Nate laughs as he sits down at his desk. "Girl, you were off in La-La Land. What were you daydreaming about? Abby?"

Since I haven't told Nate about the dreams and swore Isaac to secrecy, I don't have to play at being shocked. "What? No, of course not. What did Isa— What made you think I'd be thinking about Abby?"

"Oh, come off it, girl. You've been hot for her for months now. I saw the way you looked when you were dancing with her at our engagement party. Not to mention your little freakout when you saw her in that tux at the bridal shop." He gives me a knowing smile. "And don't worry, Isaac didn't have to say a thing."

"I…uh…" I'm quite literally speechless.

He rolls his desk chair over, then spins mine so we're facing each other and our knees are mere inches from touching. "Now that you know I know, dish. Tell me absolutely everything."

Seeing the earnestness, but also kindness, in his eyes, I don't hesitate for long. I start from the beginning and leave nothing out. The dreams, the panic attack at the symphony where I told Isaac, the déjà vu I've been feeling, being overwhelmed by seeing her in the tuxedo. Every single detail.

When I'm finished he sits back, looking spent. "Wow," is all he says.

"Please tell me you have something to say other than 'wow.'"

He puts his hand up. "Give me a minute. That's a lot of information to get all at once. I'm processing."

I nod and we sit in silence for several moments while he digests all I've told him. Finally, he looks back at me and says, "You have to tell her."

"I know, and I keep trying to, but—"

"No, like, you have to tell her now," he insists. "Isaac told me he ran into Abby, and she said that her parents are setting her up on some blind date with some lawyer chick they know. You have to get in there first."

"Why haven't I heard anything about this?" I'm genuinely surprised that Isaac—or Nate, for that matter—would know something like this before me, her best friend and roommate.

"It just happened today right before he and I had lunch." He waves his hands dramatically. "But that's not the important part. She said yes to going on this date, which means she's either just doing it to get her parents off her back or she's genuinely interested."

I scoff. "Obviously it's the first one."

"Do you really want to take that chance?"

I shake my head. "Of course not. I'll talk to her tonight."

"Good girl. Now, get back to work before your boss hears you've been slacking off." He winks before he slides his chair back to his desk.

"Thanks, Nate."

"You're welcome. Now go get her!"

* * *

When I get back to the apartment that evening, Abby's sitting in the living room doing something on her phone. I put my things down in my room, then join her on the sofa.

"Hey," she says, finishing whatever she was doing, then looking up at me. "Have I got a story to tell you."

Not wanting to lose my nerve or get derailed again, I plunge forward. "Actually, there's something I've been really wanting to talk to you about for a while now, if that's okay."

She looks at me, concerned. "Is everything okay?"

"Everything is fine. It's nothing bad." I hesitate. "It's good. At least I hope it will be."

"Great, I'm always in the mood for good news." She tucks her legs underneath her and faces me expectantly. "Spill."

Suddenly I'm more nervous than I thought I would be, and my palms are sweating. I wipe them on my pants and swallow the fear down. *You can do this.* Just as I'm getting ready to speak, Shelley jumps up on the sofa and curls up next to Abby. To say I'm shocked is an understatement because she doesn't sit with anyone but me. Abby reaches down to pet her, and Shelley purrs contentedly. "Have you always been able to pet her?"

Abby looks down at the cat like she doesn't realize what she's doing. "Oh, no, this is pretty recent. She's been more affectionate with me lately. Or maybe the better way to put it is not standoffish."

This is huge. It's another sign this is the right time to finally tell her. "So, you know all those dreams I've had since my mom and dad died?"

"The ones where a faceless person does all sorts of romantic things for you?"

I'm hit with another feeling that I've heard her say those words before, but I tamp that down because I need to get this out if it kills me. "Yes, those. Only, lately, the faceless person has morphed from this genderless figure into someone distinctly female."

Her eyes widen with interest. "Really? That's crazy. Does she have a face or like hair or something where you can tell who she is?"

My heartrate starts to speed up, but I take a couple deep breaths to calm myself down. *You are okay. This is Abby and you can tell her anything. You are not going to have a panic attack right now. You are okay.* "Still no face or anything like that, but with the last few I've had this intense feeling that she's—"

"Oh my god!" Abby exclaims. "You have to be kidding, right?"

Has she guessed? Is she mad? Happy? "Um…" is all I'm able to eke out before she continues.

"I can't believe you'd consider going back to her just because of some dreams. Seriously, Clare? I mean this in the kindest way possible, but she isn't right for you." She takes my hands in hers. "There is someone right for you, and maybe these dreams have something to them, and maybe they don't, but she's not the one in the dreams."

"Hold on," I say, realization dawning. "You thought I was going to say Suz?"

She nods. "Yeah. You weren't? Then who were you talking about?"

"Well, I was going to say that she's…you." There, it's out. I finally did it. Go me!

Abby's features cycle through the annoyance she had when she thought it was Suz, to relief that it isn't Suz, finally landing on shock mixed with confusion. "Me?"

I squeeze her hands. "I know. It's crazy. I have been so uncertain about whether to tell you or not, but then Nate said that Isaac said that you were going on some blind date your parents set up with some lawyer, and I—"

My ramblings are cut off by the sound of Abby's musical laughter. She releases my hands and throws her arms around my neck, still racked with giggles.

"I'm glad you're taking this so well," I say.

She pulls back, composing herself, and replies, "I'm sorry. I didn't mean to laugh. It's just that…well…I've sort of had feelings for you for quite some time."

I have no words, but I'm sure she can tell from the look of shock on my face what I'm thinking.

"I know. I'm actually kinda surprised that of the two of us, you had the guts to actually say something. Good for you!" she enthuses, playfully punching me in the shoulder.

"How long?" I ask.

Hand on her chin, she looks up at the ceiling for a moment like she's counting. "Probably since college."

"Since college? This is insane. Why didn't you ever say anything or do anything?"

"I don't know. At first, it was because I assumed you were straight 'cause you only seemed interested in guys in high school and college. Then, when you did show an interest in girls after you came out, you were drawn to the more—how do I say this without sounding mean?—stoic, goth types."

I open my mouth to object but shut it when I realize she's right.

"Once you started seeing Suz, I figured it was all over 'cause you seemed in it for the long haul—although I knew she was never right for you. Then when you did break up with her, I wanted to give you space to deal with the breakup. And here we are," Abby concludes.

"Did you ever tell anyone else how you felt?"

"I never outright told them, but I think Nate and Isaac might suspect something," she says.

"Of course they do, which is why they both pushed so hard for me to tell you," I muse. *Or she thinks they suspect something because I've been talking to them about my feelings lately.*

"Probably," she replies. "And oddly enough, your parents seemed to know 'cause your dad said something about us making a cute couple once. But that was all they ever said about it."

I'm even more caught off guard by this last news. *My parents knew?* I don't get too long to digest it though because Abby continues.

"But the more I thought about it, the more I wasn't sure I should do anything about it. We're best friends. I don't want to be all cliché here, but I don't want to lose that if this doesn't work out," she says gesturing between the two of us.

"I completely understand," I say, but I'm not sure I mean it. "I don't want to ruin what we have either because you are my best friend and that means more to me than anything."

"But don't worry, I'm not going to fall in love with Belinda, the lawyer my parents set me up with. I talked with her, and she sounds nice and all—not like that Lily—but she's also being pressured by her parents to date more, so we're really only doing the blind date to get them off our backs."

I feel my shoulders relax a little. "Sounds like a good idea."

"Hug it out?" she asks with arms spread wide.

And we do, but I'm devastated. I really think Abby is the one in the dreams, but if she's going to go on a blind date with this other woman even though she's liked me for years, what does that say?

We pull apart and Abby gets up to go to her room. I, on the other hand, am rooted to the spot.

Part 11

"Remember When it Rained"

July

I stood in the middle of Main Street U.S.A. staring at Cinderella's Castle. I shook my head wondering what I'm doing at Disney World. Crowds of people walked all around me—the usual hustle and bustle of the theme park. It was a beautiful day. Blue sky, a nice breeze and soft music played from somewhere near the castle. The music gradually faded out and a brief moment of silence preceded a trumpet blast. I thought maybe it was time for the parade to start, so I moved over to the sidewalk to get out of the way, and saw others following.

As I walked closer to the castle, I could see a small crowd gathering behind The Partners Statue. I heard some music playing, so I continued walking closer. Eventually I saw there was a man standing on the ramp in front of the castle holding a microphone. I figured there must be some sort of concert going on and thought about turning around, but something drove me forward still. The man began to sing, and I realized it was my favorite song, "Possession," though I couldn't actually hear it in the dream. Looking closer, I realized it was him, the faceless man, and he was singing to me. People around me noticed I was the one he was singing to, and they ushered me up onto the ramp.

Listening to him sing, I realized I had no idea he had such an amazing voice, so strong and deep. I felt tingles up and down my spine, and goose bumps ran up and down my arms. It was a little embarrassing standing in front of all these people at Disney World, of all places, having someone serenade me. All too soon, though, the song was finished. He placed the microphone back onto the stand and looked into my eyes.

"Clare, you are the most wonderful woman in the world and I would do anything to make you happy." He got down on one knee. "Would you make me the happiest man alive and be my wife?"

"Yes!" I heard myself say.

He swept me up into his arms and kissed me. When we pulled apart, he placed a ring on my finger. I tried and tried to see it, but it was just as blurry as his face.

* * *

"Well, the score was great, I'll give it that," Roddy says as we leave the movie theater, hand in hand. "That's about all I'll give it."

"Really? I mean, I didn't think it was the best movie ever, but I thought there were some redeeming qualities," I reply.

"Yeah, and I think I know what those 'redeeming qualities' are: Rachel McAdams and Oscar Isaac."

I grin up at him. "Well, you should have known better than to let me pick the movie when either of them have a movie out."

"I think I've learned my lesson." He kisses my hand and smiles.

We get into his car and drive the short distance to my favorite Mexican restaurant, picking apart the subtleties of the movie as we traverse the streets of Cary. This being the first movie we've gone to see together, it's very interesting to see what Roddy likes and doesn't like. He listens almost exclusively for the soundtrack, and not the pop songs sprinkled here and there, but the score. I'm sure it comes from him playing in an orchestra for so long, but it's intriguing to me that he seems to listen for that while sacrificing understanding of the dialogue and plot. Whereas I am all in it for the dialogue and plot. And the super-hot actors.

We arrive at the restaurant and are escorted to a booth on the side. We sit under a mural of Cancun, which is just one of the many places I'd love to see someday. I pick up my menu on the pretense I need to figure out what I want, when I almost always get the same thing: two cheese enchiladas with rice and guacamole salad.

"Ah, señor," our server, Miguel, says as he sees Roddy. Then he notices me and smiles even wider. "And señorita. I did not know that you knew each other."

"I come here a lot," Roddy says, at the same time I say, "I've been here just a couple times." All three of us laugh.

"And you are dating. How wonderful, my friends!" Miguel replies. He takes our orders and hurries off to the kitchen.

"Strange that we've never run into each other, since we both frequent this place," Roddy says.

I nod. "Yeah. Strange." Of course, I know it is strange. Everything to do with our meeting and not meeting is more than strange. I've been at North Carolina Symphony donor functions with him, I've been to innumerable concerts that he's played in, we both apparently love Fiesta Mexicana, and who knows what else. I mean, I've had dreams about him for years, then meet him in real life, and find we've crossed paths many times before.

"Clare?" I hear Roddy say above the screaming inside my head.

I shake the thoughts from my head. "Sorry, did you ask me something?"

"No, you just looked pretty far away there for a minute. Just making sure everything's okay."

"Yep, everything's fine."

* * *

My enchiladas were wonderful, as usual, and Miguel even brought us some celebratory queso on the house. After we devoured our meals, Roddy paid the check and now we're on the way out to his car.

"Do you have to get home right away?" he asks, holding the door open for me.

"No. What did you have in mind?"

"I was wondering if you wanted to come back to my place. Camille baked me this chocolate cherry cheesecake and I thought you might want some dessert."

"Sure. I love cheesecake," I reply, perhaps a little too enthusiastically. I want to go to his house so badly, but I'm not sure if I'm ready yet because of the expectations that implies. Or at least I don't think I am. I have no idea. It feels strange that I've been to his parents' house, but I haven't seen his place. But with the fact that he's been coming to my place to take care of me all the time during my testing and after surgery, I guess it makes sense.

So, it's not like I'm a prude or a virgin or anything, but Suz and I didn't do much intimate stuff when we were together, and I haven't actually *been* with a man before, even though I'm bi. But I really like Roddy a lot and after seeing his tattoo and the kiss afterward, it's all I can do to not think about sex with him. Plus, everything is going to change for me once I start chemo. I could be thrust into premature menopause, even temporarily. I may be too tired or not have a sex drive at all during that time. This could be the perfect opportunity to have sex before my treatment. God, that sounds romantic: "Yes, let's get it on now before I start chemo and don't have any interest anymore." *What is wrong with me?*

Roddy's townhouse is about ten minutes away, so I have plenty of time to work myself into a frenzy before we get there. He lives in a really nice development off Tryon Road. Each unit is three stories, and the first floor is brick, while the rest is white siding. There are brick stairs that lead to the front door, but Roddy parks inside the garage, so we enter the house that way. He leads me into the kitchen and asks me to sit at the little bistro table in the corner while he slices the cheesecake. I do and take a look around. He has beautiful cherry wood cabinets with granite countertops. He doesn't seem to have a lot of clutter on his counter, whereas Abby and I have several small appliances scattered about in our kitchen.

There's a small window next to the table where I sit that overlooks the backyard, and he has some fairly non-descript cream-colored curtains on it. I look further, past the kitchen, and can see what I assume to be his living room, but there's barely any furniture in it. Just a couple of chairs and a piano. I guess if you're a bachelor, you don't need a ton of furniture, unless you have people over.

"Here we go," Roddy says as he puts a plate in front of me. "Camille is an excellent baker, and this is one of her specialties. It's actually a recipe from Bake Off."

The cheesecake looks amazing, and I can't wait to dive in. I sink my fork into the thick slice of cake, making sure to get a whole cherry and some of the crust. I take a bite and the flavors of the chocolate and cherry blend so deliciously with the cream cheese and graham crackers. I even taste a hint of cinnamon, most likely from the crust. Before I can stop myself, I've taken three more bites and I'm sure my eyes are rolling back in my head with pleasure.

"Good, huh?"

"Scrumptious," I reply. "Do you think Camille would make me one of these every week?"

"Probably. She adores baking, especially for other people." Roddy takes a particularly large bite, and I can tell he is as blown away by the dessert as I am, even though it sounds like he's had it before.

"Of course," I add, "I'd be as big as a house if I ate one of these every week, so maybe I should just settle for one for my birthday."

Roddy smiles. "I'm sure she'd be happy to. And when, may I ask, is your birthday? You know, so I can get it on Camille's calendar."

"It's March tenth."

"I will let her know. And I'm sure she'll be happy to bake you whatever you like while you're going through treatment. If you're feeling up to it, that is." He places his fork on the side of his clean plate and wipes his mouth with a napkin.

"That would be very sweet of her. I'll let her know." I take another bite of the delicious dessert and realize my plate is clean too.

"Speaking of Camille, does she know the sex of the baby yet?"

Roddy shakes his head. "She wants to be surprised. She won't even let Dilip find out either."

I laugh. "And I'm guessing he wants to know?"

"Desperately," he answers. "Everyone except Camille is dying to know, but she won't let the doctor tell anyone. Our mother even tried to call the doctor's office to get them to tell her—and she can be pretty persuasive—but they wouldn't budge. HIPPA practices and all that."

I could almost see Sabine trying to use her charms to get the doctor to tell her the sex of her daughter's baby and being sorely disappointed when they didn't. "I think it's cool that she wants to be surprised. I mean, it wasn't too long ago really when you couldn't find out even if you wanted to. Of course, people resorted to all kinds of tricks and listened to old wives' tales to predict the sex of the baby. And ultrasounds aren't always one hundred percent accurate. I was supposed to be a boy."

Roddy tilts his head to one side and smiles. "I'm so glad they were wrong." He leans forward and kisses me warmly. We part and he sits back in his chair and just looks at me for a long moment. "Well, let me clear these dishes and then I can give you the grand tour."

"Great," I say, wondering if the finale is going to be his bedroom. My palms are getting sweaty.

* * *

Turns out, what I thought was his living room is actually his music studio because it has better acoustics than the family room downstairs.

"Do you play the piano too?" I ask, thinking I couldn't imagine being able to play one instrument, let alone two.

"Sort of. I can play enough to get by with accompanying my students," he says, sitting down at the piano and playing my favorite song, "Possession" by Sarah McLachlan. Just like with his cooking skills, he's undersold himself.

I love this song and can't help but sing along. He glances at me in surprise because I guess I haven't sung around him before. It's fun singing with someone playing live versus just in my room or the shower or the occasional sing-along with Abby in the car.

Somewhere around the second verse, it hits me that this was the song the faceless man sang for me in the latest dream I had. My mind whirls, but I will myself not to falter as I continue singing. Somehow, I make it through.

Roddy relaxes his hands on his lap when he's finished and looks at me. "I had no idea you could sing. That was amazing."

I blush. "Thank you. My dad had a beautiful voice too, so I guess I inherited it from him."

"You could be singing in concert halls," he says, and my blush deepens.

Wanting to change the subject so I don't fully combust, I point to the two cello cases next to the piano. "Are those both yours?"

"Yep. The one in the black case is the one I use for the symphony because it has the best sound quality."

"And the one in the brown case?"

"That one was my grandfather's. I keep it mostly for sentimental reasons, but it has the best feel of any cello I've ever played." He looks off into the distance for a moment, thoughtful. "Do you have a favorite pair of shoes that are maybe not the best looking anymore, but they're so comfortable you can't bear to part with them?"

I nod. "I've had a pair of loafers since college that I still wear even though they're all scuffed. I've never been able to find another pair that are as comfy as those."

"Well, that's how this cello feels to me. It just fits better than any other cello, probably because it's been so well broken in by three generations of Vaughn men. But since it's older, it doesn't project as well as my newer one, so I can't use it for performances."

"Would you play it for me?"

In response, he opens the well-worn brown case and takes out a beautiful cello. I can definitely see the wear in spots, but I can also see the craftsmanship. I hear my father's voice in my head, "Craftsmanship is the cornerstone to a stringed instrument. If it doesn't have craftsmanship, it's just piece of wood with some strings on it."

Roddy sits down and does a bit of tuning. "Anything in particular you'd like to hear?"

I shake my head and sit down on one of the other chairs. "Surprise me."

And that he does. I can tell from the opening notes that he's playing "El Cant del Ocells," one of my all-time favorite cello solos by Pablo Casals. I close my eyes and just breathe in the music. The sound is mournful, but also hopeful at the same time. I can hear that the tone is not quite what you would hear in a concert hall performance or a recording, but it's beautiful all the same.

When he finishes, I open my eyes and find that I've been crying without noticing. I was so involved in the music I didn't realize tears were streaming down my cheeks. All the memories of listening to this with my dad and the moving nature of the piece in general just overwhelmed me.

After Roddy puts away the cello, he comes to stand next to me and sees me wiping my eyes. "Are you okay?"

"I'm fine. It's just that that piece reminds me of my dad. He loved this piece as well, and we went to see a performance of that with the symphony about a year before he died."

"About six years ago?"

"I think so. I know there was an out-of-town soloist playing with the symphony. He was absolutely amazing, and my dad couldn't stop going on about how wonderful of a performance it was."

Roddy looks down at his hands, sheepishly. "That was actually...me. I was the visiting performer for that show."

"You're kidding." If I wasn't sitting down, I would have fallen down.

"Nope. That was me," he says. "I was doing a lot of solo touring at the time, but all the travel was wearing on me. Plus, Camille and Dilip were getting married and talking about a family, so I thought it would be good to settle back down here. When I came for that show, I talked with the powers that be at the North Carolina Symphony and they had an opening they were auditioning for. I finished my tour a few months later, moved back to Raleigh and have been playing with them ever since."

Without thinking, I blurt out, "I've been dreaming about you." My heart races with panic as soon as I realize what I've said.

He cocks an eyebrow. "You have?"

You have two choices, Clare: spill the beans, or lie through your teeth. In the end, I choose truth. I motion for him to sit back down, and I tell him everything. Well, maybe not every single dream, and definitely not the proposal ones, but enough. He listens quietly while I go through everything from my parents' deaths to the dreams in the hospital that I thought were drug-induced to the more recent ones where the faceless, tuxedoed person morphed into a man.

"So, yeah, that's about it," I conclude, dropping my hands into my lap.

"That's...a lot to take in," he replies.

I bob my head. "I don't know why I blurted that out. Maybe my shock at knowing my father would have been so closely connected with your guest performance. I mean, he literally talked about that until the day he died." So many memories are resurfacing. "And I'm now remembering him saying something about being glad 'that guest cellist's audition went well so we have him here for good.'"

Roddy laughs. "It's always nice to hear you're wanted."

He gets quiet again, and I know I've totally killed any good vibes we had going tonight. "Sorry to ruin the evening. If you point me toward the nearest bus stop, I'll make my way home." I stand up to leave.

He grabs my hand kindly but firmly to pull me back to him. "No, Clare, you didn't ruin anything. I just need a moment to digest everything you told me. It's a lot to live up to, if I'm the one in these dreams or even if I'm not."

I shake my head. "No, you don't have to live up to anything. They're just dreams, not expectations. I mean some of them are so far-fetched they couldn't happen in real life. Where would you get a dinosaur to ride?"

We both laugh. "Yeah, I doubt that one's going to happen."

"And I'm not checking things off on a list or anything. These dreams aren't a bucket list of romance for me." I pause. "But I do feel like my parents might have sent them to me to point me in your direction. Especially with all the ties my father had with you and the symphony."

When he doesn't respond, I add, "That's the real reason I ran after you and kissed you in the street that night. I saw you in your tux and was overcome by a feeling I couldn't explain and I–"

He closes the short distance between us in a moment and puts his fingers to my lips to quiet me. "I think I understand now," he says. "And it's okay. Whatever it was that brought us together is amazing because you are amazing, and I want to keep exploring everything together with you."

A contented sigh escapes my lips. "I'd like that too."

Something unspoken passes between us and we both stand up. We're staring into each other's eyes, and neither one of us cares about the rest of the house tour. I reach up to run my fingers through his curls, feeling the softness, and pull him toward me for a kiss. Our lips touch gently at first, but the kiss deepens quickly, becoming more insistent. Soon, it feels like our hands are everywhere: my hand around his back, his hand in my hair, my other hand grasping his strong bicep and his other hand tracing a line down my spine.

All my previous worries and trepidations are gone, and when he whispers, "Do you want to go upstairs?" in my ear, I don't have to think before telling him yes.

* * *

After, while we're laying in his king-sized bed, I ask him to tell me more about his tattoo. Now that I've gotten a chance to see it close up, it's more than just a cello. It's a side view of a cello from his left shoulder blade down to his right lower back, at the angle where one would play it, and you can almost imagine the bow is moving across the strings. Coming out from the instrument are lines of music across his upper back and right shoulder blade.

"Well, I wanted the cello, obviously, but not like just a flat cello on my back," he replies as I trace the lines of the tattoo. "So, I had Camille draw the design of the side view with the bow. Then I had them add some lines of a piece my grandfather composed for cello back in the seventies."

"Oh, wow," I say. "That's lovely. Is your grandfather's piece anything I would have heard?"

He turns around to face me. "No, he never published it because he wanted it to stay in the family."

"What's it called?"

"*Clarus Amor.* Bright Love in Latin," he says. "And it just occurred to me that clarus is the root of Clare."

I'm too dumbfounded to reply, so I snuggle into his warm chest and hold him tight.

Part K

"About Damn Time"

August

The smells of spiced apple cider and freshly baked pastries filled my nostrils. I looked around and saw that I'm standing near Norway in the middle of World Showcase at EPCOT, which is decorated for the holidays. I must have been at their Festival of the Holidays celebration, which is something I've always wanted to see.

"Try this," a voice said in my ear as they embraced me from behind and offered a Scandinavian pastry to me. I took a bite and it's like a cinnamon and cream-filled wonder, wrapped in very thin dough. When I turned around, I saw the faceless woman there, back in her tuxedo, taking her own bite of the treat.

She took my hand and pulled me off to try more delicacies of the event. We ate and laughed and thoroughly enjoyed ourselves, to the point where I forgot she has no face and just reveled in her company.

As we were exiting the park, she turned to me in front of Spaceship Earth and kissed me. Her lips tasted of cinnamon, even though I couldn't see them.

* * *

"It's not too late to turn around," Abby says as we pull into the parking lot and see the red walls and white roof of the Angus Barn.

"Well, considering I see your mom waving to us from the entrance, I think it is," I reply, waving back at Mrs. Cassidy.

"Damn," Abby says. Once she parks, she looks at me sincerely and adds, "Have I thanked you enough for coming with me?"

"Yes, but you'll really clinch it when you take me to Element for a proper dinner I can actually eat next week." The Cassidys have a penchant for selecting restaurants with hardly anything I can eat. At least the last one had a few options. At this one, I can only get one thing.

"And you can order anything you want. Appetizers, entrees, desserts. Get something to take home for the next day. I'll get you anything you want for eating with them again. Especially here."

We gather our things and reluctantly walk to meet up with Abby's parents. Abby's mom is all dressed up like she's going to a formal event with a red cocktail dress complete with beaded clutch and stiletto pumps. Mr. Cassidy is wearing a full suit with a tie that matches Lynnette's dress perfectly and pristinely shined wingtips. On the other hand, Abby and I are both wearing dress pants with nice blouses like we're just here for a nice dinner and not heading off to meet foreign dignitaries.

"Hello, dear," Lynnette says to Abby, then leans forward to give her a quick air kiss.

"Hi, Mom and Dad." Abby grudgingly turns to her father and gives him a hug.

Jack pats Abby's back once, then releases the embrace. "Hello, Abigail."

I also exchange pleasantries with the Cassidys, then we head into the restaurant for our reservation. We're led to our table by the fireplace and handed menus by the hostess. Jack immediately hides behind his menu, perusing all the offerings of meat. As I take a quick glance at the menu I've already surveyed online, I can't help but think about how Abby called this place "Big Steak Meat Palace" the other day, and I start to giggle to myself.

"Clare, that's a lovely top," Lynnette says. "Where did you get it?"

I look down at my blouse as if I've forgotten what I'm wearing. "Oh, I think I got it at Torrid. But that was ages ago."

Lynnette frowns as if that's not a shop she'd ever conceive of shopping in, but she says, "If they have things as cute as that, I'll have to check it out sometime."

I hear Abby mutter, "Sure you will, Mom," under her breath.

After several moments of complete silence from the table, I attempt another ice breaker. "So, what is everyone going to get for dessert?"

"Dessert?" Jack says with barely disguised disdain. "Who is thinking about dessert right now? I haven't even ordered my steak yet."

Abby grabs my hand under the table. "I think Clare was just trying to make conversation, Dad. Also, as you know, she's vegetarian, so there's not a lot she can eat on the menu here."

"Good thing you brought her, then," he replies.

Both Lynnette and Abby seem poised to come to my defense, but the server appears to take our orders. Thankfully, Jack doesn't try to steamroll the ordering process this time and we each get to order for ourselves. I order the three-cheese ravioli and a side salad, while Abby gets the grilled chicken, and Lynnette and Jack get some kind of extremely expensive steaks. They, of course, order a whole bottle of wine to share, even though Abby and I say we're going to stick with water.

"And we'll get the chilled seafood tower for the table," Jack says.

As the server walks away, I surreptitiously roll my eyes and keep my mouth shut because I really don't care. The main thing is to get through this evening as calmly and quickly as possible, then hope to not have to repeat this nonsense for quite some time. Considering the emotional abuse piled on by her father especially, I wish Abby would cut them out of her life completely, but I also understand how that would be very difficult since they're her parents.

No one says anything for the longest time, but you could cut the tension with a knife. I take a sip of my water and survey the interior of the restaurant. The walls are dark brown paneled wood, as you'd expect from a barn, and all the tables are clothed in gingham. The chandeliers are made of antlers, and there's various country décor and hunting memorabilia decorating the walls. It's homey and the fireplace adds a nice ambiance.

The server arrives back with the seafood appetizer and everyone else tucks in. Abby gives me an apologetic smile as she takes a couple shrimp from the platter, and I just nod for her to enjoy her food.

"How did your date with Belinda go, dear?" Lynnette asks, finally breaking the silence.

Abby swallows her bite of shrimp and wipes her mouth before responding. "It was fine. She was nice and all, but we didn't have a lot in common."

"Typical," Jack coughs around a mouthful of crab.

Lynnette puts a hand on Jack's arm. "Did you make plans to see each other again?"

Abby shakes her head. "No. Like I said, we didn't really hit it off."

"That's a shame. I was so sure she'd be perfect for you."

"Well." Abby shrugs.

"Well, what?" Jack asks. "Your mother found you a wonderful girl with a *future* and all you can say is 'well'? Did you at least get some tips from her on planning for your future? Going back to school? She went to Duke, you know."

"No, we didn't really talk about our jobs that much," Abby responds meekly.

Every time I see her around her parents, I'm surprised by how much she lets them get away with. Why can't she just stand up to them? She's not this timid in her day-to-day life. She stands up to people all the time in her line of work and has no problem with it. But get her around these people and she's a mouse.

"Well, have you even given any further consideration to law school?" Jack asks. "Let me just take a wild guess at that answer: no."

Abby looks down at her plate.

"Your father and I only want what's best for you," Lynnette chimes in. "We're only concerned for your future. We won't be around forever to bail you out."

"I haven't ever needed bailing out, Mom. I'm doing just fine," Abby replies.

"Fine is just not good enough. We set you up with that college fund for you to go to law school. I went to law school. Your grandfather went to law school. Your great-grandfather went to law school. There's a legacy there and you're not living up to your potential." Jack grabs his wine glass too forcefully and some of it sloshes onto the tablecloth. "I knew we should have tried for a boy," he mutters.

That's the last straw. "What did you just say?" I ask.

Jack looks taken aback. Apparently, he thought none of us heard his last comment. "Nothing."

"I heard what you said, and it was far from nothing." I set my water glass down deliberately and look directly at Jack. "This woman"—I put my hand on Abby's shoulder—"is perfect just as she is. She has a heart of gold, and she would do anything for her friends and her family, even though you've never supported her in the slightest. She works hard at her job, and she's been promoted several times to become one of the most trusted property managers at Marshall Realty. Her apartment is beautifully decorated because she has an eye for design—but you wouldn't know that because you've never seen it. She manages her money well so she will have money for retirement but still be able to enjoy her life now. Which, again, you wouldn't know because you don't take the time to know anything about your daughter's actual life, just the life *you* decided was right for her. Most importantly, she has done all of this on her own, without even touching your precious money."

I don't know how, but Jack looks like he's shrunk about two feet, and Lynnette won't look up from her plate. But, when I look at Abby, she's smiling but also looking at me like she's never seen me before. And maybe she hasn't.

Abby stands up and throws her napkin on the table. "We're leaving." She puts her hand out for me, and I take it. "Clare is right. You don't know or understand my life because you've never tried to. And I'm tired of it. When you come to your senses, you know where to reach me. Until then, I'm done." She pulls me to my feet, and we walk hand-in-hand out of the restaurant. On the way out, she grabs one of the mints on the host station, unwraps it and pops it into her mouth in triumph.

Once we're out in the parking lot, I gush, "Oh, I'm so proud of you. You were absolutely brilliant. The way you stood up—"

All of a sudden, she pulls me to her with such force that I forget to breathe for a second. Then, suddenly, her lips are on mine, and they taste of cinnamon, just like in my dream. And I know she's the one in the dreams, beyond a shadow of a doubt now. There's the very real feeling that we've both been longing for this for ages, and embers have ignited into flames.

When we pull apart, we're both panting like we've run…well, any distance really. She smiles at me, and I smile back.

"Clare," she whispers, "will you be my girlfriend?"

Part 12

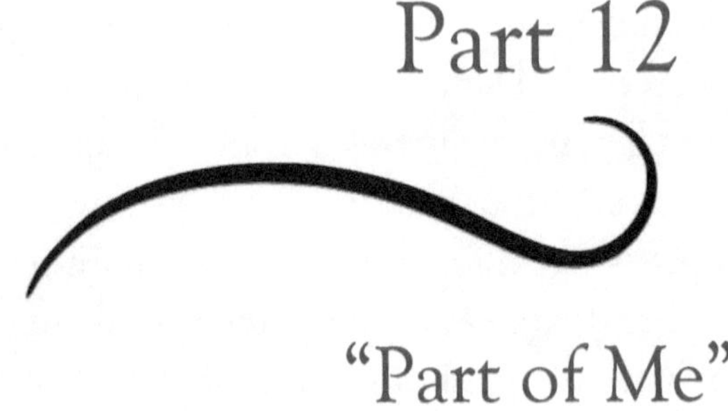

"Part of Me"

August

"Are you ready to get started, Ms. O'Donnell?" Amy, the oncology nurse, asks as she gets ready to access the chemo port in my chest. I've already been given a selection of various pre-meds to keep me from having an allergic reaction and to hopefully help with some of the more annoying side effects, like nausea.

I grab Roddy's hand and squeeze it tightly. "As I'll ever be."

Amy accesses the port—which doesn't hurt much more than a simple shot thanks to the numbing cream my doctor prescribed—and gets everything all set up for the first of two drugs I'll be getting for my first four sessions of chemo. This one, Adriamycin, is nicknamed "The Red Devil" because it looks like red Kool-Aid and because of the potential side effects.

"Alright, I'm going to get started, so get your popsicle ready," Amy says.

The only silver lining with this particular drug is that you have to keep your mouth and throat really cold to prevent mouth sores, so you get to eat popsicles while they infuse it. I unwrap my favorite flavor, cherry, and start eating it. Roddy sits in the chair next to me and holds my other hand. I'm so used to having to carry on conversations with nurses while having blood drawn or other tests done, that it is strange to me to be completely silent while she's infusing the drug directly into the line, but my only job right now is to keep my mouth cold with the popsicle.

Finally, after about fifteen minutes, the nurse gets me started on the second drug. This one, cyclophosphamide, will take a couple of hours to infuse through the IV connected to my port, so Roddy and I can sit in my little cubicle in the chemo area and read, watch something on my laptop, talk quietly, or nap. My chair is a recliner with massage and heat, and there are tables that lift up on the sides so I can set my eReader, my water bottle and my snacks on them. Roddy's chair is a fairly standard hospital chair, but he says it's comfortable.

"You're all set to go," Amy says, closing the door to the IV machine. "Would you like some warm blankets?"

"That would be great," I reply. I'm not normally cold-natured, but it's pretty chilly in here and after eating three popsicles, I'm freezing.

She grabs two blankets from the warmer by the nurses' desk, and Roddy helps her cover me up with them. "If you need anything else, I'll be around. And you can alert any of the nurses in here if you start feeling anything unusual. And sir"—she addresses Roddy—"if you notice any symptoms of an allergic reaction like…"

I tune out the rest as I can't handle thinking about having an allergic reaction right now. Going through surgery was relatively easy. I was a little scared—as anyone who is going under the knife should be—but mostly I just wanted the blasted cancer out of my body. But chemo is a whole different ball game. I'm not ready to feel bad all the time or to lose my beautiful hair. I'm not ready to think about any of the long-term side effects, like heart damage, that I could have from this. Yet here I am. The cancer didn't give me a choice.

Thankfully, I have a great support system with my friends and Roddy to help me through everything. I haven't had to go to a single appointment alone, and I know that's not simply because I don't drive.

"You doing okay so far?" Roddy asks after Amy walks away to help another patient. "You look lost in thought."

I look over to him and put my hand out, which he takes. "I was just thinking about how much I don't want to be doing this right now." The corners of his mouth turn down and his eyes soften. I continue, "But also about how glad I am that you're here."

"I wish you weren't doing this either, but I am glad that I can be here for you too," he says, then he raises my hand to his lips and kisses it.

* * *

The rest of the time at the cancer center passes uneventfully and Roddy drives me home. I'm so drowsy from all the pre-meds that I fall asleep hard as soon as we get back. He stays with me, reading in my mother's rocking chair, throughout the afternoon. When I wake up, he makes me lunch, just like he did when I had the last biopsy. Thankfully, I haven't had any nausea yet, so I'm still able to eat.

"If you have students to see or a rehearsal, you can go. I think I'm probably fine," I say after I finish eating.

"No rehearsal today, and I took the day off from lessons. I told my students last week that they'd have a week off, and they were thrilled," he replies. "Not sure what that says about my teaching, though."

I laugh. "I'm sure they love you and your lessons, but kids love a day off now and then."

"I'm sure you're right." He takes the tray of dishes to the kitchen. "Go ahead and pick something to watch, and I'll be there in a couple minutes."

We spend the afternoon watching brainless movies and more baking shows. Nate checks in to see how I'm doing via text and tells me he's working on some proposal for some big Ireland trip that he'll fill me in on later, and Isaac calls to check in as well. Sophia texts to check on me too and says she's mailing a care package with some essentials. Abby comes home eventually and joins us until she leaves for a date. Her parents set her up with some lawyer lady named Belinda, and though they didn't really hit it off on the first date, they both agreed to give it a second shot just to prove to both sets of meddling parents that they'd tried.

"She's nice enough and at least we have the psycho parents thing in common," she'd said. "Maybe we'll discover something else we share this time around, or at the very least, we can have a nice meal together and that will be that."

Now, as night begins to fall, I feel a thrumming in my head, and I don't think it's just from the music in the movie we're watching. I close my eyes and rub my temples, but this does very little to alleviate the worsening pain.

"Clare, are you alright?" Roddy asks through the pounding in my ears.

"My head hurts." I can't think enough to say more than that.

"The nurse said headaches were a potential side effect. Let me go get the binder to see if there's something you can take for it." Roddy gives my shoulder a quick squeeze before he runs off to get the binder the cancer center gave me before I started chemo. It has all the emergency numbers, non-emergency numbers, home remedies, medicines you can and can't take while on chemo, recipes, exercise guidelines, and more. It was a lot to digest when I got it and right now, I can't remember anything specific.

I feel Roddy sit back on the sofa next to me and hear him leafing through the binder. "It looks like you can only take Tylenol, but I wonder if there's anything stronger you can take. Do you want me to call the on-call nurse to see?"

"Yes, please, anything," I say.

All at once, the nausea hits like a wave crashing onto a rocky coastline. I get up quickly—even though that act makes my head pound even worse than before—and rush to the bathroom, sure that I'm going to throw up at any moment. I collapse onto the floor, heedless of my knees on the hard tile, and open the toilet lid. The nausea is still there, but nothing happens. Roddy rushes in the room after me, obviously worried.

"Clare?" he says, panicked.

"Uunnhhh..." or some variation thereof bursts forth from my mouth.

"Clare, just hold on, I'm going to talk to the nurse and get you some help." Then into the phone, "Yes, yes, hello. My girlfriend had her first chemo treatment today and she's got a massive headache. ...Yes...yes. No, she hasn't taken anything yet. We wanted to find out what she can do. Tylenol isn't going to help this..."

This conversation goes on for a while. Meanwhile, I'm still crouched over the toilet because I don't want to throw up on myself or the floor, and I'm also painfully aware that I might throw up in front of Roddy, but my head feels like it's going to split in two at any moment so at the same time, I don't really care. I have never in my life felt pain this bad before. Not after the car accident. Not after my lumpectomy. Never.

"I can't do this," I whisper into the toilet bowl, tears streaming down my face. Even through the incessant pounding and the sound of Roddy on the phone, I still hear the *plink plunk* of my tears hitting the toilet water. Shelley comes and curls up behind my bent legs, purring softly. I half-heartedly pat her head, then return my arm to the rim of the toilet.

Suddenly, I feel Roddy's hand on my back, and I feel a shiver go up my spine. "Clare? The nurse says you can take Excedrin Migraine. I've got some in my bag. She also said you should take your anti-nausea pill to help with that. I'm going to go get those and some water. I'll be right back, okay?"

I hear myself mutter something incomprehensible in agreement and he runs off to get the drugs. Some amount of time later, he returns with the three pills and a cup of water. It is all I can do to swallow anything because of the overwhelming nausea, but I manage to, one by one. Roddy sits on the floor next to me, looking completely lost.

I hand him back the cup and return to my death grip on the toilet. "I can't do this," I repeat, this time loud enough so an actual person can hear me.

"Oh, darling, yes you can. This is just a minor setback," he says in an attempt to be reassuring.

"Roddy, I feel like my head is going to break apart right now." I'm crying in earnest, the tears flowing faster. "If I have to go through this every treatment, I don't want to. It's not worth it. I can't."

"Clare, look at me."

"I can't."

"Look at me." He doesn't say this as a command, but as an entreaty. He strokes my hair. "Please, look at me."

Finally, I turn to look at him. Instead of the pity I thought I'd see in his eyes, I see hope...love even.

"You are so strong. I know it doesn't seem like it right now, but you are more powerful than chemo. You are more powerful than cancer." He caresses my tear-stained cheek.

"And you don't have to do it alone. I'm here with you. Abby, Nate and Isaac are here with you. We will be with you every step of the way to make sure you kick cancer's ass and come out even stronger on the other side. Because we believe in you, even if you don't believe in yourself right now. And, because we love you."

Through the pain, I feel my heart skip at the sound of those last words. I know he said "we" including my friends, but he still said it. However, I don't have the bandwidth to process the implications right now. And he doesn't give me a chance to respond anyway.

"Now, let's get you to bed to see if that helps any. The nurse said sometimes laying down will help these headaches. Something about blood pressure."

He puts his hands out and slowly helps me up to my feet. We walk over to the bed and I climb in, settling my aching head onto my pillow. Roddy goes around to the other side, undresses and climbs in behind me. He runs his fingers gently through my hair for a while.

"Feeling any better?" he asks quietly.

As I'm about to answer, I open my eyes and notice an apparition in my bathroom. I squint, but the images don't get any clearer, but I'd swear it was Abby helping another me to get off the floor. As they come closer to the bed, I notice that Other Me doesn't have the same port scar on her chest. They disappear quickly, and I turn the little amount of focus I have back to Roddy's question.

"Yes," I whisper. "The headache is almost gone."

"Good."

"Will you..." I hesitate.

"Stay?"

"Mmm-hmm."

"Of course."

He kisses me tenderly on my shoulder, then rubs my back until I fall asleep.

Part L

"Broken Pieces Shine"

August

In the words of Carrie Bradshaw, "and just like that," Abby and I are dating. Or maybe "together" would be a better term since we haven't had time to go on an official date yet. The night of the "Big Steak Meat Palace Disaster" as we've been calling it, we got in her Mini and drove to the closest restaurant that had vegetarian-friendly food and wasn't packed on a Friday night, and while I love Greek Fiesta, it's not what I would call "first date material." Especially not the kind of first date Abby and I have been building up to after so much time.

So, we've basically been going about our lives the same as we were before, but now with kissing and cuddling on the sofa. Gearing up for Nate and Isaac's wedding in a couple of months has taken up a lot of our time, plus Abby has been throwing herself into work lately, which I assume is a reaction to the blow-up with her parents. I've tried talking to her about it, but she's shut it down cold. Though I did have some flashbacks of Suz, I'm giving Abby time to process and not bugging her about it. I can't imagine what it must be like to have told your parents off—quite rightly, I might add. But, when she's ready to talk, she knows I'm here.

I'm super busy with work as well because we had a large group contact us who wants a private, custom tour of Ireland for next July, and Nate and I are preparing a proposal for them. It's a group of thirty-four seniors who are all of Irish descent wanting to go to Ireland to trace their roots. However, they all seem to have different budgets and very different ideas about how a tour like this could work. Nate also gets the feeling from speaking to the group leader, Mr. Walsh, that they might be interviewing other travel agents. So, we need to knock their collective socks off if we want to win this business.

"Do you have the quotes from CIE Tours or Brendan Vacations yet?" Nate asks in the office today.

"Not yet. I emailed both of the reps this morning and they said they should have them to us by the close of business today," I reply, clicking through my emails.

Nate sighs. "We really need those quotes so I can put the finishing touches on this PowerPoint. And, oh my god, what if the other companies are working with CIE and Brendan too? Should we quote another company? Should we build something from scratch? I don't think we have time for that. We have to present in literally seven days and I'm losing my mind here."

"Deep breaths. We'll get them and I know they'll be great. Even if the other company or companies are quoting CIE and Brendan, they may not quote the exact same itinerary," I reply, attempting to soothe him. "And a week is plenty of time to finish the PowerPoint."

"Clare, you just don't even know how important it is that we get this booking. This could really put Nerds on a Plane on the map!" His voice has gone up about three octaves and several decibels. He drops his head into his hands.

I pat his back. "Nate, seriously, I need you to breathe. Or, maybe, go take a walk. Something." If he's going to be like this for the next week, I'm going to lose it. "I do know how important this is, and we're both working as hard as we can to land this client. We'll do our absolute best, and that's all we can do. But you know what else? We have something those other companies don't."

He looks at me from one eye peering through his hand. "Yeah, like what?"

"Us," I answer. "We're the best nerdy travel agents around, and that's exactly what this group needs. They need people who can find them the unique experiences they're looking for that are off the beaten path so they can see more and do more. We're those people."

He raises his head and smiles. "You're right, girl. We are exactly what they need, and we are going to win this!"

"That's the spirit," I enthuse. "Now, seriously, go take a walk or something to get out of your head for a bit, and I'll hold down the fort."

"Thanks, Clare," Nate says, hugging me. "I don't know what I'd do without you."

"Probably drive some other poor sap crazy. But, it's okay, 'cause I love ya."

"Love ya back." He releases me, then heads out for that walk.

I'm just finishing up a welcome home email to one of our clients who just returned from their trip to Spain, when my cell phone rings. The number isn't familiar, but it is a North Carolina area code that isn't coming up as Spam, so I decide to answer it. "Hello?"

"Clare? This is Mrs. Cassidy. Abby's mom. Lynnette," she says as if I need that many names by which to know my best friend's mother when she calls. Come to think of it, Lynnette has never called me on my cell phone before, which would be why I didn't have her number programmed.

"Oh, um, hi," I say, not sure at all what to say to this woman. It's only been about two weeks since our fateful dinner, and I certainly didn't expect her to call me.

"I…I know you're probably busy," she begins, "so I won't take up too much of your time. I just wanted to see how my dau—how Abby was doing. Is she okay after…everything?"

There are two ways I could play this: beat around the bush and tell her everything's hunky-dory or give it to her straight. After my part in the restaurant disaster, I feel like the latter is the best option, and probably why Lynnette called me in the first place. "Mrs. Cassidy, Lynnette, she's *acting* mostly okay. She won't come out and say anything because I think she's still processing everything that happened, but I know she's really hurting right now."

Lynnette sighs heavily through the phone. "I thought as much. I hate that I hurt our little girl. I never meant for this to happen. I love her and only wanted what was best for her."

"Forgive me for saying so, but if that's truly the case, then why did you treat her the way you have for forty-one years?"

"I don't…I didn't mean to. I really do love my little girl. But she never seemed to take the path we laid out for her. She always wanted to go her own way, even if it was harder. That's hard for a mother to watch." There's a hitch in her voice. "I only wanted her to have what I never had."

Intrigued, I ask, "And what was that?"

"Love," she replies simply, and I hear her soft sobs through the line.

It's then I realize maybe Lynnette and Jack's marriage wasn't what it seemed on the surface. Perhaps the same pushing Jack does with Abby, he does with Lynnette as well. Maybe she settled. Maybe she had no choice. Maybe she loved him in the beginning and maybe part of her still does, but perhaps it's changed into something different, unmanageable.

"Why are you telling me this instead of talking to Abby?" I ask.

She takes a ragged breath before she answers. "I wanted to see if you thought she'd be open to seeing me. Just me." I have to hold myself back from prying more at that point. She continues, "I've tried calling and texting, but she hasn't responded."

That tracks. "I can ask. No promises, but I can ask. You might just need to be patient."

"I truly appreciate anything you can do."

"Okay, well, I need to get going," I say.

"Sure. I'm sorry I kept you," she says. Then when I don't say anything else, she adds, "Oh, and Clare?"

"Yeah?"

"Abby is lucky to have you as a friend."

Tears well up in my eyes as I put down the phone, and I realize that she doesn't know Abby and I are dating.

* * *

"Do you think you're ready to get out on the open road?" Abby asks as I drive around a quiet neighborhood with very few cars around. Over the last few months, I graduated from the empty parking lot to neighborhood driving, and I've been doing really well, if I do say so myself. Abby's been such a great support through all of this, even more so now that we're dating.

"Yes, I think I am," I reply, really meaning it. The scariest part seems to be behind me now and I feel confident behind the wheel like I never thought I would be again. I drive to the entrance of the neighborhood and signal for a right turn onto Wade Avenue.

"You got this," Abby encourages.

I smile but keep watch of the traffic. Once it's clear, I pull out and I'm driving again on a busy street for the first time in five years. But now is not the time to celebrate because I need to maintain my focus. There are a lot of cars and to some extent, I still feel like a student driver.

Everything is going smoothly until I realize I'm in an exit-only lane for Capital Boulevard. I check my blind spot to the left, but the traffic is bumper to bumper, and no one is letting me over. I feel like Dionne in *Clueless* getting on the freeway, although Capital Blvd is not quite the same as a freeway in L.A., I'm still petrified. I always hated Capital Blvd when I drove before, and going this direction means I'll be driving in downtown Raleigh with the narrow one-way streets and even more traffic.

"It's going okay, sweetie," Abby says. "Just keep going, you can't stop in the middle of the exit ramp."

I hadn't realized I'd slowed down quite so much and cars are honking behind me. I hit the gas and proceed onto Capital. The cars behind me fly past me as soon as they can, leaving me to merge once they've gone by. "I hate Capital Blvd!"

"I know. Everyone does. It's not too much farther to Edenton, then we'll just go down Hillsborough and be almost home."

Abby sounds so calm whereas I want to jump right out of this moving vehicle. I don't, though, and keep driving at exactly the speed limit until we get to Edenton Street where I turn right. Thankfully, Abby knows the quickest way to get us home, avoiding most of the narrow streets. However, things aren't much better until we get past the traffic circle on Oberlin Road and I know we're almost home. Once I've parked Abby's car in the garage, I drop my forehead onto the steering wheel and sigh heavily.

"You did it!" Abby pats me on the back. "I'm so proud of you."

"I never want to drive on Capital Boulevard again," I mutter into my chest.

"Well, I'm not sure I can promise you'll never have to do it since it is a pretty major street in Raleigh, but at least you know you *can* do it if you have to. I think you're ready to get your license again."

I turn to Abby, who is positively beaming with pride, and I can't help but smile. "Really?"

"Yes, really. Sure, you might want to practice some more with me or someone else, but other than that tiny moment of panic on the exit ramp, you handled yourself really well out there." She pumps her fist in the air. "You didn't let the fear overtake you this time."

"I didn't, did I?"

"You did not."

I lean over and kiss my girlfriend—I mean, I might as well keep in line with what Dionne did after getting off the freeway, right? Well, almost. Abby and I aren't quite there yet considering we haven't had a first date.

When we finally pull apart, she sits back with a satisfied "Mmm" sound. "I should take you on Capital more often."

We both laugh, then get out of the car and head up to the apartment. In the elevator, my phone bleeps with a text from Abby's mom asking if Abby said anything about meeting with her. I roll my eyes at the fact that it's only been a few hours since I spoke with Lynnette. However, it also makes me realize that with all the hubbub with driving, I haven't mentioned it to Abby yet.

As we enter the apartment, I say, "So, I got a phone call from your mom today." I have no idea how Abby's going to take this.

She turns to me, accusing. "Why would she call you?" At my step back, her gaze softens. She puts a hand on my arm. "I'm so sorry, Clare. I didn't mean to direct my hostility to you. I was annoyed that she would call you instead of trying to communicate with me directly."

"It's okay," I reply. "She said she's tried to reach you but hasn't gotten a response. She wasn't sure what else to do."

Abby crosses her arms across her chest. "I just need time."

"I know. I told her that." I'm not sure how much to reveal of my conversation with Lynnette, so I only add, "She really seemed sincere in wanting to mend fences. And she only mentioned herself, not your dad."

Abby's head tilts to the side, pondering for a long moment. "I'll think about it, but I'm not ready to commit to seeing her right now. It's still too raw."

"I completely understand." I wrap her in a hug. "Whatever you need, I'm here for you. And if you want to meet with her, I'm there."

Abby rests her head on my shoulder as she cries.

* * *

The next evening, I'm eating dinner in front of the TV because Abby had a final fitting for her tux after work, and my head starts to pound. I get a few headaches from time to time, but this comes on very suddenly and with brute force. I wonder if this has anything to do with the stress of the Ireland trip Nate and I are working on. Sighing, I put down my fork and walk to the bathroom to get some ibuprofen. I nearly trip over Shelley when I do so because she's collapsed on the floor half on the bathroom tile and half on the bedroom carpet. Silly cat.

When I lean over to open the cabinet, the pain almost knocks me out, it's that strong. Unlike my normal little tension headaches, this feels like my entire skull is going to crack open. And I'm suddenly nauseated. I never feel nauseated unless I've got a stomach virus. *Did I eat something weird? Do I have a stomach virus? But a stomach virus wouldn't give me a headache.*

I grab for the bottle of pills, but the pain is so bad I can't see straight anymore. I fall to the floor, clutching my head. I'm seeing double and also hallucinating. There are two Shelleys—one where she was a moment ago, and another right beside me. I put my hand out for the one beside me, but it goes right through her. Then, a man enters the room, but he's not really there either because he walks through the "real Shelley." *Am I seeing ghosts?*

I hear the front door open, and Abby announcing that she's home. I cry out something unintelligible, and I hear her rapid footfalls as she runs into my room, calling my name.

"Oh my god, Clare!" she cries when she sees me. "What happened?"

"My head. It hurts so bad."

"Did you fall? Do you need to go to the hospital?" she asks, concern etched all over her face.

I shake my head. Big mistake. "No fall. Headache. Really bad. Nauseated."

"Maybe it's a migraine," Abby says. "I've got some Excedrin Migraine in my bathroom. I'll be right back."

She runs out around the same time that the ghost man does also—and I know I've seen him before, but I can't place him. I close my eyes because I can't take whatever this is. I try massaging my temples, but somehow that makes it worse.

Abby's back quickly, and she hands me two pills and a cup of water. I take the pills one by one and set the cup down on the floor where Ghost Shelley used to be.

Abby takes my hand. "Any better? I mean, I know you just took the pills, but…"

"Not really," I say.

"Why don't we see if lying down helps?" She puts out her hands to help me get up.

Over her shoulder, I see Ghost Man helping a ghost me into my bed. *What the hell?* I watch the ghost scene as Abby helps me up to standing. As Ghost Me turns around, I notice a definitive scar on her chest that looks like what you would get if you were getting chemo. My mind reels and my kneels buckle. Abby barely manages to keep me upright.

"Clare?"

"Sorry, I…sorry," I say knowing that this headache is not going to allow me to put into words what's going through my head right now.

"It's okay," Abby consoles, helping me make it the rest of the way to the bed. She pulls back the covers and I crawl in, resting my head on the pillow. She sits on the side of the bed, watching me breathe. "Is that any better?"

Somehow, it is. I don't know if it's just lying down or that—and I can't believe I'm even thinking this—Other Me's headache is going away, but the pounding has ceased and there's just a dull ache at my temples. "Yes," I reply.

"Oh, good." She sighs with relief. "I wasn't sure what else to suggest other than a compress. That, or a trip to the ER."

I roll over onto my back and rub my hands over my face then up over my head. "Yeah, I wasn't sure what else to try either."

"You know," Abby begins, scrunching her face up in a quizzical expression, "it's really strange that it went away so suddenly. I mean, the medication hardly had any time to get into your system."

I hesitate briefly, but I also know I can tell Abby anything, especially now. I push myself up to sitting. "I have a theory."

"I'm all ears."

"You know those sensations of déjà vu I've been having?"

She nods. "Yeah, with the dreams and the faceless person that's none other than yours truly." She flips her hair over her shoulder, grinning.

I chuckle, which brings back a little of the pounding in my head from before. "Right. So, I haven't only been having that because of the dreams."

"No?" she asks.

"I've also been…seeing visions or hallucinations—whatever you want to call them—of myself in like another timeline or something."

"Oh my god, like one of Suz's movies with the parallel universes?"

"Like a multiverse, yes." I still can't believe I'm thinking this, let alone saying it out loud.

"In the words of Keanu Reeves, 'Whoa,'" she says.

"Exactly. And I think that this timeline, universe, whatever is somehow connected to another one, and I'm experiencing some of what that me is going through. Probably vice versa as well."

"This is… I mean, I don't know what to say. This is nuts."

I nod and sink my face into my hands. Abby's said she believed me about the dreams, but I don't know how much she really did. But this? This is a whole different level of crazy. I'm sure she's going to have me committed to an institution or at least suggest I go back to therapy like I did right after my parents died.

She puts a comforting hand on my shoulder. "Clare, it's okay. I didn't say *you* were nuts, I said *this* is nuts. I believe you."

"Really?" I raise my head cautiously.

"Sweetie, I'll always believe you, no matter what. You've never given me any reason to doubt you and I know you wouldn't make up something this serious. If you believe this is happening to you, then I believe it too." She holds up a hand. "Don't get me wrong, though, I have tons of questions. Like tons."

I laugh and give her a big hug. "Thank you for believing me and in me."

"Always," she says. When we pull apart, she asks, "So, why do you think you got this headache then? Does Other You have migraines or something?"

It's time to say the really hard part. "No. Actually, I think Other Me has cancer."

Part 13

"Shut Up & Dance"

October/November

This would be the point in the movie version of my story where they'd show a montage that illustrates what chemo is like, because no one really wants to know what chemo is like. Chemo is messy and it's awful and it's so effing hard to get through. There were days during those first four treatments when I didn't think I would make it through—like when I had that massive headache the day of the first infusion—and times when I just wanted to stay in bed all day.

But there is no montage for those going through chemo. So, now I'm home after receiving my first of four infusions of the last chemo drug. This one, Taxol, is supposedly not as bad as the other two, but it is supposed to come with some severe bone and joint pain, so my doctor has given me some vitamins and supplements to help counteract the side effects. Oh, and the really fun part is that I have to wear these frozen gloves and booties the whole time it's being infused so I don't get peripheral neuropathy. Isn't that just great?

"How are you feeling so far?" Abby asks as she hands me a bowl of salted popcorn for movie night.

Nate and Isaac have been coming every Friday following my infusion for a movie night to lift my spirits, especially since Roddy usually has concerts on Friday evenings and can't be here until late. Nate brings over his collection of popcorn seasonings so everyone can experiment, but because I don't know whether I'm going to feel nauseated or not, I stick with plain, lightly salted popcorn. But it's still nice that I can participate.

Roddy's mom and Camille have been dropping off food during my off weeks from chemo, when I feel more like eating. I had to tell Sabine to bring some actual food instead of just pastries, though, because I was going to gain so much weight by the time all this was over with all the steroids, the butter and the sugar. "You need the sugar to keep your strength up, chérie," she said. But she did start bringing some savory foods as well.

"The bone pain is getting pretty bad," I reply, shifting in my seat on the sofa. I'm in my comfiest sweats, but my body aches like I have the flu. Instead of wearing one of the fun wigs I got—an emerald green one, a funky red one and a lavender one—I'm wearing a teal chemo cap because I'm just sitting at home with friends and even my scalp hurts.

"Let me get the heating pad for you," Isaac says, grabbing it from the end table next to him. He plugs it in and helps me get it situated. "Do you need some more Tylenol?"

"Thanks. No, I can't have any more yet." I punch the button on the heating pad and wait for it to heat up. Although, my bones already feel like they are on fire, so I'm not sure if the heating pad will help or hinder. "Let's go ahead and start the movie. Hopefully the distraction will help."

Abby presses play on *13 Going on 30*, which is a favorite of all of ours, and everything is going fine for a while, until the pain gets to be so much, I can't stand to sit still anymore. I stand up and start marching in place while we watch the movie. Somehow, it helps a little, though my body still feels like it's been pulled apart and sewn back together again.

Eventually, we abandon the movie because they can all tell how much pain I'm in, and Abby draws me an Epsom salt bath—another of the home remedies my doctor mentioned. The simple act of taking my clothes off is on the one hand exhausting and on the other freeing because nothing is touching my skin anymore, which also feels like it's on fire. I get in the tub and instantly the burning goes away. However, once the water turns cold, the aching in my bones is back again.

When I go back out to the living room around nine-thirty, Nate and Isaac have gone home to let me rest, and Abby is reading her book in her chair. She puts her book down and sits up when I sit gingerly down on the sofa.

"Any better?"

"Not really. It was fine while the water was warm, but now it's just as bad as before." I turn the heating pad back on to see if it will help at all this time.

"I'm so sorry. Did they say how long it could last?" she asks.

I shrug. "'Everyone is different.' But from what I read online, it could be several days each time."

The doorbell rings and Abby gets up to answer it. I don't even have the energy to look over and see who it is. I do hear her say, "She feels pretty bad."

"Hey, Clare," I hear Roddy say as he walks into the apartment. I can't help but smile at the sound of his voice. "I came as soon as the concert was over."

"I'm going to go read in my room," Abby says, picking up her book from the chair.

Roddy comes and sits down beside me. "Abby said it's bad." He takes my hand in his and I wince. "Sorry."

"It's not your fault. I just ache all over. They weren't kidding when they said I'd have bone pain."

"Is there anything I can do?" The way that he looks at me, with some amount of pity, sure, but also like he still finds me beautiful even though I'm pale, bald and in pain makes me know in my heart he's the only one for me.

"Just being here is helping," I reply.

"Then here is where I'll be." His voice is so warm, it's like an Epsom salt bath for my heart.

* * *

Once I've completed my final chemo treatment, I'm at the post-chemo follow-up with my medical oncologist, Dr. Abiola. Roddy holds my hand as we wait for the doctor to join us in the exam room.

"Are you nervous? Your hand is shaking," he says, rubbing small circles on my hand with his thumb.

"A little. I'm scared about the side effects of the hormone therapy drug she's going to want to put me on. I mean, I'm already getting hot flashes from the premature menopause. Or should I say, 'hot flushes' as all the doctors feel the need to call them?" I reply, the last part my poor attempt at menopause humor. Sometimes you have to laugh to keep from crying at everything cancer takes away from you. I've never really wanted kids, and Roddy feels the same, but when they told me the chemo would likely throw me into premature menopause, I felt the loss of my "womanhood" all the same. Not enough to want to freeze my eggs or anything, but enough for some late-night tears. "But, in all seriousness, I don't know how much more I can take."

He squeezes my hand and wraps his other hand around it. "I know. Or rather, I don't know, but I know that this has been rough on you. But we have to trust that all your doctors know what they're doing to keep you from getting cancer again. As I've said before, you are so strong, and you will make it through this."

I nod, just as the doctor comes in. "Hi, Clare, how are you feeling today?"

We go through all the pleasantries and the oh-so-enjoyable breast exam—during which Roddy leaves the room even though he's seen them a few times by now, but I appreciate the privacy—then Dr. Abiola gets down to the crux of today's appointment.

"Your labs are still consistent with early onset menopause, though that could still be caused by the chemotherapy at this point. In that case, I'd recommend starting you on Tamoxifen for at least eighteen months. If you're still in menopause at that point, we'll reevaluate. How does that sound?"

"What are the side effects of Tamoxifen?" I ask.

"The most common side effects are those already associated with menopause like hot flushes, night sweats, mood swings, and insomnia."

I wink at Roddy when Dr. Abiola says 'hot flushes' instead of what every woman on the planet calls them: hot flashes.

Dr. Abiola looks from Roddy to me and back again, as if she's not sure if she should be sharing the rest of the information with him present. I nod for her to continue. "Other common side effects are vaginal dryness and/or discharge, loss of sex drive, joint pain, fluid retention, and weight gain."

"Dr. Abiola, will Clare get all of these symptoms? And, if so, are there things she can do to minimize them?" Roddy asks.

Dr. Abiola looks at Roddy when she answers. "No, most likely she won't experience all of these symptoms, but they are the most common. And, to answer your second question, yes, there are things we can do to mitigate any symptoms that do occur." She turns back to me and says, "Clare, I'll send you some information through your patient portal with the full list of side effects along with supplements you can take and options to help with side effects, such as Vitamin E for hot flushes and lubrication for intercourse."

My cheeks feel hot all of a sudden, and I'm not sure if it's a hot flash or the fact that my doctor is talking about needing lube for sex right in front of my boyfriend. I don't dare look at Roddy because I will either start giggling like a teenager or I will cry. The mood swings are no joke.

"If you're okay with everything we've discussed, and you don't have any other questions, I'll go ahead and send in a prescription for the Tamoxifen so you can start on that right away. If you have any major side effects or come up with any other questions, you can either reach me through the portal or call the nurses' line for emergencies."

Although I know I'll have more questions about this medication I know virtually nothing about, I nod my assent and the appointment is over. While I do like Dr. Abiola most of the time, my appointments are usually only about fifteen minutes long and it always feels like I'm being rushed through them. She does seem to know what she's talking about, but her bedside manner could use some refreshing. I've had better appointments with her nurse practitioners and PAs than I have with her. I guess that's why we have Dr. Google now, so we can look up medications and symptoms to be petrified of because our doctors won't spend more time with us.

Roddy drives me home but doesn't immediately come in when we get there.

"I'll be up in a second. I just need to send a quick text," he says.

I take the elevator up and trudge into the apartment feeling a bit deflated, if I'm honest. While chemo is over and I knew that was going to be the worst part, I still can't quite see the light at the end of the cancer tunnel knowing the hormone therapy starts as soon as I take that first pill, and radiation starts in a few short weeks. I hope someday I can look back at this as just a blip—or chapter, as Abby called it—in my long life, but right now it seems interminable.

I put my jacket and purse in my room, then come back into the living room when I hear Roddy come in. He's holding an enormous rectangular box with a big pink bow on it, and I can't imagine what it could be.

"This is for you," he says, setting the box down on the kitchen table.

"But, why?" I ask and immediately feel stupid. "Sorry, what I meant to say was, thank you, what's the occasion?"

He laughs heartily. "I wanted to get you something to celebrate being finished with chemo. And there's another reason, but you'll have to open it to find out."

I pull off the bow and lift up the box lid. Underneath the lid is a ton of crisp, white tissue paper, and I gingerly lift each sheet. I steal a glance up at Roddy and he looks like he's dying with anticipation. Finally, I pull back the last sheet of tissue to reveal beautiful emerald-green fabric. I gasp as I pull out a gorgeous dress in delicate satin.

"Oh, Roddy."

"Do you like it?"

Tears fill my eyes as I look up at him. "I don't like it. I love it!" I throw my arms around his neck and kiss him passionately.

We pull apart and he says, "Go try it on. I want to make sure it fits."

I practically run into my bedroom and try it on. It fits perfectly and I look fabulous. Plus, the green really goes well with the red wig.

Roddy comes into the bedroom when I tell him I'm ready, and he simply stares at me from the doorway as I preen in the mirror. "It looks even better than I thought it would. Camille did such a great job with it."

I stop twirling and my mouth drops open. "Camille...made this?"

"Yes. Sorry, did I not mention that?"

"No, you didn't. I can't believe she made this, and without measuring me or anything."

"Well, we might have had a little help with that from Abby," Roddy says sheepishly. "Abby measured some of your favorite clothes for Camille so she could figure out proportions that way."

The tears are coming again. "Oh, you guys are just the best." Then, I remember something else he said when he gave it to me. "Wait, what was the other reason you gave this to me?"

He walks over to me, takes my hand and spins me in a slow twirl like we're dancing. "Well, I was thinking you could wear it to Nate and Isaac's engagement party this weekend. This way, you have something to wear that really shows off your beauty."

I don't try to stop the tears this time. And I say the words that have been on my heart since practically the day I met him. "I love you, Roddy."

He wipes the tears from my cheeks and kisses me tenderly. "And I love you, Clare."

* * *

Nate and Isaac's engagement party at their favorite restaurant, Caffé Luna, is more wonderful than Abby and I could have hoped. To be honest, she did most of the planning, but I did help a little with the video montage and picking out some of the music. She told me when I kept offering to help more, "You focus on beating cancer, and I'll plan the party. Don't worry, I got this." And she did.

Everyone seems to be enjoying the wonderful Italian food, and I'm thrilled that I finally feel well enough to stuff myself with carbs. Though my stamina isn't back to where it was before and probably won't be for a while after I finish radiation, I am getting back into doing some of the slow dancing workouts with Gina B., and I hope to do at least a little dancing with Roddy tonight. He did have his sister make me this spectacularly twirly dress after all, I need to showcase it to its full potential.

"How are you doing, Clare?" Nate's sister, Sophia, asks from beside me during dinner.

"I'm doing well. So glad to have the whole chemo mess behind me," I reply. I've learned that these are the types of replies people can handle when they ask how you're doing during or after cancer treatment. They might seem like they really want to know, but more often than not, they are just asking to let you know that they care, but don't want to know the gory details.

"That's great to hear," she says. "Nate said some of the side effects were pretty awful, like the bone pain during the last several cycles. I hope you don't mind, but he's been keeping me updated. I would have contacted you more directly, but I didn't want to bother you because I'm sure you've had tons of people bugging you for updates."

I underestimated Sophia, and I feel a little guilty because I should have known she would be keeping up with my situation through Nate. "I don't mind at all. And, I wouldn't have minded if you'd reached out more."

"Hey, let's get lunch the next time I'm in town. I'd love to catch up"—she leans in closer and whispers—"especially to hear more about this gorgeous man you're seeing." She winks.

I can't help the school-girl giggle that escapes my lips. I know Roddy is engaged in conversation with Isaac's mom about music, which they could both talk about all day, so I doubt he's heard, but I steal a glance back anyway just in case. He is none the wiser, so I turn back to Sophia. "Sure. Text me when you're going to be here, and we'll set it up. I'd love to know more about how things are going with Adam too."

"Oh, he's not...I mean, we're not..." She looks completely flustered.

I hold up my hands. "Sorry. I just thought..."

"Totally fine," she says. "We're just good friends, and he's friends with Nate, so that's why he's my plus one."

"Clare," Roddy says from my other side. "Would you like to dance?"

I turn in my chair, and he's standing with his hand outstretched toward me. Over the din of people talking, I hear the opening lines of Ed Sheeran's "Perfect" playing. I've always loved this song, and I cannot think of a more...perfect...song to dance to with Roddy.

Nate and Isaac are already dancing, along with a few other couples, and we join them on the dance floor. Roddy puts his arms around my waist, and I put my hands on his shoulders. We sway and turn slowly in time with the music. And I cannot help myself, but I sing along with Ed Sheeran. But when I get to the part where Ed sings about carrying children, I do choke up and can't sing the next chorus. Even though Roddy and I are both on the same page about not having kids, the fact remains that it's something I will never experience, and it was taken from me, whether I wanted it or not.

Roddy leans down and kisses my forehead. Then he starts to sing along with the second chorus in his slightly off-key baritone. This bolsters me to start singing again as well and we finish the song together. He squeezes me tight before we make room on the dance floor for couples wanting to party down to "Get Down on It" and "Electric Slide."

When the next slow song comes on, "Truly, Madly, Deeply" by Savage Garden, Roddy and I rejoin the fray. Nate and Isaac are still out there, wrapped up in each other's arms. As we're dancing this time, I have another of those visions of another me and she's dancing with someone else. It even looks like they're at a completely different venue. Maybe...the art museum? They turn and now I can see that Other Me is dancing with *Abby*! That's an interesting turn of events. But it makes sense considering that night at the symphony when Abby's face appeared to exchange with Roddy's before I had the panic attack. Now, Abby's waving at me or, more likely, someone else at the party.

The more I've thought about what I saw the night of the massive chemo headache, the more I've realized I've been having feelings of this Other Me for a while now. It doesn't make much sense, but the only explanation I can come up with is that it's another timeline intersecting with this one. I never thought I believed in other universes or timelines, but maybe they are real. It's just not fair that Other Me doesn't have cancer.

Part M

"I Wanna Dance with Somebody"

November

"I can't believe it's finally here!" Nate squeals from the back seat of the Towncar. It's taking us to the North Carolina Museum of Art to get ready for their wedding.

"I know, it doesn't feel real," Isaac seems excited as well, but isn't about to bounce off the walls quite as much as Nate.

"Are you ready to deal with them all day?" Abby asks me behind her hand, but loudly enough for both of them to hear.

I shake my head. "I don't know. We might have to get someone else to handle Bridezilla and her husband-to-be."

Nate puts his hand to his heart and replies, "Hey, now. I won't have you talking about my Isaac that way on our wedding day."

We all erupt into a fit of laughter. "Only joking, Nate. You know we love you and couldn't be happier."

He takes one of each of our hands in his. "But seriously, you two have been amazing and we wouldn't be here without you."

"That's right," Isaac echoes. "We love you girls, and we're not only thrilled to have you as our Best Women, but as our best friends."

Tears well up in all of our eyes, and I'm grateful that we're not doing hair and makeup until we get to the museum. "We wouldn't have it any other way."

"Group hug!" Abby announces.

We skooch as close together as the awkward seating will allow and embrace each other. Just then, the car turns, we all slide to one side, and Nate lands on the floor. We explode into hysterics again and Isaac helps his fiancé back onto his seat.

Soon enough, we're at the venue and ushered off to our separate areas to get ready. Nate and Isaac wanted plenty of time to take lots of photos, so we got here three hours before the ceremony is to start. There are so many great places at the art museum to take photos, both indoors and outdoors, that it will take at least an hour or more. Thankfully, Isaac's coworker, Sarah, does photography on the side, is looking to build her wedding portfolio, and is giving them the entire photo package as a gift for their wedding. She does great work too.

Abby and I settle in for the hair and makeup team Nate hired to work their magic on us. Neither of us wears much makeup, so we've asked if they can keep it very natural. For her hair, Abby is going with a French twist with curls cascading out of the top. Since my hair is pretty short, I've asked my stylist to just add in some waves and call it a day. My stick-straight hair doesn't normally hold curl well, but if she puts in enough hairspray, it should at least hold through the photos.

We text the boys when we are ready—because of course they are finished sooner—and head off to meet the photographer at the *Mirror Labyrinth* installation for the first set of photos. We progress from there to the some of the gardens, the giant ring sculpture called *Gyre*, and finally to the courtyard before we make our way into the West Building where the actual ceremony and reception will be held.

"Thank god that's over," Isaac says, wiping his brow with a handkerchief when we're finished with the photos.

"If it's any consolation, I know I got some great shots," Sarah says, scrolling through some of them on her camera. I take a look over her shoulder and she's right, there are some stellar photos on there.

"Just think of all the fun we'll have sharing these with our grandkids someday," Nate adds, wrapping his arm around Isaac's shoulders.

"Grandkids?" Isaac looks, in a word, petrified.

"Okay, nieces and nephews. Whatever. We'll still have plenty of kiddos to torture with fabulous photos of us lookin' fly on our wedding day."

"'Lookin' fly'?" Isaac tries and fails to stifle his laugh. "Oh, honey, we really need to work on your slang."

Nate looks at Abby and I for support, but we're giggling right along with his fiancée. "Et tu, lesbians?"

"Hey"—I hold up one finger—"I'm bisexual."

"Yeah, I'm the only lesbian here," Abby pipes up and puts her arm around my waist. "My girl here loves everyone."

"So-o-rry," Nate says, adding an extra syllable to the word. "I stand corrected."

"Can't we all just get along?" Isaac adds. "All the queerness in this group of friends has a place, and I, for one, am here for it!"

"Hear, hear!" Abby responds.

"Hear, hear!" Nate and I echo in unison.

We have another impromptu group hug, careful not to ruin anyone's makeup or hair, then we go back to the boys' ready room to wait for the guests to arrive.

It's not long before the guests have arrived, and the wedding coordinator is calling us to take our places. Neither Isaac nor Nate wanted to be standing at the front waiting for the other one to walk down the aisle—and Nate would be damned if he didn't get to march down that aisle on his wedding day—so they decided they'd both do it, escorted by their Best Woman. We all decided that the only fair way to decide on who went first down the aisle was alphabetically, so Isaac and I are going first.

"Are you ready?" I ask Isaac, who doesn't look at all nervous.

"Absolutely," he replies, and we start our march down the aisle to the string quartet playing Etta James' "At Last." It took a long time for them to select a song to walk down the aisle to, and Abby found this group called Vitamin String Quartet, who has an album called *The Gay Wedding Collection*. They loved everything on it, but they both agreed that Etta is timeless, so that was that.

As we approach the archway under which the minister is standing, I glance over at the string quartet and see a familiar face. The cellist most definitely plays for the symphony, but more than that, he looks very much like the ghost man from the other timeline. I start to feel faint, but I force my eyes to look forward and to remain focused on the beautiful wedding we've all been waiting so long for. But I will be telling Abby all about this later on.

Isaac stops as we reach the minister, and we turn around on our side to face the guests. Nate and Abby are already a quarter of the way down the aisle, and I smile watching my good friend and my girlfriend walk toward us. Nate is positively glowing and smiling broadly at Isaac. And I can't get over how beautiful Abby looks in her tux, not to mention the warm fuzzies it's giving me for how much it reminds me of the girl in the dreams.

When Nate and Abby reach the front, the minister begins the ceremony. As the boys wanted, it's very short, sweet and to the point. However, they both wrote their own vows, which bring a tear to nearly everyone's eye, and some laughter as well.

"Nate, you are joy, light and energy," Isaac begins. "Ever since I met you, my life has been a fuller, richer, more beautiful place to be. Your heart reaches out to all to give them love and comfort when they need it most. I want to spend the rest of my life making you feel my love and comforting you when you're down. I will be here as your friend, your lover and your husband, until death parts us. Forever, my love." He puts the wedding ring on Nate's finger.

Once Nate composes himself from hearing Isaac's beautiful words, he pulls the ring out of his pocket. "So, when I started working on my vows, I was struggling. Then, I started looking up stuff on Google to see if it would help. And, you know what? It did!" Everyone laughs. "I looked up our names and found out that Nathan—and no one on this earth is allowed to call me that except my parents—means 'gift of God.' And Isaac means 'one who rejoices.' Which means, that we're perfect together because I'm God's gift and you rejoice about it!"

Isaac's booming laugh fills the hall, and everyone else joins in. He leans forward and gives Nate a hug and whispers something in his ear. When they pull back, Nate continues.

"But, in all seriousness, Isaac, you are my gift, and I rejoice in you. You have my whole heart. You have since the moment we met, and you will until the day we die. Together. At the exact same time, because you're not leaving me here on this planet without you." Another smattering of laughter from the crowd. "Forever, my love."

I cannot see anything for the tears flowing out of my eyes as Nate puts the ring on Isaac's finger. The minister pronounces them married and everyone cheers as the happy couple kisses passionately in front of some of Rodin's masterpieces. The quartet plays Madonna's "Like a Prayer" as we exit, with Nate and Isaac leading, and Abby and I following also arm in arm.

The reception begins quickly since the guests stood for the short ceremony and the food is directly behind everyone. The boys opted for the buffet option to keep things a little cheaper, and it also gives more options for dietary restrictions. There are both high and lower tables around so guests can stand or sit as they please, but still have somewhere to put their food and drinks. The ceremony space is perfect for dancing, and the DJ is getting set up now that the string quartet has packed up.

When I start to sing "Only You" and they dance to it now, it's magical. The way the dimmed lights create shadows of their intertwined bodies moving around the dance floor, it's like an art installation in and of itself.

The DJ takes us from their song directly into mine and Abby's: "Truly, Madly, Deeply."

I walk over to where Abby is talking with Isaac's parents and tap her on the shoulder. "Sorry to interrupt, but may I have this dance?"

She excuses herself from the conversation and takes my hand. Isaac's parents wave us on, smiling. We make our way onto the dance floor, and I wrap my arms around her waist as she puts her arms around my neck. "You remembered," she says as we start to sway.

"Of course I did."

I'm entranced by this beautiful woman in my arms and lost in the feeling of this wonderful day. Abby grins at me as if she can feel it too. *Could this be any more perfect?*

Suddenly, I see something over her shoulder. It takes a moment before I can figure out what it is because I can tell it doesn't belong here and now. In the distance, I see Ghost Me dancing with the cello guy from the quartet, only they aren't in the art museum. I lean closer to Abby—which she mistakes for me wanting to dance closer, not that I mind—and squint to see if I can figure out where the apparitions are. *Is that? Are they? Yes, they're at Caffé Luna!* They must be at the engagement party.

"Abby," I say. "Can you turn around slowly and see if you can see Other Me behind you?"

She pulls back abruptly and starts looking every which way. "What? Now? Where?"

"Yes, now, but maybe don't be so obvious about it. I don't need everyone at this wedding thinking I'm insane or that we're looking at them. And keep dancing."

She nods, looking back at me and continuing to dance. "Ah, yes, got it."

"Now, over your left shoulder, right behind where Sophia and Adam are standing, you might be able to see Other Me."

She looks nonchalantly over her shoulder, gives a brief wave to Sophia, then turns back around. Not great, but passable. "No, I only see Sophia, Adam and a bunch of sculptures."

"Darn. Okay, well, it was worth a shot. I guess I'm the only one who can see them."

"Them?" she asks.

I realize I forgot to tell her about the cello guy. "Yeah, apparently the me from that timeline is with the cello guy from the string quartet tonight."

"What?!" she exclaims then quickly realizes it was entirely too loud when several people look over. She mouths, "Sorry," to them. To me, she says, "Sorry, what?"

"Other Me seems to be dating the cello guy from the quartet, who also plays for the symphony, because I saw him there too."

"Wow."

"Yep."

"This parallel universe stuff is…wild."

"Tell me about it." I sigh.

Abby wraps her arms around me tightly and we dance the rest of the night away.

Part 14

"Padam Padam"

January

I was sitting in an apartment and the doorbell rang. I looked around and realized I was sitting in Ross' apartment from Friends—not the first one he was in, but the former apartment of Ugly Naked Guy. I noticed the walls are the nice blue color, instead of the brown Ross painted it after he moved in. My mind felt sort of hazy and I couldn't remember what I was getting ready to do. Answer the door. I opened the door to reveal a delivery man holding a rather large rectangular white box.

"Can you sign here, please?" he said, holding out a clipboard.

I signed and he handed me the package. I closed the door and walked over to the coffee table to put the box down. Grabbing some scissors out of the end table drawer, I cut the tape on the box and opened it. Inside was something wrapped up in tons of white tissue paper—and not the kind you buy at Target, but the really fancy acid-free kind. On top of all the tissue paper was an envelope. I opened the envelope and read a handwritten note that said:

I thought you could wear this on our date tonight.
Love,

I could not read the single initial written below "Love." I puzzled over this for a moment, then set the note aside and started peeling away the tissue. Tears sprang to my eyes as I realized it was a dress. And, not just any dress, but an exact human-sized replica of the dress from a Peaches and Cream Barbie—only my favorite Barbie and favorite Barbie dress of all time. Delicate spaghetti straps, a shimmery white bodice and yards upon yards of peach chiffon for the skirt, with just a single ruffle at the bottom. The tears were mixed with joyous laughter as I twirled through the apartment holding the dress close. I finally stopped twirling and went to my room to try the dress on. It fit perfectly and looked even more amazing than I'd ever dreamed.

I reluctantly took the dress off and hung it up on the back of my bedroom door so it wouldn't get wrinkled or damaged before our date. The phone rang and it was "him"—the guy who was in love with me who sent the dress—but, I couldn't make out what he was saying, because it sounded like the teacher on the Charlie Brown cartoons. I could tell it was him by how my heart beat faster hearing the sound of his voice on the phone.

* * *

All the radiation from my treatments must be going to my head. I've never had a dream about the faceless man where "the thing" has already happened. Or maybe it was the chemo that scrambled the dreams. Who knows? Either way, it was still a beautiful dream that I did not want to wake up from at six-thirty in the morning to go to yet another radiation treatment.

Roddy and my friends have been taking turns driving me because these treatments are literally every single weekday, and while the treatment itself doesn't take that long, I know the drives to the cancer center and back every day are taking their toll on everyone. I know they are on me. But my friends are amazing and patient, and not one of them has suggested that I get over myself and get my damn driver's license again. However, I have decided once I'm finished with treatment and feeling better, I am going to learn to drive again. It's time.

Today, Roddy slept over—which might explain the dream—and is going to drive me to my treatment, then we'll go get breakfast and he'll drop me off at physical therapy after. The physical therapy is a preventative measure my radiation oncologist recommended to help me reduce the risk of lymphedema, something I really don't want to get and something I'll be at risk for the rest of my life. Yay. The therapist walks me through various ways I can break down the scar tissue from the surgery and radiation, perform self-massage if I feel any tingling or swelling, and wrapping techniques if I do experience lymphedema in my arm.

When I get out of bed, I see Roddy is in the bathroom scooping Shelley's litter box. I needed someone to do this for me when I was going through chemo, but my doctor said I should be okay to take the task over again now that chemo is finished.

"I can do that," I say, walking up behind him and giving him a pat on the back. "But thanks."

"I know, but I don't mind." He puts the scooper back in its spot, washes his hands, then turns around to kiss me.

I cover my mouth with my hand. "Eew, no. I've got morning breath."

"Yeah, and so do I. Who cares?" He pulls my hand down and gives me a tender, closed-mouth kiss. "Was that so bad?"

"No," I acknowledge. I nuzzle into his chest, and he wraps his arms around me. I feel his chin stubble atop my still-bald head.

"Hey, you know what? There's a decent amount of hair coming in now," he says, giving the crown of my head a little kiss before releasing me.

I turn toward the mirror and see that he's right. There is some peach fuzz coming in up there. It feels soft as I run my fingers across it, and my scalp tickles a little. So much better than being painful to the touch when I was completely bald and going through chemo. "Yay! I mean, I still look bald, but it's a start."

Roddy wraps his arms around me from behind. "Hair or no hair, you're beautiful."

I melt in his embrace, leaning my head back to relish this wonderful moment with this man whose eyes always echo what he says. I never thought I would find someone who would love me or see me so completely, yet here he is. "I love you."

"I love you too, Clare." He says, kissing the top of my head again. "Now, we'd better get ready or you're going to be late for your treatment."

* * *

At the cancer center—god, I'm so tired of seeing this place—Roddy sits in the main waiting room when I'm called back to change into a gown and sit in the smaller patient waiting room. Thankfully, the gowns here are nice and soft, unlike those at the radiologist's office. Although, considering the fact that I basically have to drop my top as soon as I get in the radiation room anyway, the pretense of the gown is almost comical.

"Clare," Nurse Stacey calls. She's one of my regular radiation nurses, along with Kim and Jeremy. Since I'm here every day, I've given them permission to use my first name instead of saying Ms. O'Donnell all the time. "We're ready for you."

I follow her into the treatment room, remove my gown, and lay myself down onto the table. It's essentially like an MRI or CT table, but they have a mold they made especially for me to lay on that keeps me in the right position and a bolster for my knees since I'm on my back for my treatment. There's a whole host of other molds hanging up in racks on the side of the room for everyone else coming later. There are also more bolsters and blankets to the side to help them keep everyone in position and as comfortable as possible.

"Let's get you centered here," Stacey says, adjusting me along with Jeremy. They both call numbers and measurements to Kim who is sitting in a booth with all the computers adjusting the radiation equipment.

The machine itself moves around me and has points they need to line up with specific points on my body. To achieve this, I had to get my first and only tattoos which consist of four dots: two on my sternum and one each on the outsides of my ribcage.

"Looks good," Jeremy says. "Alright, Clare, go ahead and put your right arm above your head."

I follow his instructions as I've done every day. Stacey puts a rolled blanket under my arm to keep it comfortable since it will be up there for the duration of the treatment. They make some additional adjustments since the movement of my arm has moved my ribcage slightly. Once everything is lined up again, Stacey and Jeremy go into the booth with Kim.

What follows is a series of instructions to hold my breath and to breathe normally as the radiation machine moves around me. I don't feel anything physical while it's happening, with the exception of soreness in my shoulder from being in that position for too long.

However, I'm emotionally and physically exhausted from all the treatments and the feeling that all this will never end, even though I know I'm almost done with the main treatments. Don't get me wrong, chemo was the worst part, but daily radiation treatments have their own physical toll because you're reminded every single day that you're going through cancer treatment. You can't escape it. Not to mention the copious amounts of greasy lotion I have to keep on the skin on my breast, chest and underarm from the radiation burns. I'm basically wearing the same old clothes most of the time because everything is getting coated in the stuff that I'll just have to throw them out.

I've only got seven more treatments to go out of twenty total, and believe me, I'm counting down the days.

* * *

After my treatment, Roddy takes me to Denise's Café for breakfast. We introduced Roddy to Denise's, and he loves it now as much as the rest of us. We get a booth in the corner, and we give our orders to the server because we both knew what we wanted before we got here.

"I'm so glad radiation is almost over," I say, taking a sip of my water.

"I can imagine," Roddy replies. "And I know you won't be done with all treatment then, because you'll be on the hormone therapy for years, but at least the more active treatment will be finished."

"Hallelujah!" I do some jazz hands and we both laugh. "I cannot wait to start feeling normal...or whatever the 'new normal' is going to be."

"Speaking of, there's something I've been meaning to talk with you about," he starts.

"A good something or bad something?"

He shrugs. "It could be a great something...for both of us."

I'm intrigued, and trying not to jump to too many wedding-type conclusions as my mind races to figure out what he's going to say. "Go on."

Of course, the server arrives at that moment to bring our food and drinks, so we take a few moments to shuffle plates around, thank her and get settled again. I start buttering my toast while I anxiously wait for Roddy to continue.

He finishes putting honey in his tea before passing the golden bear to me. "You remember when I went to New York a few months ago?"

"Sure." I take a bite of my buttered toast, then prepare my tea.

"So, while I was there, I was performing at one particular show, and Josh Groban happened to be there in the audience."

I stop stirring my tea to look at him agape. "You're joking."

"Wait, it gets better." He grins. "After the show, I'm told that Josh Groban would like to meet me. So, of course, I say yes."

I am literally about to bounce out of my seat right now. "I can't believe you didn't tell me this before!"

"I know, I'm sorry. So, Josh and I talk for a while about the show and music, and he says he's having auditions for cellists because his current cellist is going on maternity leave soon, but he's heading out on a European tour for four months." He takes a sip of his tea and continues, "He asked me to audition for his whole orchestra while I was in town, so I did."

I set down my fork and glare at him. "I seriously cannot believe you not only met Josh Groban—my favorite singer in the whole world—but you auditioned to go on tour with him, and you didn't tell me!" I lean forward and playfully punch his shoulder. "Is there more you didn't tell me?"

"Actually, yes, there is." He looks down at his plate of half-eaten cheese omelet, then back at me. "They picked me, and I leave to go on tour with them in three months. And I'd like you to go with me."

* * *

I'm still shell-shocked when we get to my PT appointment. I told Roddy I'd need to think about it, and he completely understood. Not only that, but I'd need to speak to Nate to find out if I could work remotely from Europe for four months or if I'd need to take a sabbatical. Plus, so many other considerations I can't process right now. Our ride from the café over to the physical therapist's office was silent. I'm actually grateful he simply dropped me off and I can walk home from here, because I need some alone time to clear my head. Plus, in the back of my mind, there's this feeling that my other self is going through something similar, so there's that to process as well.

I go through the motions with my therapist, and it's my final appointment there, so he's basically just reviewing everything we've done so far. He gives me a bunch of handouts, and a bag full of wrapping supplies, just in case I need them. I thank him for all the information and assistance, and he congratulates me on being almost finished with treatment.

I'm so in my own head when I walk out of the appointment that I don't notice someone calling my name until they tap me on the shoulder. "Clare."

I turn to see Suz standing right behind me. I haven't seen nor heard from her since the breakup, and she looks different. Not bad per se, but like she's been going through something. "Suz. What are you doing here?"

"I could ask you the same thing," she says, but instead of leaving it there like she normally would, she continues, "I just finished with my physical therapy for today. You?"

I shake my head to clear it. "Um...yeah...same."

She asks, "What are you doing therapy for?" at the same time I ask, "How've you been?"

We both laugh, and I gesture for her to answer first. "Still working on some of my fine motor control, you know, since the accident."

I am completely taken aback. "Accident? What accident?"

"The car accident I was in the day you left," she says, matter-of-factly. "Did no one call you? I thought you were still my in-case-of-emergency person."

"No. I didn't know anything about it," I say honestly. "What happened?"

"I should have known that's why you weren't there. Even though stuff was...weird between us, I still thought you'd come." She runs her hand through her hair, which I realize isn't cut in her normal severe bob but is now shoulder length with long layers and no bangs. "Yeah, I went out that night and got hit by someone driving too fast in the rain. I don't remember much, but I hit my head pretty good and had some internal bleeding. Had some surgeries, stayed in the hospital a long time, went to a rehabilitation center for a while, now I'm home, but doing lots of PT."

"Oh my god, Suz! I'm so sorry I wasn't there. I had no idea." I want to reach out and hug her, but I don't know how things stand between us now. "I tried texting a couple of times after I left, but I never heard back. I guess I know why now."

She nods. "My phone was toast after the accident, so I had to get a new number."

"Again, I'm so sorry I wasn't there. And I'm sorry for how I left things with us. I shouldn't have just left like that." I search her face and there's a softness there I can't read because it was never there when we were together.

"I didn't give you much of a choice," she says. "Things weren't good, and we were never right together."

"Wow. I...never thought I'd hear you own up to us being together at all," I reply.

She shrugs. "I've had a lot of time to think, and I've been going to regular therapy as well as physical. Gotten things in perspective."

"That's great. I'm really happy for you." And I really am. "And you're good now, or, at least, getting better...physically?"

"Yes. I'm doing much better," she replies. "Still working on some fine motor skills with my hands, but I'll be released from PT soon."

"Good. That's really good." I'm still so shocked by seeing her and her news that I don't know what to say next.

She gestures to me. "So, if you don't mind me asking, why are you here?"

"Oh, yeah...um...I just finished doing some preventative PT for lymphedema," I reply. "I'm in the middle of my radiation treatments and my doctor thought it would be a good idea."

She looks as stunned as I felt. "You have cancer?"

"Well, technically I'm what they call NED or No Evidence of Disease—what most people refer to as cancer-free. But I'm finishing up my radiation treatments next week."

"Clare, I'm so sorry. I didn't know."

"That's pretty much on me 'cause I didn't bother to tell you before I walked out. That was the day after I got the results."

She looks up at the sky for a moment. "I guess it's been a tough ten months for both of us, hasn't it?"

"I guess it has."

"Oh," she says, gazing over my left shoulder, "I see my girlfriend pulling up now, so I need to run. But it was really great to see you."

Girlfriend? "Yeah, it was great to see you too," I reply, not asking the thousand questions that are swirling around my head at the thought of Suz with a person she actually calls her girlfriend.

"Hand me your phone." I do and she updates her number in my contacts. "Send me a text and we can catch up some more sometime. Maybe over dinner?"

"That would be nice," I say, meaning it.

"Bye, Clare," Suz says, dashing off to the car waiting for her at the curb.

"Bye," I repeat, feeling better about one thing today, at least.

Part N

"Hold on to Now"

November

I was in the cemetery again—standing under the funeral tent—and I was all alone. Everything was black and white, but it suited my mood. I looked down at the graves. I stood there for several moments before I got the eerie feeling that I was being watched. I turned my head slowly to the left and saw a woman standing there. I wondered if she was with the funeral home urging me to leave so they could take down the tent and put all the chairs away. I told her I'll only be another moment, but she didn't respond. I turned back to the graves and spoke a few last words to my parents, then I turned and walked back to the car. Halfway there, I realized the woman was following me. I walked faster, but she did as well, and she was catching up with me. I turned back again and saw, to my horror, that she had no face. Though, in the back of my mind I knew this shouldn't bother me because I felt like I'd seen her before. I stood there and watched as she got closer and closer, my heart beating faster and faster.

Then, suddenly, she took my hand, and we walked through a stained-glass window into a world full of color. The green of the grass and the blue of the ocean were startling compared with the shades of grey from the last world. She pulled me along and we practically danced among the hills and cliffs, though our feet didn't touch the ground. When we were both out of breath, she kissed me sweetly and I felt at home...

* * *

"Why would they want me?" I ask, incredulous.

"Why *wouldn't* they want you, Clare?" Nate replies. "They were so impressed by your enthusiasm and your hard work on the presentation that they want you to lead them on it. Your passion for your homeland really shows through, girl."

"I…um…" is all I can say.

When I came into the office this morning, Nate was brimming with excitement. I thought it was just because he and Isaac were finally married, but that wasn't the only thing. Apparently, Mr. Walsh, the leader of the Ireland seniors group we did the presentation for a couple months ago, called, and they want to hire us. But only if I agree to go with them on the tour as their tour guide. Since then, I've been overwhelmed by this feeling of Other Me getting a similar proposition. I get the feeling that she doesn't know what she's going to do about it either.

"I've never even been to Ireland, and I'm not a tour guide," I finally manage.

Nate dismisses my protestations with a wave of his hand. "You won't be guiding everything because we'll have guides for the more specific historical sites prebooked, but you'll be there to coordinate them getting on the bus on time, making sure they all get the right rooms, and stuff like that. You're great at organization and I'm sure you'll be a natural when it comes to herding sheep around Ireland." He laughs at his own joke. "See what I did there?"

"Ha ha. Very funny." I've dreamed of going to Ireland my entire life, but this seems like a huge undertaking, and I don't know if I'm up to the challenge. Plus, I haven't really been anywhere. I can push buttons on a computer all day long and be called "organized," but that's totally different from organizing actual human beings. "I'm just not sure if I'm ready for something like this."

"Clare, can I be real with you here for a moment?" Nate asks, coming to sit right next to me.

"When are you not 'real with me'?"

"Touché," he concedes. "Anyway, what I want to say is that I think you are ready for something exactly like this. You've been wanting to go to Ireland forever—even more so since your parents died—and you deserve the chance to get there. You've just tackled the daunting task of getting your driver's license again. If you can do that, you can certainly do this. Plus, if you go with this group, you'll be going for free and getting paid for it. Can you name a better scenario?"

"Not really, no," I reply. "It's still a lot to think about, especially since they're wanting to go for a whole month. Can I have a bit to mull it over? I should probably talk it over with Abby too."

He pats me on the back. "Of course you can! They aren't going until next summer, and I told Mr. Walsh that if you didn't go, then I would take them, and he seemed okay with that. Not thrilled since I'm not you, but okay enough to still book with us."

"But you and Isaac have your honeymoon cruise to Alaska in July."

"We could always reschedule it for June or August, if necessary. I'm sure Isaac will understand." He gets up and heads back over to his desk. "Seriously, either way will work, but I think this would be good for you. As a travel agent, as an Irish-woman, and as someone who needs to get out there and live!"

* * *

Later that day, Abby and I are at the coffee house waiting for her mom to get there. It took two months, but Abby finally agreed to meet her mom to see what she had to say. In the meantime, I received many a text or phone call from Lynnette asking what else she could do and eventually told her again that she needed to be patient. Abby was hurt and needed space.

"I just don't know if I can trust her," Abby had said when we talked last month. "And I don't want to get my hopes up, only to be disappointed, yet again. I'm too old and too tired for this shit. Pardon the language."

"I hear you," I'd agreed. "I can only tell you the feeling I got when I was on the phone with her, and I really felt she was being sincere. But you know her better than I do. And I don't want you to get hurt again."

We went over it from every angle, and finally, Abby called her mom and arranged to meet here, with me present. I sort of feel like the middlewoman in a negotiation, but the only negotiating is for Abby's trust, and I can't help with that. We have each other's already, and her mom is going to have to win it back all on her own. Through all this, not a single one of us has mentioned Jack.

"Yeah, so Nate says I can have a while to decide, but what do you think?" I've just explained to Abby the whole leading-a-tour-group-in-Ireland-for-a-month thing to see what her thoughts are. She hasn't said a word the whole time I've been talking, and I don't know if that's a good or a bad sign.

"A month…that's…quite a while," she replies.

"It is. And I've never been overseas before, so it's a lot to think about. Plus, being away from you." I take her hand and rub little circles on the back of her hand with my thumb.

She doesn't say anything for a long moment. "Yeah. A month is a while," she repeats.

I realize this might not have been the right time to tell her about this when she's already nervous about meeting up with her mom. She's just looked up again expectantly at the front door to see if her mom is the one entering. "How are you feeling?" I ask.

"I'm good. Yeah…I'm fine," she replies, her leg dancing a jig under the table.

"Would you like something else? A muffin or a scone?"

She fidgets with her napkin for a second while she thinks. "Sure. A scone would be good. I don't care what flavor."

I pat her on the shoulder. "Coming right up."

While I'm up at the counter ordering the scone and a muffin, I glance at the front window and see Lynnette approaching. I let out a sigh of relief because I was starting to get scared she wasn't coming, and that would crush Abby. The barista hands me Abby's blueberry scone and my lemon poppyseed muffin, and I make my way back to the table.

"Hi, Clare," Lynnette says as I sit back down with the food. "I was going to go up and order, then I'll be back, but I wanted to say hello first."

"Hi, Mrs. Cassidy. It's nice to see you," I reply because after speaking with her the last couple of months, I really do think she wants to turn things around with her and Abby's relationship.

Lynnette goes off to order, and I start eating my muffin. Abby picks at her scone, more playing with it than actually eating it. She has a far off look in her eyes, so I don't disturb her and continue eating my muffin and drinking my English breakfast tea. We sit like that for a few minutes before Lynnette comes back with a cappuccino and croissant.

"Abby," Lynnette begins, "I'm not going to beat around the bush. I want to start with how sorry I am for how I've treated you over the years. I have always wanted the best for you, and I thought I was doing what was right for you to set you up for the best life possible. Obviously, I was wrong. I hope you can find it in your heart to forgive me."

"Mom, I…" Abby trails off. She looks off into the distance and squints as if she can't think of the right words to say back to her mother's apology.

"Sweetheart, I know it will take some time—"

Abby shakes her head. "No, sorry, Mom, it's not that." She turns to me and points to a table in the far corner of the coffee house. "Clare, isn't that Suz over there?"

I look where she's pointing and it is Suz at a table by the window, sitting alone with her laptop. "What should I do?" I ask, panicked. I think about ducking under the table, but it never works in movies or on television.

"Well, I don't think she's seen you, but it's only a matter of time," Abby says. "She has to walk past us to get to the exit."

"Crap. Are you okay here? Do you want me to stay?" I ask Abby, glancing at Lynnette knowingly.

Abby shrugs. "No, I think we're okay. Might be good for us to have a few moments alone. Go ahead and talk to her. Clear the air, maybe." Then, pretending to pick her napkin up off the floor, she says quietly to me, "Mom seems really sincere."

"If you're sure." I push back from the table and stand up slowly. "Sorry for the interruption, Mrs. Cassidy."

"That's okay, Clare," Lynnette says, generously.

I most definitely didn't want to see Suz today—or really ever again, if I'm entirely honest—but it was inevitable. Made more so by the fact that we're literally at the coffee house across the street from Suz's apartment. My old apartment.

Wait a minute. Suz doesn't even like this place. What is she doing here? I start marching over to Suz's table, chicken out once, then turn around when I see Abby shooing me on, and finally make my way there. True to form, Suz doesn't bother to look up when I approach. She has the intense look of concentration she gets when she's writing code or playing a particularly difficult level in a game.

"Hey," I say.

She types a few more words on her keyboard, looks up with no change in expression and says, "Hey."

I sigh. Same old Suz. "How are you?"

"I'm fine. You?" Her face softens ever so slightly, but not enough to express a change in mood or happiness to see me.

"I'm fine too. Hey, I thought you hated this place." I gesture at her table and the detritus of food and beverage scattered around.

She shrugs. "My coffee maker broke, and I haven't had a chance to get a new one, so I've been coming here to work. It's not so bad."

Wow. "Okay, well I just came over to let you know that Abby and I are dating now. I thought you should know, and I didn't want you to hear it from anyone else." I don't know who else she'd hear it from, but it seems like the polite thing to say.

"Good for you?" She says this like a question. "And, thanks, I guess."

I don't know how I expected this conversation to go, but this was probably all I could have hoped for from her. "Okay, well, I guess I'll see you around."

"Yeah. See you around," she says then dives right back into her computer.

She'll never change, I guess. I stand there for another few seconds before I walk straight back to my table. When I get there, Abby and Lynnette are hugging, which I take as a great sign, so at least one of the interactions in this coffee house went well today.

"Awww, did things go well?" I ask.

Abby is the first to respond. "Yes. It's going to take some time, but we're going to go see a counselor and work on our mother-daughter relationship."

"That's wonderful news," I say, thrilled for both of them, but mostly for Abby.

"I'm so glad Abby has taken it into her heart to hear me out and work on our relationship with me. I love her so much." Lynnette gives Abby another squeeze. "And I'm so glad to hear about the two of you being together."

I blush and feel Abby's arm draw me into a side hug. "We couldn't be happier," she says.

"Great news all around," Lynnette says. "This has filled me with so much joy."

"Me too, Mom," Abby replies.

The three of us have a group hug before Lynnette leaves to head back home. Abby sits back down and actually eats a couple bites of her scone before turning to me. "My mom kicked my dad out."

I nearly choke on my cold tea. "What?"

"That night at the Angus Barn." Abby nods. "Right after we left, she had it out with him, and she gave him an ultimatum: either apologize to me or get out. He left the next day."

"Oh my god, you're kidding!" I exclaim.

"Nope. She said he's staying with Uncle Mark until he finds a place."

"Good for her, I guess. How do you feel about that?" I ask.

She thinks about this for a moment. "Honestly, I'm kinda glad. We both deserve better. I mean, I'm sure there will be a lot more to unpack when Mom and I go to counseling, but for now, I think it's a great thing for both of us."

"Wow. I just can't believe it." I shake my head.

"Yeah." She pushes away the rest of her scone, then rests her head on her hands. "So, do you think I could come with you on this Ireland trip, if you go?"

"Dream On"

January

This time, I'm in one of those dreams where I know that I'm dreaming. I look around and the ground—floor?—seems to be made of opaque glass, and everything surrounding me is white. It's not a room, per se, but a vast expanse of nothing. Almost as if the whole world is...blank. I turn around to see if there's anything or anyone here, and I see nothing. I can't hear anything except my own breath.

I'm just about to try and wake myself up when I hear footsteps behind me. I look back and see my father coming toward me. Tears spring to my eyes because he looks exactly the same as before he passed away. As he gets closer, I see he is beaming at me and his arms begin to open. Sparing no further thought, I run to him and wrap my arms around him as tightly as I can. He squeezes me back just as tightly, and I don't fight the sobs that explode from my lungs. I realize I have no sense of smell here because if I did, I'd be able to smell his familiar scent of aftershave and vanilla.

"My darling Clare," he says, finally pulling back to look at me. "Oh, how I've missed my beautiful girl."

"Daddy," I manage through my sniffles. "What's going on? Is this real? Am I dreaming this?"

He waggles his head noncommittally. "Yes and no. You are dreaming, but at the same time, this is real. I am here in this dream together with you. Your mother's here too, actually, but she's with the other version of you."

My head is spinning. "Mom's here too? And my other self?" I look around to see if I can see them.

"They are, but we're going to have a chat first before we meet up with them," he says. "They're having a chat now too."

I'm really wishing I had a chair to sit down on, and suddenly, a chair just like my mother's rocking chair appears beside me. Sitting down, I feel a little better without the burden of standing. "What did you want to talk with me about? There are so many things I'd like to tell you. Or do you already know them?"

Dad laughs as he too takes a seat in a chair that's appeared for him. I've missed the way his eyes crinkle at the corners when he smiles and the baritone sound of his laugh. "I know, darling. I've been keeping an eye on you and helping you out, or couldn't you tell?"

"I was right? You sent the dreams? You and Mom?"

He nods. "Yes. We knew our smart cookie would be able to figure them out."

I ask the question I really want to know. "So, you want me to be with Roddy?"

He takes hold of my hands, and they feel warm even in this dream state. "From the moment I saw his passion playing El Cant del Ocells, and speaking with him at the donor event later, I knew he would be the one to take care of my darling Clare in my stead."

"Does that mean you knew I was going to get cancer?"

He looks down at our hands and his mouth turns down into a frown. "Yes. We knew one of you would and one of you wouldn't. So, we had to pick the best fit for each of you depending on your circumstances."

"I feel like my head is going to explode," I say. "Are there only two universes or timelines or whatever, or are there more?"

He shrugs. "To be honest, I don't know. Your mother and I can only see these two, so we thought maybe they are the only ones we're connected to. Maybe this is the only set where we died in the car accident. We really have no idea."

I nod. "I wish I understood, or maybe I don't, but that's helpful, at least." I squeeze his hands. "God, it's so good to see you again, Dad. I've missed you so much."

"You have no idea how much your mother and I have missed you." His eyes glisten with tears about to fall, which makes me start tearing up as well. There's nothing like seeing your father cry to make you cry too.

"I wanted you with me so badly when I was going through treatment," I say, choking back the tears. "But Roddy was there for me, along with Abby, Isaac and Nate, and I felt so supported and loved. They all got me through treatment, and I don't know how I would have made it without them."

"That's why we chose him to be the one with you in this timeline to support your other friends because we knew they would be there when we couldn't be. We've also seen how wonderful Roddy's family is and how much they love you. And of course they do because who wouldn't love our beautiful Clare?"

The other question that's been weighing on me suddenly doesn't seem to be a question anymore. "So, I should go with Roddy on the tour."

"I think your heart will tell you what is right. But I will say that your mother and I want you to get out there and live. Don't live for us—we lived our lives—live for yourself. Make the most out of your life and live with no regrets. We had no regrets when we died, other than not getting to spend more time with you." He pats me on the cheek.

I lean over toward him and throw my arms around his neck. "I love you, Daddy."

"I love you too, Clare. My darling angel."

We hug for several minutes, until my father says, "Alright Clare, it's time to go see your mother."

*　*　*

I'm standing in a completely white room by myself. There's no one else around, and you could hear a pin drop, it's so quiet except for the beating of my heart. Other than sight, sound and touch, my other senses seem to be dull. It's eerie and at the same time, relaxing. My mind feels clear after the last few weeks of discussions and trying to make a decision about the trip.

Suddenly, I hear a voice beside me say, "Clare," and I'd swear it was my mother. I turn my head and there she is. I close my eyes tightly and open them again, but my mother is still standing there in front of me, looking just as she did before the accident.

"Clare, dear," she says again.

My eyes moisten with tears, and I run to her, wrapping her in a hug. Her embrace feels so warm, even in this cold, uninviting place. I never want her to let me go. "Mom, where are we?" I ask into her shoulder.

"We're here together in your dream," she replies, finally pulling back from the hug, but still holding onto my arms. "Your father and I have been watching out for you, you know."

My hands fly to my head as if to keep it intact. "In my dreams? You've been…so you did send me the dreams like I thought?" I can't believe I was right about that, but at the same time, it makes perfect sense.

"We did. We always said we'd watch out for our dear girl wherever we were. You didn't think we'd go back on that promise, did you?" She puts her hands on her hips and cocks her head to one side, but I see the familiar twinkle in her eyes.

"No, of course not. I just wasn't sure how you'd do it," I reply. "I also didn't know there was a way to manipulate dreams of the living from beyond the grave."

She puts a finger to her lips. "Shh. That's our little secret."

"My lips are sealed." I bite my lip. "But I might have to tell Abby."

My mom chuckles, and the melodic tinkle of her laugh reminds me of how she used to laugh at the silly jokes I would tell as a kid. "Yes, you can tell Abby. And Nate and Isaac, if you want. Just don't go spreading it far and wide."

I nod. "Did you send me the dreams to tell me that I'm supposed to be with Abby and not Suz?"

Mom looks thoughtful for a moment before responding. "Now, we didn't want to make that decision for you. We'd never do that. But we did want to give you a little nudge in the 'right' direction, so to speak." She uses air quotes around the word "right."

"Thank you. I needed that," I reply honestly. "I don't know if I ever would have left Suz without those dreams."

"You probably would have, but who knows if Abby would have still been single by that point. Or, if her relationship with her mother would have been salvageable," Mom says, shrugging.

Another question pops into my mind. "Do you know about the feelings I've had of Other Me? This other version of myself that's in some different timeline who did get cancer."

She nods. "I do. We didn't have anything to do with you having those feelings, but we were able to see both timelines. Your father is here as well, speaking with the other Clare."

"They're here?" I look around, but don't see anyone or anything else. "Where?"

"They are, and you'll see them once we're all finished with our individual chats," she says.

"Are there other timelines than these two?" I wonder aloud.

She shrugs. "I really don't know. Your father speculates we can only see these two because maybe they're the only ones in which we *died in this way. It's a mystery I can't hope to comprehend, but I'm so glad to have been able to keep an eye on my dear girl since we've been gone."*

I'm overwhelmed with everything she's told me, and just with the fact of seeing her again after all these years. "Oh, Mom, I've missed you so much."

"And I've missed you." She wipes a tear from her cheek as I do the same. "Is there anything else you wanted to ask me before we go see your father and your other self?"

It feels so trivial now, but my heart is telling me to ask her anyway. "Should I lead the Ireland tour group?"

My mother smiles. "I think you already know the answer to that question, but here's my advice: grab the reins of life and don't let go. You only get one chance, and you should do whatever will make you the most happy, even if it scares you. Your father and I tried our best to live that way, and we want the same for you."

I throw my arms around her and cry for the time we've lost, but also for all the time we had together. "I love you, Mom."

"I love you too, my dear girl," she says, rubbing my back like she used to.

We cling to each other for a few moments before she says, "It's time to go see the others."

* * *

Without warning, my mother and my...Other Self are here. I'm torn between wanting to hug my mother and stare at this person who both is and isn't me. I opt for the former, and Other Self does the same with my/our father. My mom's hug is just as I remember, warm and cozy. If there was scent here, I imagine she'd still smell of lemon verbena.

We share the "I missed yous" that we did with the other parent before, and tears are shed anew. Finally, when we're all hugged out again, the four of us step back in a circle, alternating with Dad then me, Mom then Other Self. It's so strange seeing her there with her full head of hair, looking completely normal, like I used to before...everything. I'm sure she's thinking the opposite about me with my peach fuzz—though it is coming in nicely now to the point where I don't wear the wigs all the time anymore—and the dark circles under my eyes that won't go away.

"Clare," Dad begins, and I wonder if he should have addressed us as "Clares" instead since he's speaking to both of us, "I know you're wondering why you're both here."

Both of us nod, and Other Self says to me, "Yeah, although it is nice to finally see you in person."

"Likewise," I reply.

Dad continues, "Now that you both understand the point of the dreams, your mother and I feel that you aren't in need of them anymore."

I gasp. "Does that mean you won't still be watching out for us?"

"Of course not," Mom says. "We'll be watching out for you just as we always have been."

Both Other Self and I release deep sighs of relief.

* * *

It's strange seeing myself without my hair and with obvious signs of prolonged illness, but she looks pretty good considering all that she must have been through. Her hair is starting to come back, and I would totally rock that as a hairstyle by itself, though she might still be wearing wigs in the day-to-day.

"Right. We just won't be sending you more dreams like we have been," Dad repeats.

"What about the connection to each other?" I ask.

Mom and Dad both shrug. "We're not sure," Mom answers. "Since we didn't have control over that connection, or even of you two being here today, we don't know what will happen after this."

"You might have the connection forever, or you may never notice one another again," Dad adds.

"That would be a shame," Other Me says, frowning. "It's been nice to know there's a universe out there where I didn't have cancer."

This brings a tear to my eye. "I'm sure, but I also appreciate knowing that I'm strong enough to get through anything if I can get through that. And that I have amazing friends who will help me through it."

Other Me nods. "That you are and that you do."

I'm reminded of what Mom said about the trip and realize that even though it scares me, I'm strong enough to do it. If Other Me can get through cancer, that means that I could too, and if I can get through that, then I can certainly escort a group of seniors around Ireland for a month. And do a darn fine job at it too.

"I'm going to go on the tour," Other Me says at the same time I say, "I'm going to Ireland."

The four of us look around at each other and start laughing. Dad's deep laughter nearly drowns us all out, but us women hold our own, and soon we're cackling at how wonderful it is to laugh together again.

Dad is the first to break the merriment. "I'm so sorry, my darling Clare, but your mother and I have to go. And you need to wake up soon."

Other Me and I sober up quickly, and both run to hug the parent closest to us. We switch, then get to the good-byes. The most-likely forever ones.

"We're so proud of you, Clare," Mom says, stroking her hands through our hair. "You are our beautiful girl, and we will love you forever and ever."

Dad takes one of our hands in each of his. "Take care of yourselves, and let Roddy and Abby take care of you. And know that we love you, darling Clare. And we're always here if you need us."

A group hug, and they're all gone...

I wake up in bed, holding onto Abby and know I'm home.

* * *

When I wake up, tears stain my pillow, but I feel Roddy's warmth as we spoon and feel comforted.

Chapter 2

"Come What May"

June

Roddy and I have been on tour with Josh Groban for a month now and it's been...in a word...exhilarating. We're in a different European city every other night or every few nights, and I can't believe I'm getting to experience each of these amazing places finally. Though Roddy has rehearsals in each venue and prep before each show, he's been able to take some time to explore with me or show me the sights if he's been to a particular place before. But, even when I'm on my own, I'm having an amazing time trying to see everything I can before we pop off to the next city. I am no longer the "travel agent who hasn't travelled"!

My stamina has slowly, but surely, come back. It's not quite where it was before I started treatment, and my doctors say it may never get back to that place, but I seem to have reached my "new normal" as they call it. The hormone therapy drug and lower level of estrogen in my system from the premature menopause does make me feel like I'm about eighty instead of forty-three, but I'm not letting that stop me from enjoying life, and this tour, as much as possible. If I can beat cancer, I can do anything!

The tour began in Paris, and Roddy asked me to book a few extra nights ahead of time—as his personal travel agent—so we could really experience Paris. We, of course, visited the Rodin museum, the Eiffel Tower, the Louvre, Musée de l'Orangerie so I could see Monet's *Water Lilies*, Sacre Coeur and Notre Dame. But he also took me to some of his mother's favorite markets—both for food and clothing—and some amazing cemeteries that aren't as well-known as Père-Lachaise.

Not to mention the gastronomic adventures we've been having all over Europe. From flaky croissants in Paris to melt-in-your-mouth chocolates in Belgium to käsespätzle in Germany. And the tea and cocoa are so much better here than in the US. Thankfully, I've been doing so much walking or else I'd have gained thirty pounds by now.

Now, we're in Dublin and I'm soaking in everything I can. I already know two nights in Ireland won't be enough for me, but at least I'm here in the country of my heritage, and I'm already making plans to come back. Soon.

Roddy is at rehearsal, and I'm winding my way through EPIC The Irish Emigration Museum this morning, learning so much about why so many people have left Ireland and where they've gone. I'm reading through some of the letters they've collected from emigrants when my phone bleeps with a text from Roddy.

Roddy: Are you busy?
Roddy: Can I call you?
Clare: I'm in a museum. Let me step outside and I'll call.
Clare: Everything okay?
Roddy: Too much to text, but you're not going to believe it.

I make my way past all the other cool-looking exhibits to the exit. When I step outside, I call Roddy's number. He answers on the first ring.

"Hey." I can hear sounds of instruments tuning way in the background like he's walked to the other end of the concert hall from the stage.

"Hey. What's going on?" I ask.

"You know Odessa, the woman in the opening act who usually does the duet with Josh?"

Of course I know her. She's absolutely amazing and definitely won't be in an opening act for long. "Sure. She's fantastic."

"Right. Well, she just showed up to rehearsal with laryngitis. She can't sing!" Roddy exclaims.

"Oh no! What are they going to do? Can her partners go on without her?" I assume there's some sort of contingency plan since she's part of a band that has other singers and they can just play other songs that don't feature her or something.

"They're trying to figure that out, but I think they will just perform different material until she's better. Clare, hang on just a second." Roddy mutters something unintelligible to someone nearby, then comes back to the line. "Sorry about that. It's crazy here."

"I can only imagine."

"The reason I'm calling is, Josh still needs someone to fill in for Odessa for the duet. It's the big finale to the show—other than the encore—and he doesn't want to change it midway through the tour. They're scrambling to find someone, and I immediately thought of you."

I'm rendered speechless. I cannot do this. Absolutely not.

"I know it's a lot to ask, but you know the song cold, and you have the most beautiful voice I've ever heard." The earnestness in his voice is threatening to break through my resolve. "I know if Josh heard you sing it, he'd agree that you're the one to do it. Would you at least try?"

"I...I don't know," I reply, a waiver in my voice. "I've never sung in front of that many people before. And with all the lights and...everything..."

"The lights actually help," Roddy says. "You won't be able to see the audience because they basically blind you."

"I guess that helps a little."

"Please, Clare. Will you try?" he asks again. "If you don't feel one hundred percent comfortable, you don't have to do it. No questions asked."

I think of what my father said in the dream I had with my parents a few months ago, "*Make the most out of your life and live with no regrets.*" I haven't felt my other self since that dream, but I think she'd be cheering me on to do it as well. I know I will regret not at least trying to see if I can do this. Josh Groban is one of my favorite artists of all time and to sing with him would be another dream come true. Another dream Roddy made come true.

"I'll do it."

* * *

What feels like minutes later—but in reality, is almost ten hours later—I'm backstage at the concert hall waiting to go on. I've seen some of the concerts from this vantage point before as sometimes I'm allotted a seat in the audience and sometimes, I get a seat backstage, but never before have I been waiting to go onstage in any capacity. I'm wearing the dress Roddy bought me for Nate and Isaac's engagement party, and the hair and makeup team has had their way with me. Of course, I still don't have a ton of hair to speak of, but they worked some kind of magic to make it look like I have a lot more than I do.

Even though I rehearsed the song with Josh, and the whole orchestra, about a dozen times, my insides still feel tied up in knots. I hope Roddy is right about the lights blinding me so I can't see the sheer volume of people out there, but I know I'll be able to hear their reaction if I totally muck this up. While Josh is finishing up "February Song," I close my eyes and take deep breaths in and out, in and out. I visualize my parents standing beside me, bolstering me through this. Slowly, I start to feel better, and by the time Josh introduces me, I feel, if not calm, at least not like I'm going to throw up.

I walk out on stage on cue and the crowd cheers. I steal a glance at Roddy who beams at me and mouths, "I love you." I stop right on my mark opposite Josh, who gives a friendly smile. I smile back and nod that I'm ready. Josh signals to the band to begin the familiar chords to "All I Ask of You" from *Phantom of the Opera*.

Josh sings Raoul's lines, and as I come in as Christine, all my fears evaporate, and I am wrapped up in the notes and the music. The passion and lyrics of love flow through me, and even though I'm supposed to be looking at Josh the whole time, my eyes drift to Roddy as we sing the dramatic climax of the song and Roddy's eyes lock back on mine as well. When the song is over, the audience absolutely erupts, and Josh asks for the house lights to be brought up so I can see the standing ovation they're giving us.

"Clare O'Donnell, ladies and gentlemen," Josh says, gesturing for the audience to sit back down as the house lights are turned off. I'm about to make my way off stage again when Josh adds, "Clare, stay out here for a moment, would you?"

Confused, I turn back and nod.

"So, not only is Clare the hero of the hour for stepping in on that duet, but she's also the girlfriend of our amazing cellist, Roddy Vaughn." Josh gestures to Roddy behind him.

"Roddy's become a great friend over the course of this tour, and when he asked me for a favor today, I couldn't say no. Roddy, would you like to come up here?"

I'm panicking. *What favor? The favor of me singing in place of Odessa? Was it all a big mistake?* But Josh just called me a hero for doing it. Then the thought flies through my brain and discards itself just as quickly. *No, he couldn't be. Could he? When did he set his cello down?*

Roddy walks over to us and takes the microphone Josh offers. "Thanks, Josh," he says. Then to the crowd he adds, "I hope you'll indulge me for a couple moments, then I promise Josh has got some more amazing music for you."

He turns to me and takes my hand. "Clare, I've been wanting to do this for some time now. I've actually been planning to do this in Dublin since you decided to come on the tour with me, and the fact that you were going to be on stage tonight is, well, fortuitous to say the least."

Oh my god, oh my god, ohmygod, ohmygodohmygod!

He gets down on one knee and there is a collective gasp from the crowd. Tears fill my eyes, and I want to scream "Yes!" even though he hasn't asked me anything yet. With everything this past year has brought, he's been one of the main lights in an otherwise dark time. I know our light will only continue to grow as the years go on.

"Clare, you are my Bright Love. And I want to keep loving you no matter what life throws at us. I want to go everywhere with you, hold you when you're sick, laugh with you, cry with you, and make music together for the rest of our lives. I want to make all your dreams come true." He releases my hand to pull a ring out of his pocket and offers it to me. "Clare, will you marry me?"

"Yes, Roddy," I say without hesitation into my own mic. "I absolutely will marry you."

The crowd erupts again. Roddy hands the mics to Josh, then puts the ring on my finger, picks me up and twirls me across the stage as the orchestra plays Mendelssohn's "Wedding March." He sets me down so we're off stage and away from the prying eyes of the audience.

"I love you, Roddy," I say into his ear. "No matter what."

"I love you too. No matter what," he says. He pulls me to him, and we kiss behind the curtain until he has to return to the stage to play Josh's encore, "You Raise Me Up."

As I listen to the song, I think of my parents and how they got me to this moment, and how I'm going to live like they want me to, with Roddy by my side.

* * *

"Are you sure they'll be alright?" I ask Abby as she tries to pull me along the path at the Cliffs of Moher in my namesake county. It's still surreal that I'm here, finally, and I'm absolutely soaking in all the beauty that is County Clare and Ireland in general. I can see why my parents wanted to remember it through me.

Now, we've stopped at the famous cliffs and Abby wants us to leave the group for a walk by ourselves down the left side while my group goes down the path on the right. We haven't had a lot of time alone on this trip because leading a group of seniors is...a lot of work. They're wonderful people, but there are logistics to sort out each day with the driver, maps to look over, tickets to hand out, and more questions than I could have ever imagined. I don't know what I would have done if Abby wasn't here to help me. I mean, I would have muddled through, but she's been fantastic at fielding questions and herding the group places.

She waves her hand over her shoulder in a dismissive gesture. "They'll be fine. I asked David to keep an eye on them for an hour or so. We need a break!"

David Doolan is the driver for our trip and has been fantastic. He was born and raised in County Roscommon, and now lives in Galway with his family. He does private driving tours like this one six months out of the year, then does walking tours in Galway the rest of the year. The group has had so much fun peppering him with questions about Ireland and getting him to say things with his "cute accent," and he's been a great sport about it.

"You're right. They'll be fine with David," I relent. We hold hands as we walk along the path on this uncharacteristically sunny day. The country is beautiful, but the weather has been swinging wildly from warm to chilly, cloudy to rainy, all in the span of a day sometimes. "How do you think the trip is going so far?"

"I think it's going wonderfully. Everyone is having a great time, and you're doing a fantastic job," Abby replies. "But I don't want to talk about the group. We're taking a break, remember? It's not a break if all we do is talk about the group."

I nod. "You're right. What would you like to talk about?"

She's thoughtful for a moment, looking out at the Atlantic Ocean. "What's been your favorite thing we've seen so far?"

"Oh, wow, I have no idea how to answer that," I say. "I loved seeing the hustle and bustle of Dublin and the GPO was one of my favorite museums. And the Ring of Kerry was one of my favorite days so far with all the sweeping views and rolling hills—although this view right here is climbing right up there. But the most memorable thing, and the part I'll probably treasure the most, was yesterday afternoon in Tulla." Tulla is where my father grew up and where my grandparents are buried. The group was so kind to allow me to build in a few hours of my own ancestry search into their trip.

Abby squeezes my hand. "Those are some great highlights. And, I agree, yesterday was very special. Even though I don't really know my ancestry, I can see how beautiful those experiences have been for everyone throughout the trip."

I wipe a tear from my cheek. "So, what's been your favorite part?"

"Honestly, every moment I've gotten to spend with you," she replies, smiling. "Sorry, was that too cheesy?"

I smirk. "Just cheesy enough, I think." I lean over and give her a kiss on the cheek.

We walk along in silence for a few moments and stop to take some pictures, because Nate would kill me if I didn't have tons of photos of the Cliffs of Moher for our socials when I get back. Every viewpoint shows us something different, and I'm relishing this time alone so much so that I'm thinking of doing something impulsive: proposing.

As we walk on, I'm thinking this through. I'm not the spontaneous type, and I actually had a plan to wait till we got home where I'd have a chance to book a table at a lovely restaurant—where we could both enjoy the food—have the ring hidden in a dessert or something. But I'm not sure if she cares about all that. I don't know if I care about all that. I've been wearing the ring around my neck the whole trip. It's my mother's engagement ring, and I've been wearing it to feel her presence with me while we're in Ireland. I don't need anything more than that and my love for Abby, do I?

"…it just hit me that everything can turn on a dime." I realize Abby's been talking this whole time and I haven't been paying attention.

I throw out an, "Uh huh," so she knows I'm listening now.

"I mean, my mom just threw him out. And, I don't blame her at all, don't get me wrong, but it was just like that"—she snaps her fingers—"and they're over. It's been a lot to digest."

"I know it has. I can't even imagine what that must feel like."

"And you'd think that I'd be opposed to marriage or long-term commitments after something like that, but I'm not," she continues. "I think people should really look at the person they're thinking about committing themselves to, though, before making that leap. I don't think my mom did that. She's said as much in our therapy sessions."

Abby hasn't opened up to me this much about her therapy with her mom before. She's told me the sessions are going well, and she and Lynnette are working through things, but this is the first I've heard of anything specific. I've told her it's up to her how much she wants to share with me, and I'm thrilled she's doing so now.

"That's why I'm glad you and I are so stable, connected and real with each other. I know I can tell you anything and you'll stand by me. You'll have my back, and I'll have yours. We really *get* each other, you know?" She pulls me closer to her as we walk. "I love us."

"Absolutely," I reply. "I love us too."

We arrive at the south viewpoint, and we stop to take more photos. I don't know if it's the conversation we're having or the sun blinding me, but I swear I can hear the wind telling me to "go for it." Maybe it's my parents or maybe it's Other Me—even though I haven't felt her at all since that last dream we had months ago—but I know this is the time. This is the moment.

I unclip the chain from around my neck, slide the ring off and turn toward where Abby was standing a second ago taking pictures, only she's not there anymore. I scan from side to side and don't see her. *Where did she go?*

"Clare?" Abby's voice comes from behind me.

Turning around, I see her down on one knee holding up a silver ring with a princess-cut emerald in the center. I gasp in shock, then start laughing hysterically.

"What? Do you hate the ring?" Abby asks, obviously scared by my laughter. "Isaac said I should've gone classic with a diamond, but I thought you'd appreciate an emerald more than some silly—"

I wave my hand to stop her rambling. "No, it's just that I also have a ring." I'm still laughing as I hold out my mother's engagement ring. "I was going to propose too."

She slowly takes in this new information, then starts laughing as well. "Oh my god. I can't believe it!"

"I know. I've been planning to for a while now and I was going to wait until we got home so I could plan the perfect moment, but today just seemed so perfect already that I decided to do it."

Abby stands up and grabs my free hand. "I've been planning to propose here for a month. I talked to David back in Dublin about taking the others for a walk on the other side so I could have time alone with you."

I shake my head at the ridiculousness of it all. "Do you want to start?"

"Is there even anything to say other than I love you and I want to spend the rest of my life with you?" she replies.

I shrug. "Maybe 'will you marry me' would be good to add in."

"Maybe," she says laughing.

We put the rings on each other's fingers, marveling at how perfectly suited for each other they are. I feel a warmth in my chest seeing my mother's ring on her finger and know that my parents would be—are?—so happy.

"I still can't believe—" she starts to say, but I interrupt her by pulling her to me in a passionate kiss. The wind blows our hair around so much so that it's getting tangled together, but neither of us cares. Everything about this moment feels like home to me and I hope the feeling never ends.

"You were right," I murmur into her lips.

"About what?"

"It *was* only a chapter," I reply, caressing her cheek and seeing how my new engagement ring catches the light. "And I want to spend all my remaining chapters with you."

SONG LIST

Music has always been a huge part of my life—from listening and enjoying to singing in the choir to playing piano to dancing in my living room. Going through my cancer journey, certain songs hit me in new and different ways and helped me through. The same can be said for other emotional aspects of my life like the grief of losing my father to the joy of being married to my husband for over twenty years.

If you haven't noticed already, each chapter/part title is the name of a song. The songs for the corresponding parts of the two timelines have some connection to each other—be it the same artist, a similar theme or both. See if you can spot them all!

Below is the list of all the songs referenced as chapter/part names (in the order they appear in the book) along with the artists I had in mind. Explore some you didn't know before or create your own playlist on your favorite streaming media app/program. Most of all, enjoy!

- "Unwritten" by Natasha Bedingfield
- "Set Fire to the Rain" by Adele
- "Here Comes the Rain Again" by Eurythmics
- "Sail On" by Commodores
- "Curse the Love Songs" by The Hawk in Paris
- "Uninvited" by Alanis Morissette
- "Unintended" by Muse
- "Déjà Vu" by Dionne Warwick
- "Taking Over Me" by Evanescence
- "Shivers" by Ed Sheeran
- "Touch of Your Hand" by The Nylons
- "Umbrella" by Rihanna

- "That's What Friends Are For" by Dionne Warwick, Elton John, Gladys Knight, Stevie Wonder
- "Falling into You" by Celine Dion
- "Truly, Madly, Deeply" by Savage Garden
- "All of the Stars" by Ed Sheeran
- "Written in the Stars" by Vertical Horizon
- "Easy on Me" by Adele
- "Between the World and You" by The Hawk in Paris
- "Where the Light Shines Through" by Switchfoot
- "Dare You to Move" by Switchfoot
- "Remember When it Rained" by Josh Groban
- "About Damn Time" by Lizzo
- "Part of Me" by Evanescence
- "Broken Pieces Shine" by Evanescence
- "Shut Up and Dance" by WALK THE MOON
- "I Wanna Dance with Somebody (Who Loves Me)" by Whitney Houston
- "Padam Padam" by Kylie Minogue
- "Hold on to Now" by Kylie Minogue
- "Dream On" by Aerosmith (or Blacktop Mojo)
- "Come What May (from *Moulin Rouge*)" by Nicole Kidman, Ewan McGregor

Other songs or pieces of music mentioned in the text:
- "Black or White" by Michael Jackson
- "Love on Top" by Beyoncé
- Requiem in D minor by Wolfgang Amadeus Mozart
- Symphony No. 7 in A major, Op. 92 by Ludwig van Beethoven
- "Livin' on a Prayer" by Bon Jovi
- "True Colors" by Cyndi Lauper
- "Get Down on It" by Kool & the Gang
- "Electric Boogie (The Electric Slide)" by Marcia Griffiths
- String Quintet in C major by Franz Schubert

- o   "I Love Rock 'n' Roll" by Joan Jett & the Blackhearts
- o   "Faith" by George Michael
- o   "Girls Just Want to Have Fun" by Cyndi Lauper
- o   "(Theme from) New York, New York" by Frank Sinatra
- o   "Possession" by Sarah McLachlan
- o   "El Cant del Ocells" by Pablo Casals
- o   "Perfect" by Ed Sheeran
- o   "At Last" by Etta James (or Vitamin String Quartet)
- o   "Like a Prayer" by Madonna (or Vitamin String Quartet)
- o   "Only You (And You Alone)" by The Platters
- o   "February Song" by Josh Groban
- o   "All I Ask of You (from *The Phantom of the Opera*)" by Josh Groban with Kelly Clarkson
- o   "Wedding March" in C major by Felix Mendelssohn
- o   "You Raise Me Up" by Josh Groban

Finally, the series title is a reference to the song "These Dreams" by Heart.

ACKNOWLEDGMENTS

No one publishes a book by themselves, just as no one goes through cancer by themselves, so I'd like to take this opportunity to thank those people who helped me through both.

First and foremost, I'd like to thank my mom, Becky Barnes, for her unconditional support from my first breath, through cancer treatment and everything in between. She's been there, rooting me on, being a shoulder to cry on, an ear to rant to and a pal to laugh with for 45 years, and I don't know what I'd do without her. And, to my dad, Bill Barnes, who left us too soon. I know he's looking down and saying, "You always make Mom and me real proud." Love and miss you more than words can say, Dad.

Second, I'd like to thank my doctors and nurses in the UNC Rex system who were and are amazing! To Dr. Rougier-Chapman who saw my "chunky" lymph node on the diagnostic mammogram and decided to biopsy it even though it could have been a vaccine reaction, I will be forever grateful to you for saving my life. To Nurse Chitsaz, NP for being so caring and helpful through all the early testing and beyond. To Dr. Natesan for your thoroughness and thoughtfulness through my radiation journey. To Dr. Thawani for explaining the surgical options so well, for being a badass surgeon, and an amazing doctor all around. To Dr. Olajide for really listening to your patients and showing that we're not just numbers to you. And to all the nurses who are too numerous to name individually, but are no less important: Thank you for <u>everything</u> you do every day to care for your patients.

Next, I'd like to give a shout out to special friends who have been there through thick and thin, and are the definition of "found family": Tara Gazak, Courtney Brooks, Rachel Goffin, Cass McClellan, Glendyne Reinmiller, Dhara Jones and Julie Burroughs. Thank you for all your encouragement, pebbling of random memes, thoughtful gifts during my treatment, reading of very early drafts of this book (you know who you are), Zoom calls, friendship and love. Thank you also to all my other friends and family for your love and support both through cancer treatment and throughout my life.

To my pink siblings in the North Carolina Breast Cancer Support and Triangle YSC Thrivers online support groups, I appreciate your support, your knowledge, your candor and your hope. That last one is a big one, and my hope is that there will be a cure someday. But, for now, giving each other the hope of life during and after cancer is huge, and I send my love to you all.

A shout out to Gina B. of Up to the Beat Fitness for her daily encouragement since 2020 when I stumbled upon her workouts on YouTube. They are a daily mood boost and stress relief, plus they are so much fun! I'm pleased to call you my friend. Seriously, everyone, check out her workouts on YouTube or on her website. You won't regret it.

To my beta readers, J.S. Fields, Natalie Ingram, Tara Gazak, Glendyne Reinmiller and Rachel Goffin, thank you for your feedback. Your support of my work in this manner is invaluable, as were your comments, edits and pointing out of my foolish errors. Copy editors are not infallible.

Which brings me to my next thank you: to Courtney Brooks for editing this novel because I am incapable of editing my own work. You're amazing, and I've trained you well, young Padawan.

To my brilliant cover designer, Abra Millsaps of Abra Millsaps: Art & Design, thank you so much for the beautiful cover. The way you were able to take the thoughts (and faceless people) in my head and translate them to this art is nothing short of amazing!

Finally, to my amazing husband, Bill Tracy, thank you doesn't begin to express how I feel about the love and support you've given me over the last twenty-six years. Your support of my writing and of me through all of life's trials—not to mention running two small businesses and seeing each other all day, every day for the last five years!—is unending, and I hope I give even half of that support back to you. Come what may, my love.

ABOUT THE AUTHOR

Heather Tracy (she/her) is a travel agent by day, and a masked copy editor and writer by night. As a travel agent, she plans Nerdventures—travel for the nerd in all of us. These can be anything from visiting New Zealand to see as many *Lord of the Rings* filming locations as you can to visiting castles in Europe to following in the footsteps of your favorite author.

As a copy editor, she's found hundreds of typos, comma splices, and other grammatical nitpicks for Space Wizard Science Fantasy since before 2016. With over 30 titles copyedited, she's now turned her hand to her first published short story in *Fiery Deeps*, and her first novel, *Only a Chapter*, which features some of her personal journey surviving breast cancer.

Heather lives in Raleigh with her husband of over twenty years, William C. Tracy, where they have two rambunctious cats and several beehives. They enjoy taking their own Nerdventures—as much as they can be away from their small businesses—and cosplaying at various markets and cons throughout the year.

You can find her on Facebook as @heathertracyauthor, on Bluesky as @heathertracyauthor.bsky.social and on Instagram as @hunnyjar319. For her travel agency, Melvin's Travel Adventures, you can find her on Facebook and Instagram as @melvinstraveladventures or on Bluesky as @melvinsta.bsky.social.

Please take a moment to review this book at your favorite retailer's website, Goodreads, or simply tell your friends!